INCAS

Book Two

The Gold of Cuzco

INCAS

The Puma's Shadow
(Book One)

The Light of Machu Picchu
(Book Three)

INCAS

The Gold of Cuzco

A. B. Daniel

Translated by Alex Gilly

POCKET
BOOKS

LONDON · SYDNEY · NEW YORK · TOKYO · SINGAPORE · TORONTO

First published in Great Britain by Simon & Schuster UK Ltd, 2002
This edition first published by Pocket Books, 2003
An imprint of Simon and Schuster UK Ltd
A Viacom company

Original title
Inca
Princesse du Soleil

International rights management for XO Editions: Susanna Lea Associates
© XO Editions, 2001. All rights reserved.

English translation copyright © Alex Gilly, 2001

1 3 5 7 9 10 8 6 4 2

Simon & Schuster UK Ltd
Africa House
64–78 Kingsway
London WC2B 6AH

www.simonsays.co.uk

Simon & Schuster Australia
Sydney

A CIP catalogue record for this book is available from the British Library

ISBN 0-7434-1605-8

Typeset by Palimpsest Book Production Limited,
Polmont, Stirlingshire
Printed and bound in Great Britain by
Cox & Wyman Ltd, Reading, Berkshire

Tropic of Cancer

Atlantic
Ocean

Panama

Orinoco

Equator

Quito

Tumebama

Tumbez

Amazon

Cajamarca

Madeira

Hatun Sausa

Lima

Cuzco

Titicaca

Paraguay

Pacific
Ocean

Tupiza

Tropic of Capricorn

1000 kilometres

Furthest extent of
the Incan empire

·········· Pizarro's route

Machu Picchu

Wilcamayo

Ollantaytambo

Salcantay ▲

Yucay

Calca

Huchuy Qosqo

Vilcaconga

Jaquijaguana

Rimac Tambo

Cuzco

Apurímac

20 kilometres

nnnnnn Gabriel's route

Lima

Cuzco

Lake Titicaca

Titicaca Island

Pacific
Ocean

Grand
Salar

Tupiza

400 kilometres

PROLOGUE

The Huaylas Cordillera, 5 April 1533

ON FOOT, LEADING HIS HORSE BY ITS BRIDLE AND carefully picking his way through the crumbling rocks, Gabriel pressed on. He was preceded only by two porters bearing tent poles and canvases. The path was just wide enough for his bay horse to follow him without shying.

They had been travelling cautiously along a clifftop since dawn, pressing on through fog so thick that they hadn't been able to see either the sky above or the river that they could hear grumbling angrily far below. But now the fog cleared from the bottom of the cliff as though it had been suddenly inhaled into a giant's mouth. It stretched itself thin, coiled into wisps and shredded itself to nothingness on the sharp rocky edges. A warm breath of air caressed Gabriel's face.

He blinked, put one hand on his horse's shoulder, and came to a halt. In an instant, the light became dazzling, the sky a pure blue.

And in this sudden clarity Gabriel realized that the expeditionary force had only come halfway along the clifftop. The path didn't lead up into a great valley as they had imagined, but rather into a breach in the mountainside, a gully so narrow that it seemed merely to have been cleaved open with a giant axe. Drops of moisture on the leaves and fronds of a myriad luxuriant plants clinging to the cliff face sparkled in the sun's rays. Six hundred feet below, the swirling river, fattened by the recent rains, growled like a wildcat. It was so full of earth and pebbles torn from its banks that its water was now a dark ocher colour, the same hue as the mud that the Incas used to cob walls. Although from this height it was difficult to make out the finer details, Gabriel knew that tree trunks, branches, clumps of grass, orchids and *cantutas* occasionally floated by in the turbid current.

He glanced back at the long column following some way behind him. It looked like an immense, variegated snake against the verdurous rock face. The column was headed by a hundred or so porters stooping under their loads of gold, while following them were almost as many llamas, packed like donkeys. Then came the Spaniards, leading their horses along by the reins, with Hernando Pizarro's blood-red feather sticking up from his silver-plated morion clearly visible even at this distance. Finally, the big dais of their favorite 'guest', the Inca general Chalkuchimac, was borne along at the column's rear.

Gabriel had left Cajamarca five weeks earlier to join Hernando, who had gone south in search of gold – as much gold as he could possibly get his hands on. This was the return journey, and the goal of their mission had been more than adequately achieved.

Hernando was as crafty as he was violent. He cheerfully used both lies and brutality to achieve his ends, and somehow he had persuaded the captured Inca Atahualpa's chief general to accompany the conquistadors. Consequently, Chalkuchimac, famous for his ferocity, was following them in his palanquin all the way to Cajamarca, with the intention of joining his master there. He had a mere twenty warriors escorting him. Gabriel couldn't help but admire Hernando's feat, despite his contempt for him – a contempt that grew more pronounced with each passing day. Certainly, the peaceful capture of the Inca general might lessen – perhaps – the men's constant fear. Ever since what the Spaniards had taken to calling among themselves 'the Great Battle of November', not one soldier had woken in the morning without dreading an attack by Atahualpa's army during the day that lay ahead. The rumor was that it was still a large and powerful force.

'*Hola!*' grumbled Pedro the Greek behind Gabriel. 'Would his lordship deign to move forward, or must we stay planted on the spot until Christmas?'

Gabriel smiled without replying. The Greek giant had been grumpy since morning. He was tired of leading his horse instead of riding it. Or perhaps it was the absence of his usually inseparable companion Sebastian the African, who was walking a little further back in the column, that was the cause of his ill humour.

They set off again, still moving cautiously, holding the horses' bridles close to the bit to prevent the animals bolting.

Soon enough they fell into a regular rhythm of climbing up and up, happy to feel the sun warm on their faces at last. A shadow passed over Gabriel before veering off and travelling across the cliff face like a gust of air made visible.

Gabriel turned his face skyward: an enormous bird was gliding slowly, lazily between the two sides of the canyon, not once beating its wings. It looked huge to him, even though it was so high up and far away.

Gabriel measured in half-day blocks the passing of the remaining time that stood between him and Anamaya. It went by excruciatingly slowly. He would look ahead at each mountain ridge that they came to and hope in vain that it would be the last, that beyond it they would at last begin the descent towards Cajamarca.

He missed everything about Anamaya: her voice, her mouth, the nape of her neck, her skin's fragrance of dried grass and peppered flowers. He longed to kiss her shoulders and her belly, but his mouth tasted only the mountain's cold breath. He would wake in the night yearning for her caresses and her whispers, for the infinite blue of her eyes, eyes whose gaze he would lose himself in when they made love. He dreamed of her body whose delights she knew how to deny and give to him simultaneously, of her savage tenderness, of the way she would tilt her head forward and half close her eyelids when she whispered that she loved him. He laughed at the memory of her timidity when he had taught her that word in the language of Spain.

Gabriel would awake, a bashful lover, and go outside, wrapped in his damp blanket, to wait for dawn. He would look for Anamaya through the fog and the rain, on the mountain tops and in the depths of the valleys. It was at those moments that Peru, that unknown country as strange as a distant planet, would appear to him as magnificent: magnificent because it was hers. And sometimes, during the course of the expedition's long, long daily marches, he would look into the dark and fearful eyes of the porters and try to find something of her in her people's features.

'Oi! The dreamer there!' Pedro de Candia muttered brusquely from behind. The Greek pointed his gloved hand and said, 'Have a look at what's up ahead.'

Three hundred paces up the path, set above a bend in the river, a rope bridge joined the two sides of the canyon. The bridge was so long that it sagged like a necklace on a flat chest.

Gabriel slowed the pace. The giant Greek, his cheeks pale under his bushy beard, came up beside him and muttered:

'I don't like it. And the horses are going to like it even less.'

But Gabriel didn't hear him. Instead, he whistled appreciatively through his teeth.

'By Santiago! How in the world did they build that thing?'

'Who gives a damn, friend? Ask yourself instead whether it's going to hold and how you're going to get across it . . .'

'By placing one foot in front of the other, I imagine,' teased Gabriel, 'You're not frightened, are you, Pedro?'

'I'm not frightened, *compadre*! I just don't like it, is all.'

'Well, old friend, I'm afraid that all you can do is learn to like it. But perhaps your horse will learn to fly, a veritable Pegasus . . .'

Pedro looked unconvinced.

They pressed on to the end of the path. There they discovered the massive pillars to which the ropes were attached. Delicately woven strand by strand, each rope was as thick as a man's thigh. The guard rails were made of a complicated system of thinner ropes and knots. The bridge was wider than the track that they had just come up.

Gabriel stood transfixed, full of admiration. The Inca builders and architects had managed to create a structure as elegant as it was beautiful, without recourse to any iron tools at all: no saws, no gouges and no planes. Three of the gigantic rope cables supported a roadway built of meticulously laid-out logs. A layer of twigs and leaves had been spread on top of the logs, making the way across less dangerous and slippery, and smoothing the surface.

'By the Sacred Virgin,' groused de Candia. 'Look there! Look, Gabriel, it moves! It sags . . .'

'Yes,' said Gabriel. The bridge was indeed a heavy structure suspended over a very deep ravine, the river growling far below, and the whole thing was undeniably swaying gently in the slight breeze.

'It'll never take the weight of the horses!' insisted Pedro.

'Hola, Pedro! I've known you more heroic than this! But rest easy. See the size of those cables and logs? It's a solid piece of work . . .'

A group of Indian guards appeared on the other side of the chasm. The rest of the column arrived in straggling groups and now the porters hung around the near end of the bridge apathetically, only interested in seeing how the Strangers and their horses would cross it.

Gabriel removed a long blue scarf (the same colour as Anamaya's eyes and which until now had never left his neck) and began to wrap it around his bay's eyes.

'Do like me, Pedro. Blindfold your horse so that he sees neither the river nor the height . . .'

Gabriel murmured comforting words to his horse – reassuring himself as much as the animal – and, with infinite caution, he set off between the support pillars, holding the bay's bridle high. A few steps later and he found himself above the abyss. The further he advanced, the more violent became the rumbling of the river, like a sustained roaring rising from far, far below.

Glancing back through the rope-work he saw the column of men and horses, the Inca general's palanquin, and Hernando, recognizable by the feather in his helmet, gathered at the end of the bridge. Everyone was watching him. He roared out:

'Follow me, Pedro! All's well – she holds!'

'I'm behind you!' bellowed de Candia in his stentorian voice. 'Did you think that I'd let you play the hero all by yourself?'

Gabriel grinned and quickened the pace a little. The bay was doing well and appeared confident. They descended easily enough towards the lowest point of the bridge's roadway. Here, though, the slope became even steeper. Gabriel had to throw his shoulders back to keep his balance as though with each step the heels of his boots were sinking into sludge rather than landing on a bed of branches.

The din of the river below was now deafening. Looking down, Gabriel could see whirling, muddy water and enormous waves crashing on the rocks to produce an explosion of foam so violent that it created a heavy mist in that part of the canyon.

He heard a muted sound, a cry. His bay bumped into his shoulder, snorting heavily. As he turned, Gabriel heard Pedro bawl:

'Goddamned bitch of a bridge!'

Gabriel nearly laughed aloud. The Greek had slipped and was flat on his ass, legs splayed and one boot already lost into the abyss. But his hand hadn't let go of his horse's bridle and the animal, its neck arched, its hind legs dug in, had saved its master from a long, long fall to certain death.

Heaving himself over, de Candia grabbed a guard-rail rope and got back up onto his knees, breathing heavily. The pink feather in his morion had snapped clean in two and now fell away and floated into the void, swirling around gently in the canyon's air currents. A long time elapsed before the furious river swallowed it up.

'Are you all right?' asked Gabriel.

'Why wouldn't I be?' bellowed de Candia.

Gabriel saw Hernando smiling. The leader of the gold-seeking expedition stood surrounded by his henchmen up at the near end of the bridge. Gabriel could see the hateful disdain concentrated in that smile even at that distance, despite the concealing effect of the Governor's brother's beard.

'Let's go,' Gabriel growled to himself.

But the incident of Pedro's fall had altered the bridge's equilibrium, and the movement of the structure had become much more vigorous, almost as though it were alive. Now it was not only swaying horizontally but had also developed a new rolling movement like that of a wave, as though the logs of the roadway had been caught in a heavy swell at sea. The more the two men and their horses advanced, the more violent the motion became. The bay baulked when the bridge jolted at the peak of each 'wave'. Gabriel yanked on its bridle, but was himself soon overcome with a desperate feeling of sickness. In an instant, cold sweat had his shirt and doublet clinging to his body.

And then, suddenly, it was all over. They were close enough to the other side for the supporting cables to become taut. The Indian guards waiting there grinned at them. With nausea churning his guts and with his heart in his mouth, Gabriel speeded up and completed the crossing at a sprint. He yelled unwittingly as he did so, as though charging into battle. Seeing his contorted features, the Indian guards stopped grinning and scurried away in a group, seeking refuge behind a wall surrounding a nearby group of buildings.

The Greek caught up with Gabriel on the big platform at the end of the bridge. They smiled broadly as they embraced one another and slapped each other's backs.

For almost an hour, the llamas and Indian bearers streamed across the bridge without further incident. The deftness with which the porters of the Inca general's palanquin negotiated the crossing was truly impressive. They seemed to slide gracefully along the bridge's roadway, completely unmindful of its steep angles. The palanquin itself remained stable and horizontal, and even its curtains barely fluttered.

As for the Spanish cavalrymen and foot soldiers, their own skill was no match for that of the Indians. They urged one another on with loud, pointless shouts, and their movements lacked the measured precision of the Indians'. Some even vomited, and most reached the other side of the canyon much paler than they had been when they'd started to cross.

Sebastian negotiated the bridge without mishap and positioned himself next to his two friends, greeting them with a simple wink.

The sun would soon reach its zenith. A light breeze scattered the last remaining clouds heaped in the sky over the western end of the valley. The green of the vegetation acquired the depth of emerald in the sharp new light. Now not just one condor soared through the intensely blue sky but two, three, ten and more whirled high above in a majestic airborne ballet. Gabriel could not help but admire them, and was delighted to see them coming closer and closer. He could make out their long necks quite distinctly, as well as their enormous beaks that were curved like Turkish cutlasses. But their wings were what impressed him most. They were entirely and perfectly black, reflecting the sunlight like immense sheets of damask steel. The birds seemed never to flap those wings at all, save for the occasional slight quiver as they hovered on a gust of air. As far as Gabriel could tell, the wingspan of the largest condors was easily greater than the length of a horse.

Now the drama of their whirling began to intensify. They fell into steeper and steeper dives, and they flew further and further upstream. On their return flights they came in so low that Gabriel could hear a sort of screeching sound whistling through the air, audible even through the rumble of the river below.

It happened when the last of the porters were halfway across.

A dozen Indians were advancing prudently in pairs, carrying between them the carcasses of young llamas, suspended from bamboo poles. The Spaniards had grown to enjoy the meat of these animals, roasted for their feasts. Most of the bearers had already made significant progress and had adapted to the rhythm of the bridge's undulations. But a couple of stragglers seemed to be having trouble keeping their balance.

Suddenly, the lead porters came to a halt and looked up anxiously at the sky. It was then that Gabriel understood. One of the condors had glided so low and so close to the heads of the last pair of porters that it looked as though it was going to hit them. The two Indians, taken by surprise, raised their arms to protect themselves. They lost their hold on their llama carcass and it fell into the chasm, twisting and turning as it went, chased by a second condor, before disappearing into the rapids.

Immediately, the first massive bird of prey turned gracefully and climbed high, only to dive once again at the bridge. The superb and insolent creature seemed furious at having lost its prey. Its fellows joined in its aerial dance. One after the other, their wings angled forward and their necks pulled back into their spotless ruffs, they dived at the porters, who were now lying flat and shrieking with fright.

Gabriel heard them cry:

'Kuntur! Kuntur!'

As everyone who'd crossed already looked on, dumbfounded, two Indians brandished a llama carcass above the rope cables.

The last condor came at them majestically, so slowly that it looked as though it was going to land. It unfurled its talons, its claws as long as a man's fingers, grabbed hold of its prize and carried it away into the sky.

Gabriel, short of breath, heard the Indians chant as the great birds flew away:

'Kuntur! Kuntur!'

'Mother of God, what's got into them?' asked Pedro the Greek, still wide-eyed.

'They consider the condor a sacred animal,' explained Gabriel. 'The Incas see them as messengers from their sun god, and—'

But he didn't get a chance to explain further. A furious roar made him turn around.

Hernando, standing at the end of the bridge, was hurling insults at the porters as they finished crossing at a run.

'Bunch of fucking idiots! Frightened of birds! Who gave you permission to let go of those llamas?'

The porters, their eyes still full of fear, stopped dead a few steps away from the Governor's brother. Hernando grabbed Felipillo, the interpreter who had been with them since the landing at Tumbez, roughly by the shoulder and said:

'Tell these monkeys that I will *not* have food wasted!'

Felipillo mumbled a few words. With his head lowered, the oldest of the Indian bearers replied almost inaudibly:

'They say that one has to feed the condor when it is hungry, or else the Sun God becomes enraged.'

'Damned bunch of savages!' screamed Hernando. 'Feeding birds

– what next? Who gives a damn about the sun's rage? It's *my* rage that you should be worried about . . .'

In three quick steps, Hernando was past the pillars. He grabbed the old porter, and in a single movement lifted him and threw him over the rope cables with the ease of a lumberjack tossing a log.

Gabriel couldn't believe his eyes. He saw the stupefaction on the porter's face, his hands grasping futilely at the empty air as he tumbled into the abyss, his mouth gaping in a silent cry. In an instant the man looked like nothing more than a tiny, gesticulating puppet. He struck a sharp edge of rock and bounced off it into the river as though he was made of dough, as though he had no spine.

Silence. Hernando turned towards the Spaniards and grinned.

'Well, it seems there's one at least who can't flap his wings and fly,' he said with sinister sprightliness.

The Indians remained dumbfounded. They dared not even look at the river. Sebastian couldn't hold back a surprised gulp, and his customary grin had given way to a grimace: the African slave, his face gray beneath its normal dark brown, trembled with impotent fury. Gabriel, overwhelmed with rage himself, approached Hernando. He stood firmly in front of the Governor's brother, so close that the man could feel Gabriel's breath on his face.

'Don Hernando, you are filthy pig's shit.'

Hernando made no reply. His eyes narrowed so venomously that all that could be seen of them were two slits through which his hatred glowered: a deep, infinite hatred. After a pause, he said:

'I don't think I heard you right, you whoreson bastard.'

'Your presence poisons the air, Don Hernando. You are no man, no Christian, and you bring shame upon your family's name. Your blood is mud and your brain rotted into sewage long ago.'

'By the blood of Christ!'

Hernando drew his sword swiftly from its scabbard. Gabriel had just enough time to jump back to avoid having his throat sliced open.

'Haaa!'

With a cry of rage, Hernando whipped his blade through the

air again. But once more Gabriel was too quick for him, leaping back with his arms held away from his body as though dancing. Hernando, hitting nothing, swung back around on himself.

'The day you die, Don Hernando,' said Gabriel, his voice shaking less and carrying a slightly amused tone, 'even the carrion crows won't touch you.'

'Defend yourself!' growled Hernando, throwing aside his morion. 'Unsheathe your sword, you bastard scum!'

Everyone around them had drawn back. Gabriel's pliant blade hissed and glinted as he drew it from its scabbard with an easy movement of his wrist. For a moment, the two men seemed to be moving in slow motion, as though an invisible and impenetrable block had formed between them.

And then Hernando lunged. His blade slid along Gabriel's and Gabriel parried, his knees and waist bent, lifting the locked swords above his shoulder. The weapons' hilts slammed loudly together. Gabriel shoved Hernando back and turned as their blades disengaged, a grim smile on his lips. The Governor's brother was heavy, breathless with rage, drunk with an uncontrollable urge to violence. He whipped the air with his sword like a rabid dog wagging its tail. Gabriel contented himself with parrying his opponent's slashes and thrusts with small strokes. He could read the mad rage in Hernando's eyes. Then, with a sudden jump, he was in close, his torso side on to Hernando. He slipped his blade beneath Hernando's – and now Gabriel had the upper hand. With all the strength in his arm, he heaved on the interlocked swords, and with a powerful flick of his wrist flung his arm wide to the right.

Hernando's sword tinkled like a bell as it landed at de Candia's feet. The Greek couldn't help but smile.

Gabriel pushed the point of his sword into the cloth of his adversary's doublet, forcing him back. Hernando's mouth twisted, his eyes communicating an emotion that Gabriel had never seen in him before. *He's frightened*, Gabriel thought with pleasure.

'You forget that suffering has two faces, Don Hernando,' he said in a low voice, breathing heavily. 'You enjoy seeing fear in the eyes of others. But how do you feel now? What have you to say to that wrench in *your* guts? One or two more steps and you too might learn to fly.'

Gabriel forced Hernando further and further back as he spoke, right to the edge of the canyon, to the very spot from where the Governor's brother had thrown the unfortunate porter.

'Gather your wits, man. I'm not going to kill you. But know that the Governor, Don Francisco, shall be the one to judge your misdeeds. Certainly, you are bringing a lot of gold back to Cajamarca, together with an important general who serves the master of that place. But none of that shall buy you your redemption.'

'By the Virgin, threaten me all you want! We shall see who will be the one who suffers in the end.'

Hernando had said this with a contemptuous snigger, but everyone present perceived that his bravado was a façade. The humiliation he had just suffered had been too great, too public, and too spectacular.

'Peace, my lords. The point has been made,' interrupted de Candia as he laid his hand on Gabriel's arm. 'God is my witness, and I say to you that two conquistadors cannot fight one another: it ain't dignified, it ain't natural, and it goes against the good fortune of the Conquest! Don Hernando, here is your sword. Let us be on our way, if you please.'

Hernando and Gabriel eyed one another scornfully. Gabriel lowered his sword. But it was Hernando who lowered his gaze.

Behind them, the hanging that enclosed General Chalkuchimac's palanquin fell back down silently.

As the column set off, Sebastian took Gabriel by the arm. He walked with him for a while in silence. Then he leaned over to speak into his ear and murmured:

'Thank you.'

PART 1

CHAPTER 1

Cajamarca, 14 April 1533: dawn

'I LOVE YOU,' MURMURED ANAMAYA IN THE PALE DAWN rising over Cajamarca. The darkness of night still lingered, but the smoke rising over the thatched roofs was now slowly turning blue in the growing light.

Anamaya was alone.

She had stolen away from the palace in which Atahualpa was being kept prisoner. She left it behind her now as she moved like a quick shadow along the narrow streets laid out on the slope overlooking the main square. Soon she arrived at the river and the access street to the Royal Road.

'I love you', she repeated. *'Te quiero!'*

The language of the Spaniards came to her so easily that everyone was amazed, whether conquistador or Indian. It had also roused an old mistrust among her own people, and once again there was whispering behind her back. But she didn't care.

She ran stealthily alongside the houses, staying close to the shadows of the walls in order to evade the guards watching over Atahualpa's palace and its ransom room piled high with treasure.

The mere sight of this precious haul intoxicated those who had won the battle of Cajamarca and who had had the audacity to lay their hands on Emperor Atahualpa. It was as though they imagined that gold would yield to them the magical powers that they lacked.

The plunder inspired a deep and silent sadness in Anamaya.

The strangers were insatiable. In search of still more booty to stuff into the large ransom room, Don Hernando Pizarro had gone to sack the temple at Pachacamac, far, far away on the shore of the southern sea. And because his brother was late returning, the Governor, Don Francisco Pizarro, had sent Gabriel and a few reliable men after him.

Gabriel . . . she let his name settle into her heart, the sound of it so foreign, yet so tender to her . . . she called to mind his face, his image . . . the Stranger with sun-coloured hair, with pale, pale skin, with the mark of the puma crouching on his shoulder, the mark that was their bond, their secret link that she would reveal to him one day.

Gabriel had no love of gold. Many times she had watched him stand by, indifferent to, even irritated by his companions' delirious rapture at the mere touch of a few gold leaves.

Gabriel did not accept that an Indian should be beaten because of a trifling offence, even less that they should be chained or killed.

Gabriel had saved the Emperor from the sword.

Anamaya recalled Atahualpa's words, the words he had spoken when he had still had all the power of an Emperor. On the eve of the Great Battle, seeing the Strangers for the first time, he had murmured, 'I like their horses. But as for them, I don't understand.'

Like him, Anamaya could have said, 'I love one among them, the one who leaped across the ocean for me. But as for the rest of them, I don't understand.'

Now Anamaya had left behind the high walls surrounding Cajamarca. As she ascended the lower slopes of the Royal Road, her pace slowed. The adobe-walled houses were fewer now, and set further apart. Dawn was lighting up the mountainsides, breathing life into the corn and *quinua* fields that rustled in the morning breeze. Occasionally she saw a peasant, already bowed beneath some burden, silhouetted against the growing pale radiance of day.

Anamaya's heart would fill with an uneasy tenderness. She would feel an urge to run to the man and help him carry his burden. She thought about the suffering weighing on her people.

Her people! Because now she who for so long had been the odd child with blue eyes, the awkward girl who was too tall and too thin, now she knew how much all those who lived in the Inca Empire formed what she called 'her people'. They didn't all speak the same language or wear the same clothes, and only superficially did they believe in the same gods. Often they had warred among themselves, and the spirit of war was within them still. Yet, in her heart, Anamaya would wish them all to be blood brothers.

By the time she reached the pass, the day was well established. Light shimmered on the marsh and spread across the immense plain, right up to the mountains that concealed the road to Cuzco.

As happened each time she returned here, Anamaya couldn't stop the flood of her memories. She remembered those days in the not so distant past when the entire plain had been covered by the white tents of Atahualpa's invincible army. It had been the army of an Emperor who had known how to defeat the cruelty of his brother Huascar, the madman of Cuzco.

The steam rose from the baths over on the opposite slope. Atahualpa was resting there, giving thanks to his father Inti by fasting. Her breath short, her heart constricted, Anamaya remembered, as though they were forever tattooed into her skin, those endless days when news of the Strangers' slow approach was brought to them. She remembered that time when everyone had scoffed at them, and the fear that she had felt bloom within her. And then she remembered that dawn when all of a sudden *he* had appeared: him, Gabriel. He was so handsome, so attractive that his beauty had been incomprehensible to her.

She didn't want to contemplate what had happened after that. The Emperor Atahualpa was now but a shadow of his former self, a prisoner in his own palace while his temples were destroyed.

Thus had been accomplished the will of the sun god.

Thus had been fulfilled the terrible words of the deceased Inca Huayna Capac, who had once come to her in the form of a child and said: 'That which is too old comes to an end, that which is too big shatters, that which is too strong loses its force . . . that is what the great pachacuti means . . . Some die, and others grow. Have no fear for yourself, Anamaya . . . you are what you are meant to be. Have no fear, for in the future the puma will go with you!'

Thus, from the other world, the former Inca had simultaneously announced to her Atahualpa's fall and Gabriel's coming!

In truth, ever since her lips had kissed Gabriel's, ever since she had kissed his strangely marked shoulder, there had been many things that Anamaya hadn't been able to understand. There were so many sensations, so many unknown emotions now living within her. And living with so much strength that it seemed as if the claws of a real puma were lacerating her heart.

There were those emotions that urged her to say, 'I love you,' the words that Gabriel had stubbornly laboured to teach her. He had become angry as she had sat there smiling while she listened to him, refusing to repeat the words after him.

And then there was the mystery: how could a Stranger, an enemy, be the puma who would go with her into the future?

Anamaya walked slowly to the end of the plateau that stretched across the head of the pass. She wrapped her cloak about herself and lay down on the still-wet grass covering the slope. She gazed at the highest peaks in the east, contemplating the sun's first rays.

Anamaya closed her eyes. She let the light caress her eyelids and drive away the tears that had formed under them. And as soon as the sun had warmed her face, the image of Gabriel appeared to her against the red underside of her eyelids. Gabriel, the handsome Stranger with eyes like coal, who laughed as innocently as a child, and whose touch was so tender.

Once more her lips formed the words. She whispered them as though they could fly above the earth like hummingbirds: 'I love you.'

As they approached Cajamarca, Gabriel, unable to hold himself back, spurred on his horse. He rode to the head of the column at a full trot. His blood surged. He hadn't slept a wink since his encounter with Hernando three days earlier. Three nights spent contemplating the stars or sharing the watch at a campsite or a *tambo*. But today it was finally over.

He was going to be with Anamaya once more.

In a little while he would be gazing into her blue, blue eyes, he would be able to touch her tender mouth, so tender that her kiss melted him, making him oblivious to reality. Only two more leagues and he would be able to see her tall and slender figure, unique among Indian women. And the awareness of this alone aroused his very soul.

He hoped as well that nothing had happened to her during his long absence. There had been talk, as he was leaving Cajamarca, of the arrival of *mariscal* Diego de Almagro, Don Francisco's old brother-in-arms, bringing with him yet more troops and horses . . .

Gabriel was trembling with joy and yet, had he dared, he would have yelled his lungs out in order to banish his apprehension.

He passed stretchers, borne by Indians, on which the heaviest treasures lay: a great gold bowl, a gold statue, a gold chair, and gold mural plaques torn from temple walls. Gold, gold, and yet more gold! It was everywhere – in wicker baskets, in hide sacks, in woven saddle-packs. The porters were bent double, bowed under its weight, and the llamas had all but disappeared beneath their burdens. The column had slowed because of it, as though the entire expedition had, since Jauja, become weighed down with all the gold and silver of Peru . . .

And to think that this was all only a sample: rumor had it that these treasures were nothing in comparison with what would soon arrive from Cuzco. The Governor had sent three men there on a reconnaissance mission, including the execrable Pedro Martin de Moguer.

The Spanish cavalrymen were permanently on the alert. Their nerves frayed, their dark gazes mistrustful of everything, they watched for the slightest sign of unrest among the ever-docile Indians. Gabriel hadn't many friends in that group. They were all Hernando's men. The personal enmity between him and the Governor's brother had been well known by everyone for some time . . . and their recent duel had frozen the two men into an icy mutual hatred. The Governor's red-plumed brother now went out of his way to avoid Gabriel, more from caution than sensitivity.

As he arrived alongside the palanquins of two high priests from the Pachacamac temple, priests whom Hernando had bound in chains, Gabriel heard a familiar voice hailing him:

'Would Your Grace be in a great hurry, then?'

Gabriel pulled on the reins. With a graceful volte, his horse compliantly came up alongside Sebastian. The big black man, one of Gabriel's few intimate friends, had been on foot for twenty days now. The price of horses had become prohibitive, but what was more to the point, two days before they had left Pachacamac Don Hernando had forbidden Sebastian to take the horse of any dying or even already dead man.

The memory of his insult still rang shrill in the two friends' ears: 'Holà, darkie! Who do you take yourself for? Have you forgotten that horses are reserved for *caballeros* carrying the sword? Just because you kicked a few Indian asses you don't have the right to regard yourself as a man!'

Leaning forward along his horse's neck, Gabriel reached down and warmly shook the hand that Sebastian was holding out to him. The African giant might have had no horse, but his leather doublet was brand new and as supple as a second skin. His breeches were tailored with all sorts of fabrics sent from Spain to Cajamarca. These were of the latest Castile fashion: large green, red, yellow and pale blue stripes of felt or satin, and even a little lace on the cords of Sebastian's boots. The extravagance of his outfit made Gabriel (who always dressed soberly) feel like he was travelling with a retinue of Toledo maidens, their bosoms squeezed into their bodices!

'So where are you trotting off to so quick?' asked Sebastian.

'There's a stench round here,' growled Gabriel, looking directly at Hernando's escort. 'I need to breathe fresher air.'

The black giant gave him a wicked grin.

'Ahh . . . and there was I thinking that you were spurred on by an urgency of, how shall I put it, a higher order!'

Gabriel gave a hint of a smile.

'Why, what else could there be, other than my haste to present the Governor with *my* report of the mission?'

'Hoh! I see nothing else, indeed.'

Sebastian nodded. Then he fell silent, not bantering anymore. Gabriel's gaze fell upon the mountain ridges surrounding Cajamarca. A few months earlier, this alien landscape had harboured nothing but menace. Now it had become familiar, almost friendly. And now, of course, it also held for him the most wondrous promise.

Gabriel suddenly pulled his feet from the stirrups and jumped nimbly to the ground. While he led his horse using one hand, he wrapped his other arm around Sebastian's shoulders and leaned in close to his friend.

'You're right,' he said in a low voice, his eyes aglow. 'I *am* in a hurry . . . and it has nothing to do with that whoreson Hernando . . .'

'Well?'

Gabriel made a vague gesture towards the mountains.

'Anamaya says that she can't marry me. She is some sort of priestess in their ancient religion. Marriage is forbidden her, even marriage to an Indian. But still . . .'

'But still?'

'But still, I love her. Damn and blast it, Sebastian! Just thinking of her makes my heart explode like a volley of grapeshot. I love her as though I had never known the meaning of the word before.'

Sebastian burst out laughing.

'Do like me, my friend! Love many of them at once! One here, one there, but always and everywhere one to want you. A tender bed here, a fiery one there . . . then you will know what it means to love!'

There was a certain restraint in Gabriel's smile as he returned to his saddle.

'There are times, *compañero*, when I wish you weren't so witty.'

Sebastian seemed about to smile, but his expression remained as dark as his skin.

'I too wish it. And then again . . .'

'And then?'

The column had slowed and grown longer, and now it ground to a halt. The royal road had grown narrower at the approach to the last peak before Cajamarca.

'And then what?' insisted Gabriel.

Sebastian shook his head. He motioned to Gabriel to gallop on ahead.

'I'll tell you some other time, when you're in less of a hurry.'

The hammering that startled Anamaya from her sleep was not that of her heart. It was the stamping of men and horses and the noise was thrumming through the ground. She sat up, rose and went to hide in a hedge of acacia and agave close to the Royal Road.

A herd of llamas that had been grazing quietly in a neighbouring pasture now shot past her and fled, bounding nervously as they went, to the other side of the ridge. The instantly familiar clinking of the Spaniards' iron weapons rang through the balmy air. It slowly increased in volume, along with laughter, bursts of speech, and the click-clacking of hooves on flagstones.

Anamaya caught sight of them coming out of a small wood at the foot of the slope. She saw the lances and colourful plumes of the horsemen first, then their somber bearded faces beneath their morions, before the Indian porters and the Spaniards on foot finally appeared. She could now see the entire slow-moving column that was led by the Governor's brother.

Anamaya breathed in quick, staccato gasps. She looked for *him*.

But scrutinize each face, each man's apparel as she might, she couldn't see Gabriel among the men approaching the ridge. She couldn't make out his black doublet, nor his reddish-brown horse with the long white stain on its hindquarters. Neither could she make out the blue scarf he invariably wore around his neck in order to 'carry the colour of her eyes' with him, as he said, and that normally helped her pick him out from afar.

Anamaya's fingers trembled without her realizing it. Her heart beat strongly – too strongly. She was ashamed of her fear, and she pulled a low branch aside to see more clearly, despite the risk of being seen herself.

At last the blue patch of the scarf appeared fleetingly behind a palanquin. She caught a brief glimpse of the bay. She let out a little spontaneous laugh.

And then she froze.

Her gaze didn't linger on Gabriel. Rather, it remained fixed on the hangings that enclosed the palanquin. She recognized the markings and colors, the slanted lines of blood-red and sky-blue rectangles and triangles.

It was General Chalkuchimac's palanquin. Atahualpa's most powerful warrior.

So, the Strangers had convinced him to travel all the way to the Emperor's prison. By what ruse, what treachery had they accomplished this?

Anamaya watched Gabriel pass, riding in front of the palanquin as though guarding it. Her heart was no longer beating so fast at the prospect of seeing him. A shadow loomed over her joy.

She understood how things stood. She knew, better than any, what was to become of the Emperor.

A cry from behind caused her to turn around. A small group of riders was coming from the other side of the ridge, negotiating the very steep slope with some difficulty. Leading them was Governor Francisco Pizarro, the leader of the Spaniards, dressed in black, his grey beard standing out against a strange white garment full of holes. A little way behind him came de Almagro, an undersized man riding a mare far too big for him. He had a frightening appearance. A green bandana covered one eye. The pockmarked and chapped skin of his face was covered in rusty blotches that the sparse hairs of his beard failed to hide. His too-wide mouth had few teeth. Yet when he spoke his voice was often gentle, almost doleful.

Another cry rang through the air, followed by others. Laughter echoed; lances and pikes were raised and waved about. When the long column of horsemen was just a stone's throw away from him, Don Francisco jumped agilely from his horse and walked, his arms flung wide, towards his brother.

Before they had even embraced, Anamaya had already reached the long grass and was running towards the town along the shepherds' steep path.

The ridge's last slope was very steep for the horses. Gabriel guided his steed cautiously, holding the reins chest high. The flagstones were slippery, and the porters faltered. Their talking ceased as he approached; it was known among the Indians that he spoke a little of their language.

Calls and cries rang out from the head of the column. Gabriel urged on his horse and moved away from the Inca general's palanquin. He saw Hernando Pizarro meet his brother Francisco high up on the narrow plateau at the ridge's crest.

Gabriel couldn't help but grin mordantly. Don Francisco had donned his most impressive finery in which to welcome his brother. He wore a Cadiz lace ruff around his neck, an item that must have cost him its weight in gold, though it contrasted nicely with his meticulously trimmed beard. But whatever sartorial efforts the Governor had made, it was still his brother Hernando, bigger and seeming more assured in the power of his body and his eminent origins, who looked like a genuine prince.

The two brothers embraced enthusiastically in front of the entire company. The Governor's two younger brothers stood in the background: the handsome Gonzalo, with his dark curls, and the diminutive Juan, with his beauty spot on his neck, watched the proceedings with their hats in their hands and grins on their faces.

Gabriel knew what those grins were worth. What really grabbed his attention was the ill-looking fellow with a scowling face that was ugly enough to frighten children. Although Gabriel had only laid eyes on him a few times previously, years ago before they had left for the Peruvian coast, he recognized him instantly.

So, Don Diego de Almagro had indeed come from Panama during Gabriel's absence! He who, out of his own pocket, had paid for Don Francisco's most ambitious adventure, who had given of himself for it, who had dreamed of becoming an *Adelantado* alongside his old companion – now called Governor – he on whom King Charles the Fifth had only bestowed the title of Lieutenant of Tumbez, with a miserable salary and a *hidalgo*'s title: Don Diego had come to claim his due!

The porters began to move forward again. They advanced cautiously down the broad, slippery steps that plunged down to the outskirts of the town. The interpreter Felipillo, his thin lips shut tight, his eyes darting and evasive, stayed close to the most richly decorated palanquin, that of General Chalkuchimac.

When the palanquin and its retinue reached the square where the Governor, his brothers, and Don Diego de Almagro had already arrived, the litter's curtains opened slightly. Through the gap, Gabriel saw a powerful hand appear, large enough to crush a llama's throat.

Felipillo scurried up to the gap, bent double and murmured a few words that Gabriel couldn't hear.

He stood upright again and barked an order. The porters stood still, their eyes lowered. The hanging enclosing the palanquin slowly rose.

General Chalkuchimac wore a magnificent blue *unku* made of a blend of cotton and wool. The tunic's weave was strewn with gold sequins. Very fine *tocapus* outlined a crimson band around the general's waist. His long, thick hair fell to his shoulders, partly concealing his gold earlobe plugs. They seemed smaller than those worn by other nobles that Gabriel had seen. Yet Chalkuchimac's face commanded respect. It was difficult to guess his age: he had the power and impassiveness of a statue, as though he had been sculpted from a block of sacred rock hewn from the mountains.

He moved forward and glanced at Gabriel. He growled a few words:

'I must see my master.'

Gabriel wasn't sure if he had understood him right. Felipillo was bustling about at one end of the palanquin. The Inca general raised a hand, pushing the interpreter back without even touching him.

Then Chalkuchimac approached one of the porters. He took the man's load from him. The porter trembled, staring fixedly at the ground, his hands empty.

Chalkuchimac placed the enormous basket on his back. Bent double under its weight, he entered the town.

'Now,' Atahualpa affirmed slowly, 'they will free me.'

The Emperor was seated on his royal tripod, a cape of fine wool hanging over his shoulders. His voice was muted, hardly breaking the silence.

The room was large and permanently dark. Neither light nor drafts found their way in, and smoke from the braziers had blackened the stones, the tops of the crimson tapestries and the building's beams. Many of the niches were empty, or else contained only carved wooden ceremonial vases, albeit magnificent ones, for holding sacred beer. Most of the gold pots, silver goblets and statues of the gods had all long since been added to the heap in the ransom room.

The Emperor had his servants, wives and concubines leave the room every time Anamaya visited. These moments of intimacy were all that remained of their lost liberty.

Atahualpa's silhouette, radiating pathos, appeared from the shadows. Anamaya couldn't help but shiver when she thought that he who had been the Inca, the very brightness of the sun, was slowly slipping towards the Under World.

The *llautu*, the royal band, was still on his forehead, and in it were fixed the black and white feathers of the *curiquingue*, the symbol of the Emperor's supreme power. Anamaya noticed that he no longer wore gold plugs in his earlobes. His left lobe, a gaping ring of dead flesh, hung down to his shoulder. His wives had woven him a bandanna of the finest alpaca wool in which to wrap his hair, and he wore it so that it concealed the torn lobe of his other ear.

Anamaya averted her gaze from the pitiful signs of a power in decline. It seemed to her that a little more of Atahualpa's soul left him with each passing day. The virgins still wove his tunics for each new day. He was still served his meals in earthenware that no one else used. His retinue, whether they were men or women, and including the few noblemen who were his fellow prisoners in the Cajamarca palace, still feared his word as they had always done. The Strangers bowed before addressing him, and the Spanish Governor accorded him the respect due an Emperor. And yet, Anamaya couldn't help but see it all as a masquerade playing itself out. The Emperor had developed a stoop, his face had grown sallow, and the red of his eyes had become even bloodier. His mouth was less beautiful, less imperial. His whole body seemed to have shrunk.

The conqueror in him, the son of the great Huayna Capac, had disappeared. Atahualpa was still the Emperor who lived in the Cajamarca palace, but he was no longer the powerful progeny of the sun who had defeated his brother, the madman of Cuzco. He was merely a prisoner without chains who dreamed of his liberation.

Anamaya wanted to tell him what she had seen on the mountain road. She wanted to warn him that Chalkuchimac had been there in his palanquin. But she didn't dare, and Atahualpa repeated:

'They have their gold now. They will let me go.'

'I'm not sure,' replied Anamaya, looking away.

'What did you say?'

'I'm not sure,' she repeated.

Atahualpa gestured irascibly in the direction of the ransom room.

'I chose the biggest room in my palace, I designated a line on the wall to mark the height of the ransom pile. It has now been reached.'

'I remember, my Lord,' agreed Anamaya gently. 'The Strangers laughed – they thought that you had been seized by madness.'

'I told them where to find our gold and silver. I told them that they could take it all, from every house except my father's.'

'I know, my Lord.'

A sly smile lit Atahualpa's face.

'I realize that I'm talking to the wife of my father's Sacred Double . . .'

Anamaya let a moment pass, and then replied:

'My Lord, those who went to Pachacamac have returned today.'

'How do you know this?'

Anamaya made no reply. She didn't want to emphasize the weakness of his position.

Again, the Inca grinned:

'Isn't that what I was telling you? I am going to be freed.'

'My Lord,' Anamaya said in a voice so low that it was barely audible, 'the big room is filled with gold, with all our sacred objects, both the most ancient and those that the smiths have only just finished. But the Strangers will not leave your kingdom. They will want to go to the Sacred City. They will fill the biggest room, and then they will take the gold of Cuzco. And even if they swore to you by their god and their king not to touch anything belonging to your father Huayna Capac, the mere sight of the gold will make them forget their promise. You know it, my Lord . . .'

Atahualpa lowered his gaze.

Anamaya didn't want to stop talking now. She continued gently:

'More Strangers will arrive in your kingdom, my Lord. They too will bring weapons and horses, and they too will want gold.'

'Yes,' murmured Atahualpa. 'I don't like that new one, that very ugly one-eyed man . . .'

The words came out of Atahualpa's mouth with difficulty, as though he was a hesitant child once more.

'His name is Almagro.'

'I don't like him,' repeated the Inca. 'His eye lies. He and those who came with him take my women without my permission. They laugh when I forbid it. He says that he is Pizarro's friend, but his eye tells me that it isn't so . . .'

'Why would these men be here, my Lord, if not to take yet more gold?'

'Pizarro's brother will protect me,' affirmed Atahualpa. 'He is powerful.'

'Hernando? Forgive me, my Lord, but don't trust him. His heart is false.'

Atahualpa shook his head.

'No! He is powerful, and the others are frightened of him.'

'You say that because he has great bearing, because he has a

proud eye and he dresses more carefully than the others, who
are slovenly and as dirty as the animals that they have brought
with them and that now infest our streets. The feather above his
helmet may be red, but his soul is black.'

A look of shameful hope came over Atahualpa's face.

'He promised that he would help me. If he doesn't . . .'

His voice lowered slightly. He motioned to Anamaya to approach.
A glow of naive excitement had returned to his eyes.

'If he doesn't, the thousands of warriors mobilized by my loyal
generals will deliver me. Chalkuchimac is at Jauja, waiting in
readiness. He will tell the others . . .'

Anamaya stifled a cry.

'Oh, my Lord . . .'

As she hesitated, they heard shouts echoing across the patio.
A servant bowed at the threshold of the room. Anamaya knows
what he is going to say, and her blood ran cold.

'My lord . . . General Chalkuchimac is here. He asks whether
you deign to look upon him.'

At first, Atahualpa didn't move. Then the full meaning of the
words reached him, and the colour drained from his face.

'I am a dead man,' he whispered.

'May he enter?' asked the servant again, who hadn't heard
him.

'I am dead,' Atahualpa repeated.

At the palace entrance, Chalkcuchimac hadn't taken off the load
weighing on his back. Gabriel watched the Inca general, who was
bent double like a supplicant carrying his cross.

De Almagro muttered:

'Let us be done with this damned comedy! The only thing
this monkey has to do is tell us where he has hidden the rest
of the gold.'

Don Francisco raised his black-gloved hand.

'Patience, Diego, patience . . .'

The Inca warriors guarding the entrance to the patio had
retreated respectfully as Chalkuchimac had come forward. Water

spouted from the mouth and the tail of a stone serpent set in a low fountain in the centre of the patio. All around bloomed the bright red corollas of the *cantuta*, the Inca flower. A servant whose only job was to collect the wilted petals stood by them.

Once Chalkuchimac had crawled on his knees into the middle of the courtyard, Atahualpa came out of the room. Gabriel had trouble recognizing him. Behind the Inca, in the shadows that half hid her features, he saw Anamaya.

When at last she lifted her face towards him, it was only with the greatest of difficulty that he managed to restrain himself from going to her.

Atahualpa seated himself slowly on a red wood bench, about a handsbreadth from the ground. It was his usual seat. Some women approached, ready to serve him.

Chalkuchimac at last unburdened himself of his load, giving it into the hands of a porter who had followed him from the outskirts of the town. He removed his sandals and raised his hands toward the cloud-veiled sun, his palms turned skywards.

Tears ran down his rugged face as words escaped from his mouth. Gabriel made out a few offerings of gratitude to Inti, and some mumbled expressions of love for the Inca.

Then Chalkuchimac approached his master. While continuing to weep, the general kissed Atahualpa's face, his hands, and his feet.

Atahualpa remained as still as if Chalkuchimac were only a ghost brushing past him. His eyes gazed at an invisible point in the distance. Gabriel had often seen the Inca, but he had never managed to fathom his reactions or his facial expressions.

'You are gladly received, Chalkuchimac,' said the Inca eventually. His voice was monotonous and cold.

Chalkuchimac straightened up and again raised his palms towards the sky.

'Had I been there,' he said in a resonant voice, 'none of this would have happened. The Strangers would never have laid a hand on you.'

Atahualpa turned toward him at last. Gabriel was trying to

attract Anamaya's attention when Don Francisco grabbed his shoulder. Impressed by the events, the Governor asked:

'What are they saying?'

'They are greeting one another,' Gabriel replied.

'Strange way to say hello,' muttered Don Francisco.

Chalkuchimac stood up. His face had regained its usual impassive and noble composure.

'I waited for your orders, my Lord,' he said in a low voice. 'Each day, each time that our father the Sun rose into the sky, I felt the urge to come to your rescue. But, as you know, I could not do so against your wishes. And the *chaski* bearing your command never came. O my Lord, why did you not order me to annihilate the Strangers?'

Atahualpa made no reply.

The Inca general waited silently for an answer, for some encouraging words. They didn't come. They would never come.

Don Francisco asked again:

'What are they saying now?'

Gabriel felt the infinite and magnificent blue of Anamaya's eyes speak to him, and in that moment he suddenly understood. It was anger that made Atahualpa so still, that had frozen him in that terrible silence.

'The general regrets not having served the Inca better,' murmured Gabriel. 'He regrets that he has been taken prisoner . . .'

Chalkuchimac took two steps back.

'I waited for your orders, my Lord,' he repeated. 'We were alone, isolated. Your generals – Quizquiz and Captain Guaypar and the rest – were alone. If you do not order it, they will not come to liberate you.'

And with that Chalkuchimac turned his back on his master and walked slowly from the patio, his shoulders sagging as though they now bore a heavier load than the one he had entered with.

Gabriel advanced carefully through the dark, feeling his way past the sacks, baskets and jars.

The secret passage began from the very heart of the palace,

from the end of a small room in which the *mullus*, those pink shells so important during Inca rituals, were kept.

Anamaya had revealed it to him shortly after the Great Battle. He had had to promise her to keep it secret. He remembered jesting with her, saying, 'So, would you mind if I brought the Governor here?'

Back then, the words they spoke to each other were still uncertain. Action had taken the place of talk. They could only express and share their love physically. But they did not always have the chance to escape to the cabin by the hot springs, the hut where they had spent their first night together. So this passage had become their trysting place.

As he crossed the room, Gabriel sank his hand into a large jar of shells. Doing so evoked an oddly pleasant impression of the sea. The trapezoid niches now so familiar to him surrounded the room. All the gold statues they had once contained had been removed at the beginning of the Spanish occupation, and the alcoves were now covered with cotton hangings. He lifted one, his heart racing.

The tunnel had been dug at a slight rising angle. A thin layer of beaten earth covered the rock. Anamaya had explained to him that, during ancient times, the tunnel system had crisscrossed through the entire hill, passing through the *acllahuasi* and reaching the snail-shaped fortress, the one the conquistadors had demolished upon their arrival.

The passage was remarkably clean and dry, and chests in which reserves of food and clothes had once been stored still sat in recesses at intervals along the way. A rumbling rose up from the belly of the earth: it was the sound of the underground rivers flowing beneath the mountain.

Gabriel's eyes had not yet adapted to the darkness, and he uttered a surprised cry when a hand landed on his own as lightly as a butterfly.

'Anamaya!'

Her hand fluttered against his face, tapped lightly on his full lips, caressed his cheeks half hidden under his beard, and gently stroked his eyelids, his forehead. Gabriel tried to kiss her, to hold her, but she embraced him and then dodged away from him immediately. They laughed softly.

The moment he stopped grasping for her, she stopped evading him. Now he felt her breath close to his own lips and at last he could make out her proffered face. They both smiled even though they were unable to see one another clearly through the darkness.

'You're here,' Anamaya whispered.

Gabriel sensed in her voice a timidity, or rather a sense of modesty so profound that he was overwhelmed by it. Those simple words had travelled far in her heart and her soul before reaching her lips.

She was so close that he could smell her scent.

When he drew her to him, she surrendered herself demurely. Gabriel's arms closed around her; he felt her firm breasts against his chest, her lithe legs pressed along the length of his own. Suddenly the two lovers were clutching at one another, their loins afire, their senses made dizzy by the vertigo of passion.

All the energy and desire within them, all the accumulated self-constraint of their waiting was released in an instant. They felt a sudden, quivering thrill that they sustained by caressing each other's bodies.

Gabriel wanted to be the embodiment of tenderness. He ran his hand through Anamaya's thick hair. They held one another still for a moment. Their hearts pounded so strongly that it felt as though one pulse beat for both of them.

Anamaya took the lead in their lovemaking, placing her lips on his, touching him, undressing him, pushing him back with gentle but insistent motions so that he bent his knees and slid slowly down to the ground.

Gabriel felt her mouth travelling over his body, running across his face, his neck, his chest, a wave of warmth on his skin.

Then he allowed his own hands their freedom. They gripped Anamaya's smooth, strong thighs, naked under her fine wool tunic, parting them gently but firmly. He thought he heard a new sound, a groan that blended with the subterranean murmuring of the rivers.

Anamaya whispered a few lively, happy sounds into his ear, words that he didn't understand.

She is so light, Gabriel thought to himself as their naked bodies burned and melted into each other.

And then, overwhelmed by her caresses, he soared away with her.

CHAPTER 2

Cajamarca, 14 April 1533

ANAMAYA WAS RESTING IN HER CHAMBER. THE SMALL room was bathed in a gentle half-light. In the Inca's palace, the *Coya Camaquen* was entitled to a room of her own. But unlike Atahualpa's, hers had been emptied of ornaments and tapestries – all its niches were bare. Delicate stone snakes slinking up the walls were the room's only decoration. The light played on their undulating forms, and in its movement the snakes sometimes appeared very real.

Anamaya dreamed of the day when she and Gabriel would be able to sleep alongside each other the whole night through, as wife and husband. But would it happen? There was so much against it becoming a reality.

She was still light-headed from the passion of their reunion in the flesh: her body felt both heavy and weightless with the well-being of love. The door hanging fluttered in the balmy breeze. It was as though the breeze was stroking her with one final caress, an ephemeral touch of her lover's hand.

A sudden gust of air startled her.

'*Coya Camaquen!*'

It was a whisper, barely a murmur. She propped herself up on her elbows.

'*Coya Camaquen!*'

Anamaya made out a figure crouched in the shadows like some frightened small animal.

'Who are you?' she asked quietly.

'*Coya Camaquen*, I need your help . . .'

'Who are you?' repeated Anamaya.

All she got in reply was a tense, quick sound of breathing. She sat up on her matting and extended her hands towards the huddled shape.

'Come closer . . . don't be frightened.'

The form slowly and timidly straightened itself. Two dark and lively eyes appeared beneath a head of dishevelled hair. It turned out to be a young girl, almost still a child. Her face was triangular, and she wore a simple tunic, splattered with mud, under a gray cape too large for her. She advanced, bent double as though she was carrying a load, and stopped at the edge of the mat. In a trembling supplicant gesture, she knelt, bowed her head and placed her two tiny hands on it, the palms facing upwards.

'What are you doing here?' asked Anamaya.

The black eyes stared at her but no reply came.

A feeling of infinite tenderness towards this fragile stranger beset Anamaya. She imagined the dread she must have felt while slipping past the guards and running across the patio to be here now.

'If you don't speak to me,' she continued with feigned severity, 'I will never know if I can help you!'

'My name is Inguill and I come from Cuzco,' said the young girl in one burst of breath. 'I am from the Great Lord Manco's clan.'

Manco! Anamaya felt a constriction in her throat.

Manco: her ever-loyal friend, loyal to her despite the wars and the animosity between the clans. Manco, who had taken her advice and fled into the hills above Cajamarca, along with the golden Sacred Double, on the terrible night following the Great Massacre and Atahualpa's capture.

Manco, he who the deceased Inca Huayna Capac had designated as the *'first knot of the future'* the last time he had visited her from the Other World.

Suddenly anxious, Anamaya gripped Inguill's shoulders.

'How is he?'

'He told me to come to you,' replied the very young girl, a little frightened, 'He told me: "Go to the *Coya Camaquen*, she will find a way to keep you near her. She sees the future unfurling before us . . ."'

Anamaya suppressed a sigh. If only it were so! What would she say to Manco if she saw him today? Would she be able to tell him 'No, I no longer know how to communicate with the Other World, and Emperor Huayna Capac stopped visiting me once a Stranger made my heart beat and touched me in a way that no other man has ever done? A Stranger unlike any other, a man marked by the puma?'

She allowed herself one small smile as she lightly stroked the young messenger's shoulder.

'So he is well!'

Inguill nodded her head, finally relaxing.

'He also told me that you must not worry about him or the Sacred Double. Each is where he is meant to be.'

Anamaya lowered her gaze in approval and asked:

'Now, tell me your story. You can trust me.'

'As you know, Huascar, who wanted to be Inca instead of Emperor Atahualpa, died shortly after your city was defeated by the Strangers. But the vengeance ordered by Emperor Atahualpa against the Cuzco clans loyal to Huascar was terrible. The order came from here, from the Cajamarca palace. My family was annihilated. Emperor Atahualpa's soldiers entered the town and killed all its men. They crushed their heads while they slept, crushed them with bronze bludgeons. Then, while instead of sacred water our men's blood flowed down the street gutters, they took us. They took the children, the girls and the women. They shoved us forward with the tips of their spears. They struck us with the handles of their axes and laughed. They told us that they would feed our flesh to pumas, and that condors would read the future in our entrails. They . . .'

Inguill's quiet, timid voice hesitated for the first time. She didn't break down so much as speak even more softly, and Anamaya had to lean forward to hear her.

'They tore a baby from its mother's womb. As she lay dying they chopped it in half while she was forced to watch.'

Anamaya didn't reply. She could no longer make out Inguill: tears blurred her vision, and now she too was trembling.

A vision from the distant past came to her mind's eye, a vision that broke her heart and awoke a torment she had thought gone long ago. She saw the tender loving face of her own mother. She saw the misshapen catapult stone, hurled by an Inca soldier, pierce her mother's temple. She watched it happen unbearably precisely and slowly, and once again she saw her mother tumble into the mud, never letting go of her hand. She saw her child self, standing alone, lost.

The pain choked her. Now the *Coya Camaquen*, the great Huayna Capac's favorite, the one who had saved Atahualpa, had ceased to exist.

For a few seconds Anamaya was once more that young girl terrified by the brutality of warriors, that lonely child for whom the night brought no rest. She hardly heard Inguill add:

'One night the soldiers drank *chicha* to thank the Sun our Father and Illapa the lightning god for having defeated Huascar's clans. I fled when they fell asleep. I didn't know where to go, so I returned to Cuzco. The Great Lord Manco was living there, hiding in his ancestors' temple. His brother Paullu had just fled to a hiding place near Lake Titicaca . . . I no longer had a family or home to go to, no more brothers or sisters, so Lord Manco told me that you would help me if I came to you.'

'And so I shall,' murmured Anamaya.

She took hold of the young girl's hand. Inguill's fingers were still stiff from fear, and she hesitated briefly before curling them around Anamaya's. She leaned forward and pressed her head against Anamaya's belly. Her chest heaved, and sobs punctuated her speech:

'Many moons have passed since I left . . . I thought I would never make it. It snowed when I crossed the Jauja Mountains. I was sure I was going to die . . . but then one day I saw the column of Strangers . . . with General Chalkuchimac. I hid myself among the porters . . . no one said a thing! All I had to do was carry a *manta* full of gold goblets all day . . .'

'It's over now,' said Anamaya, stroking the nape of Inguill's neck. 'It's over.'

Inguill straightened herself, suddenly proud, and wiped the tears away from her eyes with the back of her delicate wrists. She tried to smile as she said:

'Once here, I had to watch out for the Strangers. That was why I could not come to you sooner. At first I was very frightened of them. Whenever they saw me they guffawed and tried to catch me. But they're not quick enough . . .'

Inguill paused, as did Anamaya, allowing the silence to return and calm their breathing. The northerly breeze had strengthened. The door hanging swung more regularly now.

Anamaya was still holding Inguill's hand. She felt the girl shudder. She nodded, feeling almost serene, and said in a low voice:

'The Great Massacre erased all that was before. The old order is dead. Those who claim still to know what is and to foretell what will be are like blind children who see night when it is really day. No one here realizes that they are blind. The world has been turned upside down and that which once was strong is now weak. Tomorrow is like the blackness between two stars in the night sky . . . our Father the Sun and our Mother the Moon are watching us in silence, without telling us what we should do. Everyone here is doing as he pleases, and many are those who are misguided. The Strangers think only of gold. And among those who serve Emperor Atahualpa, many are still consumed by the dark fire of vengeance that goads them on against the Cuzco clans . . . you must hold your tongue from now on, Inguill. Tell no one else your story.'

'I know. Lord Manco warned me, he said: "Talk only to her, she'll know how to hear you."'

'From today onwards,' added Anamaya, 'you must hold back your tears. You must smile and show how happy you are to serve the Inca.'

'I will do anything you ask if you let me stay close to you, *Coya Camaquen*.'

Anamaya stood up, and Inguill jumped to her feet.

'First, I shall find you some clothes . . .'

Inguill looked at her adoringly.

'You are so beautiful . . . Lord Manco told me that you were the most beautiful woman in the whole Empire of the Four Cardinal Directions . . . I thought he told me that because he feels so strongly for you. But you *are* beautiful, and your eyes—'

'Stop! Don't say those things!' protested Anamaya, a little too sharply. 'Don't forget: when there are others present, you must speak to me only if I allow you to . . .'

As though to mitigate the severity of her words, Anamaya took the young girl's face between her hands and brought it close to her own, placing her cheek against Inguill's.

'Everyone knows that I do not have a sister. I need you to pretend that you are my servant. But remember that in my heart you are a sister sent to me by the Powerful Lord Manco.'

'I am not pleased,' growled Governor Francisco Pizarro, looking Gabriel directly in the eyes. 'And you know the reason.'

'Tell me, Don Francisco, so that I may hear it from your own mouth.'

Pizarro sighed. He had steered the young man out of the palace and away from the square, across an alley running along the length of the Inca's palace and towards the hill on which stood that odd building that from habit they called 'the fortress', even though no soldier or weapon had ever been found there.

'You seriously offended my brother Hernando, and you provoked him into a duel in front of the men—'

'Is that the cock-and-bull story he told you?'

'I forbid you to speak thus!'

But despite the severity of Francisco's tone, Gabriel was not really worried. Had Hernando's tale convinced the Governor, Gabriel would not be strolling through town – he would be facing a tribunal. Ever prudent, the Governor must have checked the facts with de Candia.

'Let us save time, you and I, Don Francisco. Tell your brother that you threatened me with the worst punitive measures. And I

will take upon myself the humiliation of admitting that I presented
you with my most sincere repentance . . .'

'If only it were so easy.'

The Governor's air of despondency intrigued Gabriel.

'What the devil is this all about, Don Francisco? Has your
brother perhaps been touched by the grace of God? And
now, ruing his transgressions, does he threaten to retire to
a monastery to atone for his sins, and so die in the odour of
sanctity?'

'Hold your jeering tongue, schoolboy. My brother is a hero in
the eyes of everyone ever since he returned with that general. My
brother is admired and feared by all the Indians. And my brother
insists upon an apology . . .'

Gabriel roared with laughter.

'Your brother still does not know me very well. I had thought
that with the tip of my sword—'

'Enough!' cried Pizarro, placing his hands over his ears. 'I don't
want to hear any more.'

'Then ask nothing more of me, Don Francisco.'

The two men had reached the high point overlooking the plain
that stretched beyond Cajamarca. They could make out the steam
rising from the hot springs in the distance, from the Inca's baths
where Atahualpa was waiting for them.

'I sympathize,' murmured Pizarro in a subdued voice, 'and if I
were in your place I would no doubt refuse. But I'm asking you
nevertheless . . .'

The change in Pizarro's tone alerted Gabriel to what was to
come, and he stiffened as he listened.

'I need my brother. I know him to his core, and I know all of
his failings. But I need his lack of scruples, his natural authority
– and I need his money . . .'

'But the treasure is piling up!'

'You really *are* an innocent, aren't you! All that treasure is
nothing in comparison to the mountain of debt that I have
accumulated, nothing compared to what my esteemed associate,
the one-eyed de Almagro, is owed, nothing compared to the
promises that I had to hand out like bread when the conquest

was still nothing more than a madman's dream inside my head.
If Hernando abandons me, I'm . . .'

Rather than finishing his sentence, Pizarro made a slicing
motion across his throat with his hand. The gesture spoke more
eloquently than a thousand words. Don Francisco's sincerity
rattled Gabriel far more than his attempts to threaten him
had.

'And if I don't offer my apology—'

'Publicly.'

'. . . Publicly, Hernando threatens to abandon everything.'

Pizarro nodded. Gabriel's heart beat hard, and a cold sweat
dripped down his spine.

'I don't know about this, Don Francisco . . . I really don't
know . . .'

Pizarro nodded again.

'Do as you wish, my boy.'

Gabriel said nothing, but he knew in the bottom of his heart
that he had already accepted. An odd fusion of relief and rage
made him tremble.

He didn't see the slight smile that played across Pizarro's
face.

Chalkuchimac was standing still on the square, as large and as
furious as a bear.

'What is the meaning of this?' he bellowed.

None of the few nobles of his retinue dared reply. They stared
straight ahead, wide-eyed.

Where once there had stood the elegant pyramid of the *ushnu*,
there now remained nothing but a pile of stones. The Strangers
were building an outlandish structure with this rubble, something
with too many walls and roofs, an edifice of a type never before
seen in the Empire. Its walls were thin and twisted, and the
stonework was so awkwardly chiseled that it looked as though
a mere gust of wind, one small expression of rage from the sky
would knock it all down and reduce it to dust.

Chalkuchimac turned to Felipillo and barked once again:

'What is this monstrosity?'

'It is a temple that they are building for their Heavenly Father. That is the name they give Him who allowed them to defeat Emperor Atahualpa,' the interpreter replied with an exaggerated deference.

'And who authorized them to destroy the *ushnu* to build this horror?' growled Chalkuchimac, his face dark with rage.

Felipillo looked warily at the nobles, looking for support that did not come.

'Nobody.'

Chalkuchimac gestured angrily, but at that precise instant a rider emerged from one of the buildings that faced onto the square. The Inca general stood frozen, stunned.

'But . . . he was in the temple of the Sun . . . with his animal . . .' he murmured, disbelieving the evidence of his eyes.

The noblemen and Felipillo stood around him in absolute silence, their heads lowered. Without taking his stare from the horseman, Chalkuchimac extended his arm towards him threateningly and howled.

'He was in the Temple of the Sun with his animal!' he repeated. 'Is someone going to tell me what is going on here?'

Felipillo bowed almost to the ground.

'Governor Pizarro – their *Machu Kapitu* – has decided to take the temple as his house, and—'

Felipillo broke off. The sound of the horse's hooves on the flagstones of the huge square rumbled louder and louder. The rider had taken his horse to the far end, by the entrance to the baths, and there had turned it sharply around. With a jab of the spurs glinting on his boots, he launched his animal directly at the group of Incas. Riding high in his stirrups, the brim of his hat pressed flat against his forehead by the speed of his passage, he pushed his steed into a full gallop. Felipillo and the noblemen couldn't tear their stares away from the animal's gaping chops; they were transfixed by the sight of its gaping nostrils and its eyes bulging from their sockets. Chalkuchimac slowly closed his own mouth and stood motionless, a haughty look on his face.

The Indians felt the drumming of the galloping hooves rever-
berating in the hollows of their chests. When the beast was
only a hundred paces away, the Inca noblemen cried out fearfully and retreated from its path. Felipillo jumped back, taking refuge behind them. With its lips pulled back to reveal
its yellow teeth, and with foam spraying from its mouth and
nostrils, the animal panted as it lifted its fetlocks high. Now
it was only fifty paces away, and still General Chalkuchimac
didn't budge.

He looked at its rider, a small grimacing man who was obviously
having trouble keeping himself in the saddle. He was a one-eyed
man of extraordinary ugliness, the skin of his face scarred by
disease.

With the rider – and his horse's hooves – approaching rapidly
from dead ahead, Chalkuchimac pulled back his shoulder blades
sharply, as though trying to make himself wider. Hatred and
disdain creased the corners of his mouth. Now he understood
how the Strangers had dared destroy the *ushnu* in order to build
their ridiculous house. Now he knew what they were capable of.
He understood what it was that had turned Emperor Atahualpa
so soft and spineless. In that fraction of a second, as he heard the
cries of the wretched noblemen behind him, his fury became so
immense that he seemed to turn to stone.

Just above Chalkuchimac, the rider flinched, his fleshy lips
trembling in consternation. He jerked his left arm, pulling at the
reins at the very last moment, and the horse's hooves kicked up
a shower of stones against the general's legs. The Inca general
felt the rider's boot slam into his shoulder, and the animal was
so close that he could smell its acid stench. The horse flicked its
tail through the air above him.

Chalkuchimac hadn't budged an inch. He didn't even move his
eyes as the Stranger, laughing now, trotted his animal around him,
so close that the horse trampled the general's shadow.

Chalkuchimac remained absolutely still. His blood had turned
to ice. His hatred for the Strangers and his rage against Emperor
Atahualpa, who had allowed this infamy to occur, were all that
lived, burning, within him.

The horse turned and turned again. The beast's slobber and pungent sweat, along with the dust, dirtied General Chalkuchimac's alpaca *unku*. But he no longer heard the rider's laughter.

All that insignificance had ceased to matter.

Only Inti and Quilla were real, along with the Apus, the stone Ancestors who lived beyond the hills, in the mountains by the sacred roads.

A ray of sunlight burst through the layer of cloud that hid the sky.

The rider placed himself directly in front of Chalkuchimac. With a squeeze of his knees, he made his mount rear up on its hind legs. The horse neighed, furiously swiping its hooves through the air just above the defeated general's head.

Chalkuchimac remained motionless.

He turned his face toward the Sun God. He smiled. His face furrowed like the slopes of a mountain being born at the start of time.

And now it was the one-eyed stranger's turn to be afraid.

Compared to the palace in which his brother the Governor had taken up residence, the one that Don Hernando Pizarro had taken as his own already resembled an opulent Spanish mansion. By some miraculous means he had managed to have a great number of cases delivered to him, and his residence buzzed constantly with the noise of Indian artisans at work. With varying degrees of brutality, the Spaniards directed the rare expertise of these craftsmen.

The area that Hernando had transformed into his dining room attempted to imitate the regal splendor of one of Charles the Fifth's palaces: it had a massive if crudely sculpted table, a candelabra, and a gold and silver dinner service. He had even got up his servants in a distinctive livery – red, like his morion feather. Don Hernando had set out to make it clear that he was not just anybody . . .

When Don Francisco and Gabriel entered, Hernando was already seated at his table, entertaining his young brothers Gonzalo and Juan, de Soto, and most of the Spanish lieutenants, de Candia being the only notable absence. The two new arrivals were greeted by laughter.

'Ah, my brother,' said the usually timid Juan. 'Don Hernando was just telling us how he flung that monkey into the river, advising him to fly like a bird.'

Silence followed Juan's forced laugh. All stares were focused on Gabriel.

'Don Juan, did your brother tell you the rest of the story? Rumor has it that it's most amusing.'

'I don't recall it,' declared Hernando. 'But perhaps you might enlighten us, sir?'

'My knowledge of such things is far too limited, Don Hernando, and I wouldn't dare remember what you have forgotten.'

Don Francisco stood stiffly beside Gabriel, who could sense the Governor's extreme tension.

'I see that you have met with a belated sagacity, sir,' said Hernando angrily.

'Merely prudence, your lordship, or else feebleness of spirit. I shall not bestow the noble name of "sagacity" on such a lapse of memory.'

'Yes. Clearly something is lacking, however – something essential.'

Gabriel laughed good-naturedly.

'I lack so many things, your lordship, too many to come even close to what you imply . . .'

'Come now, make an effort.'

'No matter how hard I try, I cannot do it. It's that simple.'

'Simple, sir, yes, very simple,' growled Hernando, frowning darkly at his brother. 'Simpler than I can describe . . .'

His fists clenched on the table, Hernando could no longer control himself. He jumped to his feet, knocking over his chair, and moved swiftly toward Gabriel.

Gabriel turned nimbly on his heels and headed for the door hanging.

With his back to Hernando, he muttered:

'I offer you my apologies, Don Hernando.'

And with that, Gabriel disappeared so quickly that Hernando
found himself standing stupidly in front of the flapping hanging.
He turned, furious, towards the others.

'What did that whoreson say?'

'He presented you with his apologies, brother,' replied Juan in
an embarrassed tone. 'Will you tell us why?'

CHAPTER 3

Cajamarca, June 1533

AN AWKWARD SILENCE REIGNED OVER EMPEROR
Atahualpa's court.

Women were placing gold, silver and terracotta serving
vessels – the Inca's meal service – on a mat woven from green
cane set in front of Atahualpa's bench. As they had before the
Strangers' arrival, these containers held the finest meats, as well
as fish brought from the distant ocean. Yet this delicate ritual of
pleasure to come was performed in a dance of total silence.

A few paces away, Gabriel and Anamaya stood next to each
other in the shadow of a wall, far from the braziers. They stood
side by side, but not quite face to face, nor yet shoulder to
shoulder. They had acquired the habit of standing thus whenever they were under the scrutiny of others. But nothing could
prevent them from feeling the invisible attraction of their private union: not even the sadness that pervaded every corner of
Atahualpa's palace.

In a low voice, Gabriel told Anamaya how Hernando Pizarro
had duped Chalkuchimac with lies, and how the conquistador
had assured the Inca general that his master Atahualpa needed
to see him. He described the general's contemptuous indifference
in the face of the Governor's brother's insistent demands for
gold and silver; Hernando's massive greed and veiled threats;
the excitement of the troops when the rumor reached them
that de Moguer and his companions had reached Cuzco, and

that from there they were sending a treasure even more fabulous than anything they had found thus far.

'You should have seen the madness in their eyes – they couldn't have been more excited if they'd been promised eternal life. Some even refused to sleep in case the treasure arrived at night . . .'

'The ransom room is already almost full,' murmured Anamaya.

'Anamaya, it's not a roomful that they're after, not a palace full, but a whole *town* built entirely of gold . . . and even that probably wouldn't satisfy them . . .'

'Your people are very strange. I never stop watching them. I'm always trying to understand in which ways they differ from you and in which ways they are similar . . .'

Gabriel couldn't think of a reply. He looked at Anamaya as she stood with her head lowered. Her blue eyes looked mainly at the ground, but she occasionally flashed glances at his animated expression.

'Emperor Atahualpa will never be free,' she murmured.

'Don Francisco promised him that he would reign peacefully in the north – from Quito, where he was born.'

'That will never happen,' said Anamaya, slowly shaking her head.

'The Governor made a promise,' insisted Gabriel, his brow furrowed. 'All of us must obey his command. That is how it is with us. Even our king, who is high above Governor Don Francisco, wishes that Atahualpa should remain your master . . .'

'You just told me that gold was your only law . . .'

'*Their* only law!' replied Gabriel proudly.

'Are you saying that you can change their law?'

Once again Gabriel didn't know what to say. Anamaya looked deeply into his eyes. He felt lost, floating, almost dissolving in the power of her gaze, in that beauty as fresh and as simple as a still lake. She was able to communicate her convictions to him wordlessly, showing him in this way her unshakable knowledge of the truth. Each time she did it, he thought he detected a power that he had never suspected existed until then.

Like a child unwilling to be convinced, he protested once again:

'If they try to harm him, I shall prevent it!'

He spoke so loudly that he startled the women. Anamaya turned towards them, and the servant girls dispersed like a flight of birds. Gabriel blushed, then continued in a quieter tone:

'Ever since the day he was captured, when I prevented him being killed, the Governor has requested that I watch over your king's life.'

Anamaya tightened her cape, pulling its hem further up her delicate neck.

'You cannot oppose what must be . . .'

Since she didn't continue, Gabriel asked, more harshly than he intended to:

'And what is that?'

'Time flies. There are forces against which it is useless to fight. Even you, who are good, cannot . . .'

Gabriel lowered his head, touched by the tenderness of her words. He didn't notice Atahualpa coming out of the main room. The Emperor wore a cape of very fine brown wool, clasped across his chest by a gold *tupu* encrusted with jewels.

A woman rushed forward to sweep the small stretch of floor between him and his bench. Even from behind Anamaya recognized Inti Palla's broadened form: Inti Palla, Anamaya's false friend and real enemy who had so often willed her ruin. Despite living under the same roof, they hadn't spoken to one another more than twice at the most since many moons.

Anamaya rose and, in a low voice, asked Gabriel to make himself scarce.

At that very moment, a cry that echoed as far as the distant hills tore through the silence: a shout, or rather a roar, so powerful that it froze them with shock. Everyone stiffened and then the strident bellow came again, rending the air.

'Chalkuchimac!' whispered Anamaya, turning towards the Inca.

Gabriel felt his guts churn.

Atahualpa carried on as though he hadn't heard the cry. He pointed toward one of the golden bowls, and Inti Palla bent over to pick it up and bring it to him. As yet another shriek ripped through the sky over Cajamarca, the Inca brought a thin shred

of vicuña meat to his mouth. Some juice dripped from his lips
and a drop of boiled blood fell on his tunic.

Without waiting any longer, Anamaya and Gabriel rushed
towards the entrance, ignoring the rule of the Inca's sacred
court. Half drawing his sword from its scabbard, Gabriel pushed
aside the Inca warriors and Spanish soldiers guarding the palace's
entrance.

As Inti Palla continued to hold the bowl of meat, her gaze
turned toward the door through which Anamaya and Gabriel had
disappeared. Atahualpa barely lifted his face to watch them go.
He remained there for a brief moment, chewing on a few grains
of corn. Then he stood up from his bench and disappeared into
the shadowy interior of his palace, walking with the slow and
measured pace of a man with a mandate over time and space.

A crowd had gathered on the square outside the erstwhile Temple
of the Sun that was now Governor Francisco Pizarro's residence.
The surrounding cob wall was, as always, planted with *quinua*
hedge. Gabriel and Anamaya passed through the silent group of
Indians. At the entrance, Gabriel caught a glimpse of Pedro the
Greek's huge silhouette and hooked nose.

'What's going on, Pedro?'

'De Soto asked that fellow where the gold is – asked him most
genteel, like – but he didn't care to answer.'

The Greek glanced over Gabriel's shoulder and saw Anamaya.
He grinned knowingly.

Gabriel moved on, pushing aside a few men. He crossed the
hall, furnished more or less in the Spanish style now, and reached
the light of the courtyard. There he heard Anamaya at his side
utter a little cry of surprise.

A stake had been erected in the middle of the courtyard.
Chalkuchimac was tightly bound to it. Under his feet was a
pile of straw and deadwood. Although it hadn't yet been lit,
smoke was rising from the general's slightly burned tunic, and
his calves were blackened. De Soto stood in front of him, the
interpreter Felipillo at his side. Gabriel could only assume that

someone had tried to frighten the Inca general into talking by passing a lit torch across the lower hem of his robe. *A bit like the Inquisition just showing suspected heretics the instruments of torture to get them to confess – it can work if the subject's scared enough*, he thought grimly. The barrel-chested, stumpy-legged captain was stamping on the ground with his hobnailed boots as though he was trying to shatter the courtyard's flagstones. His face, its expression normally so self-contained and smug, glowed with rage. He was pointing his index finger at Chalkuchimac's chest.

'Let me make myself clear: You are brave, General, as strong-headed as a bull, and as stone-hearted as a crow. But I, who am only a humble captain, I want to know where your gold is!' he yelled. 'I also want to know where your troops are, and what orders you have given your lieutenants. I want to know, and I *will* know, or else you will be roasted like a pig on a spit!'

The interpreter Felipillo leaned reluctantly over the straw, as though frightened of falling there and burning with the general. He kept his eyes closed as he murmured into Chalkuchimac's ear. The Inca general's face remained unfathomable, but a vein pulsed visibly in his neck.

Gabriel came forward.

'De Soto!'

The captain turned towards him, his eyes bulging with rage.

'Stay out of this, friend.'

'The Governor—'

'—Ordered me to interrogate this damned fool, and I am doing so,' de Soto cut in, his tone menacing.

Gabriel knew the man well enough to know that he never lied.

At that moment, the cry that they had heard when they'd been in Atahualpa's palace cut through the air again. It came from Chalkuchimac. Gabriel could hear him saying something, but what it was he couldn't tell. He turned to Anamaya, who was now being lewdly eyed by the Spaniards. She didn't notice him. Her blue-eyed gaze was fixed on Chalkuchimac's face. Her lips moved silently, mouthing the word that the general had cried out. This time Gabriel could discern it.

'Inti! Inti!'

The Inca general was not howling in pain or fear. What came from his throat was a powerful call, like that of a trumpet resonating from a mountaintop.

'Inti!'

Chalkuchimac was invoking the Sun God. He was offering himself to Him with all the assurance of his unshakable faith. His gaze fell upon Anamaya, and he said to her calmly:

'*Coya Camaquen.* Have my lord, the Emperor, come to me.'

'Burn him until he's a pile of ash,' Gabriel growled to de Soto. 'He'll tell you nothing. You can't frighten him any more than a fly can. He is asking for an audience with his king. Only he can decide whether Chalkuchimac speaks to you or not.'

The captain glared at Gabriel, his anger barely contained. But he lowered his gaze and, shrugging his shoulders, sighed deeply in resignation.

A tense calm, an uncomfortable sense of waiting, fell upon the courtyard after Anamaya had left bearing her message. Gazes darted around nervously, except for that of the Inca general, who stared fixedly at de Soto with contemptuous defiance.

A noise from behind caused Gabriel to turn, along with the rest of the gathering. The Governor had arrived, with Atahualpa beside him. As Don Francisco looked from Gabriel to de Soto, a smile appeared on his face, scarcely discernible beneath the hair of his beard. He gestured toward the Inca and announced:

'Lord Atahualpa deigns to speak with his general. Perhaps he will succeed where your persuasion has failed, de Soto . . .'

Gabriel noticed Anamaya's hesitation. She'd had to remind herself not to walk ahead of the Inca as he approached Chalkuchimac.

From his torture post, the general looked hard at his master. He who had earlier shown himself so submissive and loyal to Atahualpa now didn't bat an eyelid as the Emperor approached. He showed no sign of affection. Quite the opposite: his mouth curved in an expression of growing contempt.

Atahualpa stopped a few steps in front of the pile of straw and wood. He spoke in a low voice, but not so low that Gabriel couldn't hear.

'They threaten to burn you, but you mustn't believe them. They will not harm you, because to harm you would be to harm me. They do not have that blasphemous audacity in them.'

Chalkuchimac remained silent for a short moment. He looked the Inca up and down, and then turned his heavy gaze towards Anamaya, ignoring the Spaniards as though they were nothing but shadows. He asked:

'My Lord, do you still know the will of your father the Sun? Are you still our Inca?'

Atahualpa quivered as though he had been slapped in the face. He straightened his spine, and in that instant the Spaniards could see in the expression of his rage the proud and powerful man he once had been.

'How dare you speak to me thus?' he snarled.

'It seems to me that you are frightened of dying, my Lord,' replied the general, now bent on provoking him. 'Is that the case?'

'You have lost your wits, Chalkuchimac. You would do better to keep silent in front of the Strangers. You are more frightened of their flames than I am of death. None will lay a hand on Inti's son.'

'They already have.'

'Do not see. Do not hear.'

'Why not?' the general asked severely.

Gabriel felt Atahualpa's discomfort. No one among the Spaniards understood what the general meant, but Atahualpa and Chalkuchimac seemed to understand one another perfectly clearly.

'Shut up,' said the Inca finally.

'Why didn't you call for me, even though I was ready? Why did you refuse to let me die to free you? I came to you, my eyes full of tears and affection, and you gave me only silence. I look at you and I see you tremble in front of the Strangers. They are nothing but temple pillagers, low thieves lusting after gold. It is not these robbers who are destroying the Empire of the Four Cardinal Directions, Atahualpa, but your own fear!'

Growling harshly, Chalkuchimac spat upon the heap of kindling. Atahualpa turned on his heel. The blood in his eyes seemed

to have obscured even his pupils. Anamaya kept her gaze lowered
to the ground, her neck bowed. Gabriel had to clench his fists,
so great was his desire to take her in his arms. But he knew that
doing so would cause more harm than good.

With a signal from de Soto, the Canary Indians who were there
to do menial tasks for the Spaniards set their torches to the straw.
Instantly, it burst into small, bright flames.

The sinister silence in the courtyard was broken by the growing
crackle of the fire. Anamaya heard it and lifted her face, her mouth
gaping as though she was going to cry out. Pizarro's hand gripped
Gabriel's arm before he had a chance to make a move.

'Don't fret, my boy,' Don Francisco murmured. 'The Inca is
right. This is just a ruse to loosen his general's tongue.'

The flames jumped from the straw to the deadwood, crackling
and spluttering as dense, acrid smoke billowed. It whirled up
around Chalkuchimac, who stared straight ahead, his lips only
very slightly parted.

Atahualpa turned toward him once again and stared imperturb-
ably through the flames leaping up from the fire.

As the fire took hold, the wood cracked loudly. Anamaya
clenched her hands so tightly that the blood drained from her
knuckles. Now Gabriel could feel the fire's heat on his face.
Chalkuchimac looked at Atahualpa and once more shouted furiously. Only this time he said:

'Take this lord out of my sight! Make him leave! Take him away
from me! I'll talk – I'll tell you what you want to hear.'

He had barely finished speaking when Felipillo shouted out
the translation.

'Do as he asks, and put out the fire,' ordered Don Francisco
calmly.

As the Canary Indians threw large pots of water on the burning
pyre, soldiers gently directed Atahualpa out of the courtyard. He
left without once turning around.

The blaze became a foul-smelling white steam. Only now
did Anamaya turn her blue-eyed gaze on Gabriel. The *Coya
Camaquen*'s lovely face was as sad as it was serene.

Gabriel preferred to turn away rather than meet her look.

He found the sight before him, and all that it meant, unbearable.

Chalkuchimac was black with ash, and his harsh breathing was all that could be heard as his ropes were untied. Below his knees, his legs were just shrivelled lengths of burned flesh oozing blood, and his scorched hands and arms were covered with blisters, many of them burst and weeping. And yet, when a mat was brought for him to rest on, the old warrior refused. He was carried a few paces away from the pyre. There, he elbowed the Canary Indians away, refusing their support and refusing also to show his pain – although his hoarse gasps hinted at it. He stayed upright and waited for the Governor to come to him.

Now it was de Soto's turn to shake his head. He looked at the general as though the Inca soldier was a madman.

The indomitable Chalkuchimac unloosed a torrent of words.

Yes, there was more gold, a lot more, in the city of Cuzco. Yes, there were many more treasures there. If Atahualpa had forbidden that his father's, the Inca Huayna Capac's, possessions should be touched, it was because his father had been the most powerful and the richest of all the sovereigns: he had died in this world, but still lived on in the other. There he drank, he ate, and his temple overflowed with gold . . .

But there was more: He, Chalkuchimac, had approached Cajamarca four times at the Emperor's request. Four times the Inca had ordered his retreat at the last moment. Four times he had failed to give the order to attack, and he, Chalkuchimac, had had to retreat, his heart enraged.

Gabriel barely noticed that Anamaya had left the patio. The smoke from the dying pyre irritated his eyes, and filled the air with the odor of burnt flesh and of shame.

Chalkuchimac talked and talked, and he spoke the words that de Soto and the Governor wanted to hear. But they were words inspired by a desire for vengeance, and no one knew if they were remotely true.

*   *   *

The fires of the forges lit up Cajamarca's nights. The sharing-out of the spoils had begun and continued day and night. Now that the pile of treasure had reached and even passed the line drawn by the Inca in the ransom room, loot was brought directly to the forges. They glowed red as molten gold streamed from them, a glinting, magic liquid. Then it cooled and became ingots, tangible measures of jubilation. These were packed tightly into sacks and baskets, filling them entirely with gold.

At first all the Spaniards stayed close, their faces as red as the burning braziers, their cheeks as swollen as the smiths' bellows. Some even burned their fingers in their impetuous desire to fondle those bricks of happiness before they had cooled. With their stares fixed obsessively on that soup of gold that the *plateros* poured from their smelting ladles, the Spaniards consigned everything else to oblivion. They forgot their bad memories, their fears, the diseases that they had suffered, their enmities – and their friendships. And as the molten gold flowed endlessly, its smelting soon became an event as ordinary as the rising of the sun.

So much so that eventually the soldiers became reluctant to stand guard over the forges, claiming that doing so only offered a man a mug's choice: whether to roast his ass or his balls. But as even the most unusual gold ornaments were ruthlessly melted down – images of corn ears and llamas, decorative jugs, necklaces, earlobe plugs, idols, and ornate plaques – no Indian, not even one of those most loyal to the Spanish invaders, was ever allowed to approach the forges.

Sebastian observed the pile of assorted gold objects that had just been dumped outside a forge. There were the usual vases and plates, but also tubes taken from fountains, chairs, and even gold stones.

The treasure gleamed scarlet in the light of the moon and the flames, reflecting on his face.

Gabriel grumbled to those around him:

'There are evenings when I am happy to have been deprived of a share of the plunder, overjoyed to have nothing to do with it at all. My horse remains my most precious treasure!'

'Ha! But a real treasure he is, though: I'll give you three thousand *pesos*, going rate!'

'Forget it, he's not for sale.'

'Now don't be getting sentimental about him. Why, you haven't even given him a name . . .'

Gabriel thought for a moment.

'It's not that I don't want to – it's just that I don't seem able to, for some unknown reason. No name seems to suit him . . . but he's my horse, and that's enough for me.'

Sebastian nodded.

'Well, I wouldn't mind it at all if they gave *me* one – but Hernando forbids it . . .'

'That damned jackass!'

The curse escaped from Gabriel at the mere mention of that hated name.

'Well may you grouse, my friend – though between you and me and the devil, you made me most uncommon happy when you cut him down to size the other day – but still, that doesn't relieve me of my bondage: a slave am I, and poor must I remain.'

'Bah – you're bound to pick up a few scraps from the forges, here and there.'

Sebastian laughed a silent laugh so hard that his whole body shook. He pointed his thumb at the smiths at their forges.

'If you think that they're leaving any scraps for the picking . . .'

'Patience,' grumbled Gabriel. 'You're bound to find a Good Samaritan who'll slip you some of your cursed gold!'

'Is that right? Yet I have only two friends here in this forsaken land: You and de Candia. And, curse my luck, you have to be the only conquistador in existence who is denied a share of the spoils, and what's more who doesn't even care for gold! A madman who loves only some Indian girl's blue eyes!'

Gabriel stared at his comrade, ready to explode in anger, but he saw in Sebastian only affection, amusement and admiration. He let out a gentle laugh.

'De Candia loves you as much as he loves his gold.'

'Alas! You might as well say that he's no better than you and that he'll never be rich!'

Gabriel sighed, his smile still upon his lips.

'Who knows, Sebastian? Perhaps *you* will become the richest among us!'

The black giant burst into laughter, holding his sides.

'With no horse? No sword?'

'You'll get your sword: everything in its own time and at its proper price.'

Gabriel fell silent. His gaze followed a small group of Spaniards who were herding two Indians along. The Indians were carrying a golden idol the size of a large doll. Don Diego de Almagro was behind them, his lips pursed, surrounded by a few of his followers.

'Don Diego won't be able to watch all this gold pass under his nose for much longer,' murmured Sebastian. 'He's been as mad as a bull ever since he arrived.'

The Indians painstakingly set the statue down on the ground as though it was a delicate child.

'The rule was established long before he arrived,' replied Gabriel in a low voice. 'The Cajamarca gold goes only to those who took part in the Great Battle, to those who captured the Inca!'

'Rules are made to be broken,' murmured Sebastian. 'All you have to be is stronger than the other.'

'What do you mean?'

'Just that it won't be long before Don Diego improves his own lot.'

'He would take on the Governor?'

Sebastian shrugged his shoulders.

'They're all here for the gold. All of them will have to get a share.'

Gabriel watched de Almagro as Don Francisco's associate moved around agitatedly over by the statue. He was obviously excited, squatting down beside it, caressing it and laughing, his only eye aflame with gold-lust.

'Is it true that you saved his life?' Gabriel asked Sebastian, nodding toward Don Diego.

'That was a long time ago. And until now, it has given me more trouble than reward.'

'Perhaps he could make you rich.'

Sebastian burst out laughing.

'No. He could make me *free*, however. He owns me. He only lent me to the Governor's expedition. His gold represents my freedom.'

There was once a time, thought Gabriel as he walked through the shadowy but bustling streets, *when this city was inhabited by men busy only with living and with worshiping their gods. But now we are here, and like birds of ill omen we have brought with us our fevers and our lust for gold and glory.*

Occasionally he came across a torch burning on a street corner, a torch belonging to one of the fifty cavalrymen on night duty. These latest arrivals, de Almagro's men, were the most aggressive because they were the poorest. They had no *pesos*, no women, and barely enough liquor.

'Soon, very soon, you shall see . . .' the Cajamarca veterans would tell them, who paid their way with gold ingots.

Coming out onto the square, Gabriel took the route heading towards Pizarro's palace. He noticed, across the square and behind the church that was being constructed, a gathering in front of the largest of the town's buildings, or *kallankas*, as the Indians called them, the one that Hernando had chosen as his abode.

That was where Chalkuchimac was resting that night, his hands and feet burned, his nerves frayed.

A few soldiers stood guard at the entrance, tense in front of the crowd of Indians, who were themselves quite calm, speaking to each other in low voices. It was difficult to gauge their mood.

A hand gripped his shoulder. He jumped, his hand already on the hilt of his sword.

'Don't be frightened—'

'Anamaya!'

They laughed together at his surprise. A white *añaco* was wrapped about her waist, held by a crimson sash. She was gorgeous, like a star fallen to earth. She stood beside him, refraining from touching him.

'What are they waiting for?' asked Gabriel, pointing at the Indians.

'They want to serve Chalkuchimac.'

'Why?'

She turned to face him, her own expression unfathomable, yet she spoke with a teasing tenderness.

'They have lost their Inca, and they need a master.'

'But the Inca lives yet.'

'Yes, but his father the Sun no longer rises for him . . .'

'You mean that Inti rises for him instead?' asked Gabriel, pointing at the palace door behind which, somewhere, Chalkuchimac lay.

'No. I only say that they want to serve somebody.'

'But serve who, if not the Inca?'

Anamaya made no reply. Her gaze wandered over the distant hills, toward the moon, toward the mountains with their eternal snows.

When her gaze eventually came back to Gabriel, she allowed herself to fall gently against him.

'Come with me,' she whispered.

Blind, for now, to the Indians' sadness and the Spaniards' drunkenness, they made their way along beside the square's wall and took the road leading to the Inca's baths. It was there that, in the autumn, Atahualpa's magnificent cortege had come to meet, in one short day, his glory and his end. It was there that Anamaya and Gabriel had fled together to discover the first night of their destiny.

As they went deeper into the shadows, their murmuring mingled with that of the waters. Soon, they were one with the night.

CHAPTER 4

Cajamarca, 25 July 1533: dawn

IN THE SHY BLUE OF DAWN, GABRIEL RODE ALONG THE
well-made stone path overlooking the Hatunmayo River. A
great stand of trees protected him from the morning wind,
and in the distance he could see the rising sun cast its pale
light over the hills. It was a fine day, and last night's dew was
evaporating slowly from the leaves.

Gabriel's heart grew lighter as Cajamarca slowly fell away below
him. The will-o'-the-wisp wind, the intoxication of the breeze . . .
It was as though he was at last escaping, in a clatter of hooves,
from the tension reigning over the conquistadors.

Hernando, the Governor's brother, had returned to Spain,
accompanied by a few *hidalgos*. He bore with him the good news
of the victory at Cajamarca, as well as the proof of it: The King's
quint, a ship filled entirely with gold.

Yet Gabriel hadn't regained his high spirits since his hated
adversary's departure: The Governor's younger brothers were
Hernando's equals in treachery and villainy. In town, the tension
between the haves and have-nots prevented any hope of tranquillity. Their only thought was gold, gold, and yet more gold. Yet
the more they acquired, the more their avidity increased. Those
already rich wanted to be richer, and those who weren't were
ready to kill to become so. What was more, it was rumored that
the ill feeling between de Almagro and Pizarro, once comrades
in Panamá, had reached its lowest ebb.

And the spread of fresh rumors unnerved them further. It was said that the Indians were amassing troops in the mountains surrounding the city, and that these forces were being commanded secretly by Chalkuchimac even from within Hernando Pizarro's palace where he was detained. The interpreter Felipillo claimed that the Inca's army was so big that his generals had had to divide it into three or four regiments so that it might be resupplied more easily.

Once again Chalkuchimac was interrogated. This time, however, he maintained a steadfast silence. To reassure himself, Don Francisco had sent a reconnaissance mission, commanded by de Soto, down the road to Cajas.

Cavalrymen reconnoitred the roads around the city daily, on the lookout for an Inca vanguard preparing an assault.

Little by little, an insidious fear returned to plague the Spaniards.

It wasn't the same as the terror that had gripped them that past autumn when they had discovered the extent of the Empire's power, nor did it resemble the panicky fear that they had experienced on the eve of the battle when they had known that they were vastly outnumbered. It was a more muted dread, one that took hold of their guts and wouldn't let go. At night it feigned sleep, only to return hidden in a gust of wind or in the sound of an animal moving stealthily through the undergrowth . . .

The sound of hoofbeats from behind him caused Gabriel to turn around swiftly in his saddle.

'Don Gabriel! Don Gabriel!'

Gabriel recognized the dark green velvet doublet and the piebald horse with its silver-studded bridles. Pedro Cataño might have been a dandy, but he was one of the few Spaniards on this expedition whose company Gabriel could stand. They were of the same age, and could have easily known one another at the University. Cataño was one of the few men of the expedition who could read and write. Indeed, he spent a lot of time writing an account of his travels, as though enamoured of his own story. He was also one of the few who had behaved with dignity during the November battle and had never attempted to insult the Inca. This attitude, in conjunction with his swarthy skin tone and cheekbones so high that he could easily have been mistaken for an Indian himself, had earned him the epithet *Indio*.

'*Holà*, Pedro! What a hurry you're in! Bad news?'

Cataño shook his head, smiling. He was breathing hard.

'I should say not! It was only that I saw you leaving, and the desire came upon me to accompany you.'

'I am not so certain that I need your company,' said Gabriel, but not unkindly.

'Gabriel,' replied Cataño, still seated on his horse's back, 'I thought that we had been ordered not to wander into the hills alone . . .'

'Ah yes, orders . . .' Gabriel sighed fatalistically.

Riding at a slow walking pace, the two men reached the first peak. The river meandered gently down below. The day was well advanced, and a light breeze prevented the heat from becoming oppressive. It was hard to believe that thousands of men armed with axes and slings were hiding in the surrounding splendid landscape.

Cataño brought his horse up alongside Gabriel's. The two men sat shoulder to shoulder in silence, admiring the beauty of the city, watching the smoke of hundreds of cooking fires rising from its roofs.

'What damned inventions these rumors are,' griped Gabriel. 'I wager you all the gold I don't have that there isn't an Inca warrior within leagues of here!'

Cataño grinned.

'Now there's a wager that can't be lost!'

'They're lying to us, Pedro! And we know why, don't we?'

Cataño pondered. Deceptively timid in manner and appearance, he was actually very audacious, and his speech was on occasion, disarmingly direct.

. 'Are you inferring that de Almagro's people want to rid themselves of their Inca, the sacred Atahualpa? That they are so impatient to reach Cuzco and make their own fortunes that they would contravene the Crown's orders?'

'Atahualpa's ransom has been paid, even overpaid,' said Gabriel. 'Those recently arrived, Don Diego most of all, find that they cannot wait any longer. Atahualpa's continued presence, and the supposed risk of an assault by Chalkuchimac's troops to free him, frays their nerves. And the fact is that we really can't remain holed up here forever. Is that not your own opinion?'

Cataño hesitated slightly.

'Don Francisco will not allow it to happen. Will not let the Inca be killed, I mean.'

Gabriel stroked his horse's neck. Whenever anyone mentioned the Governor's rectitude to him, he couldn't help but remember the smell of burned flesh when Chalkuchimac had been tortured with fire.

'By the faith, I hope so.'

'Is he aware of this danger?'

'Don Francisco understands and is aware of everything that goes on here. No one has a better view of the situation than he. And everyone knows that he has cheated Don Diego a little. They set out on this adventure together ten years ago, against the winds and the tides, and were close friends. But today one is rich and a Governor, whereas the other has lost his fortune and is a mere captain.'

They admired the splendor of the plain in silence for a few moments, while the implications of Gabriel's words sank in. Then Cataño nodded his head, smiling wearily.

'I understand now why the Governor's brothers hate you as they do, Don Gabriel. Until now I thought they were merely jealous of your intimacy with Don Francisco. But your eye is too sharp. They will not let you off the hook . . .'

Gabriel laughed quietly and gave his companion a friendly look.

'Well, may you be the only judge of whether your own eye becomes too sharp, Pedro. Do not forget the tribulations that such a fine, clear view can bring you.'

Pedro considered this silently. But his half-smile, one of affectionate appreciation, told Gabriel that he had already decided.

Gabriel said a short goodbye and, without another word, set off at a full gallop toward the town.

As she put on her straw sandals, Anamaya found a massive spider on one of the straps, its long, thick legs covered in hair. After an initial involuntary movement of repugnance, she let the arachnid crawl up her bare leg. It hesitated for a while on her knee before climbing back down and fleeing across the flagstones. As silent as a shadow, it disappeared nimbly beneath a mat.

Anamaya remained still for a moment. She no longer enjoyed mornings as she once had. She often awoke these days in a cold sweat, her heart racing, terrified by premonitions, her spirit confused by the lies and the heavy silences weighing down the palace's *cancha*. Things were being hidden from the Inca: news of his servants who died or fled, any hint of the imperceptibly gradual crumbling of everything. Atahualpa existed in the center of an invisible shrinking circle, drawn around him by others, within which he was still an absolute ruler. But outside it chaos, confusion, and disorder reigned.

Anamaya existed in a strange state now, and Gabriel's love brought her no security: on the contrary, it caused her even greater disquiet.

'Are you dreaming, Anamaya?'

Inguill had never lost her habit of slipping into Anamaya's room with the stealth of a *viscacha*. It had helped her survive so far, and she continued to move thus all over the palace. In all the chaos, few questions were asked about the sudden appearance of another servant girl. All spare hands were needed.

'Yes, but I'm trying to reach the conscious world,' said Anamaya cheerfully.

'May I have permission to speak to you?'

Inguill had the serious manner of a child: it always made Anamaya feel like a mother.

'You have heard, as I have, the rumors that are being spread about Inti Palla . . .'

'I'm not interested in Inti Palla.'

Anamaya spoke, despite herself, with venom in her voice. Her hatred of that woman who had once been such a very beautiful princess had never subsided. Inguill stared at her, taken aback.

'Forgive me,' said Anamaya, more gently. She took Inguill's hand in hers.

'So tell me, what are these rumors?'

'They say that Inti Palla allowed herself to be seduced by he who serves the Strangers and translates all they say.'

'Felipillo?'

Inguill nodded her head.

'Inti Palla goes to Felipillo's bed?'

'You mean you didn't know?'

Anamaya shrugged her shoulders in a gesture of contempt.

'But such a thing is impossible! Inti Palla is a wife of Atahualpa! How could she dare?'

Inguil's demeanour grew stubborn. She squeezed Anamaya's wrist, insisting in her certainty:

'But it's true! I saw them! I couldn't sleep last night and I went to the *cancha* before hiding in the Temple of the Divinities. And I saw them . . .'

'Them?'

'Felipillo had his hands on her, and she was happy . . .'

The glowing ember of Anamaya's dormant but still living hatred towards the false-hearted princess flared in her heart. She asked coldly:

'Did they see you?'

'I don't think so.'

'I told you to watch out for yourself, Inguill!'

'But *Coya Comaquen*! I heard them utter Atahualpa's name! I had to tell you!'

'Yes, that's true . . . thank you. But don't forget to be very careful. And now let me be, little one.'

Inguill's eyes lingered a moment on Anamaya before she reluctantly obeyed.

Once she was alone, Anamaya sat perfectly still. She felt a pain rising in her soul. Shame, fear, and a sense of having been deceived ran through her body like poison. She should run to the Inca and tell him, she thought; warn him of the danger as she had on so many previous occasions.

But this time, she felt only sorrow and a longing for solitude.

'Fucking idiot! Damned fool!'

Gabriel heard the insults through a gap in the wall. He dismounted and handed the reins to one of the Indians who were always hanging about in front of the *canchas*. He entered the courtyard. A Spaniard was hitting an Indian with the pommel of his sword, hammering him on his head, his ears, and his neck. The Indian, bleeding, howled in pain.

'What's going on here?' demanded Gabriel.

The Spaniard turned around, his dishevelled brown curls framing his cherubic face. Gabriel hadn't immediately recognized him from behind: it was Gonzalo Pizarro, the Governor's youngest brother and the most handsome man in Cajamarca. But his good looks were just a mask for his black soul.

Gonzalo smiled with feigned amicability, and pointed with the tip of his sword at a table. There was an adze propped against its legs.

'What's going on is that I ordered this monkey here to make a table. A table, do you hear? Not a rood screen or a damned pulpit, but a table! And this is what he does!'

Gonzalo leaned on the table. It wobbled very slightly.

'Well?' asked Gabriel, forcing a smile as false as Gonzalo's.

'Well, it wobbles.'

Gabriel approached the other end of the table and pressed his hand down on it.

'It doesn't wobble,' he said quietly.

'I tell you that it wobbles.'

Gabriel bent down to pick up the adze. He handed it to the terrified Inca.

'Here, take it,' he said in Quechua. 'Don't be frightened.'

The man hesitated an instant, then timorously took the tool and glanced fearfully at Gonzalo.

'In my opinion this table doesn't wobble,' said Gabriel, keeping his voice low for Gonzalo's benefit. 'Yet even if it wobbled so much that everything slid off it and shattered on the ground, your brother the Governor would agree with me that it wouldn't be worth a poor wretch's life.'

Gonzalo's hand gripped the hilt of his sword tightly. The mention of his brother's name, the Governor's name, made him thoughtful.

'Be very careful,' he said eventually.

'Santiago!' continued Gabriel in his friendliest tone. 'I'm on tiptoe night and day.'

Gonzalo reddened at the jeer.

'I shan't be as kind to you as my brother Hernando was,' he spat.

'I hear you, Gonzalo. It's just that I miss your big brother and his big red feather. But I'm as frightened of you now as I was of him then. Do you not see how I tremble?'

And with that Gabriel turned on his heels and left the courtyard. He slipped a fruit to the Indian who had looked after his horse.

Gonzalo gave the artisan one final thump. The poor man kept his gaze turned toward the ground.

'Make it again, you confounded idiot!' he shouted. 'And this time make sure that it doesn't wobble!'

He turned around and shook his fist at the door through which Gabriel had left.

'Be very careful,' he repeated to himself.

And then he smiled.

Seated on his *tiana*, his royal throne, the Emperor had his eyes closed. His face was impassive, and he sat utterly still, as though he was already his own mummy.

When he opened his eyelids, his pupils were two tiny black points in the middle of two blood-red lakes. Anamaya remained silent. An old feeling, stronger than her anger against Atahualpa, or her sadness, or her bitterness, overwhelmed her.

It was tenderness.

But suddenly, as though he had detected that emotion, the

Emperor did something astonishing. He slipped from his bench towards the floor that was covered with guanaco skins and vicuña wool blankets. He reached out his hands towards Anamaya. He murmured so low that his voice sounded barely louder than his breathing:

'*Coya Camaquen!*'

She crawled to him on her knees and placed her own hands in those of the Sun King, palm against palm.

The Emperor trembled. His entire body trembled – his lips, his hands, his chest, everything in him trembled from the apprehension he felt at the unhinging of his world. He trembled so much that his teeth chattered. He trembled like the stones in the temples, their edges polished a thousand times, did whenever *Pacha Mama*, the Mother Earth, moved from deep within.

And so the Inca wrapped his arms around Anamaya and held her close. He held her as tightly as his father Huayna Capac had once gripped her hand for the entire night before he died. He held her against his heart as he had in the old days when, guided by the comet, she had foretold his destiny of glory and triumph.

They heard boots stamping in the courtyard. When Don Francisco Pizarro crossed the room's threshold, he found them thus entwined.

Pizarro hesitated, embarrassed. Behind him, the wily Felipillo stood aghast, flabbergasted at what he saw. The Governor waited a few more seconds and then, as though nothing out of the ordinary had occurred, he called out gently and with respect:

'Lord Atahualpa!'

The Inca opened his arms. Anamaya rose to her feet with no particular haste. She stood behind Atahualpa, who had returned to his *tiana*. She stared at Felipillo. The interpreter looked away, ill at ease, and she wondered about what Inguill had told her. But then the three words that came from the Governor's mouth completely captured her attention, driving all other thoughts from her mind.

'You are free!'

She was not sure that she had understood clearly.

The Governor, his expression intent and, at the same time, puzzled, stared at Atahualpa.

'You are free,' he repeated. 'But I don't understand you.'

Felipillo translated, looking furtively at Anamaya as he spoke.

'What is the meaning of this?' asked the Inca. 'What is the *Machu Kapitu* saying?'

Anamaya repeated Felipillo's words, looking hard at the Governor as she did, unable to fathom him.

'I hear rumors, Lord Atahualpa!' Pizarro continued, more comfortable now. 'I try to ignore them, but they keep on coming . . . almost every day your *caciques* come to my palace and tell me that you're sending orders to every province in the Empire to mobilize your troops against us . . . your general, Chalkuchimac, is here with us, but you send orders to your other lieutenants, Quizquiz and Ruminavi. But I like you, and I don't believe everything my ears hear. Nevertheless, I ask you: Am I right not to believe them?'

Anger flashed across Atahualpa's face.

'Of course you are right! It is all rubbish.'

The Governor listened to Felipillo's nervous translation and nodded his head.

'So much the better. In that case, you will soon be able to go to your northern kingdom as I promised, and there rule in peace – with my protection, of course – for the glory of and in the name of our Emperor Charles the Fifth and Our Lord. Meanwhile . . .'

Atahualpa was listening intently. He waited. But Pizarro fell silent suddenly, showing no intention of continuing.

'So, I'm going to die,' said Atahualpa eventually.

'How do you mean, die?' asked the Governor, astonished.

'I shall soon be with my father.'

Pizarro didn't deny his words or protest at them.

Anamaya suddenly saw Gabriel's silhouette through the door hanging. He came in to stand next to the Governor.

'Forgive me, Don Francisco,' he whispered, out of breath. 'I couldn't come more quickly.'

Pizarro didn't look at Gabriel. He didn't take his gaze from the Inca.

'Please don't say such things, my friend,' he said gently to Atahualpa. 'You are not going to die. If you have enemies, we shall protect you against them. And we shall guard you from those Christians who don't understand you. I value your friendship too much.'

'I am weary,' replied the Inca, his voice calm.

'Then rest. Be at peace, and relax as best you can.'

Pizarro bowed, bending his lean body low, then left, followed by Felipillo and Gabriel.

'Where are they?' he asked when they were all out in the courtyard.

Two soldiers approached. Gabriel was puzzled to see Sebastian, his expression tight, carrying a chain, each of whose links had a circumference as wide as that of a child's wrist.

'What in the name of God are you doing with that?' he asked.

Sebastian made no reply. Gabriel turned to the Governor.

'Don Francisco, please tell me what's going on.'

'Come,' said Pizarro to Gabriel after he'd directed the two soldiers to the Inca's room. 'We need to talk.'

Anamaya had remained standing behind Atahualpa. When she saw the door hanging rise once more to reveal the chains in the Spaniards' hands, she stepped back involuntarily.

'Don't worry,' said Atahualpa. 'All is as it should be.'

Sebastian approached the statue-still Inca. He looked quickly to one side, caught Anamaya's blue-irised gaze for a moment, then glanced away again.

'Tell them to do what they must do,' said Atahualpa calmly.

The African giant placed an iron collar around the Inca's neck. He made sure not to set it too tightly. A chain was hooked onto the collar, then looped around the room's lowest supporting beam and padlocked.

Atahualpa still hadn't moved. A wan smile lit his face and even his eyes.

'You see, Anamaya. I am free!'

CHAPTER 5

Cajamarca, 25 July 1533: evening

THE STRANGERS HAD TRANSFORMED, WITH WHAT SMALL means they had at their disposal, the biggest room in the Temple of the Sun into something approximating the interior of a lavish Spanish palace. They had even made some rudimentary Spanish furniture – such as tables and high-backed chairs – albeit mostly rickety. Faded tapestries hung on the walls above stacks of travel chests. In the niches stood statues of the Virgin Mary, so cherished by Governor Pizarro. They had taken the place of puma masks and model llamas made of gold or silver, long since smelted down into ingots. As for the pottery, that had all been stolen or smashed.

Four places had been set around the big table onto whose surface candelabras were dripping wax. At the moment there were only three guests, however. Don Diego de Almagro sat facing Gabriel, while Pizarro remained standing.

Don Diego wore no eye patch on his pockmarked face that evening. Gabriel wasn't sure which eye to look at. The one that had been destroyed by an Indian spear was oddly fascinating in its unsightliness. It was a dry, black mass, which sometimes seemed to move in coordination with the good eye. Don Diego (who, it was said, was as courageous as ten men) was, in fact, beneath his boorish, rough-hewn façade, a sophisticated and wily man, and he knew how to make the most out of his disability.

'I saw him,' he said, his accent betraying his La Mancha roots. 'I went to his cell and told him to calm down.'

'Who are you talking about, Don Diego?' asked Gabriel.

'Pedro Cataño! Your friend, apparently. He kicked up a fuss at the Council this afternoon, interrupting Don Francisco to claim that you and he had foiled a plot against the Inca! Why, in the name of God, he went so far as to declare that he would give his life for him! One would think that he was one of the Inca's twelve hundred sons, to hear him say such things! Though I can't help but wonder, given the color of his skin.'

Pizarro grinned. Gabriel went pale, and had to grind his teeth hard to prevent himself from speaking out and insulting the one-eyed man.

'The Governor had him thrown in a cell to cool off,' said Don Diego, laughing. 'What else could he do?'

'He could've let him be,' growled Gabriel, 'and simply advised him to hold his tongue.'

'Enough, gentlemen!' intervened Pizarro, rubbing his hands together. He had removed his gloves, for once. 'I have invited our friend Cataño to sup with us. Was that not a good idea of mine, Don Diego?'

Rolling his only eye, de Almagro raised his arms towards heaven.

'I know too well the depth of your magnanimity, Francisco. It is unfathomable indeed, and also, if you will forgive me for saying so, dangerous.'

Pizarro's face lit up. Despite the causes and the bitterness of their rivalry, de Almagro had the privilege of being one of the few men able to draw a smile from him.

'If your lordships, in all your beneficence, would be so kind as to grant me an explanation?' asked Gabriel sardonically, wary of what he would no doubt hear.

'At the Council of War that your friend Cataño so rudely interrupted, we were discussing what to do with the Inca. Father Valverde and I are of the opinion that he is a human being and that we can make a Christian of him, but there are some . . .'

The play of the candlelight cast sinister shadows across de Almagro's face.

'. . . There are some who feel that it is a dangerous situation,' finished de Almagro in his shrill voice as he toyed with a goblet of bad wine. 'And there are others who think that it is no longer possible to launch an expedition against the Empire's capital. De Moguer and Bueno were adamant on their return to Cuzco. There are treasures to be found there that are worth far more than anything we have seen up to now – I mean anything *you* have seen up to now, all of you who were with my cherished friend the Governor, Don Francisco, the treasure that *you* have amassed, melted down, and carefully stashed away in *your* pockets—'

'Nonetheless, none of us are in doubt that we must demonstrate a very Christian spirit throughout this adventure,' continued Pizarro impassively. 'We must ensure that our Emperor Charles the Fifth is gladdened by our efforts when news of them reaches him.'

'The royal decree is clear,' Gabriel broke in. 'It dictates that we protect as far as possible the lives of all kings, princes and lords of the Indies.'

'As far as is possible, so therefore not in the case of treason,' said de Almagro hoarsely.

'What treason?' demanded Gabriel, raising his voice.

'Easy, Gabriel . . . none so far,' said the Governor quietly, approaching the table. 'It is possible, merely *possible*, that there may be a case of treason, Diego. In the absence of any solid evidence of it, we must continue to protect the Inca's life and await de Soto's return.'

'But we *do* have evidence!' shouted an exasperated de Almagro, slamming his goblet down on the table.

'What evidence?' asked Gabriel.

'The Indian witnesses!'

'Lies, Don Diego! You know very well that that is all the result of their internal politics and intrigues.'

'Lies yourself, sir! You want truths? I'll give you one: we can't march along the roads to Cuzco with that feathered monkey on our backs! All the Indians in the world would fall on us!'

'How do you know? He appeases them with a mere word. I've seen him do it.'

'You've seen nothing at all, comrade. I have but one eye, but I've seen far more than you can imagine! I've been seeing what this rabble is capable of for more than forty years! And Francisco knows them as well as I do, don't you?'

'I like to do things according to the law, Don Diego. I like there to be order.'

'Ha! Is that so? Then put things in order, Governor! Set a date for our departure to Cuzco, and make sure that Featherhead can't come up behind us!'

'But that's disgraceful!' yelled Gabriel, standing up, 'You cannot—'

Don Francisco waved him back down, and then turned to face a statue of the Virgin.

'The Inca is under my protection. If he is guilty, it shall be a court of law that decides, just as in Spain.'

De Almagro shook his large, misshapen head, angrily bit into a piece of corn bread, and howled with pain.

'Diego! What's wrong?'

'By the devil! I've broken a tooth,' he mumbled, furious. 'Forget about your damned Virgin, and have them bring us meat, Francisco. I'm hungry!'

Don Diego de Almagro spat his cracked canine onto the floor.

Shadows reigned in Atahualpa's palace. The Emperor had given the order that no torches were to be lit. He had refused all his meals; declined visits from his *curacas*; and turned away from the attentions of his wives and concubines.

He wanted only Anamaya for company. While the light of day still reached the gold puma in its niche, he remained silent. It was only long after nightfall that he said:

'I am a jungle cat who no longer knows how to pounce.'

There was no bitterness or sadness in his voice. It was a simple observation. He touched the collar around his neck, and shook the links chaining him to the wall.

'Come nearer, *Coya Camaquen*. Put your arms around me . . .'

Anamaya laid her hands on the Emperor. She felt his exhausted body through the softness of his clothes, the heat already draining from him. He was dying of his own volition. He was a man who already belonged to the Under World.

'Now I know everything,' said Atahualpa calmly. 'It is too late now. I regret nothing, because my life is the price I pay for this knowledge. I know what my father said to you the night before he died because I am in that same night now, and soon I shall be at his side. It is his voice, not mine, speaking to you. So listen – behind mine there is my father's! My voice is infinitely older than I am, and it will continue to speak long after I'm gone. *Coya Camaquen*, gentle young girl with eyes the colour of the lake, never forget to heed the voice of the son of Inti!'

'I have known for many moons that you would be leaving us, my Lord,' murmured Anamaya. 'Yet now that the moment is upon us, I'm frightened.'

'I am not. Stay with me as you stayed with my father.'

Anamaya's breath mingled with Atahualpa's, and they were one in the night.

'There are no more Cuzco clans,' whispered Atahualpa. 'I carried out my vengeance like a drunken fool, an unjust man ruled by anger. There are no more brethren; no more enemies . . . The children of the Empire are today bound in chains, just as I am. They cry tears and suffer, and it is my fault.'

His knees gave way and Anamaya tried to hold him up, but the collar dug into the Inca's neck. A groaning of pain sounded hollowly in his chest. He said hoarsely:

'The North and the South have been weakened by my actions. The blood of the Sun has been shed because of me. Chalkuchimac was right: This is not the doing of the Strangers! They are like the birds that wait for their prey to exhaust themselves. I, Atahualpa, son of Inti and of the great Huayna Capac, I have fractured the Empire of the Four Cardinal Directions, and the Strangers are making the most of it. But they know nothing of the power of the Other World. They are building with mud on a mountain of fire that will, one day, wake and so utterly consume them that their ashes will be blown back to the ocean that brought them here.'

Atahualpa's voice no longer came from his chest. It was as harsh as winds blowing from the bowels of the earth. It was the voice of all the Ancestors, of all the fathers and sons who had carried the lineage since the birth of the world.

'I have long renounced my brother Manco. Now I see what you have always seen but never dared tell me: that he is the first knot of the future.'

'And the Puma?'

The question came from her mouth despite herself. Yet there was no surprise in Atahualpa's voice when he answered:

'The Puma is no longer with me, but you must place your trust in him. Follow my father's orders, and heed his advice . . .'

Anamaya felt the shackles of silence that had been constricting her throat break now, thanks to the relief his words had brought her. At last, the Emperor had managed to see and understand what she had seen and understood for so long. At last, he was close once more to the Ancestors of the Other World. Now he was truly on the path that ended with the death of the body.

The Emperor and the *Coya Camaquen* shared their joy long into the night, with their eyes closed and their spirits lightened. The barriers between their dreams and their consciousness, between night and day, between flesh and its absence had been removed. Like transparent birds they spread their wings and travelled above the mountains and plains of their beloved country, into its past and into its future, into the lake of its origin, into the Sacred River in the sky, into the silver of the Moon and the gold of the Sun.

Prisoners once, they had now found freedom.

The other Spaniards were already peeling their fruit when Pedro Cataño walked unsteadily into the Governor's dining room. Rage and fear at having been locked up ruined his features. Don Francisco rose and placed a hand on his shoulder, a gesture that Gabriel knew well, for it was the Governor's way of calling for submission under the guise of showing affection.

'Calm yourself, Pedro! Sit down and eat something.'

Cataño slid into a chair and promptly launched into a tirade that he had clearly been preparing for a long time. He glared at de Almagro who was seated directly opposite him.

'Gentlemen, Governor, I thank you for bringing the justice that Lord Atahualpa deserves upon his head.'

De Almagro chuckled and picked at some shreds of mango flesh caught between his teeth. Pizarro, acting as though he hadn't heard, asked:

'What do you say to a round of cards?'

'Cards!'

Gabriel couldn't believe his ears.

'Does our noble Gabriel consider himself above such amusements?' jibed Don Diego.

'Excellent,' continued Don Francisco, making a sign to the Indian servant girls. 'Diego, you team with our friend Cataño, but first let him eat his dinner . . .'

De Almagro took the deck of cards, a bored expression on his face, while Cataño ate ravenously from his pewter porringer.

Just then a disturbance started outside, and angry voices could be heard. Gabriel went out onto the threshold. The palace guards were standing in the way of three men: two Spaniards and an Indian slave brought from Nicaragua. Gabriel recognized one of the Spaniards as Pedro de Añades, a small man with a sparse beard who never stopped sweating. If ever there was anyone loyal to de Almagro, it was him.

'Well, de Añades,' called Gabriel, 'what's going on?'

'They're preventing me from getting through,' shouted de Añades, indicating the guards. 'I need to see Don Diego de Almagro this instant.'

'This instant? That's a little presumptuous, isn't it? Don Diego is playing cards with the Governor.'

De Añades's face lit up at the news.

'Then Jesus is watching over me, Don Gabriel. I need to see the Governor as well.'

'May I ask why?'

'I feel that their lordships would be somewhat displeased with me were I not to bring them this fellow's testimony directly,' he said with a grandiose air, pointing at the Indian.

'What testimony?'

De Añades put his finger to his lips.

'Forgive me, Don Gabriel, but this matter is of such import that I can allow this man to speak only in front of the Governor and Don Diego.'

Smug satisfaction was writ large all over de Añades's face. Gabriel reflected on the small fellow's expression for an instant, thinking that there was something cruel in it. He gestured at the guards.

'Let them in,' he ordered.

'Your lordships,' began de Añades pompously, once he was in the dining room, 'it is of the utmost importance that—'

'Get to the point,' cut in Pizarro.

Disconcerted, de Añades glanced at the table, the dishes, the cards, as though looking for the quickest way to reach his goal. In the end he thrust forward the reluctant Indian and said:

'Speak, then.'

The Indian remained silent, rolling his terrified eyes. His lips moved but no words came out. De Añades, his forehead glistening, said:

'This man says that he saw a multitude of Indian warriors three leagues from Cajamarca marching on us . . .'

'From what my own ears hear, this man says nothing at all,' remarked Pizarro coldly.

'Hold on, Francisco,' intervened de Almagro, throwing his cards down and jumping up from his chair. 'By all the saints, we are in danger of annihilation and you speak as though we were in a Seville court of law!'

'This man either speaks or he doesn't. I want to hear what *he* says.'

'Talk to us,' Gabriel said gently to the Indian. 'Just tell us what you saw, and we shall be satisfied.'

The slave pulled himself together. He spoke in short, clipped sentences:

'I saw those warriors. Many, very many of them . . . from the

North . . . I was hiding in a village . . . they razed a cornfield. They were singing. They spoke about attacking the town tomorrow night . . .'

Gabriel frowned, pursing his lips as he listened to the Indian continue his story. Pizarro nodded at each sentence.

'And so?' asked de Añades, still looking smug.

His question met with silence.

Then de Almagro's voice echoed sarcastically:

'Does your lordship wish that we should all die for Cataño's love?'

Pizarro looked at him blackly and replied:

'Spare me your idiocies, Diego, I've heard them all before!'

He squeezed his fist into his glove and left the room without even glancing at Gabriel. Almagro, already standing, went after him, followed by de Añades, his companion, and the slave. Despite the light of the flames, young Cataño's usually tawny face had turned grey.

'It's over, then,' he murmured. 'They're going to murder Atahualpa. We've lost, haven't we?'

Gabriel shook his head gently. 'Pedro,' he said in a low voice, 'you were with me this morning, yes?'

Cataño nodded his head unhappily.

'You saw what I saw, didn't you? Pastures, air, silence. There is no army outside Cajamarca.'

'But that man said—'

'That man is lying!' Gabriel barked.

CHAPTER 6

Cajamarca, 26 July 1533: morning

'PROVE TO ME THAT HE'S LYING!' BARKED PIZARRO.

'I don't need to prove it: I saw the mountains and fields with my own eyes, and there is no army there! I give you my word on it! I tell you: That fellow is lying. God's blood, Don Francisco! Is not my word worth more than that of a mere slave?' said Gabriel, deeply vexed.

He had forced his way into Pizarro's room at the hour when the Governor was dressing. Don Francisco was carefully setting his white lace ruff around his neck. Along with a few coloured feathers in his hat, it was the only finery he wore that counterbalanced the perpetual black of his other clothes.

'Don Francisco,' Gabriel continued, 'at least wait until de Soto returns! We shall know more then. He and his men will have explored every ravine between here and Cajas. If there are more than three armed Indians gathered anywhere, he will have seen them, or at least heard of them.'

Gabriel's voice was hard, his stare furious. He wished he was calmer, more measured. He knew that the Governor hated being pressured. And in any case, Pizarro rebuffed his proposition merely by raising his eyebrows disdainfully.

'Wait? But, my boy, what shall I tell the Council this morning? What could I say to de Almagro and to the King's officers?'

'My Lord, if my memory serves me well, you were hardly so concerned with the King's officers at our departure from

Seville . . . and even less so with the Council or with Don Diego!
You wished things to happen according to your own lights, and
that events followed rather than preceded you . . .'

An expression of mirth flashed across the Governor's wizened
face. He liked being reminded of that caper. Nevertheless, he
shook his head.

'The past is behind us, my boy. Henceforth I am responsible
for this town, for you, and for your companions. I am Governor,
and this country must abide by Spanish law.'

'Precisely!' said Gabriel bitterly. 'If the King learns that Lord
Atahualpa was executed without proof of treachery—'

The Governor's fingers quivered where they gripped the edge
of his hat. His exasperation showed when he rapped out:

'How many times must I tell you? You haven't given me
any proof that Don Diego's Indian is lying. No more than you
have that Atahualpa isn't feeding us poppycock to lull us into
complacency!'

'Just give me the time to find that proof and you shall have it!'

'Enough!'

For the first time, Pizarro raised his voice and his black-gloved
hand against Gabriel.

'Enough! That will do, Gabriel Montelucar y Flores! You forget
yourself! Remember who you are and what you owe me! And
remember your promise!'

Gabriel stiffened. The allusion to his illegitimate birth and to
that hated name made him grow pallid with rage. As for the rest
of it, he remembered it as though it had happened yesterday.

But the Governor was already biting his lip, feigning embar-
rassment, and now he said, more calmly:

'Oh, I don't give a damn where you come from. I'm like you. But
as for the rest, don't forget . . . you promised to submit yourself
to my judgement. And this condition makes you . . . yes, it makes
you a son of mine.'

The Governor's voice faded as he voiced that secret, ambiguous
affection that bound them together. *Cunning old dog . . .* thought
Gabriel, unable to hold back his emotion.

'I need your trust, Gabriel,' continued Don Francisco as he

took Gabriel's arm. 'Don't let yourself be overly influenced by that Indian girl, that sorceress from Atahualpa's entourage. It doesn't bode well.'

'That is my affair and mine only, Don Francisco!'

'I'm not so sure . . .'

They sized one another up for a moment, eye to eye. In the end Pizarro waved his hand as though brushing aside a fly.

'Bah – women, they're not important. I only tell you this because my brothers are disappointed to see you with that strange girl.'

So, here we are then, reflected Gabriel, almost amused. *The old dog is trying to change the subject and get at what he thinks is my weak point.*

'You know my opinion of your brothers, Don Francisco. I decline to have an opinion of their Indian women, whom they take and discard according to their whims.'

Gabriel was almost sure that he detected a gleam of amusement on Pizarro's haggard face. He used the opportunity to add:

'We were discussing serious matters, your excellency.'

'Yes . . . yes, you're right. In that case, listen to me carefully. I'm not just exercising power here, enforcing the King's authority. You know me well enough to know that that doesn't suffice. No one has a greater sense of duty and justice than I. No one, d'you hear?'

'I know, Don Francisco.'

'Do you think that I spend my nights praying for no reason, merely making sounds with my mouth? Or do you believe that I listen to what the Sacred Virgin tells me?'

'I know,' repeated Gabriel.

'I am not here for the gold, Gabriel, nor to grab myself enough land to work thousands of slaves on. I leave that to Don Diego de Almagro and the rest of 'em . . . no, I'm here to write into the annals of history a legend dedicated to the glory of Our Lord Jesus Christ and our King Charles the Fifth.'

'Then do not stain that legend with blood.'

Pizarro pulled his hat low on his forehead and stared into the shadows. Briskly, he tightened the buckle of his scabbard and placed a hand on the hilt of his sword, as though he was about to sit for a portrait.

'You insist that de Añades and his slave lie?'

'Yes.'

'Find me the proof.'

'And then?'

'And then nothing. Just find me that fucking proof, that's all.'

Gabriel was taken aback by all the nervous activity taking place on the square at Cajamarca at such an untimely hour. Groups of Indians murmured amongst themselves, and Spanish patrols walked about menacingly.

The guard roster had been doubled. A hundred troopers had taken it in turns to patrol the roads and streets on the outskirts of Cajamarca. All the Spaniards had slept with their weapons to hand. At dawn, Father Valverde had given a Mass in the unfinished church. His sermon reminded the Cajamarca veterans, the expressions on their pale faces affirming their devotion, of the one given before the Great Battle of November.

'Gabriel!'

The call startled him. Sebastian approached. His perpetual grin showed his teeth, the whiteness and health of which made the European conquistadors jealous.

'Walk with me for a minute, will you?'

Side by side, they walked around the church. The walls of the nave were still only waist high. On the stone altar a simple wooden crucifix had been erected. The as yet roofless columns reaching for the blue Andean sky had an ethereal quality about them.

'Why did you put the Inca in chains?' asked Gabriel harshly.

'Because they ordered me to,' Sebastian said simply.

'*They*?'

'De Almagro, and the Governor himself.'

'But you? Why you?'

Sebastian gave a sinister chuckle, and his voice was full of bitterness when he said:

'My friend, why do you always need to be reminded of the most self-evident truths? They chose me because I am Don Diego's possession, because my skin is black and because no God-fearing

Spaniard wants to sully his hands by chaining a King, even a Peruvian King wearing feathers! You never know what tomorrow's mood will be, especially if you're white, Spanish, and your name is preceded by *Don*. But I know what *my* tomorrow will be like: The same shit as yesterday and today.'

Gabriel lowered his gaze. There was so much pain in his friend's voice that each word hit him like a fist in the gut. The initial stonework of the church seemed to him in that moment as repellent as a rosary made of lies.

'It was a stupid question. Forgive me, my friend.'

'There is an ocean between you and me, Don Gabriel,' said Sebastian unhappily. 'And sometimes friendship isn't enough for us to navigate between its shores.'

'I told you: I know what it is like for you, and I ask you to forgive me. Do I have to get on my knees and beg you?' said Gabriel, feeling guilty. 'God almighty, very well! You are not to blame. It's just that I'm tired of having the wool pulled over my eyes. What's more, last night seemed to me blacker than most . . .'

Sebastian's smile returned.

'As for that, I can bring some light to bear on it. That Indian who testified yesterday—'

'De Añades's man?'

'Exactly: That Indian – that *slave*, above all, who doesn't even know who he belongs to, the bugger! Anyway, last night I drank with him – some of that beer of theirs that slips smoothly down your gullet and unties your tongue in no time at all – and by the third goblet, he was no longer sure whether what he had seen had seen an Indian army or a herd of llamas. By the fourth, he wasn't sure if he had even been out gallivanting in the highland pastures at all. And by the fifth, he was showing me the lovely gold pin generously given to him by de Añades for telling his tale.'

'You are my guardian angel, Sebastian. Where is he?'

'If only I knew . . .'

'How do you mean?'

'As he sobered up he grew frightened and regretted what he'd told me. Now I can't find him anywhere.'

'Christ's blood!'

'Yes. And if you don't get him to spill his guts to the Governor, than I shall play Judas: They have chosen me to garrotte the Inca.'

Gabriel stared into his friend's eyes. Had it been ten minutes earlier, he would have exploded into a rage. But now he felt only immeasurable bitterness. Only one last hope kept his heart alive.

'You're not going to ask me why?' asked Sebastian, his tone surly.

'Don't start!'

Sebastian took hold of his friend's wrist and fixed his dark-eyed stare on Gabriel's face as he declared, his voice sharper than a saw ripping through a piece of old wood:

'If I break the Inca's neck, Don Diego will personally present me with a sword, and Don Hernando Pizarro himself will no longer forbid me to place my noble behind on a horse's back. De Moguer will call me *Don* Sebastian. Not a bad deal, don't you think?'

Gabriel held back the fury bursting from within. He ground his jaws together to prevent his mouth spitting useless words. Sebastian was right: It was not a bad deal.

Anamaya watched blankly as the crowd of Strangers entered the Inca's chamber. She recognized all of them: The Governor led, followed by the one-eyed de Almagro, the priest Valverde, his Bible in his hand, and the King's officers. Then came the interpreter, Felipillo, and the Governor's two younger brothers, the diabolically beautiful Gonzalo, and Juan, that odd mixture of pride and timidity.

She hadn't left Atahualpa's side all night.

Pizarro motioned to a soldier to remove the collar from around the Inca's throat. Atahualpa rubbed his neck. He eyed the Strangers one by one, regarding them first with disdain, then with distaste, finally with indifference. He looked at the Governor.

'Why did you do that, my friend?'

Pizarro made no reply. He kicked aside the iron collar as though to distance it from the Inca and to erase its very existence.

'You've come to play chess, haven't you?' said the Emperor.

A murmur rose among the Spaniards as Felipillo translated. Anamaya wanted to smile. Atahualpa had spoken with such quiet assurance . . . the Emperor had found consolation in the night . . .

The Emperor signaled a servant to bring a table made of pleated bulrush. A bench was brought for Pizarro, and then the chessboard was placed on the table. Atahualpa had developed a fondness for the game during his captivity. Not far from the Palace, beside the now-empty weaving workshops, his people made chess sets for him. The materials for and sizes of the pieces were carefully chosen by him.

'You be white,' declared the Emperor, 'and I shall be black. It is in keeping with the natural order of things.'

If the Governor was surprised, he didn't show it. He removed the black glove from his right hand. Anamaya watched that small, dry hand nervously set up the pieces.

Still standing, the Emperor removed the accessories that symbolized his power and handed them to Anamaya: The breast plate of pink and red *mullus*, an astonishing piece of workmanship; the *llautu*, the royal head wreath; and even the handkerchief that hid his torn earlobe. There was total silence. All the Spaniards had their stares riveted on Lord Atahualpa. The more royal adornments he removed from his body, the more regal he became.

When he was wearing nothing but his tunic, he said quietly to Pizarro:

'Let's play.'

All Atahualpa's servant girls and wives and all the noblemen of his entourage crowded into the recesses at the back of the room. The Spaniards drifted back out onto the patio, leaving the two players to their game. Felipillo remained prudently behind Pizarro, occasionally glancing furtively at Anamaya.

From the brightness of the patio, another Spaniard was persistently trying to catch her eye: One of the Governor's brothers – but which one? Gonzalo? Juan? Each time she thought she had intercepted the stare that was meant for her, she received only a slanted smile in return, as though they were just playing with her.

Outside, the Spaniards were talking among themselves. They kept interrupting one another, their conversation growing increasingly heated.

Atahualpa ignored their squabble and advanced his pawns with calm self-assuredness. Pizarro's moves were less regular, less well thought out. Soon, one-eyed de Almagro entered the room. He came and stood so close to the Governor that he brushed his shoulders with the pommel of his sword.

'Don Francisco, we are not here to watch a game of chess.'

A murmur of agreement rose from the patio. Anamaya noticed that the Governor had already lost a lot more pieces than Atahualpa.

'Don Francisco!' insisted de Almagro.

Pizarro barely turned his head.

'What is it, Don Diego?'

'Bloody hell, Francisco! I mean, really, your lordship! We are not here to play but to notify the Inca of his sentence.'

Felipillo had stopped translating. Anamaya took over, murmuring in a low voice into the Inca's wounded ear. He stiffened slightly at the word 'sentence'. Then he nodded his head.

'Well then, do so, my friend, do so . . .' growled Pizarro.

As de Almagro turned his head toward the Spanish officers and shook his head in vexation, the Governor stared hard at the indecipherable enigma spread out in front of him on the chessboard. His hand fell haphazardly onto one of the few pieces that he had left before fluttering indecisively to another.

When Pizarro eventually raised his gaze toward the Inca, Anamaya was taken aback to discover that his expression was terribly confused.

But now the youngest of the Spanish officers had entered the room and had unrolled a parchment scroll. He began to read, pausing after each long phrase or clause to recover his breath. Ridiculously, Felipillo did the same. With a click of his tongue, the Emperor ordered the interpreter to stop. The Spaniard carried on reading the litany of accusations. Kneeling near the Inca, Anamaya translated only the most serious: Duplicity, fabrication, treason, assassination, hostile armies . . .

Atahualpa's smile broadened with each word.

When the Spanish officer had at last finished, the Inca addressed Pizarro:

'Those are not the reasons why you're going to kill me, are they.'

It wasn't a question. Pizarro was disconcerted by the Inca's statement and dropped the chess piece that he was trying to move. Emperor Atahualpa bent over, picked it up, placed it back in the Governor's hand and gently curled Don Francisco's fingers around it.

The Inca's smile was beautiful, so tender that it softened the effect of the redness of his eyes.

'Are you sure that you don't want more gold? More lovely plates, pretty statues, fine fountains?'

The Spaniards had come into the center of the room. Their breathing was the only sound audible in the heavy, threatening atmosphere.

The Emperor made one last move. Pizarro had almost no pieces left, whereas the Inca still had almost all of his.

'You are in checkmate, brother,' said Juan with contrived jollity.

Atahualpa took his own king and lifted it above the board. He turned it around in his fingers as though it was the first time he had ever seen it.

'He is a great King,' he said, 'with powerful forces. And yet he must have committed some grave errors.'

In one fell swoop he broke the piece against the edge of the board. Its head rolled about on the ground like a die. No one dared to pick it up.

Silence returned. Don Francisco Pizarro picked up the glove from the bench beside him and eased his fingers into it.

'A great King, but an unhappy game,' he sighed. 'There is nothing I can do.'

'Are you sure?'

The question required no answer, and got none. The Spaniards narrowed their eyes in apprehension. When the Inca reached out for Anamaya's hand, some of them even took a step back. Everyone watched that dark hand squeeze the *Coya Camaquen*'s, squeeze it so tightly that it looked as though the girl's hand might break.

The Spaniards didn't understand the true meaning of the gesture. They told themselves that the Inca was frightened and that he needed the comfort of a woman.

When the Emperor released his grasp, Anamaya advanced forward into the room and picked up the head of the chess king. She used both her hands to hold it tightly, hiding it from anyone else's gaze. Atahualpa smiled, and nodded briefly.

'There. Now, do with me what you must, my friend Pizarro.'

CHAPTER 7

Cajamarca, 26 July, 1533: evening

WHEN THEY ARRIVED AT DE AÑADES'S LODGINGS, Sebastian and Gabriel found the place empty save for an ancient, tottering slave seated in a rocking chair that was propped up against the wall. He only muttered incoherently when addressed. They had spent the entire day running through the town, searching every alleyway, every palace, every *cancha* whether rich or poor.

In the end they found their prey in a squalid courtyard, along with a horde of guinea pigs nibbling away at rotten leaves and scampering between naked children. Four groaning slaves were working a heavy millstone. Outside the *cancha*, some Indian servants were waiting for sacks of maize flour. Sebastian pointed at a man sitting on a stool:

'Here he is – at last!'

Gabriel saw the man's fearful eyes recognize him.

'Yes, it's definitely him,' he said.

Gabriel and Sebastian hastened together toward the poor fellow before he had a chance to move. Their jostling caused the guinea pigs to take flight in a cacophony of squeals to which the children added their own cries.

Motivated by a sound sense of caution, the four Indian slaves abandoned the millstone and took refuge in the shade of a squalid room.

'I'm not going to kill you,' muttered Gabriel as he pushed the fellow out of the yard.

As they appeared, the line of waiting servants fled to the end of the alleyway.

'I'll let you take care of it,' said Sebastian. 'They're waiting for me. Do it quickly.'

As the giant black man left at a run, Gabriel backed the slave up against a wall.

'What's your name?'

'I don't have one . . .'

All the frustration that had built up in him during the day, coupled with his rage at the prospect of the great injustice soon to be committed, snapped Gabriel's self-control. He struck the man with the back of his hand, as hard as if he was using the flat of a sword. Blood gushed from the slave's nose and mouth.

'You can't even remember your own name? How many *tupus* did they give you to forget what you know and to remember what you don't? How much was it?'

But what Gabriel got in reply was the same type of wry, ironic look that Sebastian had given him that morning when the black man had said: 'There is an ocean between you and me, Don Gabriel . . .' And his rage left him as quickly as it had come, replaced by a deep sense of shame and weariness that drained the strength from his arms. He let go of the man, who fell down, a crumpled heap of humanity, his dripping sweat mixing with his blood.

'What's your name?'

Two wary eyes looked up at him, two eyes blinded by fear. Gabriel bent over and held the slave by the shoulders with unexpected gentleness.

'Don't be frightened. I shan't strike you again.'

Gabriel sat down beside the Indian, on the same dirt and filth. When a guinea pig began nibbling at the tips of his boots, he made no motion to shoo it away. He caught a glimpse, through an opening in the wall, of the silhouettes of two crouching women. The sinister sound of distant trumpets came to them, carried on the breeze.

'Tell me what happened,' he insisted. 'What did your master ask of you?'

'I was ordered not to tell anyone,' said the man in a low voice.

'I know. Yet you must tell me anyway.'

'The Stranger Lord said that we would all be killed unless I said the things he wanted me to. He said that your master would be gratified and that he would spare us. He gave me a gold pin.'

'You didn't see any soldiers. You didn't see the Inca's warriors.'

The man dug his feet into the dirt, saying nothing. He picked up a guinea pig, then released it tenderly. Finally, he shook his head.

'What story would you tell if I were to take you to the Governor now?' Gabriel asked him.

'If I speak the truth, they'll kill me as soon as I'm finished.'

'No,' said Gabriel, standing up and dusting himself off, 'I can promise you that you shall not be killed for speaking the truth.'

Troops lined a path through the crowd from Atahualpa's palace to the execution post that had been erected in the center of the square. When the Emperor, chained and bareheaded, came out of his palace, the Indians threw themselves to the ground, wailing mournfully as though they were all drunk.

Atahualpa had the priest Valverde, the interpreter Felipillo and a Spanish captain at his side. Anamaya followed a few paces behind. The Inca turned to face her:

'Stay with me until I can see my father,' he ordered her.

She simply nodded, her throat so constricted that she was unable to reply.

'Ask them why they are putting me to death,' Atahualpa said calmly to Felipillo.

The interpreter became flustered. Hoping that Anamaya wouldn't be able to hear him, he said in a low voice to the captain and the priest:

'The Inca asks if he can buy his life with more gold.'

It wasn't the first time that the interpreter had mistranslated the Emperor's words. Anamaya was about to protest when Atahualpa, not bothering to wait for a reply, said in a voice loud enough for the crowd to hear:

'Ever since I have been in your hands, Strangers, what have I done other than bring you gold and yet more gold, silver, and precious stones? What have my wives, my servants and my sons done other than obey your every command? You claim that my armies are marching on you . . . you have imprisoned me and bound me in chains, and you tortured the powerful general Chalkuchimac. Is there a will here that is not your own? Now you have grown weary of me. You want to take my life from me. Take it. You are only taking my presence in *this* world. I am the Emperor of Tahuantinsuyu; nothing can prevent my reaching the Other World. Many seasons ago, my father the Sun scattered his seeds of gold on these mountains to ensure my birth. My mother the Moon let her silver milk flow into my mouth, so that I would be strong and powerful. I feel only joy and peace at the prospect of returning at last to Inti.'

When Atahualpa had finished, a heavy sense of sorrow descended on the crowd. Tears fell, shining on the Indians' cheeks. Even those who had complained of the Inca's indifference and severity were now bent double with grief. Today, like the sun at last breaking through the clouds, his courage and his suffering were theirs. With him, they bore the weight of helplessness of being citizens of the Empire of the Four Cardinal Directions, and with him they endured the wind of destruction raised by the Strangers.

Two men took his arms and tied him tightly to the cedar post. Anamaya recognized the black-skinned one, Gabriel's friend, the one who had placed the collar around Atahualpa's neck the previous evening. She looked at him closely, and read in his face only deep resignation.

'Where is the Governor, my friend Pizarro? I wish to speak with him,' said Atahualpa.

Father Vicente Valverde sighed, and motioned to the captain to fetch Don Francisco.

At that moment shouts silenced the crowd's wailing. Anamaya turned around to see Gabriel breaking through the line of soldiers, dragging an Indian behind him.

'Where's the Governor?' he yelled. 'I've got his proof! I've got the proof that he asked me for! De Añades's slave lied, d'ye hear? There is no Indian army! The Inca is innocent!'

After a moment of surprise, an irritated Valverde replied:

'What do you want of the Governor?'

'Father Valverde, the Inca is innocent!'

'Innocent of what? Of scorning God's will? Certainly not! My friend, if you want to be useful to this creature, you should be praying for him rather than shouting like a madman.'

Gabriel placed the trembling slave in front of him and shouted:

'Father Vicente, need I remind you that you are going to murder the Inca not in the name of God but on the pretext that he wants to annihilate us with his armies. But de Añades ordered this man here to lie to us. There isn't a single Indian warrior within fifty leagues of Cajamarca. Are you going to ignore this fact?'

The Dominican said nothing.

'By the blood of Christ, Father Valverde, give me an answer!'

But Valverde never had a chance to reply. A cry distracted them:

'Milords! Milords! We cannot find Don Francisco anywhere! No one knows where he is . . .'

'You see how it is,' said Valverde quietly. 'There's no reason to complicate things.'

Gabriel, dumbfounded, turned to Felipillo, who was still interpreting for the Inca. He caught a glimpse of Anamaya's lips; they too were moving. Atahualpa, slightly astonished, looked directly at Gabriel. He silenced Felipillo with a wave of his hand and spoke directly to Gabriel:

'Tell the Governor that I remain his friend and that I place my children under his protection.'

Before Gabriel could react, Valverde, his crucifix raised high, stepped between him and Atahualpa.

'Forget about your children, Inca!' he exclaimed. 'Forget about your wives! Think only of God – think of the face of God and die a Christian!'

'My children are many, and all so young . . .' insisted Atahualpa, still looking at Gabriel over the priest's shoulder.

'God wills it that you die for all the excesses you committed in this world. You have to repent them all that so that God may forgive you.'

'My children are weak, defenceless . . . they need protection . . .'

Gabriel could hear Atahualpa's voice, but the priest's arms hid the Inca's face from him. But now it was Anamaya's gaze that weighed upon him, that she touched him with as though she had placed her hands on his chest. He shouted out in Quechua, raising his voice above the sound of Valverde's sermon:

'Have no fear, Emperor, I will speak to the Governor about your children.'

Livid, Valverde turned on his heel, his cheeks crimson, menacing him with his crucifix.

'That's enough! Hold your tongue!'

Behind him, Atahualpa almost smiled.

'Am I to be burned?' he asked quietly.

'Your sentence demands that you should be,' said Valverde, sighing, 'unless you die having accepted the word of Almighty God.'

'How so?'

'Then God will forgive you and indulge you with his clemency.'

Atahualpa looked away from Valverde. For a moment he gazed at the crowd, as though he wanted to commit each face to memory. And then he suddenly declaimed:

'People of Tahuantinsuyu, I am going to die!'

A clamor rose from the crowd, a sound more profound than that of horns, more deafening than that of drums.

'I am leaving you to rejoin my Father at last! I am going to the Under World to begin my long voyage. I shall return to you in the form that I have taken once before, as a snake. The Strangers say that they won't burn me if I turn Christian, like them. They wish me to submit to their god.'

The crowd fell silent. Atahualpa's chest swelled impressively despite the ropes binding him.

'People of Tahuantinsuyu, my body must not be reduced to ashes. It is the vessel that must transport me to my Father. So I shall do what they ask of me. But remember: I am the son of Inti!'

These last words were spoken with so much pride that the crowd began to chant:

'It is so, Emperor!'

'I am the Son of the Sun!'

'It is so, Emperor!'

And it was thus, amid all the cries, wails, and tears, that Atahualpa permitted Valverde to baptize him.

Anamaya closed her eyes and let her memories rise to the forefront of her mind. She remembered the day that she had helped the Emperor flee, the dumbfounded guards finding only a snake slough in his cell. She remembered the morning of the Great Massacre, when he had hailed the crowd with exactly the same words.

The shadow of night was already upon the great valley, and the mountain peaks glowed red in the sunset. Torches burned here and there. Gabriel wanted to go to Anamaya and hold her body close to his. The Indian whom he had dragged along watched him in a daze. Gabriel motioned to him to disappear into the crowd. When Gabriel lifted his downcast gaze, he met Sebastian's stare. Despite himself, and unaware of the movement's implication, he nodded.

Sebastian placed the leather strap around the Inca's neck with singular tenderness. He slipped two withes into the garrotte's aperture. The device was a large wooden screw of the same basic design as those much smaller ones used to crack nuts. He turned the handle, and the leather began to cut into Atahualpa's flesh.

With a single twist of his wrist, Sebastian gave the garrotte another turn. The Emperor's dun skin whitened under the pressure of the strap. His glottis quivered, and his mouth opened in a silent scream, his well-defined lips curling with the pain.

Anamaya had opened her eyes, and she stared into Atahualpa's blood-filled orbs as though she wanted to melt into his last view of life. As the crowd continued to wail and Valverde chanted as forcefully as he could, she barely heard Gabriel order:

'Faster, Sebastian, faster!'

The giant black man now turned the garrotte with all the strength in his body. A cracking sound tore through the noise of the crowd.

The Emperor's upper spine had snapped. Atahualpa's eyes rolled back to see what no one else could see.

Gabriel realized that Anamaya was now so close to him that their shoulders and hips were touching. He felt the back of her hand brush against his. She murmured:

'No one can stop that which must be, not even you.'

The women's wails rose sharply into the darkening sky. The men tore their clothes and scratched at their bare chests. The torch flames danced madly. Anamaya closed her fingers around Gabriel's.

'All is well,' she said.

Sebastian sat down at the foot of the unlit pyre. His cheeks were dry, but his shoulders were shaking as though he was being destroyed by fever.

CHAPTER 8

Cajamarca, 26 July 1533: night

QUILLA, THE MOON GODDESS, DID NOT SHINE THAT night. The Inca Emperor Atahualpa's palace was drowned in a darkness that seemed as though it would never end.

Everywhere, in its vast halls and small chambers, in its court-yards and storerooms, wailing could be heard throughout the night. As recently as the previous day some of the Emperor's wives, concubines and servant girls had dreamed of serving the Strangers. They had complained about the Inca, his indifference and callousness – but now there was only pain. No amount of bloodshed would make up for it.

Anamaya felt as though she was burning up, and she stopped by the fountain on the patio to plunge her hands into its translucent water and bring it to her cheeks. But the liquid streamed off her face without cooling her.

Inguill came to her, and without uttering a word she pressed herself against her bosom.

Anamaya let her do so and tried to console her. She too, the young Cuzco girl, Manco's protégée, was grieving at the death of the man whose cruelty had caused the death of her mother and brothers.

Then, slowly, Anamaya pushed Inguill back a little. She looked at her for a moment as they stood in the shadows. Her small and birdlike face was bathed in tears.

'Leave me now, little one,' Anamaya murmured tenderly. 'I have much to do . . .'

And Inguill disappeared into the night.

Anamaya slipped into Atahualpa's vast chamber. Only one torch was lit, and that was at the far end of the room. It illuminated nothing, but gave the impression of a boat sinking slowly through the night to the Other World.

She banged her foot against something, and a metallic sound resonated: it was the collar, the one that had earlier been fixed around the Inca's neck. She squinted until her eyes adjusted to the feeble light. She saw all the things that had surrounded the living Inca. They still carried his afterglow, the marks of his now-fading power: the redwood *tiana*, the woven rush table, the overturned chessboard . . .

'So, you've come back too.'

A terrible fear streaked through her.

'Inti Palla?'

The young woman's silhouette appeared from the shadows. Anamaya stepped back and tripped over the Inca's bench.

'Don't be frightened . . .'

This wasn't the voice of the old Inti Palla, the one in whom she had originally thought she had found a friend, the one who had then betrayed her with honeyed words, words concealing a lurking jealousy.

'Please, take my hand.'

Inti Palla was almost imploring her, and yet her voice seemed to be coming from a world already faded. After a slight hesitation, Anamaya took her hand. It was icy cold, despite the balmy night's humid warmth.

'Remorse plagues me by night. Whether asleep or awake, my soul tries to escape it, but in vain. My remorse is a *quipu* whose knots are beyond undoing . . .'

Inti Palla uttered a little laugh that turned into a cough, her chest quivering.

'I am nothing, and yet I shared the Inca's bed. When you and I were together in the House of Virgins in Quito, I had no other desire than that. And I got what I wanted. And then, I no longer know how, Treason began to visit my bed more often than the Emperor: and Revenge and Deception followed in its steps . . .'

The princess moved closer to Anamaya. Her arm and shoulder brushed against her. Her skin was unusually dry and coarse, as though her body was preparing itself for the Other World.

'You saw that treason all too clearly, and I was frightened that you would steal him from me. I was frightened that I would be rejected like the forgotten concubines whom the troops share among themselves. I couldn't face it – I'm too delicate!'

That joyless laugh again.

'My remorse, you see, is not because I lied, or even because I betrayed Atahualpa with Felipillo . . . What I regret is the loss of *you*, blue-eyed girl. I admired and loved you more than I adored anyone else.'

Anamaya, startled, tried to pull her hand away. But Inti Palla tightened her grip, her nails digging into the *Coya Camaquen*'s palm.

'You don't want to believe me, do you? You're very wary of me, aren't you? You don't believe a word I say . . .'

'I believe you, Inti Palla . . .'

'I want you to so much! Anamaya, no other moment of my life torments me as much as does that day when you arrived at the *accllahuasi*. That day when you first looked at me. Your strange eyes were so beautiful, so deep, that jealousy instantly pierced my heart. You possessed something that I would never have . . . and over time I realized that your blue-eyed gaze asked only for friendship and fidelity. A friendship for life. But my pride and my fear immediately denied those things to me. And now, I am going to die. This very night, I am going to die with that remorse in my heart.'

'You *are* my friend,' whispered Anamaya.

Her own words surprised her. She wasn't lying. The words brought up a very old, long-lost emotion, something that she could give to the doomed princess.

Inti Palla's hand stiffened in hers. She seemed warmer now.

'How strange it is,' said Inti Palla, her voice even lower than before. 'I'm not frightened anymore.'

The two young girls hugged one another in the chamber-turned-prison. Anamaya felt Inti Palla's breathing subside and her body relax, driven by a renewed will, stronger than before.

'I want you to help me now,' asked the once-beautiful princess.

'Of course,' said Anamaya.

Pizarro, bareheaded, wore a black armband over his customary black clothes. He raised his silver goblet as Gabriel walked in.

'Guess what I'm drinking.'

Gabriel made no reply. His rage had been lifted from him while he had been with Anamaya but had then returned after he had left her. It had grown with each step that had brought him to the Governor now.

'Thank you, but I'm not thirsty,' he said dryly.

'Oh go on, taste it, my boy!'

The Governor's tone allowed for no refusal. Gabriel grabbed the goblet proffered to him and took a mouthful of its contents, before immediately spitting out the vile-tasting liquid. Don Francisco nodded soberly, without a hint of a smile, and took back his goblet.

'It's vinegar! I shall drink it all week, as will one-eyed de Almagro and all the rest of them.'

'Don Francisco, if you think that that will in any way . . . de Soto!'

De Soto walked heavily into the room without removing his hat, a usual mark of respect to the Governor. Several men followed him. The captain wore the black look of someone who had recently been through many difficult days. His eyes look tired, his beard was unkempt, and his clothes were covered in dust. Gabriel knew what he was going to say before he had even opened his mouth.

'Nothing! Nothing at all, Don Francisco! No Incan army, no marching column, not a single goddamned soldier within a hundred leagues in any direction from here. There is nothing, I tell you! The roads are as empty of Incan armies as is the back of my hand. The only weapons we saw were the peasants' spades! Nothing: we've been had.'

Pizarro sighed. His eyes half closed, he swirled the vinegar around in his goblet.

'I was lied to.'

De Soto turned to Gabriel. His tiredness made his voice hard: 'What's going on here? I'm told that the Inca is dead! As I crossed the city, I heard wails such as would freeze your blood!'

Gabriel shivered. All his muscles ached, as though he himself had been in the saddle for days on end, searching in vain.

'Garrotted,' he murmured.

'Garrotted? Without a trial?'

'With a trial.'

'But . . . since I was out on the roads—'

The captain's mouth quivered. He understood. He fell silent.

'So, de Almagro won his argument.'

De Soto lowered his head for a moment, removed his hat, and shook his head as though he was trying to shake away a gadfly.

'Governor,' he said in a severe tone, 'it is true that the Inca's presence made the Cuzco expedition difficult, but there were solutions other than execution . . . I greatly regret the Indian's death. It is a very bad thing, for you as well as for the rest of us.'

And you didn't even see it, thought Gabriel, who was still haunted by the image of the leather strap that had tightened inexorably around Atahualpa's neck.

Pizarro returned de Soto's stare for a moment, then poured more vinegar into his goblet. He sipped at it without blinking.

'I too greatly regret it, Don Hernando.'

Pizarro's voice was so full of solemnity and sadness that it commanded respect. De Soto looked at him in silence, searching his expression and waiting for him to say something more. Nothing more came. De Soto put his hat back on and left the room, returning to his men outside.

'Tell me,' said Don Francisco to Gabriel, 'tell me how he died.'

*   *   *

They were in a little room at the back of the palace, surrounded by piles of *unkus* in an astonishing variety of shapes, weaves, materials and colors. There were enough there to dress Emperors for generations to come.

The women hadn't found any agave thread in the storeroom, so Inti Palla had stolen one of those long leather straps with which the Spaniards tethered their horses. With a hint of a smile, she handed it to Anamaya.

'The Emperor Atahualpa died from a strap like this one.'

Anamaya slipped her hands around Inti Palla's neck. Adeptly, she tied a strong but movable knot into the strap. Against the princess's fine, honey-colored skin that had fanned the flames of lust in so many men the leather strap looked almost like an alluring necklace.

She looked at the princess, who gave a little nod of her head.

'Should it break,' Inti Palla said, 'I'll fall into the piles of the Inca's tunics, and I'll dream that I was the concubine whom he enjoyed during his last night on earth.'

She set a bench on top of another, and climbed deftly onto the wobbly structure. She skillfully slung the free end of the long strap around the main beam supporting the thatched roof.

'Now leave me alone.'

Anamaya left the room without looking back. From the court-yard, she heard the muted sound of the wooden benches col-lapsing.

It was the only noise that Inti Palla made during her voyage into the Under World.

Anamaya didn't check her stride at all. She went to the fountain – it was still running – and drank some refreshing water.

That night, in Atahualpa's palace, in Cajamarca's *canchas*, in the *acllahuasi*, dozens of women killed themselves, following their Inca into the Other World.

In order to fulfill the court's edict, a token pyre had still had to be lit. A few feeble flames pawed at the dead Inca's clothes and burned his skin and hair slightly. That way, the Spanish authorities would be able to say later that Atahualpa had been burned.

The stench produced by this sham was still floating in Cajamarca's air when Gabriel left the Governor's residence. The valley's atmosphere was already unbearable, thick as it was with the wails and cries of the bereaved Incas.

The execution post still stood in the middle of the square. Atahualpa's cadaver remained tied to it, looking like a sort of Indian Christ, a martyr of the night bearing the sorrow of an entire people. The suffering engendered by his death hadn't subsided. It was like a slow-moving arrow, piercing into the depths of his people's hearts, breaking them.

Gabriel moved through the crowd, his jaw clenched tight. The Indians' faces, usually so inscrutable, were glistening with tears. The nervous Spaniards had tried to clear the square a number of times during the evening, but it had been an impossible task. The Indians – both men and women – had lain down on the dusty ground like corpses, and no boot or spear could move them. They were indifferent to both fear and pain, so much so that some of them let themselves be trampled by the Spaniards' horses, even to the point of having their heads crushed.

Horns and drums sounded in the distance, echoing over the hills that surrounded the town and on further still from what had been the living heart of the Empire of the Four Cardinal Directions. Their noise reached as far as the high, distant mountains, mingling with the sounds of the rivers and the thunder of a coming storm. For above, the eternal river of stars flowed gently across the expanse of the sky.

The breath of the Inca gods passed ghostlike through the night.

Reaching the pyre, Gabriel did something that he had been unable to do for anyone until this day. Kneeling in silence in front of Atahualpa's body, he put his hands together. He, who had sworn never to pray again after his experience in the Inquisition's jails, now found the words of supplication with an ease and fervor that astonished him.

'I knew that you would come . . .'

It was only a whisper, but Gabriel instantly recognized the voice and its accent. He didn't turn around. His heart beating, his eyes still closed, he sensed the presence of his beloved.

'I did everything I could to stop them killing him . . .' he murmured. The stench of burning had evaporated now and he could smell her perfume. Anamaya wrapped her arms around him and stopped him by placing her hand lightly on his lips.

'I know.'

'I had proof. De Soto has returned . . . the Governor is convinced now. But it's no use. It's too late.'

Anamaya embraced Gabriel gently, her breast trembling against his arm.

'No. It is neither too early nor too late. It happened as it was meant to happen. I told you: All is well. The Emperor is now where he is meant to be. You did what you were meant to do. Like one of our heroes, a living warrior amid stone soldiers . . .'

'Stone soldiers?'

Anamaya nodded, peaceful, serene. Their breathing became synchronized. With all the horror around them, Gabriel was surprised by the intensity of his sudden desire to have her. Slightly embarrassed, he felt his member stiffen as Anamaya slipped her slender, agile fingers under his shirt. She traced the outline of the mark of the puma on his shoulder and whispered:

'There are some things that you should know about this mark on your shoulder. The one that I kissed during our first night together . . .'

Her caress was delicious, the tender warmth of her touch spreading throughout his body.

'I remember . . .'

'It represents an animal that dwells in our mountains, a magnificent and powerful animal that we worship because it carries the strength and will of our ancestors . . .'

'The puma?'

'Yes, the powerful Lord *Puma*. One night, many seasons ago, when I was still a frightened little girl, Atahualpa's father, the Inca Huayna Capac, called me to him. He confided to me not only the secrets of the Empire's history, but also those of its future . . .'

Anamaya spoke in a soft voice as she caressed Gabriel's hand and mouth. He let himself be carried along by her, utterly at ease and unsurprised by her revelations. She told him how she had become the *Coya Camaquen*, wife of the Sacred Double of the great Huayna Capac's mummy. She told him how she had accompanied the Sacred Double, lost him, then found him once again in the heart of the *huaca*, the labyrinth of sacred stones.

'It was there, in the shadows and the fear of that place, that I saw you for the first time. You were the puma with the glowing eyes, with the frightful claws, the puma who could cross the mountains in a single bound . . . I wasn't sure that you weren't going to devour me . . . and then I heard Huayna Capac tell me: *Trust the puma . . .*'

Gabriel wasn't sure if he fully understood what Anamaya was telling him. Her words travelled into the depths of his spirit like night birds, and they would return later in his dreams.

'When I saw you in front of me, when I saw the puma on your shoulder, I knew that you had come for me. I knew where you came from, and to where you would return . . .'

She looked up at Atahualpa's corpse.

'We have one life here, and others elsewhere, in many different worlds . . . we travel from this world to the Under World, and from the Under World to the Other World in the sky, the most beautiful and perfect world . . . we return, we transform ourselves . . .'

'You too? You've made this . . . journey?'

Anamaya didn't reply.

She turned her blue-eyed gaze toward him, looking into his eyes, and a smile lit her face. Her own eyes were the colour of the lake, the sky, the night: he dived into them, totally surrendering himself to her, and so began a journey from which he already knew that he would not want to return.

PART 2

CHAPTER 9

The Huayhuash Cordillera, 5 October 1533

'WATCH OUT!'

The cry echoed over Gabriel's head. Instinctively he raised his shield and pulled at his horse's bridle, bringing the animal up close against a wall. Rock fragments plunged into the ravine like grapeshot, the larger pieces hurtling down more like full-size cannonballs. The impacts on the road's surface and on the iron bands across the Spaniards' bucklers echoed as though the stone and metal surfaces were being struck by clubs. Every conquistador held his breath. A few pebbles pelted the horses' hindquarters, making them neigh. And then there was silence.

Almost at the same instant, de Candia and Sebastian's tall forms straightened. Like Gabriel, they brought down their shields and looked up toward the top of the gully.

The rockfall must have started just beyond the overhang that hid the summit from them. Gabriel was worried, and he turned back toward the Indian bearers following behind. But all of them had managed to take cover and only a few of the bundles they'd been carrying had been damaged.

'Very close artillery work,' muttered the Greek. 'And I consider myself an authority on the matter!' De Candia scowled, a look of suspicion souring his expression. The three friends simultaneously had the same thought: Had the rockfall been an accident, or had it been set off by Quizquiz or Guaypar's warriors? From where they stood it was impossible to tell.

'That's the third time this morning,' remarked Sebastian, grimacing ironically. 'If they didn't set this one off themselves, then they must've got one of their gods to do it for them.'

De Candia muttered an insult, but it was lost to the void.

'Let's go,' ordered Gabriel, cracking the end of his reins on his horse's rump. 'There's no point freezing to death here.'

Behind them, the long, long steaming column of men and animals stretched out across the entire side of the mountain. It was as though an entire nation was migrating. The four hundred Spaniards, led by the Governor, de Soto and Don Diego de Almagro were lost in the crowd of thousands upon thousands of natives: slaves, Canary Indians and their allies, warriors from the coast, minor local noblemen and their servants, all of whom had joined the fascinating and powerful newcomers either willingly or by compulsion.

The weather was terrible: cold and wet, with a low, heavy sky. The cordillera's peaks and valleys reared ahead of them menacingly. The mountain they were on rose up and up, its upper slopes becoming lost to sight in the fog and the icy, misty air. A cacophony of coughs and moans, of cries and curses mixed with the sporadic click-clack of hooves drifted up from the column.

Chalkuchimac's palanquin was more or less in the middle of the column, just behind the cavalry platoon surrounding Governor Don Francisco Pizarro. The rainbow arc of colourful feathers decorating it made it stand out from afar, even through the gray light. A squad of Spanish infantrymen, relieved every five hours, surrounded it from the moment the column set off in the morning to the moment its members collapsed from exhaustion in the evening. Torture had drained the Inca general of his strength but had not diminished his fearsome reputation among the Indian warriors. Not a day passed without the Governor and his men fearing that an attack to free Chalkuchimac would be made by Inca forces loyal to him.

The royal road to the capital followed ever-tighter twists down the steep and slippery mountain slope. The cavalrymen had all dismounted some time ago to relieve the overworked horses, who were snorting in strong, quivering whinnies.

The fog would now disperse, now descend at the whim of invisible gusts of wind. Occasionally Gabriel, approaching a pass, would find himself blinded briefly by the harsh light of the sun slanting through it and would then see a sky as deeply blue as an ocean.

He felt as though he was travelling into a supernatural world. Gradually the slopes became as gentle as a rolling sea swell. The short yellow grass was covered in dust worn from the rocks by years of frost. The monotony of the red and ocher earth was broken only by occasional black boulders rising from it like colossal blisters. Man was unwelcome here, and only luck could determine the success or failure of a voyage across this land.

It was almost impossible to breathe. The Spaniards felt as though they were growing heavier with every step they took, as though all the gold of Cajamarca had been melted down and poured into the soles of their boots.

The previous night had been an interminable nightmare for Gabriel. He had woken with a start at least twenty times, simultaneously freezing and sweating, convinced that he was suffocating, his mouth gasping for air. Twenty times he had dreamed that he was walking through a land devoid of air, a vacuum, and each time he woke he sat bolt upright in terror on his bedding, moaning like a wounded animal. Each time he had heard similar moans from his companions all around him, all gripped by the same dread.

He ate very little on rising. In the afternoon, he tried to banish the thought that he wouldn't have the strength to continue, that he would collapse beside the road. He had started out by counting his steps in sets of hundreds, then in dozens, but now he counted them one by one, surprised that he was still able to put one foot in front of the other.

His bay slipped on the road's smooth surface and the yank of the bridle pulled Gabriel down, making him lose his balance. He had to hold on to the pommel of his saddle while he recovered the strength in his legs.

Every move that he made exhausted him further. But the

continual effort was also what kept him from succumbing to the mental and physical numbness that occasionally overwhelmed him like the effects of a drug.

Gabriel's face was becoming frostbitten, despite the blue scarf he kept wrapped around his mouth. He could no longer feel his fingers, despite his thick leather gloves. Yet he could feel a cold, clammy sweat covering the small of his back. His temples throbbed so much that his vision became blurred. There was a burning feeling in his parched throat.

Anamaya's advice whirled around in what little remained of his mind: *Don't stop, above all don't stop, even if you feel that you can't take another step, because if you do you won't feel rested, only even more exhausted. When you feel tired*, she had added, caressing him with her fingers, *chew slowly on these leaves*.

Of course, the leaves she had given him. Why hadn't he thought of them earlier?

Gabriel's numb fingers searched sluggishly for the cloth pouch, the *chuspa* that she had strapped around his shoulder. The fabric was covered in frost. He drew a few green leaves from it and immediately put them into his mouth. They tasted slightly bitter, and he almost spat them out immediately. But he made himself chew them for a while, and eventually a sort of lightness came over him. His headache subsided.

In places the road ran parallel to a wall over thirty feet high. Its stones had been put together with the expert, seemingly almost magical masonry that he had become accustomed to in this land.

Once again his horse shied, as though it could sense its rider's apprehension. The edge of the cliff seemed suddenly dangerously close, and Gabriel, despite himself, muttered: 'Why the devil build a wall in the middle of nowhere?' Yet now he felt a sort of euphoria brought on by facing the elements thus, and he was almost indifferent to the flurries of wind-driven ice shards whipping his face.

The road took a sharp bend after the wall, and from it they could at last make out the mountain's peak. Gabriel turned around and watched the column advancing as well as could be expected. He saw horses slipping and falling, bearers struggling, the Spanish soldiers toiling through the freezing rain that went right through their clothes and got into their bones. Occasionally, a man, overcome by exhaustion or altitude sickness would collapse right in the middle of the road.

'Did you see?'

Gabriel made out Sebastian's ghostlike grin through the rain. He looked up at the peak once again. Two colossal dark blocks of stone marked the way, looking as though they'd been chiseled by giants. He nodded, and grinned. Each climb that they had undertaken had been longer than the descent preceding it, and he could not help but feel a sort of absurd hope that this would be the last.

When they had left Cajamarca a few weeks earlier, the rivalry between Pizarro and de Almagro's followers had been dangerously tense. The Governor held his lieutenant personally responsible for a wrongful execution, one that might upset the Spanish Crown. De Almagro railed against Pizarro reneging on commitments made to him, and against the fact that during the distribution of the gold de Almagro and his companions had been excluded from a share since they had arrived on the scene after the battle of Cajamarca. But here in the mountains whose peaks scraped the sky, the men walking along roads that clung to the sides of seemingly bottomless cliffs, with rocks falling on them, their progress choked by snow, and in their voiceless, ever-increasing shared anxiety, had forgotten their enmities. Now there were no longer rich men or poor men, men loyal to one leader or another, but simply a group of human beings trying to survive.

Gabriel saw the sky through a breach in the clouds, a calming and vivid blue through the milky-white overcast. A huge black bird, the ends of its wings looking like fingers, appeared in this shaft of light. The condor was gliding, dancing through the air, giving an impression of strength and unbounded freedom. It was a beautiful sight, but Gabriel couldn't help remembering the ill-starred crossing of the bridge at Huaylas, the terror-struck porters there and his duel with Hernando.

For a moment he forgot about his fatigue and the cold.

Then the clouds shut out the sky as abruptly as they had revealed it, and a glacial wind brought more and more flakes of snow. He could only open his eyes for split seconds to make sure that the silhouette of the person in front of him, bent over against the wind and by the effort of keeping going, was still there.

And in that moment of extreme spiritual isolation, when all his strength had drained from him, Gabriel felt an inexplicable confidence warming his exhausted limbs and melting away his fear.

He trudged on, reassured that Anamaya was actually there, right next to him.

When the column reached the peak, the storm and the wind suddenly died away, and the sky gradually began to clear. Gabriel blinked and breathed slowly in and out, his face burning, while a few Spaniards, who had arrived just after him, took long drafts from their gourds.

The Indians laid down their burdens and squatted on the ground, their faces wearing their usual stolid expressions. One of them raised his gaze to Gabriel, who greeted him with a smile. The man grinned back, revealing his green teeth. Then he pointed at Gabriel and laughed quietly. '*Coca*,' he chortled, deeply amused. '*Coca!*'

One of de Almagro's men, a young man whose name Gabriel didn't know, was sitting against a rock a few paces away. His face was gray and bloated, and a vicious dry cough interrupted his irregular, gasping breathing. Occasionally he turned away to spit out a sort of red foam, which landed like crimson petals on the snow.

'What's wrong, *compañero*?' asked Gabriel.

'I see it . . . I see it . . .' he repeated deliriously.

'What do you see?'

The man didn't reply. Instead, he put his head between his hands and squeezed it as though he wanted to crush it, as though the pain was too much to bear.

'Gold . . . I see gold,' said the young man. 'Plenty of gold, and that knight-in-arms guarding it . . .'

His words were interrupted by more fits of coughing. Gabriel felt overwhelmed by a feeling of profound tenderness toward this young stranger who was dreaming of adventure and fortune and who, without a doubt, was now dying of some strange disease on this mountain peak, far from home.

Gabriel knelt down beside the youth and took one of his hands between his own, trying to share his own warmth with the other man. The young conquistador's hand was as cold as that of a corpse.

So Gabriel wrapped his arms around him. He placed his ear against the youngster's torso and listened to his chest through his soaked tunic. What he heard sounded like the waters of a lake being whipped up by a furious storm. The young man's breathing would occasionally stop briefly but the viscid seething inside his chest never ceased.

Gabriel moved his head away and released his hold on the sick youth.

'Where are you from?' he asked in a tone that he hoped sounded encouraging. 'What's your mother's name?'

The young man had closed his eyes. He could no longer control his convulsing body. When he coughed, his whole frame shook violently.

As the rest of the column arrived, the other men kept their distance. Only Gabriel stayed at the youth's side.

The youngster fell asleep for a while, as though worn out by his body's shudders and paroxysms. Yet Gabriel could still feel his pulse beating in his wrist.

'Extramadura,' the young man murmured eventually, so softly that Gabriel had to lean closer to hear him. 'Maria . . .'

'Why, I come from the same part of the country, and my mother has the same name! Don't be frightened, I'm with you.'

The other man's fingers clenched around Gabriel's, and he grimaced as a bout of unbearable pain racked him. His whole body arched upwards, as though he wanted to tear himself away from the earth.

'I'm boiling,' he gasped. 'I'm suffocating! Open the window!'

'You're going to see our sunburned native land long before I do, *compañero*, and your mother will look upon you as she did when you were a child,' Gabriel said soothingly.

The young conquistador gave a final shudder as he died. He was beyond suffering or joy now. He had seen, before dying, either his mother's face or that of the knight guarding the gold. He was dead.

Gabriel stood up. Slowly, he became aware again of his own life force, of his own freezing, sweating, lamentable present existence. Life was a strange field of combat on which one never overcame anger, or fear, or greed.

He walked unsteadily toward the crowd of men who had closed their ears and eyes to the sad scene.

The storm sped away in the gathering dusk. Gabriel looked to the sky and saw one black dot, then another. The condors, in all their sinister majesty, had returned to drift above the mountain.

One of the great boulders at the entrance to the pass had had a cavity hollowed out in the side that faced away from the road, a nook not unlike a niche in a church. The rock stood out sharply against the blue-black sky, and Gabriel's heart skipped a beat as he looked at it: it was exactly the same shape as the mountain on the horizon whose snowcapped summit now glowed gold in the last rays of the setting sun. Gabriel turned toward the few Spaniards around him. They had their heads lowered, stood with their shoulders hunched, and were murmuring along with the words spoken by the priest. Under this star-speckled sky, in this thin, biting cold air, with a dead man beside them over whom they had quickly placed a blanket so that the Indians wouldn't see him, they were returning to their long-neglected God.

Gabriel found no consolation in prayer. The dead young man's inscrutable gaze haunted him, and he felt a spectral hand tugging at him from beyond the veil of night. He stared at the rock and the mountain behind it for a long time. His gaze automatically followed the pattern of the tall stones surrounding the small group before returning to the table, behind which stood the priest, that was set on two great stone blocks in the centre of the circle. It was an altar, high in the mountains.

Gabriel turned and walked away, his steps crunching through the snow. He came out from behind the natural protection of the rock and walked into a light but freezing wind. The millions of stars twinkling in the sky, which couldn't fail to fascinate the Spaniards, were now the only source of light. Whether they were from Extramadura or Castile, from Galicia or even Greece, the conquistadors had all been born under the same sky. But this was a different sky, and it looked as though a mischievous god different from the one worshiped by the priest had entertained himself by sprinkling stars around according to some divine whim. Yes, it certainly was another world.

Gabriel could hear the murmur of his companions' prayers and responses behind him. And from down below he could hear a sort of drone, a sad and monotonic music, coming from the enormous tents set up by the Indians on the natural platform just below the pass. There were no drums or horns playing. The noise was simply the collective murmur of the Indians, who had gathered in clans to tell their stories and invoke their gods.

And so, ignoring one another, not understanding one another, and divided by conflict, the Spaniards and the Indians allowed themselves – in this place, at this time – to be simply human beings, united in their fear of death and their admiring awe of the sky.

Gabriel heard voices coming from a tent set up behind a cluster of snow-covered rocks. He went to it. Three men were inside, breathing heavily and encouraging one another, trying to dig into the frozen earth with a sort of hoe that became more hopelessly dented with each strike, its blade being made of bronze rather than steel.

'Fucking useless tool,' grumbled Sebastian.

Gabriel caught a glimpse of his friend's sweating face, as well as that of Diego Mendez, a weasel-faced follower of de Almagro, whose face and eyes had become so swollen that one eye was barely visible through a narrow slit. He was afflicted with that mysterious mountain illness that chose its victims randomly, killing some while leaving others with their lives.

'Gabriel! Come break your back with us!' called Sebastian. Gabriel disappeared wordlessly, back out into the night.

The Inca tents had been set up around Chalkuchimac's. They were distinguishable by the geometric patterns that decorated their white canvas.

The Incas lowered their voices or fell silent altogether as Gabriel came nearer, the men and women wrapping their blankets tighter around themselves and diverting their gazes when he tried to make eye contact with them.

'They're not frightened of you.'

Gabriel turned around. Anamaya had come up silently next to him, wrapped in a large black and gray woolen cape. Gabriel grinned secretively into the darkness.

'I was looking for you . . .'

'I was afraid for you.'

With no firelight to see her by, Gabriel could only guess at the concerned look on Anamaya's face. But he could hear the anxiety in her voice. He could sense her body close to his, and he felt a shiver not brought on by the cold. He had to clench his jaw to distract himself from the longing to take her in his arms, to abandon himself to his desire.

'Quizquiz's warriors are in the mountains,' she continued, 'and Guaypar is with them.'

'Guaypar?'

The mention of the Inca lieutenant's name brought the image of the man to Gabriel's mind's eye: a man with a proud forehead and nose, and with eyes steeped in hatred.

'They know who you are now,' said Anamaya, 'and they know that you are not immortal. They won't be as foolish as they were during the Great Massacre. You are in their territory at this moment and here your horses slip, your swords weigh you down, whereas they hurl their stones easily and find their mark.'

Gabriel said nothing. He had been experiencing those feelings of inadequacy and anxiety she had just described for days now, as had every Spaniard in the expedition.

Gradually the Indians around them returned to their conversations. Gabriel felt surrounded by their peaceful presence,
sensing that their hostility was dormant. For the moment, at
least. He noticed silhouettes moving in front of the glow of a
fire behind a tent. He turned to Anamaya.

'They found wood to burn?'

She didn't reply, and he didn't persist with his questions.
Sometimes he felt intimidated by her silences. They walked
together toward the rock beside which the priest had earlier
said Mass.

They passed a group of Spaniards laughing and playing around
near a sort of small square fort made up of trunks and sacks. They
had attached small bells to their horses' harnesses so that if the
beasts were startled by any suspicious movement during the night
the noise would wake their riders.

'Gold,' sighed Gabriel.

'They guard it better than they do themselves.'

Gabriel made a gesture of helplessness. Because he had fled
the battle, taking Anamaya with him, Pizarro had denied him his
share of the booty. Yet that humiliation had turned out to be a
blessing in disguise, and he felt joyful in his penury and in his
total lack of interest in gold.

They reached the giant black rock, now barely distinguishable
from the surrounding night.

'Do you know this place?' asked Anamaya.

'No.'

'The mountains are gods for us, like the sun and the moon, and
like the breath of the wind. And so are these rocks, the shapes of
which mark the presence of a god. This place was shaped by the
hands of our Ancestors to indicate the presence of divinities here.
We have been making sacrifices here ever since, to give thanks to
the gods for their gifts. We call them *huacas*.'

A voice spoke from the darkness.

'The God of the Christians too has known sacrifices. But He
held back Abraham's hand against his son Isaac, He broke the
pride of man, and He sent Jesus to live – and to die – among
men to redeem their sins.'

It was a gentle voice, very different from Father Vicente Valverde's vengeful tone. But Gabriel still instinctively placed himself protectively in front of Anamaya.

'Have no fear,' continued the soft voice. 'We know one another.'

A man's silhouette emerged from the shadow of the rock and approached them noiselessly across the trampled snow. His features became clearer as he drew closer. He raised his right hand and, grinning, asked Gabriel, 'Do you know me now?'

Gabriel, dumbfounded, looked at the man's blue-gray eyes set in his clean-shaven face, which somehow looked both very young and very old, and then at the hand that he had raised peacefully above him as though to bless Gabriel and Anamaya, his index and middle fingers joined together, sheathed in the same layer of skin. Old memories came flooding back to Gabriel through the haze of recollection until he cried out:

'My God!'

'You see, you *do* call upon Him when you feel the need, friend of Erasmus.'

'Brother Bartholomew!'

'When I think,' said Bartholomew to Anamaya, 'that we spent two months together and that this fellow would have erased everything about them from his memory, except for one sad accident of nature.'

Gabriel was overcome with emotion. He hadn't thought about that jail, hadn't brought to mind his recollection of his terror of being tortured, hadn't remembered the rage and humiliation he had experienced in front of his father, nor had he recalled – and of this he was most ashamed – Doña Francesca for so long that he now felt disoriented as the familiar face of Bartholomew brought the memories flooding back.

'That was in another life,' Gabriel said.

'And yet it's the same one.'

The two men stared at each other for a long time before they embraced emotionally.

'When did you join the column?'

'I arrived in Cajamarca a few days after it had left but I caught up with it easily.'

'But then, how can it be that I haven't seen you until tonight?'

'Yes, it's odd, isn't it?'

'Don't play the theologian with me, Brother Bartholomew, by answering questions with questions.'

'When there is no answer to a question, one might as well ask another. Or else keep silent.'

'Silence . . . that was your advice to me all those years ago, wasn't it? And I still don't know if I'm capable of it!'

'Oh, you seem capable of many things to me,' said Bartholomew cheerfully, glancing again at Anamaya.

The two men and Anamaya had returned to the tent in which Sebastian and his companions were digging the grave.

'I must give the last rites to this ill-fated fellow,' said Bartholomew.

'What are you doing here, Brother Bartholomew?'

The monk didn't bat an eyelid.

'The work of God,' he said eventually, grinning.

'When there is no answer to a question . . .'

'Haven't I just given you an answer?'

Bartholomew disappeared into the tent.

Gabriel remained there for a moment, staring into the night, before Anamaya led him away.

'That man isn't like the rest,' she said. 'He isn't like you, but he isn't like the rest of them, either.'

'Yes. I too think him strange.'

'Is he capable of massacring us?'

Gabriel gazed up into the magnificent starlit sky, trying to pierce through the night in which all the birds had taken refuge, trying to feel beyond the cold.

'I don't think so,' he said at last. 'But I'm not sure.'

CHAPTER 10

Hatun Sausa, 11 October 1533

WHEN THE FIRST GRAY LIGHT OF DAWN REVEALED the field to them, all the men fell silent. It wasn't the delicate mauve of *quinua* that had been sown here, however, or the gold of corn. It was death.

The battle between Huascar and Atahualpa's men had taken place a few weeks earlier, but their warriors still lay where they had fallen – this one face down in the mud, that one with his eye sockets turned to the sky. Gabriel saw the true atrocity of this scene of eternal 'peace': the pestilent odor of decomposing bodies, the grass growing around and *through* them, the worms writhing in gaping wounds as they feasted on the rotting flesh, the hollow cavities where the corpses' eyes had been pecked out by birds. In all, over four thousand bodies lay strewn across the plain, a sinister harvest that the earth would eventually reabsorb and that vegetation would soon cover.

It was a beautiful day. And men were vomiting.

Gabriel turned his gaze away and tried to concentrate on the verdant landscape. After the harshness of the mountain passes, of the snow and the cold, this dawn seemed mild, and held the promise of warmth.

Only the Governor, Don Francisco Pizarro, at the head of the column, seemed as indifferent to the nearby scene of carnage as he was to the beauty of the more distant view. He frequently stopped the Indian guides to have them explain some feature of the terrain to him. He kept the *curaca* of the town close by him, after having made a lengthy declaration of friendship to this longhaired Huanca Indian who wore a crown four fingers wide on his head. 'We'll take care of you,' Pizarro frequently told him. 'We'll free you from the bondage of the Incas.' When this was translated to the Indian, his eyes lit up and he nodded enthusiastically.

Pizarro spent his nights praying, as he had at the beginning of the conquest. The veterans of Cajamarca felt a familiar apprehension in their guts, one that both excited and frightened them.

'We're going to fight soon.'

The mountain loomed over the town of Hatun Sausa. It was a beautiful Inca town, with its Temple of the Sun, its *acllahuasi*, its *ushnu* in the standard pyramidal shape in the middle of its huge square, its walled *canchas*, its warehouses, and its narrow alleyways. It was set in the bottom of a broad valley, next to a fast-flowing river.

It was a beautiful Inca town. And it was burning.

Higher up on the mountain, Pizarro had found himself held up by the slow progress of Chalkuchimac's palanquin. Although the general never showed himself, and although the wounds he had sustained under torture prevented him from walking, the Governor had convinced himself that Chalkuchimac was more or less secretly directing the movements of the Indian troops. That was why, as the next battle loomed closer, Pizarro didn't let him out of his sight.

The Governor had to check his brother Juan and de Almagro's impatience, and he ordered de Soto to lead a squad of cavalrymen into the town.

The days when Gabriel had had to beg to be part of the vanguard were long past, and Pizarro motioned to him to go with de Soto. 'Just in case, as usual,' Gabriel joked grimly. With a kick of his heels, he urged his bay on and took his position among the fifteen or so cavalrymen who had lined up in pairs.

When they reached the edge of town, de Soto raised his hand to halt the column. The majority of the Indian troops were massed on the other side of the river. Soldiers in colorful tunics were torching the main buildings, starting with the *collcas*, the food depots.

'They're burning the warehouses! We must hurry!' cried Diego de Agüero, one of the more hotheaded *caballeros*.

'Easy, *hombre*,' countered de Soto.

'You are unusually cautious, Captain de Soto,' said Gabriel, surprised.

De Soto grinned.

'I am simply obeying the Governor's orders: There is to be no major engagement until he arrives.'

'But everything is burning, de Soto. In a couple of hours, not a single ear of corn, nor a solitary strip of dried meat will remain in this town,' carped a *caballero*.

'De Soto,' Gabriel said, 'let me take a patrol in, just me, de Agüero and de Candia.'

'And me too,' called a cavalryman from the back.

'And him too,' said Gabriel, without turning round. 'A well-executed charge might repel them before everything is turned to ash.'

De Soto thought about it for a moment.

'By the faith, it's your head, after all! But try to stay alive, my friends, until we arrive with reinforcements.'

'Don't worry, Captain. We shall set the table. Just don't be late for dinner!'

The patrol forded the river at a trot. Then Gabriel, swiftly followed by the other three, launched his horse into a gallop toward the small group of buildings, shaped like truncated cones, where the royal road narrowed into an alley. A thick, choking smoke already billowed between the houses. At the entrance to the main square stood an Indian waving at them, his tunic torn to tatters, his face blackened by soot. He appeared completely unsurprised by their presence, and, running after their horses, he called out in Quechua, 'Save us! They're torching everything!'

The Huancas were one of the tribes conquered by the Incas who had never really completely surrendered to them. Gabriel turned toward his three companions and cried, 'They're welcoming us as liberators!'

'Well then, let's liberate them!' cried de Candia, pointing at the biggest building on the square, a *kallanka*, which the Inca soldiers were about to set alight. 'Or else everything is going to be reduced to ashes, us included!'

Gabriel, his eyes irritated by the smoke, drew his sword. Then he patted his horse, which was also finding the acrid smoke disconcerting. The soldiers coming out of the *kallanka* were armed with axes, lances, or slings. An Inca officer, catching sight of the newcomers, bellowed an order to his men. The deep sound of a trumpet echoed across the square, and twenty warriors, utterly heedless of the horses, were already running at the Spaniards before the sound faded.

De Candia gave a savage cry, a 'Santiago!' so harsh and deep that it could easily have been the roar of a huge wild animal. All four Spaniards, moved by the same instinct, bent low along their horses' necks and held their swords straight out, blades gleaming in the smoky light. The horses too seemed to find some furious stimulation as they galloped, as though now they found it easier to breathe.

The Spaniards' first charge split the group of Indians. Their steel swords sliced through the Incas' lances and the straps of their sling-shots, and cleaved through the Indian hands holding clubs and axes. One man fell to ground howling in pain, his shoulder slashed open. The others fled down the narrow alleys. Gabriel chased them, with de Candia at his side. Through the thick smoke, they made out de Agüero and his companion heading toward the river.

'Watch out!' cried de Candia.

The alley ahead of them was too narrow for two horsemen to ride down it abreast. Gabriel went first, once more bent low along his horse's neck. As he went through, he glimpsed a man stumbling and falling beneath the horse's hooves. He was horrified when he felt the man being trampled. A stone whistled past the animal's ears, and Gabriel saw the man who'd hurled it hiding in the doorway of a *cancha*. When he reached him, he forced his horse in close enough so that he was able to thrust his sword into the man's chest. The man stared at him, his eyes bulging, for a fraction of a second. Gabriel felt the death shudder of his first kill.

Soon only one man was left still trying to escape, the speed of his flight showing no sign of lessening. He was a long-ear wearing an officer's helmet decorated with blue feathers. The enormous gold plugs extending his earlobes bounced on his shoulders as he ran.

With a glance, Gabriel realized that this man was trying to reach the river. The rest of the Indian troops were already waiting on the other side. He urged his horse along the riverbank, intent on cutting off the Inca officer's escape. But when the officer realized this, he stopped running. Gabriel was astonished when he recognized the man through the dust and soot covering him. He could never have forgotten those proud eyes, nor that nose as straight as a rock edge.

'Guaypar!' he cried. 'I know who you are!'

'You speak our language?' yelled the other angrily. 'How can that help you kill me?'

'I've often thought of you, Guaypar!' said Gabriel, grinning.

Guaypar's expression remained impassive as Gabriel hesitated. Seeing this man in front of him now, the man who had tried to protect Anamaya during the massacre at Cajamarca, made him slow to react, as though his sword had suddenly turned into lead instead of steel.

'You should kill me,' said Guaypar, sensing his indecision.

Gabriel kept his horse perfectly still. Smoke drifted over the river. On the other side, the warriors had identified their officer and were gathered on the bank, crying out. Other cries rose from the village. But still Gabriel didn't move, and neither did Guaypar, who seemed gripped by his own doubts.

At that moment a thatched roof, not twenty paces from them, burst into flames. Gabriel turned his head for an instant to look at it and saw flames leap into the sky. But he didn't see Guaypar leap deftly past the horse, jump onto the sparse grass of the riverbank, and throw all his gold finery into the river.

'You should have killed me while you had the chance, because now it is I who shall kill you!' Guaypar cried, before diving in himself.

*   *   *

Everywhere he went, Gabriel met groups of men, women, and children coming out of the houses and *kallankas*, all crying tears of gratitude. He felt uneasy, and he rebuffed them with scant ceremony.

But one group of them managed to lead him to a *cancha* where an Inca soldier lay on the ground, holding an ax, his leg broken, surrounded by a gang of young Huancas who were hurling insults at him but yet didn't dare approach him. A child tugged at Gabriel's scabbard.

'I haven't the time!' he yelled.

He set off at a gallop across the square. He found no trace of de Agüero or de Candia. He headed for the bridge. Anamaya drifted into his thoughts, but he pushed her image as far away as possible, to a place of purity, away from the bloodshed.

At the river, over two hundred Indian warriors had gathered, protecting another fifteen or so at their rear. These were trying to set the straw-and-rope bridge alight. De Agüero and de Candia were already fighting, in vain, to cut a passage through the main group to prevent the others burning the bridge.

De Agüero was fighting bravely, swinging his sword in wide circles, dodging sling stones and staving off swipes from clubs, and was simultaneously handling his horse well. De Candia's movements were more deliberate but equally efficient. Gabriel, meanwhile, as he rushed to join his two companions, was struck and horrified by the resignation with which the Indians were ready to die, just like at Cajamarca, simply to gain for their companions the time to burn the bridge and so prevent the Spaniards from crossing.

In order to embolden himself and shut out his doubts, Gabriel howled like a maniac as he launched his horse into the fray. He heard de Candia laugh out loud, an outlandish yet comforting guffaw.

'Well! You took your time getting here,' said the Greek giant.

Gabriel struck out with such incredible violence, slicing off arms, piercing holes in chests and smashing faces, that he became delirious with dealing death. None of the Incas' traditional armour gave them any protection against his butchering blade. First ten, then twenty fell, powerless against him. Some died suffocating under the bodies of those who fell on top of them, while others crawled away, wounded and multilated, to drown in the river. But still their kinsmen continued the fight, clubs and axes raised high, eyes glowing with the insanity of battle.

Gabriel noticed one warrior who stood out above the rest. He was taller and seemed stronger and nobler than his companions, whom he never tired of urging on. He dodged death as though dancing around it, and many times he evaded a sword or a hoof. Then, with one agile bound, he leaped onto the rump of de Candia's horse, grabbed the Greek by the shoulder, and brought his ax up to strike him in the side.

Spurring on his bay, Gabriel charged down on them. His sword arm shot out like a bolt from a crossbow, and he felt the blade shudder as it pierced through the Inca's flesh.

The warrior cried out and straightened up, forcing all his weight on Gabriel's sword. For a moment, time and movement seemed frozen. The Indian's legs stayed gripped around de Candia's horse's back and Gabriel thought that he had pinned him there with his sword. Then the warrior let go and fell among the horses' trampling hooves.

'Fucking hell!' bellowed de Candia, rubbing his ribs. 'You're a welcome arrival, Don Gabriel!'

'The bridge has gone – it's burning already,' replied Gabriel, pointing at the rising flames.

But now the Indians were retreating, abandoning the dead and the dying behind them. The battle ended with a strange abruptness. De Agüero and his companion joined Gabriel and de Candia, their boots and breeches covered in gore. They dismounted and lifted the visors of their helmets. Their faces, drenched in sweat and blood, were still tense with fear and combat fever.

'Gentlemen,' growled de Candia, 'I have some good news: We're still alive!'

De Soto and the other cavalrymen joined Gabriel's patrol, followed around midday by Pizarro and the rest of the column. The entire town was filled with rejoicing, but the Spaniards didn't linger for the festivities, nor for the gifts that were offered to them.

Pizarro reached the riverbank along with his brothers Gonzalo and Juan, Captain de Soto, and de Almagro.

'How do we stand, Gabriel?'

Gabriel pointed to the other side of the river, where about five or six hundred Inca warriors stood facing them.

'We gave them chase, Don Francisco, and as you see we managed to discourage a few of them. But I regret to say that they still managed to destroy the bridge.'

'Treacherous coward!'

The slur had come from Gonzalo's mouth.

Gabriel wiped away the sweat still on his forehead. Then he came in right up close to the curly-haired fop. Gabriel had a menacing smile on his face, a grin that he had acquired earlier when he had been killing Incas and that remained with him now, like a knife gash across his face.

Gonzalo took a few steps back before barking again:

'We all know how you carried yourself in battle, you coward, letting their chief go . . .'

Gabriel, surprised, hesitated for a moment before he realized that Gonzalo was referring to Guaypar.

'That's enough, Gonzalo!' ordered Pizarro.

The Governor's abrupt tone invited no reply. Gonzalo and Gabriel stared one another down for a moment, pride and hatred twisting their expressions.

Don Francisco phlegmatically took stock of the piling-up of the bodies, then looked searchingly at the deep and fast-running river that ran between the Spaniards and the road down which the village's attackers had gone. Without turning around, he asked for volunteers to carry out another attack.

'We must teach them a lesson,' he said. 'We must not let them think that they can get away with this so easily.'

Gabriel didn't know himself why he was one of the first to volunteer. Rage made his blood pump faster. He barely heard the others.

'Me too!' said Juan.

'And me!' said de Soto.

'And me,' growled de Almagro, sounding as though he was waking from a long sleep.

Pizarro grinned. The four horsemen, followed by a few foot soldiers, went down the bank to the river. Some young Huanca men, eager for vengeance, jumped with them into the freezing water. They admired the horses swimming strongly, their nostrils jutting above the swirling surface of the river.

The current was strong. The conquistadors had to follow an arcing course so as not to exhaust their horses. But the slope of the opposite riverbank was gentle and easy to climb. As soon as they reached the road, de Almagro and his men marched away toward the mountain, intending to circle round and come at the Incas from behind, while Juan and a smaller group followed the course of the river. De Soto and Gabriel rode directly after the Indian warriors, intending to force them back.

Gabriel didn't feel any fatigue. Gonzalo's insult still whirled around in his brain, obsessing him and making weariness impossible. He rode tall in the saddle and his right hand, clasped around the hilt of his drawn sword, was clenched on his thigh as if the weight of the whole world was concentrated in it.

The first group of warriors rushed at Gabriel and de Soto. The Incas seemed to be waving their arms around stupidly in the air. But as de Soto cried 'Watch out!' a storm of sling stones came raining down. Gabriel's bay, struck on its shoulder, stumbled and shied. The Indian warriors were already dispersing, having learned not to stay bunched together.

But another group of Incas with slingshots had taken up position a hundred paces on, and this time they let fly at Juan Pizarro's men, forcing them to retreat.

It was at that moment that a crazy idea occurred to Gabriel. He launched his horse forward as another group of warriors, having formed up in a perfect line, reloaded their slingshots. Yelling like a lunatic, he charged straight at them. The Indians, transfixed, stared at him as he bore down on them, howling 'Santiago! Santiago!' with all the strength his lungs possessed.

He had a taste for death running through his veins now, and his spirit was seized by a violent rage. The Indians stared, gaping. As he approached them, Gabriel slipped down the side of his saddle, hanging onto its pommel with his left hand. He didn't see a bronze ax swipe through the air just above him. He kept his gaze fixed on the warriors' throats. He was keenly aware of the rhythm of his horse's galloping stride beneath him. The muscles of his right arm were harder than oak. Crouched thus, he held his sword with its blade angled back. Then he was upon them.

'Santiago!'

The steel cutting edge sliced through throats, one after another. One after another, as quick as lightning, Gabriel severed the windpipes of twelve men, letting the breath of life out of them before they had the chance to scream.

When he heaved himself back up into his saddle and pivoted his horse around, Gabriel saw twelve men crumpling to the ground. Their arms and legs thrashed about grotesquely as their blood pumped out onto the grass.

He became aware of a total silence flooding the valley. A bright white light stunned him. He had to grab onto his horse's mane to prevent himself falling from the saddle. Over to his left, the terrified Indians sought refuge in the safety of the bushes.

'Treacherous coward,' Gabriel murmured to himself, not understanding his own words.

He heard shouting from behind him. De Almagro and the Huancas were pursuing the fleeing Incas. Gabriel wiped the sweat from his face.

De Soto came up to him. They stared at one another. The captain nodded at Gabriel, and Gabriel thought he detected a perplexed fear in the other man's respectful gesture. They turned their horses around simultaneously, slumped in their saddles now like the two exhausted men they were.

An hour later, over six hundred corpses lay littered along the riverbank. Only a few fleeting, shadowy remnants of Guaypar's battalion were left. They tried, in vain, to escape by diving into the muddy, foaming river.

CHAPTER 11

Hatun Sausa, 15 October 1533

NIGHTFALL. THE ROOFS OF HATUN SAUSA GLOWED red as they burned. The air was thick with smoke and the smell of spilled blood. Jubilant victory cries echoed through the valley. A strange music could be heard, punctuated by the shrill laughter of women and children. The melody blended the notes of a deep-toned flute with the insistent chanting voices of young girls and the constant throbbing beat of drums.

Gabriel hadn't yet found the strength to cross the river again and join the festivities. His horse wandered along the riverbank, grazing on the trampled grass between the unclaimed corpses of Inca warriors.

Every now and then one of his compatriots hailed him from across the river. De Soto himself shouted a few words to him. Why would he not join them? Was he wounded?

No, Gabriel hadn't spilled any of his own blood. But he felt tainted by the evidence of the carnage that lay all around. In the gathering darkness, he saw images, still fresh in his memory, of his sword cutting through flesh, slicing off limbs, piercing lungs – killing.

No, he wasn't wounded. But he felt as though his chest was being crushed by the weight of an agonizing disgust that he couldn't shake off. He thought of Anamaya. He dreamed of her tender lips on his own, her kiss on the lids of his burning eyes. He wished he could hold her in his arms, arms that ached from the effort of killing. He wanted her to whisper a few words of love, of forgiveness to him.

And yet he knew that if she had been with him in this place, he wouldn't even have dared to utter her name. He wouldn't have been able to bear her gaze – or her touch.

Only after night was well advanced did Gabriel at last call his horse to him and cross back over the river. The freezing, turbulent water rushing past his boots chilled his feet and lower legs, rousing him from his gloomy reverie. Once he reached the other side, he urged the bay into a trot. He avoided people's glances, ignoring their exuberant cries when they hailed him as he passed, their voices made hoarse by their unrestrained whoops and cheers of victory.

He reached the town's main square just as de Almagro's men, in the presence of the Governor himself and the *cacique* of Hatun Sausa, were taking the treasures out of a smoldering *kallanka*.

Dozens of gold plates, goblets, masks and statuettes were piled up outside, by now a familiar scene. The pile gleamed in the light of the torches, despite the soot covering the priceless items. And the Spaniards' eyes gleamed even more brightly. The conquistadors were laughing and flinging gold porringers into the air, using the tips of their swords to flip them upward. The treasures had been saved from the blaze just in time by slaves, but had still been somewhat deformed by the heat. The local Indians watched the Strangers from a safe distance, intrigued.

Don Francisco's expression stayed impassive through all this. His eyes watched the gold pile up, but he seemed not to be registering it in his mind. His lips, hidden behind his perfectly trimmed beard, were moving, murmuring something. Gabriel, without having to hear him, knew that he was praying to the Sacred Virgin. Don Francisco was not one to give up old habits. He was offering the blood, the dead, the suffering, and the joy of the gold to the Virgin, reckoning that by doing so he was purifying himself. For a few moments, Gabriel envied him.

Eventually Don Francisco turned around and saw Gabriel, who

had dismounted and was holding his horse by its bridle, close by.

'Ah! There you are,' said the Governor, looking at him fondly.

Don Francisco looked Gabriel up and down, taking note of his torn and soaked breeches and his dirty doublet, its right sleeve ripped open and stained with half-dried blood. And when the Governor looked at Gabriel's face, at the cuts on his face and the vacant look in his eyes, his look of affection gave way to one of bemusement.

'What a state you're in, my boy! Not such a bad performance – for a coward.'

Gabriel acknowledged neither the compliment nor the repudiation of Don Francisco's brother's insult implicit in the Governor's words. Shivering with cold and exhaustion, he turned his gaze towards the men piling up the gold in great wicker baskets that had been brought by Indian women.

Suddenly the Governor made a motion to the trumpeter Alconchel.

'Sound "To quarters",' he said calmly.

Alconchel raised his trumpet to his lips. The town's Indians, astonished, took a step back. The noise of the Spanish instrument was very different to that of their own bronze horns. Those who had been with the Spaniards since Cajamarca laughed at them and explained to them the source of the wail rising above the smoky air in the valley.

'What's going on, Don Francisco?' asked Gabriel.

'Those whom you carved to pieces were only a small company. The bulk of their army, over 15,000 warriors, is about six leagues to the south of here. Now that the men and horses are rested, I want fifty cavalrymen to go after them.'

Gabriel was dumbfounded.

'I'm not thinking of you, my boy. You must rest now. Your day is over. Relax, enjoy the dishes and women that our new friends are offering us.'

Pizarro embraced Gabriel warmly.

A cutting snigger rose from behind them as they stepped away from each other.

'What a lovely sight that was!'

Gonzalo Pizarro was still sneering, his chest thrown out arrogantly, his doublet open over a dirty and torn shirt. His breath stank of beer. He gave an exaggerated, mocking salute.

'Well, well, brother, that was a real hero you were holding in your arms!'

'And you are another such, Gonzalo!' replied the Governor, ostentatiously opening his arms wide to him. 'And if you might find happiness in the embrace of your Governor, then it is happily that I offer it to you!'

Ignoring his brother's gesture, Gonzalo turned toward the group of cavalrymen fawning around him and spat:

'Gentlemen, please doff your hats. Having at last had the courage to gut a handful of Indians, Don Gabriel has become one of us. Welcome, bastard son!'

The Governor paled at the insult. His expression grew stern, as if the affront had been directed at him. His left hand gripped Gabriel's wrist to hold him back, and Gabriel hissed through clenched teeth:

'Gonzalo, the day shall come when you shall die, poisoned by your own venom. And I doubt that I shall be among those mourning you.'

Gonzalo's smug smile vanished instantly. He looked at Don Francisco, stupefied. He opened his mouth to reply, but shut it again as Gabriel disengaged himself from the Governor and stepped up to Gonzalo. He eyed the fop up and down.

'You're right, Don Gonzalo. There *are* some bastards here. But none of the others stink of pig's shit as much as you do.'

As he turned on his heel, Gabriel heard no more sniggers, only orders for the march being given. Don Francisco's voice was calm once more, as though nothing at all had happened.

Walking with what he hoped everyone would see as an unhurried gait, Gabriel crossed the square. His body still ached from the afternoon's violence. It was only a little later, as he was heading back to the tents set up outside the town, that he encountered Chalkuchimac's palanquin, escorted by a few warriors. Half a dozen old noblemen, members of his retinue, followed, and Anamaya was surrounded by their severe, ancient faces.

Reflexively, Gabriel ducked into a tiny alleyway that stank of stagnant water. He would not have had her see him for anything in the world, with his clothing, his soul and his vision still sullied by the blood of the Indians whom he had killed this day.

The flicker of the torches fixed to the walls at the bottom of the *ushnu*'s stairwell made the Indians' features seem indistinct and shadowy. With a mere blink of his eyelids, Chalkuchimac indicated that the tar-coated torch-poles should be brought closer.

A dozen young boys came forward so quietly that their sandals couldn't be heard shuffling across the flagstones. As there were no holders set in the nearest walls, the boys stood around the Council of Noblemen, holding the torches at arm's length, perfectly still.

Now Anamaya could see their faces more clearly.

Nine of them formed a circle around a brazier in which some coca leaves were burning: four old men, exhausted by the trip, two high-ranking noblemen from Cuzco, the governor of the region nominated by Atahualpa, Chalkuchimac, and herself, the *Coya Camaquen.*

General Chalkuchimac was the most impressive of the men. His expression showed no sign of the torments that he had endured over the previous weeks, although he still could not walk, nor even feed himself. His hands and feet, tortured with fire in Cajamarca, were still raw. The women nursing him did their best, smearing his burns with unguent and changing his bandages every morning and every evening. But still his blisters wept constantly: in fact, they were getting worse, threatening the health of the courageous warrior's whole body.

And yet, as Chalkuchimac sat there on his matting, leaning back against a chair, wrapped in a great *manta* from which only his head emerged, he seemed to Anamaya the strongest and most determined of the men present. It was he who had convened this meeting now taking place as the Spaniards celebrated their victory, feasted in the town's still-standing *canchas*, and laughed at the dead Indians rotting in the river.

Chalkuchimac surveyed each of his colleagues' grave and silent faces before fixing his piercing gaze on Anamaya. The whites of his eyes glowed red in the torchlight. For a brief moment, she saw the shade of Atahualpa in them. But Chalkuchimac turned his gaze away as he said:

'We follow them like blindfolded children. We are neither brave nor shrewd. The Strangers want to enter the Sacred City, so we lead them there by the hand! And yet we know what they will do there. Look around you: they're pillaging the clans' *canchas*, and they're stealing all the gold from the temples. And yet, noble Lords, when I see your demeanours and listen to your words, it is as though you are completely indifferent to it. Indifferent to the fate of the Empire!'

One of the older Lords raised his hand and interrupted Chalkuchimac in a sharp voice:

'You still behave and think like a warrior, Chalkuchimac. Once you spoke only the language of force. That served you well as long as Inti blessed you with his power. But now that you are weak and yield to the will of the Strangers, you speak only the language of defeat. See merely what has happened today! Hundreds of your brave warriors are dead at the hands of the Strangers, although there was only a handful of them! Whether you like it or not, their horses give them a strength that our forces don't have.'

'Chalkuchimac, listen to the people of Hatun Sausa rejoicing!' yapped another elder furiously. 'Can you not hear them singing and dancing? Your men had come to torch this valley so that the Strangers would find only ashes and smoke along their road. Listen to how happy the inhabitants of this province are now, as the Strangers empty the Incas' warehouses and help themselves to their women as though the females belonged to them! Is *this* what you want to see throughout the Empire of the Four Cardinal Directions?'

'That's enough!' ordered the highest-ranking of the Cuzco noblemen. 'There is no point in us arguing.'

They remained silent for a moment, as the sound of shouts and laughter from the tents by the river outside the town drifted into the *ushnu*.

The senior Cuzco nobleman was a round man, with very

high cheekbones and bronze skin so dark that he looked like some painted piece of earthenware. Chalkuchimac remained impassive under his gaze. The gold plugs in his distended earlobes dangled against his shoulders, gleaming. He hadn't batted an eyelid throughout the accusations made against him, and the set of his jaw gave his expression the strength and ferocity of a puma's.

'Chalkuchimac has spoken one part of the truth,' the Cuzco nobleman continued, 'and I, Tisoc Inca, agree with him when he says that we follow the Strangers like blindfolded children. It is time to elect an Emperor. It is time that Inti found a son among us.'

Anamaya watched the old men lower their faces. Chalkuchimac grinned disdainfully.

'I suppose that the noble Tisoc wants one of his clan to be chosen!'

'Your anger is pointless, Chalkuchimac. He who is elected must have the blessing of the Sun God and the support of our ancestors in the Other World. That is all I ask.'

'It surprises me that you have no one in mind,' growled Chalkuchimac.

'How can we elect an Emperor when we have neither a priest nor a soothsayer to tell us the will of Inti and of Quilla?' asked another Elder, speaking for the first time. 'How are we to choose him, since Emperor Atahualpa didn't hand down the royal *mascapaicha* to any of his sons before he died?'

'He didn't because he didn't need to,' replied Chalkuchimac dryly. 'Everybody knows that Atoc Xopa was Atahualpa's favourite son. It is he who should wear the two-feathered *curiguinge* on his head, as his father did.'

Once again Chalkuchimac's words were met with a heavy silence. Some of the Elders looked at Anamaya. She knew what they expected of her, but she bided her time, preferring to hold her tongue until all of the noblemen's words and ulterior motives had come to the fore.

'Atoc Xopa is only a child,' remarked the senior Cuzco nobleman. 'What's more, he lives in the northern capital, far from here, and far from the Strangers. How would he be able to impose his will?'

'Tisoc, you have completely missed what Chalkuchimac's words imply,' scoffed one of the Elders. 'You are right, Atahualpa's favourite son is only a child. He lives in the north, and none here have seen his face. He has never even been to Cuzco. But that is precisely what endears him to General Chalkuchimac!'

'If we choose him,' added another, 'he will be nothing more than a shadow puppet under Chalkuchimac's influence. Chalkuchimac will be the real master of the Empire, even though he isn't the son of Inti!'

All eyes were on the general. He stared back at them, his face expressionless. Anamaya couldn't help but admire his strength and composure. The tension in the room was so great that she noticed that the hands of a few of the Noble Lords were actually trembling. Then the oldest of them said, as he raised his crippled hand:

'I heard what Chalkuchimac told the Strangers' *Machu Kapitu* through their intermediary who speaks their language. He told them, on his own authority and without our consent, that Atoc Xopa should be our Emperor.'

'Chalkuchimac, is this true?'

Before replying to Tisoc Inca, the old warrior turned his gaze toward Anamaya. He looked long and hard into her eyes, as though trying to read her very soul. Then he looked up and said:

'Yes.'

An angry cry of dismay rose from the Noble Lords. But Chalkuchimac seemed to be addressing Tisoc Inca alone when he said:

'What has happened to you all? Are you like Atahualpa, who believed that the Strangers would simply leave after taking all the gold we offered them? Well, Atahualpa has gone, and no one among us knows whether he was able to join his father in the Other World!'

Another angry howl rose from the Noble Lords. Chalkuchimac, in a choleric gesture, pushed back the *manta* that was covering him. Everyone saw his blackened hands. There was no skin at all on them and the exposed tissue glistened with blood and watery fluid. The flesh on his feet and legs had been reduced to roasted shreds that oozed yellow pus.

'Why do you think that I suffered this?' roared Chalkuchimac. 'The stench of my scorched flesh fouls the air of the Empire of the Four Cardinal Directions! My agony rises into the blackness of the sky so that Inti may find it when he rises each morning! And Inti prevents my body from healing so that every one of our warriors may smell the odor of my wounds and so know that I will never prostrate myself before the Strangers. Tisoc! They are not kind and gentle! They feed on gold, and their hunger is insatiable! Tisoc Inca, don't you realize that when they reach Cuzco they will take everything and give nothing in return? They will take your livestock, your women, your children and your servants. They will take everything – and they always will, because that is why they are here! I, Chalkuchimac, tell you this: we must annihilate them while they are still few in number.'

'In that case, why designate an inexperienced child as Emperor?' grumbled an Elder.

Chalkuchimac grinned like a demon from the Under World, and Anamaya couldn't help but shudder at his terrifying appearance.

'Because then the Strangers will think themselves the Emperor's master! They will tell him do this, do that. And we shall smile at them. We shall give them their gold. But meanwhile, I shall be freed. And then I can lead our warriors into a great battle, and all the Strangers shall die.'

'Like today?' sniggered Tisoc cynically.

'You are nothing but cowards!' yelled Chalkuchimac, waving his maimed hands. 'Inti shall reduce you all to ashes!'

'Inti is not with you, Chalkuchimac!' replied Tisoc dryly. 'You forget that he who is hungry always ends up either by eating or by starving to death. Your choice is neither wise nor sound. We all know whom we should elect Emperor. It must be Manco, the son of Huayna Capac and the Lord of the northern clan. He is the wisest and strongest of those who are still alive. He will bring peace and unity to the Empire.'

Chalkuchimac's derisive chuckle sounded almost like a full-blown laugh. He turned toward Anamaya.

'Was it you who orchestrated this choice, *Coya Camaquen*? You are very quiet, it seems to me. You were more talkative when you were at Atahualpa's side.'

'Chalkuchimac!' called out one of the elders. 'How dare you taunt the *Coya Camaquen*!'

Chalkuchimac accidentally brushed his charred, skinless hands against his clothes, and grimaced in pain. He shook his head, and then said in a lower voice:

'No, no, noble Lord, I do not mock her. I know who the *Coya Camaquen* is.'

'Chalkuchimac,' said Tisoc Inca in a conciliatory tone, 'this argument is pointless. We are running out of time, and we must choose an Emperor. There is no soothsayer here, no servant of Inti who might interpret the oracles for us. But the *Coya Camaquen* can. She designated Atahualpa as Emperor even before the comet crossed the sky above Quito. He trusted her in all the decisions he took, as you know. And we all know that it was to her that he spoke the last words he uttered in this world, just as his father, Huayna Capac, did in Quito.'

'Yes!' agreed one Elder loudly. 'That is what we should do.'

'Chalkuchimac, consent to the *Coya Camaquen* choosing the new Emperor. Let her choose between Manco and Atoc Xopa.'

Chalkuchimac hadn't looked away from Anamaya for an instant. For the first time she detected fear, doubt, and even a glimmer of goodwill toward her in his gaze. Then he exhaled suddenly, like a smithy's bellows, closed his eyes and asked:

'So, what do you say, noble Anamaya?'

Anamaya's heart was beating so strongly that its thudding in her ears almost drowned out Chalkuchimac's words. She was all too aware of the immense consequences of whatever she might say. All her muscles became as hard as rock, and her sinews stiffened. But the sentences formed in her throat and came out of her mouth as though articulated by a will other than her own – as had happened on so many other occasions. Even as she uttered them, it was as if they were being spoken by someone else.

'On the eve of the great massacre at Cajamarca, Emperor Huayna Capac visited me from the Other World. He came in the form of a child. He told me: *"That which is too old comes to an end, that which is too big shatters, that which is too strong loses its force . . . that is what the great pachacuti means. The world is shrinking and being reborn. Everything has changed."'*

An astonished murmur rose from Anamaya's audience. It didn't occur to anyone to doubt her: it was as though the great Huayna Capac himself was speaking to them through her. They were on tenterhooks, and she saw from their tense faces that they were gripped by every word she spoke. She continued:

'Emperor Huayna Capac went on. *"Take care of my son whom you saved from the snake, for he is the first knot of the future."* A long time ago, when I was still an inexperienced young girl without any learning, I watched the ceremony in which the noble Manco became a man. He won the race that day. But during the course of it, a venomous snake had placed itself in his way, in order to bite him. I got rid of the snake, and saved Manco's life.'

Absolute silence reigned over the room. The laughter and singing in the night outside had ceased, as had the din out on the plain.

'And so, *Coya Camaquen*, Manco is your choice,' murmured Chalkuchimac.

'Noble Chalkuchimac,' replied Anamaya with an audacity that surprised even herself, 'it is not *my* choice. The ancestors in the Other World, it was they who chose Manco, a long time ago now. But allow me to add that he is noble and honest. He is fair, and he is no coward, as you know. He will know how to unite all the parts of the Empire without having to submit to the Strangers like a child. And to wage the war that you wish for, if it must happen, then it must happen after a reign of peace. The wounds of the civil war between the brothers that so weakened Emperor Atahualpa must be given time to heal. Yes, Chalkuchimac, you are a noble warrior. But today, war must hide under the guise of peace. Only peace will allow us to be strong when the day comes – should Inti and Quilla wish it.'

'Well said! She is right,' two of the Elders said approvingly.

'Chalkuchimac,' said Tisoc, 'all of us here agree with the *Coya Camaquen*. We trust her. Tomorrow, at first light, she will leave to meet Manco and tell him of our decision.'

With his eyes half shut, Chalkuchimac contemplated his wounds. Then he looked up at Tisoc and asked bitterly:

'What would happen if I were to disagree with the *Coya Camaquen*?'

Tisoc did not reply. The Elders' tired breathing could be heard through the heavy silence – the respiration of old men who now drew their strength only from the memory and the words of a young girl. Anamaya looked at Chalkuchimac with both admiration and regret.

'What would happen?' repeated Chalkuchimac in a deeper, more menacing tone.

Anamaya looked at Tisoc for a moment. But she didn't wait for his approval before she said, with glacial calm:

'Nothing, my Lord. Nothing would happen. I shall leave at dawn.'

Chalkuchimac stared into her eyes. For once, she saw an emotion that was neither anger nor defiance. She saw resignation.

And an infinite sadness.

Dawn rose over a thick fog that coated the rocks and the tents' canvas with moisture. The air was still full of the smell of burning. There was no noise except for the constant rumbling of the river and an occasional bird cry.

Wrapped in his long horsehair cape, Gabriel sat on a tree stump a little apart from the Inca Lords' camp. He had slept badly, waking often from a nightmare in which he repeatedly saw horrifying images of the battle of the day before. He would wake frequently, his heart beating hard with the violent desire to run to Anamaya's tent. He imagined himself taking her in his arms, losing himself in her caresses, plunging his yearning manhood between her thighs, erasing the burning memory of all the violence of war in an endless physical love. But he did not dare.

Nor did he dare join her now, as she prepared to leave on her journey.

Don Francisco had warned him that the Inca noblemen had

chosen a new king. 'With my consent, of course,' he had said, giving no other information before adding. 'Their priestess has been instructed to take the news to the Emperor-elect, and I have given her permission to leave the column.' At the word 'priestess' Pizarro's dark gaze had met Gabriel's. The young man had turned away, almost ashamed.

Now, in this damp and silent dawn, near the river, Indian bearers were preparing the *Coya Camaquen*'s palanquin. She was to be escorted by a dozen warriors, commanded by a young officer, who stood waiting a few steps away. But Gabriel stared only at the group gathered among the tents of the noblemen.

Anamaya looked resplendent as she stood in the center of a group of Elders who were paying their respects to her. She was draped in a vicuña cape decorated with patterns of blue, scarlet and bright yellow. On her head she wore a sort of gold tiara with three yellow feathers rising from it. Her lower arms were adorned with gold plaques. She held a golden replica of an ear of corn in her hand.

Gabriel had never seen her so strikingly dressed. She looked like a stranger, a princess from a world still so inaccessible to him that he experienced a pang of childish jealousy.

'Aren't you at least going to bid her farewell?' asked a voice from beside him.

'Brother Bartholomew!'

A smile spread across the monk's curiously pale face. His grey eyes displayed a degree of tenderness. He pointed his fused fingers at Anamaya, in front of whom some Elders were now bowing.

'I know what that woman means to you, my friend. But not because of any spying I might have done: everybody in the column whispers about it. As you know, lies spread as easily as truths – but then one only needs to scratch a little to tell them apart.'

Gabriel hesitated before replying:

'I can't tell if this is one of those situations where it is better to keep silent, as you have so often advocated, Brother Bartholomew. What do you think?'

'*Mihi secretum meum*, yes? Do what you heart tells you, my

friend. But you cannot prevent me from reading in your eyes the answers that your tongue won't give me.'

Gabriel nodded slowly and examined the scene in front of him. Anamaya, surrounded by Indian soldiers and three of the Noble Lords, and followed by a handful of servant girls, approached the palanquin. Gabriel knew that she had seen him.

'They say that she isn't like other princesses,' said Bartholomew, looking at Gabriel.

For the first time since the battle, Gabriel cheered up, half smiling. Bartholomew's intelligence was a welcome relief from the spite and envy of so many of his compatriots.

'She has abilities that inspire fear and respect in the Indians,' he replied, 'and the dead king Huayna Capac confided in her some secrets on which they believe their future depends.'

Gabriel paused, hesitating.

'But perhaps this all seems heathen, or even the work of the devil to you, Brother Bartholomew.'

The monk grinned.

'I'm not one to see the devil in everything, Gabriel. On the contrary, I can recognize beauty when it stands in front of me. And is not beauty always the work of God?'

Gabriel felt a real joy in rediscovering Bartholomew's subtle mind and generous spirit. And his natural smile attracted Anamaya's attention. She was only a short distance from her palanquin now. She seemed to be hesitating a little. But ritual dictated her path. An old nobleman motioned towards the palanquin, the bearers and the escort.

Bartholomew laid his hand on Gabriel's forearm.

'Let me ask you another question: Why don't you go and wish her a safe and happy journey?'

'Yesterday,' said Gabriel in a muted voice, 'I killed a lot of men. A lot of Indians.'

'Are you frightened that she will reproach you for it?'

'I don't know. But I'm disturbed by the memory I have of having wanted to kill, and even of enjoying it.'

Bartholomew laughed quietly.

'As for that, you should speak to me, not to her.'

Brother Bartholomew gazed at Anamaya's retinue with his gray eyes. He said nothing further as he and Gabriel watched Anamaya take her seat in the palanquin. Then he said in a lively voice:

'Yesterday, Gabriel Montelucar y Flores, you did your duty. You became a hero in the eyes of many of your companions, and they admire you for it today. Probably you couldn't care less about their opinion of you, because you are immensely proud and you find your compatriots a little uncivilized. But it makes no odds what you or they think. If it makes any difference to you, tell yourself that you were just returning the lives you took to God. As for the love in your heart, Gabriel, don't expect me to call it a sin.'

Gabriel was so surprised that he turned to stare at the priest.

'What things you tell me, Brother Bartholomew! That woman hasn't even been baptized! If I were to heed the words of Father Vicente Valverde, then—'

Bartholomew interrupted him impatiently:

'And if you were to heed *mine*, then you would know that to deny the force of love is a sin. The Apostle Paul says as much, and so does St Augustine . . .'

'But they're talking about the love of God!'

'And now the freethinker takes himself for a theologian! Do you claim to be able to teach me what the force of divine love is? I tell you that there is a spark of the divine in your love.'

Bartholomew's words were almost lost in the wail of the bronze trumpet sounding the cortege's imminent departure.

'Now go! Hurry!' insisted Brother Bartholomew.

Gabriel, at last released from the moral shackles that had been hobbling him since the previous day, walked through the crowd of warriors and noblemen toward the woman he loved.

The palanquin was already on the outskirts of the town by the time Gabriel caught up with it. The Indian soldiers looked a little surprised as they watched him fall into step with them. Anamaya ordered her bearers to stop.

Gabriel felt a slight shiver run up his spine as she stepped out of her palanquin and approached him. He had never seen so much nobility and dignity focused in one person. She led him a short distance away. He noticed that none of her bearers, guards or servant girls dared look in their direction.

'I am so happy that you came,' said Anamaya.

She was quiet for a moment before adding:

'I was worried that you wouldn't. I didn't want to leave without seeing your face up close.'

She raised her hand to his lips. When he tried to kiss her, however, she stepped back slightly. But she continued to smile at him.

'We can't – it's impossible,' Anamaya said gently. 'Not here, and not now.'

Gabriel's insides felt as though they were twisted into knots, and he was unable to speak the words that his racing heart urged him to say. He was trembling slightly. It seemed intolerable to him not to be able to hold her body against his before they parted.

Anamaya stepped closer to him. They were so close that their bodies almost brushed against one another. When he opened his eyes again, he saw Anamaya's blue-irised gaze looking into him, as though searching the very depths of his soul.

'I know what war is,' she murmured. 'We too kill our enemies.'

'I'm going to miss you,' said Gabriel at last. 'Not an hour shall pass when I won't yearn for you.'

'Soon we shall return to a time of peace. We have elected a new Inca. He is like a brother to me, and he is wise. He will know how to negotiate a peace with your Governor.'

The members of the cortege behind them stood perfectly still. Not one man or woman moved an inch. Gabriel thought of Guaypar, whom he had faced during the battle the day before, and whom he had let escape.

'Peace is still a long way off. Be careful.'

'You are the one who must be careful,' said Anamaya.

Suddenly her gaze was filled with such intensity, such anxiety as she looked at him that he felt uneasy.

'You have come a long way to find me. I don't want to lose you. You have revealed a weakness in me, opened a fissure that has grown into a ravine, and I'm more frightened for you than I have ever been for myself.'

Anamaya spoke these words without looking at Gabriel. Although her voice was soft and calm and her expression impassive, he sensed the depth of emotion in her.

And he found himself incapable of saying a word in reply.

Gabriel reached out for Anamaya's hand, and this time she let him hold it. She even leaned against him, her body trembling with an energy that made them both dizzy. She gripped his hand so tightly that it hurt, scratching and squeezing it: there was perhaps more abandon in this grasp than she had ever shown him during their lovemaking.

Gabriel noticed people looking at them, and he recollected her words: 'Not here, not now.' He tore himself away from her. His heart was warm and his skin cold.

They stood beside one another for a little while, feeling as though the ground itself was unsteady beneath their feet. They found themselves unable to move or speak. Gabriel smelled the scent of flowers in the air, and he took refuge in it, closing his eyes.

Anamaya started to return to her palanquin. Then she stopped and turned around.

'Look after yourself,' he said, his throat constricted.

She opened her mouth to speak, but then closed it again. He remained staring longingly at her eyes, her lips. Anamaya said:

'I love you . . .'

And before Gabriel realized that it was the first time that she had spoken these words to him, she had run back to the cortege.

CHAPTER 12

The Apurimac Valley, 30 October 1533

H E WAS A SMALL MAN. WOODEN PLUGS DISTENDED his earlobes and he wore the tunic of a bridge warden. He got down on his knees on the flagstones and prostrated himself in front of the palanquin. The officer of the guards, club in hand, watched him warily.

'Welcome to the Apurimac Valley, *Coya Camaquen*. It is my honor to help you cross the river.'

Anamaya had to smile, so much did the man seem to fear her. No day had passed since her departure from Hatun Sausa on which she had not been reminded how much her reputation and her cortege impressed both the humble villagers and the empire's officials.

The bridge warden had a few reasons of his own to be worried. Two hundred paces below them flowed the furious Apurimac River, studded with giant boulders. Its rumble echoed throughout the entire valley, which broadened substantially to the south. But in front of them, where a long rope bridge should have been hanging, there was nothing.

'Stand up,' ordered Anamaya, 'and explain to me why the bridge has disappeared.'

'Ten nights ago, *Coya Camaquen*, some soldiers came and burned it. I tried to stop them, and I ordered my guards to defend the bridge against them. But we were only ten, whereas General Quizquiz's company consisted of over a hundred men!'

'Quizquiz?' said Anamaya, astonished.

'Yes, *Coya Camaquen*. That is how they introduced themselves – as the men of the Emperor Atahualpa's great general, Quizquiz.'

'Did they say why they were to burn it?'

'To prevent the foreign gold-robbers from reaching Cuzco.'

The little man pointed toward the southern end of the valley and added:

'They say that there are troops throughout the mountains, and on the road to Cuzco.'

'But how can we cross the river now?' asked Anamaya brusquely, hoping to cut short the prattle that she sensed was coming.

The little man seemed delighted by her question. He bowed respectfully again and said:

'A messenger announced your impending arrival three days ago, *Coya Camaquen*. We have prepared the necessary: rafts—'

'Rafts?'

'Yes, *Coya Camaquen*. But we cannot cross here, where the bridge was, because the currents are too strong and dangerous. There is a better place not far from here. Will you allow me to lead you there?'

'*Coya Camaquen*,' interrupted the young officer commanding the escort, 'it is unwise to leave the royal road. It might be a trap!'

'As you can see, lieutenant,' replied Anamaya, 'the royal road across the river has ceased to exist. And I absolutely *must* reach my destination. You shall do your duty, then, and protect me.'

It took them almost an hour, hiking along a steep and tricky path, to reach the place in the river where the current ran somewhat slower.

Set between two tree-covered slopes, the Apurimac ran more evenly here. It described a wide curve between some pastures, passing through a small valley. But at the far end it broke once more into a foaming mass against a large gray boulder that marked the start of more rapids.

But right here the river broadened and flowed more calmly.

Still, one only needed to glance at it from the bank to realize that the current was only slightly less fierce than it was downstream.

'You see,' explained the bridge warden, 'the rafts must be launched from that spot over there. We must reach the other bank before we are swept past that big gray rock.'

'Where are the rafts?' asked Anamaya.

'Under the cover of those trees over there, *Coya Camaquen*. We didn't want the soldiers to find and destroy them before your arrival.'

'Have you already tried crossing the river?' asked the officer suspiciously.

'Once!' said the bridge warden, grinning broadly. 'There and back.'

'Well, then, this will be the second time,' said Anamaya calmly.

The little man, flattered by her encouragement, exerted himself vigorously in the next few moments. His men pulled two heavy rafts, made of logs and poles, from the edge of the forest. Deftly rolling them on smaller logs, they brought them across the field to the bank of the Apurimac, where they launched the bigger of the two.

A dozen men held on to it with ropes while six others set Anamaya's palanquin on it. Once the seat had been properly fastened, the Governor's men prostrated themselves and didn't get up until the *Coya Camaquen* had taken her place on the raft. Then, using long poles, they tried to keep it as stable as possible.

The current was so strong that Anamaya felt her palanquin sway back and forth. The tree trunks, tied together so as to allow a degree of flexibility, moved in an extraordinary way.

While the men struggled to keep the raft close to the riverbank, a furious argument broke out between the officer of the guards and the bridge warden.

'I must accompany the *Coya Camaquen* with at least five soldiers!' said the officer.

'Impossible! That would overburden the raft, lieutenant. We would not be able to navigate it safely. Two men at the most. Look – the logs are sinking as it is.'

'Because you made a poor job of it!'

'No, it's just that the palanquin is heavier than we imagined. But there is always the second raft. Your men can follow the *Coya Camaquen* on that one—'

'That's enough!' Anamaya interrupted. 'Lieutenant, come aboard my raft – you too, warden. If it has been badly built . . . well, then, we shall all suffer the consequences together!'

In truth, once the raft had been released into the current, Anamaya understood the concern of the men trying to navigate it. In addition to its increasingly violent rocking motion, the raft speeded up noticeably as it neared the center of the river. The power of the current seemed sure to overcome the strength of the men as they poled along with astonishing skill.

Suddenly one of them let out a cry. An unexpected whirlpool appeared, frighteningly deep. The six men quickly gathered on one side of the raft to shove it toward the right. But everything was happening too quickly. A shock of impact threw Anamaya upward. The raft's logs leaped as they ground over the hidden rock they'd hit. The palanquin was thrown upward once again, tilting to the side. The officer of the guards threw himself onto one of its shafts to prevent it from slipping away. Anamaya grabbed onto the palanquin's posts and bent herself double to counterbalance its tilt.

The palanquin righted itself with a thud, but one of its legs sliced through a cord holding the logs together, which had already been weakened by the impact with the submerged rock.

The gray rock marking the start of the rapids seemed to be getting closer at an alarming rate. The bridge warden barked an order, then another – and another. At that moment, the six men pushed together with perfect coordination.

It was like a ballet. Their poles rose, plunged, curved and slipped, then rose again, plunged, curved. Sweat pearled on the napes of their necks, and the raft stabilized. Even better, it began to move out of the center of the current. The warden's barks continued, the poles bending so much now that they seemed on the point of actually snapping. But at last, as the rumbling of the rapids rolled menacingly through the air, the raft slowed down and began gliding toward the bank.

The warden grinned. He turned to Anamaya and saluted her. Each of his men realized that the *Coya Camaquen* hadn't said a word nor cried out in fear, despite the danger.

Anamaya smiled back at him, and was surprised by the gentleness with which the raft met the bank.

As the palanquin was taken off the raft and set on the grass, she watched the men, took in the freshness of the air, and savored the odd feeling of pleasure that she had just experienced. The gazes of the soldiers and raftsmen upon her were full of admiration and a newfound respect.

'Are we far from Rimac Tambo?' she asked the bridge warden.

'Less than a day's walk. But if you would like to do us the honor of accepting our hospitality for the night, then—'

Anamaya didn't let him finish.

'I thank you, and I shall be sure to mention your competence to Lord Manco. But we must be in Rimac Tambo tonight.'

The rumble of the river rose like a soothing murmur. The mountain slopes surrounding the village seemed like sheltering petals in the gathering dusk. From the *cancha* one could see a deep, narrow valley extending to the east. The luminous fog filling it glowed pale in the failing light.

Anamaya knew today where the valley led – to the sacred city whose name must never be spoken aloud: Picchu!

Nothing had changed at Rimac Tambo. It was a strange feeling.

Many years earlier, she had stood here at just such a sunset. The beautiful, perfectly joined walls surrounding the ceremonial square had possessed the same peaceful quality then as they did now. The sharp slopes surrounding the valley, like giant geometric shapes embedded in the earth, reminded her then, as they did now, of the weavings that the virgins created daily in their *acllahuasis*. Even then they had had that same slightly alarming power. Only Anamaya had changed. She had been nothing more than a frightened little girl then, whom the sage Villa Oma had done his best to change into a vigilant and confident woman.

It had been at this very same spot and in an identical sunset that, much to their surprise, the comet identifying Atahualpa as Emperor had appeared to them, here in the hollow of the forbidden valley.

Anamaya merely had to shut her eyes to see it again.

A ball of pale yellow fire, like a sun in the night, it had climbed up between the early stars to the black Zenith. Its long hair had trailed behind it, lifted by the wind of the Other World.

She could remember the sound of the sage's voice as he had said, 'Let go of your fear, *Coya Camaquen*. Let your spirit be your guide. Remember your voyage into the rock of our ancestors. Let go of your fear.'

A screeching bird startled her and she opened her eyes.

The square around her was deserted. She felt slightly cold. Her ceremonial cape wasn't warm enough for the mountains. She had made herself wear it since two days earlier, so that she would be sure to have it on when the new Emperor Manco arrived at last. But as night fell, she felt shivers of cold run down her neck and her back.

She heard the bird screech again, closer now to the river. And then another, this time behind the *tambo*.

Night was falling fast. Now the valley seemed dark and menacing. She could still make out the flagstones of the royal road between the bushes on the steep slope that blocked the valley to the south. The road created a strange impression, as though the mountain had been cleaved by a bolt of cold, hard lightning.

Anamaya repressed a shiver, a shiver due more to worry than to the increasing cold of the dusk.

Many of Rimac Tambo's peasants had heard the bridge warden say that there were hundreds of soldiers roaming in the surrounding mountains, pillaging *canchas* and destroying villages. Their officers were refusing to obey the orders given by the Noble Lords following their peace agreement with the Strangers. Some proclaimed that they would obey only General Chalkuchimac, and that they would never allow the Strangers to reach Cuzco. The more time passed without a sign from Manco, the more Anamaya worried that he had fallen into the hands of the warrior hordes.

Would this always be the way? Would there always be violence, hatred, fighting between brothers despite the will of the Ancestors – and despite the grave danger that should have united them all?

This valley, in spite of its apparent calm, had so many melancholic memories buried in its earth that menace rose from it like mist. Anamaya remembered very well the massacre of the elders who had been accompanying the mummy of the Emperor Huayna Capac, a massacre that had taken place on this very spot.

The bird cries multiplied as the forest grew darker. In the darkening night, the rumble of the river sounded increasingly mysterious and insistent. Anamaya drew her cape tighter around her shoulders but decided not to return to the *cancha*, as though her vigilance might protect Manco while he travelled toward her.

Anamaya hadn't moved since sunset. Now it was deepest night. A brazier had been brought to her at which she might warm her hands and face. Time went by slowly as she watched the stars pass across the sky.

From time to time animal cries echoed from the dark mountainside. And although she had been listening intently, she didn't hear the steps behind her on the grass until the very last moment. She hadn't time to turn around before a broad, strong hand covered her mouth, preventing her from crying out. She felt herself embraced and lifted into the air like a doll.

'Manco!'

'Aaah!' murmured Manco as he released her. 'You recognized me too quickly!'

They stood facing one another. Her eyes shone with tenderness. Anamaya immediately forgot the official salutation with which she had planned to greet Manco. The man standing before her glowed with strength and dignity. She felt profoundly happy to see him again, and to see on his face the marks of the time that had passed since they had first met at Tumebamba. He too seemed moved by seeing her again. He took a step back to admire her better.

'It is night, and you shine like a star, my beloved sister,' he said gently.

'I'm so happy to see you, Manco. And so very happy as well to see that—'

She stumbled over what she was about to say. She wanted to tell him that he had acquired the beauty and bearing appropriate to an Emperor; that he had, in the line of his lips and in the sparkle of his eyes, the determination and self-assurance of a Son of the Sun. But she didn't dare. In a flash she remembered the eruption of her love for Gabriel. The *pachacuti* had overturned not only her world but also her heart. And in this troubled state of mind, she didn't want Manco to misinterpret her words as those of an attempted seduction.

'. . . And so very happy to see that you have arrived without mishap,' she said.

'Yes. Quizquiz and Guaypar's troops are everywhere. But those northerners don't know the mountains quite as well as I do!'

He smiled, a little disdainfully, and then went on:

'But how is it that you didn't take fright and that you recognized me so quickly? Does the *Coya Camaquen* now have eyes in the back of her head, in addition to her other remarkable powers?'

'Oh, I've been waiting for you for hours! I was worried about you, and I was listening to the noises in the night as I waited for you . . .'

She paused, grinning, before continuing:

'. . . And then, you've already surprised me like that once before – and in this very same place!'

They laughed together, both warmly aware of the other's happiness at their reunion.

'Come,' said Manco. 'Let's go into the *tambo*. I'm hungry, and we'll be able to talk more comfortably there.'

Lord Manco's arrival created a great commotion inside the buildings. The few noblemen who had accompanied him had settled into a communal room with the commander of Anamaya's guard. The servant girls fluttered back and forth, stoking the braziers, preparing food, and bringing the men *chicha*, blankets and torches.

As soon as the door hanging had fallen behind them after they had entered the room that had been set aside for Manco, Anamaya fell to her knees and prostrated herself twice.

'Anamaya!' exclaimed Manco, abashed.

'Emperor Manco—'

'Anamaya! Why do you address me thus?' interrupted Manco as he leaned down to her. 'You and I are brother and sister . . .'

Anamaya shook her head and looked up at him.

'We won't be for much longer. The Council of Noblemen met. They elected you Emperor.'

Manco straightened. His lips drew tight.

'The time has come,' murmured Anamaya.

Manco looked at her for a moment. Then he took her by the shoulders and made her rise to her feet. He looked her directly in the eyes.

'I remember the first time that I saw the colour of your eyes. We were still children. That day the blue of your eyes entered my heart. Even Paullu, my beloved brother, was a little jealous!'

Anamaya felt troubled once again, as she did every time Manco expressed his feelings for her. She pursed her lips, hoping that he wouldn't go any further. Manco, to her relief, noticed her discomfort. He remained silent, wearing a dreamy smile.

'I miss Paullu,' he sighed. 'He has been at Titicaca for three months now. He only wants to be there.'

Manco's gaze hardened as he continued:

'I also remember the last time we saw one another, my sister. That horrible night of the great massacre at Cajamarca haunted me for days and days afterwards.'

'That night, noble Manco, I warned you that Emperor Atahualpa was heading toward his end in this world, and that you would soon have to take his place. That time has now come.'

'Yes. Your words have stayed with me. I haven't forgotten. Just as I haven't forgotten that you have always marked out for me the road leading to the world of my ancestors.'

'But it's not me!' Anamaya protested. 'I'm merely the medium

through which they speak. I'm just the wife of your father Huayna
Capac's Sacred Double. It is he who has designated you Emperor.
And it is he who has placed the future of the Empire of the Four
Cardinal Directions in your hands.'

'I must try to understand, Anamaya, what happened that night.
So many things were said – that the Strangers were gods, that they
spat fire and were joined bodily with their animals. In Cuzco there
is a rumour that the sun has extinguished itself ever since they laid
their hands on my brother Atahualpa.'

Anamaya considered his words.

'I don't understand everything that is happening to the Empire,
Manco. Your father no longer visits me to offer me guidance.
My dreams are full of silences. But I have lived alongside the
Strangers for many moons now, and I can assure you that they
don't come from the Other World. They are men just like us!
But men insatiable in their lust for gold. They neither spit fire
nor possess any natural abilities that we do not also have. Their
weapons are simply more powerful than ours, that is all.'

Manco nodded, released Anamaya's shoulders, and sat on a
thick pile of matting at the back of the room.

'Come sit by me,' he said.

'Emperor—'

'No! Not yet. I'm not Emperor yet. Come, don't be frightened. I
only want to feel your warmth next to me, little sister, like before.'

Anamaya joined him, a little hesitantly. Manco held out his
hand and she placed her fingers in his palm. He closed his
hand gently.

'Tell me more about the Strangers,' he said. 'Help me understand them. Must we hate them, or can we respect some of them
and love them like ordinary humans in our own land?'

Disconcerted, Anamaya felt her heart beating frighteningly fast.
Did he know about Gabriel? Of course not. Manco was merely
curious and concerned.

'They're all a bane for us,' she said sincerely. 'Well, almost all
of them . . . they are strange and difficult to understand. They
worship their own strength as though it were a goddess. Most of
them say one thing but do another.'

'Do they frighten *you*?'

Anamaya didn't reply straight away.

'No,' she admitted finally. 'No. But they're frightened of us. Their fear makes them cruel and devious.'

'Then isn't it dishonorable to make peace with them?'

'I think that peace with them is necessary for the moment, and that peace is needed throughout Tahuantinsuyu. There has already been too much bloodshed, too many killed. All the clans and all the families are suffering, but no one knows why. We must gather our strength before leaping toward our destiny.'

Manco sighed and nodded.

'Chalkuchimac opposed my ascension, didn't he?'

It wasn't a question, more an observation. Once again, Anamaya was impressed by the future Inca's maturity.

'Yes.'

'How did you manage to convince the others to elect me?'

'All the Noble Lords, led by Tisoc, opposed Chalkuchimac. I simply acted as a medium for your father, telling them what he told me when he came to visit me the night before the great massacre. That was enough.'

Manco nodded approvingly.

'It seems that I am not the only one who appreciates your gifts, girl. But we must be careful. I don't trust Chalkuchimac. I know he controls all the soldiers in the mountains. He'll do anything to prevent me placing the royal *borla* on my head. What's more, some *chaskis* have brought me the news that Guaypar is preparing an assault on the Strangers.'

Anamaya went pale but didn't say a word.

Manco wasn't looking at her. His gaze was lost in the night as he meditated on his destiny.

'They want war. They want war with the Strangers, and they want war with us, the Cuzco clans. They value war and they don't believe that peace is in the best interests of the Empire. Anamaya, you must warn the Strangers of this threat to them. If Chalkuchimac's men attack them, it will be primarily to get to me. They hope to provoke the Strangers into retaliation against us all, and prevent me becoming Emperor!'

Anamaya said nothing. She knew that Manco was right. But she also knew, without being able to explain why, that neither Guaypar nor even Chalkuchimac could prevent Manco wearing the royal *mascapaicha*.

Manco looked at her closely. His gaze was so intense that Anamaya felt it burning into her cheeks, her lips, and on her forehead, as though it was a real caress. Manco raised his hand, and Anamaya felt it brush against her neck.

'My happiness is great when I'm near you,' he murmured. 'It makes me happy to inhale your perfume and to know that you're close by. I have missed you terribly, sister Anamaya. No woman I know is as beautiful or as strong as you.'

She smiled and bowed her head demurely.

'I have also missed you, brother Manco. But I knew that the day would come when I would have to prostrate myself before you and call you My Lord Emperor. Where is the golden Sacred Double?' she asked in order to avoid responding to the invitation contained in his caress.

'Carefully hidden in Cuzco, *Coya Camaquen*!' replied Manco, perhaps a little brusquely.

'I miss him too,' murmured Anamaya, without reacting to his ill humor, 'and I shall be very happy to be reunited with him. Emperor Huayna Capac hasn't transported me to the Other World once since the great massacre.'

'You're a consummate woman these days, I find,' said Manco melancholically. 'Perhaps it is no longer possible for you to be the Sacred Double's wife? If you were with me, your influence would be great.'

Anamaya fixed her gaze on Manco and saw in his eyes as much affection as desire. She took the young prince's hand and put it against her lips as she whispered:

'Brother Manco, you know as well as I do that that is not how things are meant to be. Tomorrow, when you leave at dawn, you will be Emperor. Tomorrow, only you will be able to prevent the Empire of the Four Cardinal Directions from crumbling into dust. No one will be permitted to touch you or even to look at you, not even me, because your father the Sun God forbids it. It's the law. You must observe the law so that the Empire is strong and united. Only then will you have the support of your father the Sun God. Meanwhile, you know that you can always depend on me, no matter what happens.'

Manco scrutinized her face. A hard look – perhaps even anger – flashed across his eyes. Yet he brought Anamaya's fingers to his lips and kissed them, just as she had kissed his hand.

'Tell me everything, little sister. Tell me everything that you have seen during the last few months. Tell me about Atahualpa's death and about the Strangers' *Machu Kapitu*. Tell me everything, until your mouth is dry and my ears are tired. Because I must understand.'

CHAPTER 13

Vilcaconga, 8 November 1533

THE INDIAN LOOKED AT GABRIEL. ON HIS FACE WAS a cool grin that indicated both fear and curiosity. He repeated his answer more slowly so that the Stranger might understand him better:

'Yes, she was here three days ago. I saw her.'

'The *Coya Camaquen*?'

'I am only a humble *hatunruna*. I don't know the names of the Inca princesses.'

'Well, then, how can you be sure that it was her?'

'Her eyes. You told me that she had eyes the colour of the sky. I have never seen another princess with such eyes.'

Gabriel nodded. He smiled faintly and almost said that he hadn't, either.

It was dawn, and the abrupt slopes of the mountains surrounding the village of Rimac Tambo were veiled in a light fog that was already rising in translucent strands. The slopes and ridges created a beautiful illusion of giant protective petals. Gabriel, disappointed at having missed Anamaya, scarcely gave them a glance. The river rumbled on. But perhaps Anamaya was not so far off; perhaps she was somewhere in the forest. During the preceding days, as he had ridden along the royal road with de Soto, he had hoped all the time to see the palanquin bringing her back from her mission. He had hoped in vain, though, and his disappointment had gradually turned into worry. Had she met with trouble? Or had she gone on all the way to Cuzco? But that hadn't been her original plan.

'She was with a Cuzco nobleman,' continued the man, as though reading Gabriel's thoughts.

'Do you know what direction she took?'

But the Indian didn't have time to reply. A voice startled them:

'Good news or bad?'

De Soto smiled amicably. Gabriel noticed that he was wearing his padded cotton vest over his doublet. What was more, his left hand, resting on the hilt of his sword, was already protected by the big leather glove covered in metal plates that de Soto wore in combat.

'Neither one nor the other, for the moment,' Gabriel said surlily.

He turned back to the Indian. He waved at the surrounding mountains and asked:

'Do you know if there are warriors in the forest?'

The man hesitated. De Soto's battle outfit bothered him. Gabriel insisted:

'Soldiers from the northern clans, the soldiers who are pillaging your villages and destroying your bridges?'

The Indian gathered his resolve. He pointed, with his peasant's hands, toward the steep mountains in the south.

'Two nights ago, just before you came, there were a lot of fires burning up there. But there haven't been any since.'

De Soto didn't need Gabriel to translate.

'Of course they're there,' he murmured. 'They must be a few days ahead of us, destroying all the bridges leading to the capital.'

The two Spaniards looked at the mountains. Less than a league from the village, the royal road ascended a slope steeper than any they had yet encountered. It was largely unpaved, and it rose so abruptly that, in the mist rising over the forest, it seemed almost vertical.

'That slope is going to be hard going, especially for the horses,' remarked Gabriel. 'The animals haven't been properly rested after the tough journey we've just made. We would do better to wait for the Governor here.'

De Soto shook his head, scowling.

'I don't like this valley, and I don't like this river. No, I don't like it at all,' he said.

With his bare hand, de Soto pointed at the strange, narrow gorge to the east, beyond the sturdy Inca buildings. Whereas everywhere else the fog was lifting to reveal blue sky, there it remained dense, immobile, threatening. Its ominous tendrils gave it the appearance of a giant, savage beast.

'Not once did the fog lift from that gorge yesterday,' de Soto went on, 'as though it led nowhere – or else straight to hell.'

Gabriel grinned, amused.

'I never knew that you were so superstitious as to fear the forms of the natural world, Don Hernando!'

'A commonplace anomaly, I'm sure. But you're unwise to scoff, Gabriel. Consider the topography of the place. Those damned Indians can remain hidden in that fog-filled valley forever, and then attack us here when we're least expecting it.'

'It's much of a muchness. We'll be equally at their mercy if we climb that slope, and the horses won't be any use to us then. Quite the opposite, in fact.'

'Then we must do it quickly. It will be worse if we wait for the weather to turn against us. Look at the sky: today is going to be beautiful, clear and blue.'

'By the faith,' muttered Gabriel, unconvinced by the serene sky, 'you're the captain.'

'Whoa, my friend!' bantered de Soto. 'I've known you to be more adventurous before. Is it that you suspect me, as our beloved leader Don Francisco does, of being impatient to reach Cuzco?'

'Certainly I suspect it,' replied Gabriel in the same jocular tone, 'and I think that this time I suspect correctly, de Soto. But it doesn't matter. It's that slope that's bothering me.'

'And it's that valley that worries me.'

'Then one of us is wrong,' said Gabriel, grinning.

'Not at all, my friend! Let us hope that we are *both* wrong.'

As they headed back toward the buildings where the Spaniards were bustling about, the Indian called out to Gabriel. He pointed at a mountain overlooking the valley from the north and said:

'Noble Stranger, the princess with the sky in her eyes left for that mountain two days ago.'

It didn't take the sixty cavalrymen long to saddle the horses and put on their padded cotton surcoats or even, for some, their mail armour. And the day was, in fact, too promising for them to worry about rain.

The three arquebuses were primed with very dry gunpowder and loaded onto packhorses. Those cavalrymen who had shields attached them to their saddles. The catgut cords of the catch-trigger crossbows had been greased the night before and, if they were stiff, changed for more supple ones. Some were already cocked, the handle pulled back on the trammel, and the quarrels were within arm's reach in the saddle quivers.

The selection of a dozen men to guard the gold in Rimac Tambo until the Governor arrived took the most time. In the end, since no one volunteered, de Soto assigned a dozen foot soldiers and the two youngest cavalrymen to the job. Gabriel and the more experienced horsemen would accompany him, including Rodrigo Orgoñez and one of their bravest, the proud Hernando de Toro.

And it was with surly, resentful expressions that those ordered to stay behind heard the order to depart, just before midday, even though the sun was as heavy and as hot as a smithy's fire. It weighed on the morions of the expeditionary force as much as it reflected off them.

Yet they began their ascent with a great deal of enthusiastic anticipation. De Soto even had to order them to slow down, lest they wearied the horses too early.

They quickly realized what they were in for, however. The paved road soon gave way to a dirt one, equally steep. Even where it wasn't muddy it still gave way underfoot. The horses found the climb so hard that they could scarcely move themselves, let alone carry their riders. Sometimes they could advance only by leaping forward like mountain goats, and they quickly exhausted their breath due to this effort and the altitude.

About a quarter of the way up the slope, the road narrowed and the forest thinned out. There was less and less shade, and the sun beat down brutally. Men and horses alike walked open-mouthed, gasping for breath, their tongues dry and furred. De Soto gave the order that they were to advance in groups of four only.

Gabriel and his three companions decided to travel alongside the road rather than on it. Their boots slipped on the grass and got caught in the thick undergrowth of bramble bushes and wild cotton plants, but the horses were more comfortable here.

Men began to unbuckle the padded armour vests under which they were suffocating. They loosened their belts and undid their shirts. They blinked in the blinding brightness of the sun. Their hands were clammy on their bridles. No one said a word, but there was still a fair amount of noise: the shuffling of boots, the thud of horses' hooves, and the laboured breathing of men filled the crystal-clear air. Their hearts beat heavily in their chests. Their veins pulsed in their necks and at their temples. They bared their gums and teeth through their beards, which made their faces look like they were gripped by the rictus of the dead.

Everyone forgot about the Indians. Their only thoughts were for the vast mountains ahead of them, mountains that they would have to overcome one by one.

By mid-afternoon, the Spaniards had conquered only half the slope.

The heat was overwhelming. There wasn't a cloud in the sky. Under the conquistadors' helmets, sweat streamed down their mud-spattered faces that were twisted with effort. They had fixed their crossbows to their saddles a long time ago. The horses were exhausted. Sweat foamed up around their jaws and on their forelegs, and the leather straps of their saddles were soaked with the same fluid. A few animals rolled their eyes and wheezed continually, as though each breath was tearing their lungs.

The soldiers reached a point on the slope so vertiginous that it gave them a bird's-eye view of the country around. Below them the narrow valley of Rimac Tambo appeared no bigger than a tablecloth. And if it hadn't been for the unremitting rumble and the sudden appearance and disappearance of foaming whirlpools on its surface, one would have thought that the gray-blue river was utterly still, like a giant sleeping snake.

De Soto, who had been urging the whole group on since the bottom of the slope, yelled a long-awaited order. The men raised their faces to see a large, flat, grass-covered ledge, a kind of giant balcony halfway up the mountain.

'Half an hour's rest,' shouted the captain.

'Make it an hour!' yelled back a man with a nose so big that it seemed to have been chiselled from a cucumber. 'It's not only the horses who need a rest!'

'Then get a horse to blow up your arse, Soytina, if it'll make you go quicker!' replied de Soto quickly. 'A half-hour, no more. Water the horses and feed 'em the corn we've carted up here: it'll do more good in their bellies than on their backs.'

The men collapsed onto the ground and removed their morions, which had become unbearable. They lay around for a few moments in a stupor before splashing themselves with water from their gourds and wetting the horses' quivering nostrils.

Gabriel remained standing in order to get his breath back faster.

His bay, although its whole barrel shook spasmodically, was holding up well. Gabriel whispered reassuringly as he made it drink slowly. The animal, its ears pricked, was too conscious of its own discomfort to pay him much attention, but the refreshing water and Gabriel's caresses eventually had their effect.

Once his horse had settled a little, Gabriel fumbled around mechanically for the cloth pouch that Anamaya had given him. He took some coca leaves from it. The tasteless, thick juice was gathering in his mouth when de Soto and Hernando de Toro joined him. Seeing him chewing on his ball of coca leaves, de Soto frowned for a moment, but then smiled wearily as he remarked:

'Another hour and I'll be proven right. The hardest part is behind us.'

Gabriel squinted up at the mountain's peak. Apart from the path, the slope was nothing but rocky scree thinly covered in vegetation.

'I'd say another league or so,' he said. 'A league of slope so steep that it makes me think we're climbing to heaven on Jacob's ladder.'

'That's a lovely image,' sighed de Soto.

'Horses don't climb ladders,' remarked Hernando de Toro.

'My point exactly,' said Gabriel, stroking his horse's withers.

De Soto pointed at the slope.

'What bothers me,' he said, 'is that we're now obliged to stay on the path. If we lead the horses off it, they'll break their legs on those rocks.'

'No doubt,' agreed Hernando de Toro, 'but that helps us as well. No man can run across such terrain without breaking his neck.'

Gabriel said nothing. He sensed that the two men were just trying to reassure themselves. All three of them stared at the slope ahead for a while, perhaps hoping that it would disappear.

'They're nowhere to be seen,' murmured de Soto. 'Not a glimpse, not even one of their damned llamas.'

Hernando de Toro wiped his face with his glove.

'It'll be up there that we'll have to be on our toes.'

'I'll lead,' said de Soto, 'and we'll go in groups of four, at intervals. You two bring up the rear.'

De Soto ordered them back on the road. They advanced in groups of four on foot, yanking their horses by the bridle. Their boots seemed heavier with each step. No one wore his padded vest anymore.

The sun was lower now, and their shadows – feeble, flickering silhouettes on the path ahead of them – were longer. Their strength, which ther'd partially recovered during the rest, quickly evaporated. In a few minutes, they were once again swimming in sweat and short of breath.

And then it happened.

They heard a roar so loud that they thought the sky was being torn in two.

They all looked up at the summit together. And they all froze in terror.

'Fucking hell!' murmured Hernando de Toro.

The entire summit was covered in Indian warriors standing shoulder to shoulder. It was impossible to tell how many of them there were, but Gabriel guessed at least two thousand. He felt his throat constrict.

Over two thousand yelling, howling warriors, banging on their shields to the same cacophonous rhythm as the war drums. Over two thousand warriors stamping their feet, waving their axes and clubs, and whirling their slingshots around. Over two thousand men forming a fringe of fierce colours against the mountain's dull green peak, like a flood of liquid poison about to carry the Spaniards away.

'Fucking hell,' repeated Hernando de Toro.

'Into formation!' ordered de Soto, sword in hand.

'Cavalrymen, mount!' shouted another voice.

The Indians up on the ridge were still shouting, but they had broken their line. The first waves of warriors came hurtling down the slope. Despite what Hernando de Toro believed, these men knew how to run through the treacherous scree.

'Watch out for stones! Watch out for their damned stones!' bawled a voice.

Gabriel didn't realize that it was his own. Panic had taken hold all around him. The men were trying simultaneously to fasten their padded vests, take advantage of a narrow rocky ledge to climb into their saddles, draw their swords, detach their morions from their shields, strap their shields to their arms, draw the cords back on their crossbows, and set quarrels in the grooves. But it was all a mess.

'The hackbuts, the arquebuses!' bawled another voice. 'By the Virgin, get the hackbuts set up!'

But it was not to be. The arquebuses were unreachable, packed too deeply in a pack animal's load behind de Soto, who was himself madly whipping his own gelding. The Indians' roar never let up, and actually became more high-pitched and frenetic. The Spaniards stumbled, fell over, and gasped for air, showing the whites of their eyes.

'Mount your horses, by the blood of Christ, mount your god-damned horses!' screamed a voice that Gabriel didn't recognize through the din.

Yet those Spaniards who were already in the saddle couldn't make their horses climb the slope. The Indians spread out through the scree, as agile and as ferociously beautiful as pumas. They were so many, so close, and so colourful that they seemed like an enormous fabric unfurled from the mountaintop.

'Watch out for the stones! The stones!'

Like everyone else, Gabriel placed his shield over his horse's neck. Hundreds of stones came whistling down onto them, hammering into their shields, thudding into their padded vests, and smashing into their exposed legs, faces and necks. It was horrific. Cries and moans erupted from the entire length of the column. The horses shied, fled into the scree, or tried to bolt down the mountainside, utterly terrified.

'Hold the horses!' yelled Gabriel and Hernando de Toro simultaneously.

Gabriel caught a glimpse out of the corner of his eye of de Soto and Ortiz at the head of the column, already fighting with the Indians, striking at them violently with their swords, which threw up showers of sparks each time the steel blades came into contact with the Indians' bronze axes.

A long period of chaos followed. The Indian warriors swarmed at them by the hundreds from all around, continually howling their demented war cries, slinging stones, throwing spears, firing arrows, aiming for the horses as much as for the men. But they were still reluctant to engage in direct, hand-to-hand combat. They danced like butterflies around the panicked horses and the Spaniards, who found themselves hindered by their armor. The Indians made terrifying faces, lunged forward and sliced through the Strangers' leather shields with their axes, or else smashed off their armor with their clubs before retreating quickly to avoid the whistling swords. And then they would start their horrific howling again.

'To the peak! Push for the peak!' growled Gabriel as he urged Hernando de Toro on.

But half the men hadn't even saddled up. They obstructed one another as they stumbled up the narrow path, unable to mount an adequate defence.

Suddenly an appalling animal shriek, followed by another, rose above the din of battle. Marquina's horse had fallen into a trap, a pit lined with sharpened stakes and covered with concealing branches. Spikes impaled its neck and belly, and its spine tore apart audibly, leaving blooms of crimson gore pooling along its back. Its eyes bulging in terror, the animal struggled desperately, worsening its agony, and pissed blood like a scarlet fountain. Marquina, unhurt, managed to clamber out of the pit with a helping hand from Soytina. They tried to climb back onto the road, but they weren't quick enough: half a dozen Indians pounced on them. An ax cleaved deeply into the foot soldier's back while a club smashed into his face, shattering his nose and instantly transforming his face into a gruel of blood, smashed cartilage and hacked flesh.

As for Marquina, he had fallen to the ground as three Indians leaped upon him. All three clubbed his head in a coordinated effort, splitting his skull in two. The Spaniards, stupefied, watched as the Indians dragged the cavalryman's corpse onto the scree, roaring with joy as his brain's blood and pulped tissue left a grisly trail across the stones.

The deafening noise echoed through the air like the nightmarish screeching of a giant flock of hellish birds.

'Stop!' Anamaya ordered the bearers carrying her palanquin.

Since leaving Manco the night before, they had taken only the less frequented mountain paths on their return trip to Cuzco in order to avoid Guaypar and Quizquiz's men.

The cacophony continued, shockingly violent. Its force made the very leaves of the trees shake.

The officer of the guard turned to Anamaya:

'Those are battle cries.'

Everyone listened intently. The violent noise persisted.

Anamaya found that she was holding her breath. She felt a knot harder than stone growing in her gut.

'There are a lot of them,' remarked the officer.

She didn't need to close her eyes to imagine the scene.

She knew that she shouldn't worry for the Strangers' safety, yet she was deeply, deeply concerned for them.

'They're at Rimac Tambo,' she murmured.

'Yes,' agreed the officer. 'The Strangers must be trying to cross the Vicaconga peak. It's a good place for a trap. Quizquiz likes it up there.'

The din seemed to subside a little, but then it grew even louder and more high-pitched, even more ferocious. In her mind's eye Anamaya imagined the innumerable warriors hurtling down the scree, down a slope so steep that even the palanquin's sure-footed bearers sometimes used ropes to cope with it.

She tried not to think about Gabriel. But the moment she had heard the battle cries she had remembered Manco's words, and the chill that she had felt when he had spoken them. Gabriel was in peril.

She felt it: her whole body felt it. She knew that he was over there in the thick of the battle.

She wanted to be reasonable with herself about it. But the love she had for him actually caused a physical pain in her heart, as though a great weight was pressing upon her.

The cries continued to echo through the cold forest air of the pass.

Anamaya was trembling. She began murmuring a prayer to herself without realizing it: 'Oh Inti, Oh Force of the Other World, Oh Sun, Father of all our Ancestors, Oh Quilla, our Mother, do not block the Puma's bound. Oh Emperor who elected me, do not abandon me on the road to which you led me. Oh you who divide day from night, do not carry him away to the Under World and leave me here alone.'

With a great effort, she regained her composure. She saw

that all the soldiers and bearers around her were watching her, utterly amazed. But they all looked away as she turned her gaze upon them.

Suddenly thunder roared above the war cries echoing through the air. Anamaya recognized the sound of the Strangers' fire-spitting sticks. Another explosion startled the bearers. Yet its echo had hardly faded before the warriors resumed their furious howling, now with even greater rage and power.

In a flat voice, Anamaya gave the order:

'Let us turn around. I want to return to Rimac Tambo as fast as possible.'

How long had they been fighting? Gabriel had no idea. The blood-covered bodies of the combatants cast long shadows.

The chaos of the battle and the noise of the Indians' cries were unremitting. The hail of stones, the blows of swords and axes, and the showers of arrows never let up. The horses' flanks shone with blood. The Spaniards had eventually managed to load their crossbows and fire them at point-blank range, sometimes killing two Indians with one shot. Yet the Inca warriors, instead of being discouraged, fought with even greater fury. They were familiar with these contraptions now: they knew that they took time to reload, and in the pauses they fell upon the cavalrymen with terrifying cries.

Gabriel maneuvered his bay around the ditch-trap and then whipped its croup hard, giving the horse its head. The animal bounded forward furiously through the fray, ploughing itself a passage to the peak. A group of Indians grabbed hold of the tail of the horse ridden by the cavalryman alongside Gabriel, hoping to stop the animal and bring down its rider. With a mad cry, Gabriel lunged forward and brought his sword whistling down, slicing clean through an Indian arm and the horse's tail. The Indian stumbled backward, howling in pain. Gabriel could see the fear in his eyes. He crossed his dagger and his sword and parried a blow from an ax, then kicked his assailant hard in the gut, sending him tumbling down the slope.

Hernando de Toro yelled from above:

'De Soto is at the peak! He's made it!'

He was interrupted by a berserk charge by a group of Indians.

He and Gabriel defended a passage beside the stake-lined pit, allowing the rest of the column to pass. The two men seemed to be everywhere at once, increasingly short of breath, blocking the strikes from the Indians' axes and clubs without ever finding the opportunity to counterattack.

Then Hernando de Toro let out an agonized cry. Gabriel saw him stagger, a pike lodged in his thigh. He rushed toward his companion, windmilling his long sword through the air, giving de Toro enough time to tear the spear out of his flesh.

'Go on!' shouted Gabriel. 'Go up to the peak – I'll guard your back!'

His voice was lost in the blast of the two arquebuses firing simultaneously.

But the Indians felled by the shots were ten paces away from de Soto at the peak. Hundreds more stood between him and Gabriel – so many, in fact, that they hindered one another.

The smell of burned gunpowder drifting through the air seemed to increase their rage.

The rear of the column was advancing at a snail's pace. The horses were exhausted. Hernando de Toro was dragging himself over the ground, pulling himself along by grabbing rocks and bushes, while Gabriel, guarding the right flank, kept the Indians at bay, hacking through their arms and chests. The veins in his temples throbbed, his pounding blood clouding his vision. His sword felt increasingly heavy and he was using it less effectively – its blade was now slicing through air more often than through flesh. He felt overcome by an indescribable weariness, as though he too was crawling on his hands and knees. He felt suffocated by the stench of blood and fear. He hardly noticed when an Indian bounded forward and leaped on Hernando de Toro.

The fight was over quickly. De Toro, in a last desperate effort to stay alive, thrust his dagger upward as the Indian brought the star-shaped head of his club crashing down on de Toro's head, one of its spikes piercing through his cheek and shattering his jaw. Wide-eyed, the Spaniard watched helplessly as the Indian brought his club up one last time to deliver the death blow.

Gabriel spun around and bounded forward. Blood streamed off his sword as he swung it through the air. Its steel blade sliced through the Indian's neck. But Gabriel had struck him so hard that the force of the impact jolted the sword from his hands.

And then Gabriel had the most odd, unearthly experience: his fear was lifted from him. Time seemed to slow right down. Exhaustion and blood-soaked weariness engulfed and insulated him.

He picked himself up slowly, his dagger hanging from his dangling hand. From his place of stillness in the center of all the chaos, he looked at the faces of the warriors of the Empire of the Four Cardinal directions. They did not wear the resigned expressions of those who had allowed themselves to be massacred at Cajamarca or at Hatun Sausa. They were the faces of fighters who had recovered their lost pride.

Gabriel heard de Soto calling out to him. The captain's voice was so faint that he could have been shouting from a great distance. But a sling stone reached Gabriel even faster than the sound of his name.

He heard the sound of its impact against his morion. And then – blackness.

Night was closing in by the time Anamaya, from her palanquin, made out the terraces of Rimac Tambo in the distance.

Shouting and drumming could still be heard from the heights of Vilcaconga. A number of wounded warriors had made it back to the river. Some were in such a shockingly bad state – their arms missing, their chests or backs cut to pieces – that they collapsed on its bank and died the moment they touched its icy water.

Anamaya had told the officer of the guard to send two men on ahead for news. Now the pair had returned and were kneeling in front of her palanquin. Despite the growing darkness, Anamaya could tell from the looks on their faces that the news was terrible.

'Speak!' she ordered, her tone studiedly neutral.

'Two thousand soldiers from General Quizquiz's army, under the command of Captain Guaypar, lay in wait for the Strangers at the mountain peak. They let the Strangers climb most of the way up so that they would exhaust their own strength and that of their beasts and so wouldn't be able to move as quickly as they usually do.'

The man fell silent, his eyes lowered, his neck bent subserviently. Anamaya could tell that he had yet to tell her the most important news.

'Continue,' she commanded.

'Five Strangers were killed by the soldiers, *Coya Camaquen*, and many were wounded. Two of their big llamas were also killed.'

Anamaya had to use all her strength to conceal her fear.

She said in a measured voice:

'And now?'

'The Strangers have managed to reach the peak. They have taken refuge there and are resting their horses. Guaypar's men have suspended their attack. But tomorrow, at dawn, the commanders will give the order to bring down a rain of flaming arrows on them, to frighten the horses.'

The drums and nighttime war songs echoed down from the mountainside. Anamaya thought about Guaypar for a moment, of his murderous rage, his insanity, and his expert knowledge of warfare and of the Strangers. He was surely up there, and no doubt he had ordered all the noise in order to prevent the Strangers from sleeping, from gaining a moment's rest through the night. At first light, massacring Gabriel and his companions would be child's play.

Anamaya caught the eye of the officer of the guard. She could see that he was troubled, and she could easily guess why: the Empire's warriors were killing the Strangers for the first time, and were on the point of winning a real battle against them. He wanted to rejoice – but he didn't dare do so in front of her.

She stepped down from her palanquin and gestured to the young officer to accompany her away from all the people. Down below, between the river and Rimac Tambo, she saw fires burning, and by their light she could make out peasants bringing food to the injured warriors as they arrived in small groups. Many seemed to have broken limbs, and they collapsed as they reached the sanctuary of the fires.

'Officer,' said Anamaya, 'you know that I have conferred with Emperor Manco.'

At the mere mention of the Emperor's name, the man bowed.

'I know it, *Coya Camaquen*.'

'He wishes for peace throughout the Empire, and for peace with the Strangers. Those attacking them up there are violating his wish.'

The officer said nothing.

'The Emperor wants us to help the Strangers reach Cuzco, where he wishes to receive them and demonstrate to them the extent of his power,' Anamaya said in a clear voice. 'And we must do this even if we have to fight our own people who are disobeying him! There is but *one* Emperor, and we must all obey his will. Do you understand me, officer?'

The officer said nothing for a moment before slowly lifting his head.

'Yes, *Coya Camaquen*. I will do as you command.'

'I thank you for it, and I shall not forget your loyalty.'

But Anamaya could see the sadness in the officer's eyes as he said quietly:

'I have learned that there is a troop of Strangers on horse-back not far from here, on the royal road to the other side of Apurimac.'

Anamaya had to stop herself from crying out joyfully.

'Then you are to send men to meet them,' she ordered. 'Let them cross the river as soon as possible. The Strangers must be here before dawn.'

As Gabriel regained consciousness, he knew that it was night. He was also sure that the hellish pain in his head was not going to subside anytime soon. He felt a fine rain falling lightly on his face.

'Dreadful blow, Gabriel, an absolutely dreadful blow,' muttered de Soto as he stood up, his fingers sticky with blood.

Gabriel sensed that there were a number of men around him even though he was unable to see them. De Soto's face was obscured by shifting shadows.

'Don't try to move, my friend,' said de Soto, his voice hoarse from shouting. 'We're looking after you, and we're all going to make it out of here.'

But Gabriel doubted it. He wanted to smile and say something to de Soto, to ask him how many men they had lost, if de Soto could mount a reasonable defence with the remainder, if the wounded could be saved. The wounded apart from himself, that was, because he was sure that he was going to die. And he accepted this fate with unusual calm, feeling completely composed. Quite the opposite of blind terror in the face of personal extinction, in fact: the idea of dying actually calmed him greatly.

But he was unable to utter a single word coherently, only a long groan that he couldn't hear himself. What was also strange was that suddenly his head no longer hurt, whereas now his left arm ached unbearably.

Gabriel couldn't remember the exact sequence of events after Hernando de Toro had been killed. He remembered being dragged to the top of the slope, surrounded by battling Indians. That was when his arm had become stuck between two rocks and had almost been broken.

But he was still sure that while his arm might be aching, death itself was eating away at his head. He had lost a lot of blood, and his face was covered in a sticky crust. His head had been bandaged with the blanket of a dead horse. But it was impossible to concentrate for long on any aspect of his condition: no part of him seemed to be functioning normally – not his hearing, not his vision, not his voice.

Gabriel could see – just about – that it was night, but he didn't know whether it would be his last one.

He wondered whether the battle was over.

He wondered whether the Indians were still howling their war cries.

Gabriel thought he could make out some cries, and the sound

of a horn. He wondered whether he was entering the realm of the dead, and whether the trumpets and cries were accompanying him into it. He mused that he was like a fragile boat being carried away on an unstoppable tide. The sound of the trumpets became increasingly terrifying, increasingly unbearable. He had but one desire left: to slip even deeper into the darkness, to be delivered from his agony by death.

Gabriel surrendered to the comfortable numbness that was reaching out to gather him into its seductive embrace.

CHAPTER 14

Vilcaconga, night of 8 November 1533

THEY DIDN'T PAUSE ONCE, NOT EVEN TO GATHER THEIR breath. Indians and Spaniards marched without respite to Rimac Tambo, stopping neither for the night's darkness nor for the sticky humidity that made their clothes cling damply to their skin.

Anamaya remembered, during her climb, the dreadful ambush in which the Elders, Huayna Capac's loyal servants had lost their lives, victims of Huascar's madness. And as she came across the first evidence of the battle – the broken weapons, the groaning wounded, the dismembered corpses – it seemed to her that that atrocity was repeating itself, or that this latest horror was a reply to the first.

She and her escort, along with the Spaniards accompanying them, came across the stake-lined pit in which the bodies of a horse and two conquistadors lay, their faces battered by the stones fired from slings. The Strangers cried out in anger, and for a moment Anamaya was frightened that they would turn their rage against her. But de Almagro was already haranguing his men, urging them to push on.

'We can do nothing for these poor souls! We must get up to the peak where de Soto is waiting for us, at the mercy of those damned Indians about to massacre them all!'

From the nearby mountain they could hear Guaypar's men shouting triumphantly, the muffled sound of their war chants, the roll of their drums, and the wail of their horns. Anamaya knew that the Incas, as a rule, never fought at night. Nevertheless, with a leader like Guaypar, anything was possible. What if, emboldened by their initial success, they had resolved to massacre the Strangers in the night?

She could hear the labored gasps of the Spanish soldiers behind her as they struggled up the scree-covered slope, leading their horses by the reins.

She shut her eyes every now and then and thought of Gabriel, imagining that she was being drawn to him up the mountain by her violent desire to be with him, to touch him, and to reassure herself that he was still alive.

When they reached the peak, Guaypar's warriors stopped their racket. Perhaps they were on the move, having been warned of the arrival of Spanish reinforcements. The horses that had come up earlier were so exhausted that they didn't even lift their heads to watch the newcomers arrive. But de Soto's men ran to meet them, crying out joyfully. Anamaya looked on as the Spaniards embraced one another, and she saw what looked to her like a gathering of shadows, standing tight against each other, utterly motionless at the very edge of the rock mantle. They were as black as the night surrounding them, and seemed to belong neither to the everyday world nor to the Other.

What remained of Captain de Soto's column had lit no fires so as to avoid creating easy targets in the darkness of the night. A horse lay to one side, and two exhausted men, lying on the muddy ground, tried wearily to get up. A faint moan reached her from further away. De Almagro rushed up to the captain.

'De Soto!'

De Soto barely moved. He was too tired to speak, saluting his compatriot with a wave instead. The upper part of his chain mail, torn to pieces, and his breeches, stiff with congealed blood, bore witness to the fury of the battle. But the icy, troubled mask of rage on his face told far more.

'How many have we lost?' asked de Almagro.

'Five, as far as I know,' sighed de Soto. 'De Marquina, Soytina,

Hernando de Toro, Ruiz, and de Rodas. And a sixth probably won't make it through the night, if he hasn't died already . . .'

'Who?'

'Gabriel.'

'Montelucar y Flores?' asked de Almagro with the thinnest of smiles. 'Francisco's protégé?'

De Soto nodded. Anamaya startled him when she grabbed him by the arm and said:

'Where is he?'

'What are you doing here?' growled de Soto, pulling his arm away.

'Her escort brought us the news of the attack,' said de Almagro.

'Please,' insisted Anamaya, 'where is he?'

De Soto nodded toward the group of shadows that she had noticed earlier.

'Over there, with the other wounded.'

Anamaya ran. The *Coya Camaquen*, to the utter astonishment of her escort, ran all the way to the groaning bodies that seemed about to blend into the night.

None of the Spaniards tending to the wounded protested when she pushed her way through them and kneeled at Gabriel's side. A blanket lay over him, covering him up to his neck. Another, rolled up, lay under his head, which was wrapped in a ragged blanket. He was breathing, albeit very shallowly, through barely opened lips, and his eyelids trembled feverishly. Anamaya brushed her fingers against his cheek, and they became coated with his cold sweat.

She was breathing heavily, searching for a calm center within herself, refusing to surrender to her fear. Yet when she felt a hand settle gently on her shoulder, she cried out in terror.

'Let me do this . . .'

She recognized Bartholomew's quiet voice, and looked up into his gray eyes.

'I can help him,' Bartholomew said.

'What are you going to do?' she asked in a low voice.

'My duty: help him pass into the Other World in a Christian manner.'

Anamaya stared at him for a moment, and then shook her head violently. She pushed him away and said:

'No! If that's your duty, then take it elsewhere and leave me with him!'

Their was no bitterness in her words, only a determination that stopped Bartholomew from replying. He watched her bend down and whisper into Gabriel's ear. He heard her murmur to him in a strange mix of Quechua and Castilian. Then she slipped her hands under the blanket and placed them on the wounded man's chest. She began slowly massaging the area over his heart. Without lifting her head, she said in Spanish:

'Light a fire to each side of him and bring more blankets.'

Anamaya seemed unconcerned about whether she had been obeyed or even heard. She repeated her order in Quechua to the soldiers of her escort, who were standing to one side and watching her, the looks on their faces as incredulous as the Spaniards'.

'Do as she says!' barked Bartholomew.

A few moments later, as the first flames rose from the piles of dry twigs, de Soto ran up, shouting:

'Have you lost your minds? I said no fires!'

Anamaya had bared Gabriel's torso and was rubbing fine mud into it. She answered de Soto without stopping her ministrations.

'The battle is over, Lord de Soto. You will not be attacked, not tonight nor tomorrow. Have you not noticed that the war drums have stopped?'

And, without waiting for a reply, she gave further orders in Quechua before lying on Gabriel as though about to make love to him. Indians ran off and came back with *mantas*, which they piled up on the pair.

De Soto's rage was stifled by his bewilderment. Bartholomew raised his joined fingers and said:

'She is right, Captain de Soto. Let her be, I beg you . . .'

Soon two great braziers were blazing beside them, flooding the rock ledge with light and illuminating the vacant, weary faces of the wounded.

Anamaya never stopped caressing Gabriel's inert body under

the blankets. She blew on his naked flesh as though trying to breathe the flames of life back into him. She took her pouch of coca leaves from her belt, chewed some quickly, and let the juice run from her lips into her lover's mouth. She continued to massage his chest, forcing his heart to keep beating. Eventually, long after the noise of the camp had subsided, she heard a faint groan rise from Gabriel's throat. Soon after, spasms shook his belly.

Anamaya made Gabriel take more coca juice. His breathing became stronger, deeper, and more hoarse. His heart beat more firmly against his ribs. Anamaya put first her lips and then her reddened cheeks to his chest. She was overcome by a timid, fearful joy, as though life was being reborn in her as much as in him.

CHAPTER 15

Vilcaconga, 10 November 1533

B ROTHER BARTHOLOMEW PAUSED JUST OUTSIDE THE tent. He could see Anamaya and Gabriel through its raised flaps.

Gabriel lay awake on a pile of blankets at the back of tent, his face washed and shaved, his head wrapped in a sort of blue turban. Wide-eyed, he was kissing the hands of his pretty friend, the young Indian girl who was some kind of influential princess among the Incas. And also some kind of magician.

For a fraction of a second, Bartholomew hesitated, unsure whether to continue or to turn back. He realized that the two young lovers hadn't noticed his presence and so he did neither, allowing himself to indulge in the minor sin of curiosity.

Bartholomew smiled. Certainly the young Indian girl was a magician! What he had seen her accomplish two nights ago would have earned her the Inquisition's stake back in Spain.

The two lovers were now kissing one another tenderly. Anamaya put Gabriel's injured arm gently to one side, and stroked his cheek, giggling. For a fraction of a second, she looked just like any young girl in love anywhere.

But in the following moment she straightened and became once more the reserved princess who controlled her movements carefully, and who wore a severe expression that did her beauty a disservice. She had seen Bartholomew.

Gabriel followed his lover's gaze and saw him too. Bartholomew

stepped forward and greeted them without a hint of embar-
rassment.

'Well now, it seems to me that we have a real Lazarus here,
brought back to life!' he said lightly.

But he did not laugh. His attempt at levity notwithstanding, the
princess's gaze never failed to sober him. Bartholomew greeted her
with a brief nod.

'Don't be afraid of me,' he told her.

Anamaya stared at him, her expression blank. In fact, *he* was
the one who was slightly uncomfortable, as though he knew that
she had the ability to see right into the depths of his soul, to see
even those darker complexities of his inner self that he himself
would have preferred to forget. He was irrationally relieved when
he thought he saw the briefest good-humored flash in her stunning
blue-eyed gaze, but it had crossed her expression so swiftly that he
couldn't be sure of it.

The princess said something quickly to Gabriel in Quechua.
Then she fastened the clasp of her silk *manta* and left the tent,
moving with a grace and poise that would have impressed the
Queen of Spain herself.

Bartholomew followed her with his gaze. He heard Gabriel say
to him from behind:

'Please don't misunderstand her, Brother Bartholomew. Anamaya
appreciates you. But she mistrusts all Spaniards.'

'Well, you shouldn't complain about that.'

'Why not?'

'You should have seen how she pushed me away from you. I,
like everyone else, had given you up for dead, whereas she still
saw the life in you.'

The monk spoke with a lightness of spirit that charmed Gabriel,
whose own spirit was still fuddled from the blows he had received
in battle. He smiled wearily as the monk continued:

'One thing is for sure, though: she saved your life. I saw her
do so with my own eyes.'

Bartholomew looked at Gabriel for a moment. He had closed
his eyes. Without opening them, he smiled as he asked:

'Pray tell me all about it, Brother Bartholomew. She wouldn't

tell me anything. And I remember nothing, except for the cold—'
he shivered as he remembered it '—and seeing the blue of her
eyes when I regained consciousness.'

'Everyone but God had given you up for dead – Captain de Soto
being the first to do so,' said Bartholomew. 'And, in fact, you were
responding to nothing. We could no longer hear you breathing. De
Soto asked me to give you the last rites. I was about to do so when
she reached you.'

Gabriel couldn't help but grin as he imagined the scene.

'And do you know what she did?' continued Bartholomew. 'She
lit a fire on either side of you and lay against you until morning,
to warm you. I must say that the two of you were quite a sight.
Everyone was impressed.'

Gabriel let his imagination run wild. His throat constricted from
the strength of the emotion he was feeling. He opened his eyes
and tried to hide his emotion with irony, asking:

'And you allowed this scandalous behaviour?'

Bartholomew nodded. He ran his joined fingers pensively across
his chin.

'Yes. I admit that it was a little . . . unorthodox, shall we say. But
amid all the chaos that night, amid all the suffering, her actions
seemed almost . . . normal.'

He paused, then added:

'Although, having said that, my friend, it would be best if
those who weren't actually there were never to hear about what
happened. Do you understand me?'

Gabriel didn't react. He felt the warmth growing in his body,
and realized that he must have been on the threshold of death
for Anamaya to abandon herself so completely to him. *To think
that I wasn't conscious enough to make the most of the opportunity*,
he thought to himself. He smiled wickedly at the idea.

Bartholomew shook his head and added:

'The next day, as soon as you were lodged in this tent, the
princess smeared a clay that she had brought from the riverbank
over your wounds. After that, she had you drink vast quantities
of some concoction of her own devising.'

'That's all?' asked Gabriel, surprised.

'That's all. And it was plenty.'

'How do you mean?'

'Because you are alive.'

Bartholomew said this in a tone that made Gabriel feel ill at ease.

'Certainly,' continued Bartholomew, 'you *were* a little delirious. But in a happy way. You thought, it seemed to me, that you were some kind of wildcat. I had trouble understanding you because you spoke the language of your pretty friend rather than Castilian. I'm learning it, as you know, but I have yet to progress beyond the most elementary level.'

'It must have been a pain-relieving decoction,' said Gabriel. 'The Indians are well versed in the anesthetic qualities of plants, and Anamaya – I mean, the princess – knows their secrets well. It's not unusual in these parts.'

'No doubt. But the strangest thing, do you see, was that your head wound immediately stopped bleeding. You can see for yourself that it is already cicatrizing, as is the gash on your arm.'

The gentleness of Bartholomew's tone made Gabriel shudder a little. It reminded him of conversations he had had – a long time ago now – back in Spain. It reminded him of that quality peculiar to men of the cloth, that insidious smile they wore when they were laying a web of words in which to trap the unwary.

'What are you trying to say?' he asked.

'The beautiful princess has led me to think a lot about our situation,' Bartholomew said earnestly. 'Is it true what they say, that she has certain powers, and that she has influence over the Inca Emperor himself?'

Gabriel straightened, his face hard. His friendliness toward the monk had completely evaporated, and his old distrust had returned.

'If you're thinking, even for an instant, of orchestrating some political intrigue, then you are completely in the wrong of it, Brother Bartholomew. Anamaya is not some sort of demon disguised as a woman.'

'Did I say that?'

'I would prefer it if you didn't even *think* it.'

'You are mistaken, my friend.'

Bartholomew seemed genuinely surprised. He laughed with real candor, placing his strangely deformed hand on Gabriel's shoulder.

'What do you think, Gabriel? That I wish your friend harm? Or else do you resent me for having helped you see clearly the truth in your heart when you would have otherwise succumbed to confusion and doubt?'

Gabriel dismissed the monk's allusion with a disdainful grimace.

'I've never seen a man of the cloth put up with what he doesn't understand for very long.'

'No!' protested Bartholomew, sitting up straight, 'No, you have not understood me at all, Gabriel. I did not come to this land to add to its suffering, but to fight against it – if such a thing is possible. You must believe me!'

'We shall see,' replied Gabriel dryly, returning to his pile of blankets.

Bartholomew looked at him for a few moments.

'As Christ is my witness, my friend, let me tell you that what interests me most is precisely that which you mention: experiencing the unknowable.'

Gabriel watched him leave the tent.

He closed his eyes, exhausted. Despite the hostility he still felt, he remembered that if it had not been for that strange monk and his disconcerting benevolence, he might never have had the courage to say goodbye to Anamaya. Then he would never have heard her say 'I love you' to him, words that remained with him still and that perhaps had saved his life.

But it was too late to call Bartholomew back.

Gabriel fell asleep with a smile on his lips.

CHAPTER 16

Rimac Tambo, 13 November 1533

'GO IN PEACE,' SAID VALVERDE.

The Spaniards, all of them armed, were standing as a group in the vast square of the *tambo*. They had listened to the Mass with exceptional reverence, and there had been none of the usual murmuring or whispered conversations – no noise at all, in fact, except for the occasional neigh of a horse and the continual murmur of the nearby brook in the background.

Despite the priest's signal that the Mass was over, none of them moved.

In the middle of the square stood a hastily built platform on which lay the shroud-covered corpses of those Spaniards who had died in battle. All those gathered there that day could not tear their gazes from it.

Gabriel was hampered by his wounded arm, stiff and in a sling. He hadn't donned his chain mail as the others had, but rather wore only his usual leather-covered, padded-cotton breastplate, now stained with his own blood.

Even the most loyal of their Indian allies averted their eyes whenever they encountered a Spaniard. As for the noblemen accompanying Chalkuchimac, it was as if they had disappeared in the mountains: the general himself hadn't left his palanquin since daybreak.

Don Francisco Pizarro walked through the ranks to stand before the bodies on the platform in the square's centre, along with

Valverde. He wore his full suit of armor, from which only his small head emerged, like that of some bird. He looked at each individual gathered there, and each man met his commander's gaze. And as their looks met, they experienced that fervor once again, just as they had the night before the battle at Cajamarca, when the distinctions between noble cavalrymen and lowly foot soldiers, between rich and poor had disappeared.

'You are grieving,' said Pizarro in a firm voice. 'And you are angry.'

He turned around and pointed at the shrouded corpses.

'They were our friends, and they were brave soldiers and I want you to remember their names: Juan Alonso de Rodas, Gaspar de Marquina, Francisco Martin Soytina, Miguel Ruiz, Hernando de Toro.'

He enunciated each name as though he was invoking the Saints.

'They came from the Basque country, from Seville, from my own dear Extramadura. Some were light-skinned, others dark. Some could read and write whilst others knew only how to fight. Some fought on horseback, others on foot. They died victims of treachery, but they died nobly, as men.'

Gabriel glanced at Hernando de Soto's impassive face. Pizarro continued:

'I know that some of you are asking why. I shall tell you.'

With a broad sweep of his arm that made his armor clang, Pizarro gestured at the mountain looming over Vilcaconga. His hand remained pointing at the peak and the horizon beyond it.

'I remember,' he said, almost laughing, 'I remember those who doubted that we would find this kingdom of gold. But I always knew that we would, my children, I always knew that we would. Well then, here we are at the gates of the capital of this kingdom of gold. Do you hear me?'

His eyes shone as though they were nuggets of gold themselves, and the eyes of his men began to blaze with the same lustre. Pizarro lowered his voice a little as he turned his gaze back to the dead bodies.

'But do you imagine that for mere gold – even for all that the capital of this kingdom of gold has to offer – do you imagine that

I can forget who killed these men, these brave soldiers, so far from their homes in Spain?'

'No! No!'

As the cries rose from the crowd, Gabriel sensed their growing thirst for vengeance.

'Then keep the memory of your fallen comrades close to your hearts, my dear, dear children,' insisted the Governor ardently. 'Keep it in the very depths of your hearts, and know that one day you shall bring it to light again – with the blades of your swords!'

As Gabriel climbed up the Vilcaconga mountain, he had the irrational feeling that ghosts lurked behind the bushes and rocks and in the riverbed. His watchful eyes kept deceiving him with images of thousands of warriors charging at him, and his ears misled him with the phantom sounds of their battle cries and the neighing of terrified horses. It was a cool day and he was walking slowly, yet he was soaking with sweat.

He had insisted on walking ahead, but his step was heavy on the slippery path and the impact of each step sent shooting pains through his injured arm.

'Does Your Grace grow tired?'

Without turning around, Gabriel shot back:

'His Grace almost had his head cut from his body trying to save your African ass!'

Sebastian, dressed in his usual spectacularly colorful outfit, guffawed and came up alongside his friend.

'My master marched us at double pace in order to reach you in time . . .'

He paused, and then continued:

'. . . But they say that de Soto is so eager to get to Cuzco that he—'

'By God! What is that?'

Gabriel pointed at the rapier dangling from Sebastian's side.

'Why, have you never seen a sword before, *caballero*?'

'Where did you get it?'

'It was presented to me with all due pomp and ceremony by

Don Diego de Almagro himself, as a reward for my past services and on the condition that I swear my allegiance to my God, my King, and to Don Diego de Almagro himself,' recited Sebastian like a schoolboy.

Gabriel whistled, impressed.

'In which order?'

'In the order of whoever asks for my services first.'

'And may one inquire as to how you intend to use it?'

'Ah! As for that, well . . .'

Sebastian shrugged. The air around them had grown darker, despite the cloudless, almost white sky. They were walking now through a thick stand of trees and could sense that the mountain's peak was at the end of it.

'I had hoped that you would give me a few lessons,' said Sebastian hesitantly.

Gabriel looked at him questioningly.

'You're determined to get yourself killed, aren't you?'

'Me? You're talking nonsense, schoolboy. What's more, I'm bound to my sword.'

'Ah yes? What does the engraving on it read?'

'*Mi dama es mi ley.*'[1]

'It's a nice thought.'

'Yes . . . still, it didn't bring its previous owner much luck.'

'Who was that?'

'Miguel Ruiz.'

The two men fell silent. Ruiz had been one of Gabriel's comrades who had fallen during the battle at Vilcaconga. Certainly, he had been a nasty piece of work, but now he was one buried in the ground. What was more, he had been the son of a gentleman of Seville and his African slave-girl.

They came out from the trees and were blinded by the brightness of the sun. As his eyes adjusted, Gabriel made out the peak.

And seven black shadows standing silhouetted against it.

*   *   *

[1] 'My lady is my law.'

Anamaya had been lurking around Chalkuchimac's palanquin all morning. She had invited Inguill to take her place in her own, while Anamaya walked alongside the Inca general's, despite the manifest hostility of the Spanish soldiers – who had put him in chains again – and despite the smell of fear and death that surrounded him.

She leaned toward the hanging of fine alpaca wool, decorated with a black and white checkered motif against a red background, that enclosed the general's palanquin.

'Chalkuchimac?'

'I hear you.'

Anamaya smiled. The seasoned Inca warrior's gruff, unyielding voice held a special meaning for her.

'I listened to the Strangers speaking among themselves this morning, and they spoke of you with particular hatred. They hold you responsible for what happened.'

'Don't worry about me.'

'If you want to escape, now's the time . . .'

A bitter laugh came through the hanging.

'If I had wanted to escape, I would have done so a long time ago.'

Because the path was so narrow, Anamaya managed to keep some distance between herself and the Spanish soldiers, who were obliged to march only in front of and behind the palanquin, not beside it. The general continued:

'They have no proof whatsoever, and only I can convince Quizquiz and Guaypar to lay down their weapons.'

Anamaya felt fear flutter in her heart.

'You know as well as I do that they don't need any proof. And since I am the one who chose Manco, and you can't—'

'It wasn't you who chose Manco, you strange girl, but our father, Huayna Capac. Today you are all going to make peace with the Strangers, but tomorrow . . .'

The rest of the general's words were lost in an inaudible murmur. The road was widening now, and already the Spanish soldiers were approaching her menacingly.

'Tomorrow, all the Incas and all the Indians shall unite to fight a war against the Strangers, and you shall lead them . . .'

A Spanish soldier pushed Anamaya.

'What treacheries are you plotting now?'

She looked at him with contempt but made no reply. The anxiety that Chalkuchimac's words had planted in her heart grew as she stepped away from the general's palanquin. She foresaw war, destruction and bloodshed.

And she saw the faces of Gabriel and Manco, so close together that they were almost touching, forehead against forehead, mouth against mouth, the blond curls of one becoming intertwined with the long black hair of the other.

'So that's him,' Gabriel said to himself upon seeing the young Emperor, wrapped in his yellow cotton cape and standing a little in front of the others, his expression somehow both proud and timid.

Over time Gabriel had learned to distinguish between the Inca's faces – faces that at first had seemed to him all identical, not unlike those gold llama figurines that the Spaniards had amassed in thousands at Cajamarca and that, each one practically indistinguishable from the next, had been melted down to make ingots.

He remembered Atahualpa's bloodshot eyes, Guaypar's arrogant gaze, Chalkuchimac's rugged features. But what he saw on this young man's face was something altogether different.

He saw an august stateliness, as well as evidence of suffering and indications of strength. He saw a youthfulness that had already lived a thousand lives, a young man who had seen death at first hand and at an age when most children were still playing games.

The small group of Incas watched the Spaniards arrive one by one on the mountain's peak. They appeared to be completely unafraid of the Strangers, or else were simply determined not to move an inch. Gabriel, the first to reach the peak, approached them straightaway, without waiting for Pizarro or the interpreters. The young Emperor said to him in a firm voice:

'I am Manco Inca Capac. I am the son of the Inca Huayna

Capac, and I have been elected by the Elders to be Emperor of
the Empire of the Four Cardinal Directions.'

'I know it,' said Gabriel in Quechua.

Manco showed no sign of surprise. He stared intently at
Gabriel.

'Is your *Machu Kapitu* far from here?' he asked eventually.

'He will be here soon.'

Gabriel took in the breathtaking view from the peak. Beyond the
steep slopes of the Apurimac valley, the landscape broadened into
a vast plateau surrounded by gentle hills. He could see the houses
of Jaquijaguana clustered together on their slopes, and a mountain
pass beyond them.

The last pass, beyond which lay the city of gold.

He turned back to the Incas, who were watching the Spaniards
and their horses stream out onto the peak. Five noblemen of
about Manco's age stood behind him, large gold discs stretching
their earlobes. A little further back stood another Indian who was
shorter and older than the others and whose skin was darker. He
wore an odd square hat over his long hair, hair that streamed down
to his shoulders. He was looking not at the Spaniards, as were the
others, but at the distant mountains.

Don Francisco arrived at the same time as his brothers, and was
followed by de Almagro, de Soto, de Candia, and the rest of the
Spanish commanders.

The Governor took Manco's hand between his own and lavished
compliments and declarations of goodwill upon him. The young
Inca smiled somewhat shyly, but showed no other emotion as he
listened to the Spaniard's formulaic diplomacy.

'The Cuzco clans and I,' said Manco, 'have had to endure the
crimes and aggression of those from the north who wished to rule
over us, in violation of my father Huayna Capac's will.'

'I know,' said Pizarro cheerfully. 'That is why I have crossed these
godforsaken mountains to help you.'

'It was they who attacked your army, not my people. We
want peace.'

Pizarro's smile grew broader.

'Then we are brothers, for I too want peace, I have not

come all this way to go to war with you or to steal your treasures!'

'To me,' said Manco, without batting an eyelid, 'peace means that I rule over my people, who are, of course, at peace with the Strangers who visit us.'

'We have the same understanding of peace, then. Please be assured that we have come to help you and your people return to your capital in peace, and to make sure that you will not have to suffer the treachery of the northern clans any longer.'

The two men smiled at each other.

'I want to tell you,' continued Manco, 'that the armies of General Quizquiz and Captain Guaypar are marching on Cuzco. They intend to raze it to the ground so that you shall find no treasure there at all, nor any food for your men.'

'We shan't let them. And we shall put an end to the treachery of he whom we had welcomed as a friend, and who has ever since been giving orders to destroy us by secret messengers. I am talking about that worthless dog, Chalkuchimac.'

Pizarro had spat out the word 'dog' like an arrow from a bow. He stopped and looked at Manco, expecting a reaction.

Manco said nothing.

'Do you not agree that it is time for that dog to die?'

Manco kept his silence. He turned his gaze away from Pizarro and looked to where the road emerged from the trees. Anamaya's palanquin appeared, carried by eight bearers. They came to a halt, and she stepped down.

'The *Coya Camaquen* must come with us,' asserted Manco. 'She must stay with us all the way to Cuzco.'

Pizarro looked at Gabriel, then nodded to Manco.

'By the faith, my friend, if that is your will, then it shall be so.'

Gabriel drew in his breath sharply. He tried to catch Anamaya's gaze as she walked past him. But she seemed determined to ignore him. So he looked straight at Manco instead. And in the young Emperor's dark eyes, he was astonished to see not only a challenge but also a sign of respect.

CHAPTER 17

Jaquijaguana, 13 November 1533: evening

MANCO, SITTING IN THE *CANCHA*'S COURTYARD, STARED into the curling flames of the recently stoked brazier. He couldn't decide whether to sleep or not. Anamaya had stayed at his side, along with the longhaired Indian whose name she now knew: Katari. She sensed Manco's disquiet. He seemed unable to get used to all the noise the Strangers made – their grating voices, their loud laughter, their indelicate shouting.

Anamaya wrapped her *lliclla* tighter around herself against the night's dampness. It was too thin for this climate. She felt her convictions slowly evaporating. She thought of Manco facing Gabriel, so close and yet so far apart, each coming from entirely different worlds and yet united together in the strange domain of her heart. For a fleeting moment, she reproached herself for not having spoken to Gabriel. But what could she have said to him? How could she explain her feelings to him? There had once been a time when her visions had given her a sense of clarity, of conviction. But now that the Spirits were silent within her, she had to walk on with her eyes closed, seeing only the path immediately ahead of her. *Trust the Puma.* Those words, spoken so long ago, now took on a fresh and mysterious significance. *Tomorrow, all the Incas and all the Indians shall unite to fight a war against the Strangers, and you shall lead them.* She could not envisage Chalkuchimac. She wondered if he hadn't been already half in the Under World when he had spoken those words to her. All those words now lived within her, and acquired power through her.

She looked at Katari.

Manco had introduced him as the son of a great Kolla warrior who had been raised by his maternal uncle. He had absorbed, during his upbringing, a great respect for and knowledge of the ancient divinities, before learning how to sculpt stone. For as long as he could remember, Manco had said, Katari had always been there to protect him and to reveal to him the presence of the Gods.

Katari had a flat face with jutting cheeks. His eyes shone out of two slits extended horizontally by wrinkles, lines that crossed his face and were lighter than his swarthy skin. His long hair fell freely to his shoulders.

'It is time,' said Katari, without looking at Manco.

The young Inca jumped to his feet and signaled to a startled Anamaya.

Everyone was asleep now, except for the Spanish soldiers assigned to guard Chalkuchimac. Manco, Katari, and Anamaya left the *cancha* and darted silently through the narrow alleyways of the mountainside town.

Soon they were alone in the night – alone with the stars and the moon that, almost full, bathed them in its gentle pearl light.

Katari led them. He seemed very confident. Soon they left the houses behind them and arrived at a natural esplanade, with four large black boulders standing at its corners.

Manco took Anamaya by the arm, holding her back to allow Katari to go on alone.

The Kolla walked ahead a few paces, removed his cape, laid it on the ground, and sat on it. He remained there immobile for quite some time, his head tilted slightly to the right, blending into the calm night.

Then Katari took a piece of cloth and spread it in front of him. He fiddled with it for a moment, arranging it so that its four corners were aligned with the four surrounding boulders.

Anamaya suddenly saw, like a bolt of lightning slashing through the night, the totality of the alignment: behind them, this side of the Forbidden City, rose Salcantay mountain, its snow-capped peak shining silver in the moonlight; dead ahead of them, beyond the pass, and far beyond the City of the Puma, lay the forbidding bulk of the twin Willkanota mountains.

The two mountains towered majestically in the night, two Apus watching silently over Cuzco as it nestled in the bottom of the valley somewhere directly in front of them, midway along the line between the mountains and where Anamaya was now standing.

The three Indians felt their souls stirred by the presence of the deities whom Katari had evoked merely by aligning his piece of cloth with the sacred peaks. They sat there in silence.

Katari next took out his *chuspa* and emptied half its contents onto the piece of cloth spread out in front of him. He took three of the best leaves, fanned them out in his hand, brought them up to his mouth, and blew on them while facing the Apus – which he invoked in a low voice – before setting down the leaves on one of the corners of the piece of cloth.

He repeated the ritual for each of the remaining three corners.

When Katari had finished, Manco came up to him and picked three leaves out for himself and blew on them, turning to face the Apus as he did so, before putting them in his mouth and chewing on them.

Katari did the same.

The two men's eyes were half closed. Wordlessly, and without looking at one another, they moved with a perfect synchronicity of action and intention. Anamaya remained perfectly still and quiet in the light of her mother Mama Quilla, the moon. She wasn't asked to participate.

Manco held a quantity of leaves in both his hands, held them over the cloth, and let them sprinkle down like rain. Katari leaned over the leaves and pointed discreetly at Anamaya.

She looked at the cloth. The stem of the biggest leaf pointed right at her.

Manco gathered up the leaves and repeated the ritual three times, letting the leaves slip from his hands onto the cloth, then picking them up again.

Each time the biggest leaf fell away from the rest and its stem pointed at Anamaya.

There were no other sounds in the night except for the shuffle of Manco's hands and the occasional beating of a bird's wings as it flew on the nocturnal breeze.

Anamaya felt light and free. That night, she was no longer the woman who had to interpret her visions, or decode the words spoken to her from the Other World. She was simply the one designated by the coca leaves, the one who offered protection and direction. The one who opened the way.

Manco took a polished black basalt stone from his *chuspa*, a pebble as hard as a sling stone. He put it in Katari's strong hands and the Kolla squeezed it between his palms so hard that it seemed as though he wanted to crush it into dust.

When he opened his hands again, Anamaya saw that the stone now shone brilliantly, as though it had acquired the luminous quality of the moon above them.

Katari slowly raised his hands, offering the stone to the night sky. When his palms were level with his face the stone continued to ascend by itself. It rose up, then became suspended in the night sky.

Time stood still.

And at that exact moment, a roar tore through the night.

Fueled by rage, Vicente Valverde scampered to the middle of the esplanade. He looked angrily at the piece of cloth for a moment, then threw it on the ground and stamped on it. He picked it up again and flung it away.

'Pagans!' he spat. 'Idolaters!'

The two young men stood still. They turned to Anamaya. Manco was wide-eyed with surprise, whereas Katari's feline eyes stayed hidden behind their lids.

Before she had a chance to reply she saw Gabriel approaching with Bartholomew, the young priest with the joined fingers.

'Fray Vicente, please . . .' began Bartholomew in a placatory tone.

'Heathen practices, soothsaying, human sacrifices . . .'

'I cannot hear the cries of children having their throats cut, can you?' interrupted Bartholomew in a slightly ironic tone. 'Please calm down, Fray Vicente, I beg of you.'

Anamaya was impressed by the young man's cool authority. But she was still in shock from the Dominican's choleric outburst, as well as being a little unsettled by Gabriel's presence.

'The alarm was raised earlier,' said Gabriel in a flat voice. 'You had disappeared. The Governor gave the order to find you.'

'We were—'

Anamaya stopped midway through her sentence. She realized that it was still too early to explain to him what they had been doing: the Apus, the coca leaves, the stone-that-makes-time-stand-still, it was all too much, too soon. They stood facing one another in silence, and the young man's confused expression dismayed her. One day, soon, she would tell him. But not now.

Bartholomew approached Katari. The contrast between the physical appearances of the gray-eyed monk and the long-haired young sage could not have been more striking. Yet the same serenity, the same spiritual energy, radiated from each of them.

'We are still learning your ways,' said Bartholomew gently, 'and we shall guide you to the Truth of Almighty God with love rather than with swords.'

Katari listened without understanding, but he smiled anyway. Bartholomew turned to Valverde.

'Fray Vicente, I understand your zeal. Believe me, I am as committed as you are to the spreading of the true faith, but—'

'But you are far too interested in their so-called customs!'

'Knowing their ways makes it easier to guide them, my brother.'

Valverde said nothing, perhaps embarrassed by his excessively violent reaction. A sort of calm returned, despite all the shouting in the night and the stomping footsteps of approaching soldiers.

Gabriel approached Manco, his heart in turmoil.

'It would be better, for your own security, not to wander off thus.'

Although Gabriel had addressed him in Quechua, Manco did not answer him directly. He turned to Anamaya instead and said:

'Tell him that the Apus watch over me. That is security enough. I don't need foreign soldiers.'

Gabriel interrupted:

'I thought you needed us to fight Quizquiz and Guaypar. Isn't that what you told our Governor?'

'Tell him that our nights are our own.'

Anamaya sensed the tension between the two men, the violent rivalry between them. They were like two wildcats challenging each other, both of them young, strong, angry, and each one sure of his own supremacy.

'We're leaving, Gabriel. Please tell the Governor that we regret the trouble we have caused. May the remainder of the night be peaceful for us all.'

Gabriel stared at her, imploring her with his gaze. It hurt her to see him so pained. Then he turned and headed back toward the town with Valverde, Bartholomew and the soldiers.

She was alone once again with Manco and Katari. Silence had returned. But her peace of mind hadn't. The marvellous serenity she had felt when she had become aware of the alignment of the mountain peaks, and when the stone had left Katari's hands, had evaporated.

Manco broke the silence:

'Who is he?'

Anamaya couldn't find a reply.

CHAPTER 18

Jaquijaguana, 14 November 1533

THE SPANIARDS HAD ORDERED, AT DAWN, THAT A STAKE should be set up in the middle of the town's square. They hadn't needed to use the whip on the Indian slaves to encourage them to bring the necessary bundles of wood.

The slaves all harboured a wicked desire for vengeance against Chalkuchimac, whom they held responsible for the attacks by the northern Incas. The prospect of seeing him burned at the stake filled them with a gruesome joy, and they carried their loads of wood as though their burdens were as light as feathers. They told jokes to one another in hushed voices as they added more wood and straw to the growing pile. They looked apprehensively at the sky, worried that it might rain and drown the flames.

But there wasn't a cloud to be seen in the vast expanse of blue above them.

The principal Spanish commanders – de Soto, de Almagro, Juan and Gonzalo Pizarro – stood in a circle around Francisco Pizarro in a dark room lit by only one torch. The palace they were in was said to have belonged to one of the Ancestors. But they saw only a sad and dark old house, each room of which had niches carved into its walls – niches that were now empty, their treasures having been pillaged. The house's guardian was a frail and trembling old woman.

'What does Manco Inca say?' asked de Soto.

'He is with us,' said de Almagro confidently.

Pizarro nodded in agreement with the one-eyed captain.

'We have all the evidence we need, should anyone ask for it: the messengers Chalkuchimac dispatched, the jewels he used to send coded messages by, as well as those cords of theirs—'

'*Quipus*,' Gabriel informed them.

Pizarro stared at him. Gonzalo and Juan chuckled.

'*Quipus, puquis*,' crooned Gonzalo. 'He's a friend of the Inca, and so we must heed what he says.'

Pizarro raised his hand authoritatively to silence his two younger brothers.

'*Quipus*, then, if that's what he says, my brothers. We also know that Chalkuchimac revealed to the Indians that our horses are mortal, and that we are too. The vast majority of their troops used to believe that we were some kind of gods without ever having laid eyes on us. If it were not for that traitor, Hernando de Toro would be with us yet.'

'But what about Manco?' insisted de Soto.

'He hates Chalkuchimac from the depths of his soul. Only his pride prevents him from asking us outright to burn him. And in any case, we don't have a choice.'

There was no trace in Pizarro's voice of the doubt and hesitation that had weighed on him before Atahualpa's execution. His guilt about that came back to haunt him at times, especially when he prayed to the Virgin in the evenings. He said to Valverde:

'Try to convert him, but do it quickly!'

'But, Your Grace!' protested the priest.

'Quickly, I tell you! I shall burn him whether his soul has been redeemed or not! After the terrible attack he brought upon us, Fray Vicente, there shall be no mercy given to that dog. And I have learned that there is no worse fate for them than to be burned to death. I want them to know that the curse of God is brought upon them by our hand!'

Bartholomew had disappeared, the morning's events being alien to his soul. Gabriel no longer felt the intimacy they had shared at Hatun Sausa, when the monk had urged him toward Anamaya.

The sympathy he felt for Bartholomew was now clouded by some shapeless unease, some indistinct disquiet.

'Gentlemen,' said Pizarro, 'we are on the threshold of Cuzco, the city of gold. I know that you are eager to live up to your roles as Spaniards and as Christians.'

There was a dark glee in the Governor's tone, and his cruel irony prevented them from laughing wholeheartedly. *How well he knows his men*, thought Gabriel, *and how deftly he fans their avidity, yet despises them for it all the while.* De Almagro, de Soto, Juan and Gonzalo Pizatte and the rest followed the Governor from the house, the only large, stone-built house in the town, which he had commandeered as his quarters for the night.

The Indians had gathered in the square while the Spanish leaders had been in council. They parted willingly to let the Spaniards through to the *ushnu*.

When the Spaniards reached the bottom of the pyramid's steps, they turned around and watched the Inca general, bound in chains, being brought forward. Chalkuchimac had declined to come in his palanquin, so that all the Indians – whether they were Northern or Cuzco Incas, allies or rebels – could see how the Strangers had treated the general, and what their vengeance was like.

He walked painfully slowly, his entire body racked with an agony that would have overwhelmed anyone else. He held his burned and blistered hands out in front of him. None of the usual Inca natural remedies applied to them had had the slightest effect, and decoctions of leaves brewed by the wisest healers had not caused them to heal one bit. They had not even helped him stand the pain.

But his eyes burned with immense pride in his inscrutable face. His tight, straight lips showed his unbreakable will.

Chalkuchimac faced death defiantly.

Pizarro didn't say a word to him. The general didn't even glance at the Spanish captain, or at any of the Spaniards for that matter. He behaved as though they didn't exist.

He had to be carried up the steps to be tied to the stake. He was so close to collapsing from exhaustion that being bound to the stake was all that kept him from falling to the ground.

Only Valverde approached him, mumbling a few words about God, heaven and hell. But Chalkuchimac didn't give Felipillo the chance to translate.

'I curse you and despise you, and your religion as well, with its foreign Gods unknown to me and which I shall never acknowledge.'

The strength of the Inca general's voice contrasted greatly with his feeble, failing body.

'Enough, Valverde!' shouted Pizarro. 'Let us get on and be done with him.'

As the torches were brought forward, and as the first flames flickered up from the bundles of dry wood, licking at the general's legs and torso, he shouted:

'Burn me, then, burn me like you have already. But you shall not kill me. And you shall not kill our Gods – Viracocha, creator of the universe, or Huanacauri. You cannot burn me any more than you can burn Inti Himself.'

Chalkuchimac was almost completely hidden by the crackling flames now, but his voice seemed to survive as his body burned, as though detaching itself from him and rising up over them.

'Quizquiz! Guaypar! All you Inca generals, captains and soldiers! Avenge me, and destroy these traitors – destroy these filthy, greedy Strangers!'

Pizarro signaled to the slaves, and they fed more wood into the fire. Now the flames danced high into the sky. The roar of the blaze was so loud that the general's voice could eventually no longer be heard as it was swallowed by the flames.

The fire reflected in the fascinated eyes of thousands of silent Indians. They showed no joy, nor did they moan and wail as they had at Atahualpa's execution. They seemed only amazed and bewildered by this furious battle between gods.

When the fire began to subside a little, and its flames began to die down, a final, terrifying cry burst from its center, a cry that fell upon them all as hard as a stone from a sling:

'NO!'

And when the echoes of this cry had faded away, the fire

subsided all at once. Only a few tiny flames still flickered away at the feet of the horrifically charred corpse, by now as black as coal. Bizarrely, Chalkuchimac's eyes were still open, staring with lifelike intensity at a distant point beyond the horizon, beyond his executioners, beyond the silent crowd, beyond the town and its mountains.

A point *over there*.

At the very moment of the Inca general's death, the sky had abruptly clouded over and it had begun to rain.

It hadn't stopped since. It was a cold rain, one that found its way through the Spaniards' chain mail and clothes, and chilled them to the bone. Black clouds bearing more rain raced through the lead-gray sky.

The Incas had built a causeway, flanked by two long ramparts, through the middle of the swampy plain. The long cortege, over a league in length, was at the foot of the last hill from the crest of which travelers first saw Cuzco.

Rumors that the city had been sacked or burned had spread through the ranks of Indians and Spaniards alike. The names of Quizquiz and Guaypar were on everybody's lips. The bearers, nervous, stumbled more than usual, and even the battle-hardened cavalrymen, weighed down by their armor, felt the twitchy edginess of their horses, which had spent the night saddled and bridled.

Manco's palanquin led the column. Bizarrely, he had inherited Chalkuchimac's, and he had had all signs of its previous ownership by the general removed. It was now crowned by a banner of yellow cloth – the same golden colour as the cape, he had worn when he had first met the Spaniards – that fluttered irregularly in the cold wind.

Pizarro's brothers, along with the other Spanish commanders, were following just behind. Gabriel rode beside Don Francisco, his gaze searching the surrounding mountains for signs of an invisible enemy.

'You seem glum, my boy,' said Pizarro. 'Would you be pining

for that young girl, by any chance? What do they call her, *coya* something or other?'

'*Coya Camaquen.*'

'That's right. And she's certainly a most attractive girl. I sympathize with you, my boy.'

Pizarro let a few minutes of silence pass. Once again, Gabriel found himself surprised by the intuition of this man who seemed completely untouched by the most horrific barbarities, yet was capable of the deepest and most surprising sensibility.

'Yes, I understand you,' continued Pizarro. 'So I shan't give you the advice that I would normally give to anyone else: that if you don't have her, than you will certainly have some other girl.'

Gabriel stiffened.

'Easy, Gabriel,' murmured Don Francisco, looking directly at him. 'Women are just women, after all, and we're not here for them.'

He nodded toward Manco's palanquin.

'You heard what he said as well as I did. He wants her for himself. I don't know why. I thought she was married to the sun or the moon or to a condor or something. But the fact remains that he's claiming her. An ally of ours is claiming her. Do you understand my meaning?'

Gabriel nodded. He understood Pizarro only too well, much to his own unhappiness.

'I need Manco,' continued Pizarro. 'He's a rebel, but a rebel who has suffered. We need to rest before the war, and to gauge the strength of this country's forces. For that, we need him as a friend, for as long as possible. Do you still follow me?'

The causeway had grown gradually steeper, and now they were climbing broad steps up to the peak. The rain had stopped, but heavy clouds still darkened the sky. Although the Spaniards had adapted somewhat to the high altitude, Gabriel and Pizarro's breathing still grew more laboured with each step.

'I'm not sure if I do follow you, Don Francisco,' grumbled Gabriel. 'I'm not sure if my spirit is open to what you are talking about.'

'My, how touchy and proud you are,' said Pizarro, with a crafty smile.

'Don't forget that I owe her my life. And this second life of mine is not the fruit of pride, but of love, despite what you might think. She must choose between Manco and me.'

The Governor was now staring at him, with a frown creasing his bearded face, and his words stung like darts when he said:

'No, Gabriel Montelucar y Flores. It won't be up to her to choose, or you. It'll be *me*. Don't forget your oath to me, nor what you owe me. Nor should you count on my indulging you, or think that I'll allow you to bring down everything that I have built in this land.'

Gabriel didn't reply. Instead, he spurred his horse into a gallop, bolting away from Pizarro. The violent movement sent pain piercing through his wounded arm, but his fury was greater than his agony. He pushed his horse harder than was wise and bolted ahead of the column, all of whose members looked at him with astonishment as he galloped up to the hilltop.

When he reached it, his heart beating furiously, he dismounted, pulled off his morion, and flung it to the ground. He followed the helmet with his eyes, watching it spin to a standstill, and it was only then that he saw the valley laid out below him.

Gabriel was so stupefied that he thought he was looking at a new world.

He saw first the washed-out, diaphanous blue sky from which the clouds had now cleared.

He saw the peaceful mountains immediately surrounding the valley, and the snow-capped peaks beyond them.

He saw the valley itself, packed with agricultural terraces stepped neatly one above the other. The sun hadn't been shining long enough to warm the wet ground.

Then he saw the city.

Gabriel had been led to expect, from de Moguer and Bueno's descriptions, a massive pile of gold. But what he saw instead was more like a magnificent ship, built of precious metals and moored in the heart of the valley.

The walls of the temples, palaces, and houses glittered iridescently in the sunlight. The whole place looked like a multicolored pile of treasure into which one wanted to plunge one's hands. Gabriel saw the two emerald rivers winding their way to the city from the far end of the valley.

His heart skipped for joy, and he had an urge to clap his hands ecstatically. He didn't notice when those at the head of the column arrived alongside him and drank in the scenery for themselves.

'*Najay, tucuyquin hatun Cuzco*.[2] Now you see it for yourself,' said a gentle voice in his ear.

Gabriel didn't turn to face her, but he could feel her breath warm against his neck, more refreshing than the still-cold morning breeze.

'Do you know what we call it?' she asked him. He shook his head.

'The City of the Puma,' said Anamaya. 'The city born of the puma. It is here where you and I shall find the path to the future.'

Standing there in the sunshine and the cool breeze, Gabriel felt all his doubts and fears evaporate as Anamaya spoke those tender and promising words to him.

---

[2] 'Great City of Cuzco, I salute you.'

PART 3

CHAPTER 19

Cuzco, 15 November 1533

THE SPANIARDS, MOVING THROUGH A GREEN CORNFIELD, noticed the contours of what they thought was a hill to their left. As they rode on, however, they realized that the hill was in fact a fortress. Its massive outer walls rose as vertiginously as natural cliffs. Three towers, one round and two square, rose at its eastern, western, and southern corners, far more imposing than any towers in Castille.

The Spaniards carried on in a strange limbo, hardly noticing the clatter of their weapons, the click-clack of their horses' hooves on the flagstones, or their leather saddle girths squeaking. Not a word was spoken. The horses clearly disliked the steep climb, and they whinnied complainingly as they threw their heads back, eliciting reassuring pats from their riders.

At the foot of the slope, facing the meticulously kept terraces, were the first houses of the town. The streets, arranged in a neat grid pattern, were lined with men and women dressed in fabulously colorful clothes, clothes that shimmered in the early morning light. Smoke rose up from fires burning among the flower beds in the courtyards. Groups of Incas stood perfectly still in the great square, a square surrounded by *canchas* and magnificent buildings. All eyes were focused on the Spanish column. Gold glittered on the walls. Gold glittered on the noblemen's clothes as they watched the Spaniards draw closer. Thousands more Incas, standing further down the valley in a tent city, an extension of the

stone one, watched the new masters of the Empire make their
way down through the sacred terraces.

Pizarro rode at the head of the column. He focused his
dark-eyed gaze on the city, wanting to absorb its every detail.
His brothers and the one-eyed de Almagro, along with his main
commanders rode at his side. No one dared to speak a word.

They couldn't see a single Indian warrior.

'Gabriel!' called Pizarro.

Juan and Gonzalo turned back in their saddles at the same
time. Gabriel, ignoring their jealous glares, clicked his tongue as
he urged his bay up alongside the Governor's black horse.

'Don Francisco?'

'Stay by me. I want you to savor the full flavor of our triumph.'

Pizarro spoke in a voice so low as to be practically inaudible.
He glanced disdainfully at de Almagro and his retinue.

'They weren't at Tumbez or Cajamarca. They're here only to
stuff their pockets with gold. But not you, my boy. You're just
like me. So stay close to me and make the most of this day, for
it is ours.'

They had come to the first houses on the outskirts of the
city. The buildings had stone foundations, and their walls were
made of sun-baked clay bricks. The Spaniards, riding up the
steep slope, looked over the dwellings' low thatched roofs from
atop their horses. Dozens of Indians surrounded them now. They
were coming from everywhere, and if they were frightened of the
newcomers they didn't show it. Gabriel was astonished by their
diversity – by their different facial ethnic features, by the variety
of their clothes and languages.

Pizarro ordered the column to halt.

'Fetch the Inca,' he commanded. 'I want him to lead us in.'

Gabriel moved back along the column at a half-trot, ignoring
his companions' quizzical looks. He could feel Manco's gaze upon
him from some distance away. Manco's palanquin, unrecognizable
as having once belonged to Chalkuchimac was of an unequaled
luxury. Its interior was decorated with constellations of jewelled
stars, a sun made of gold, and a moon crafted from silver. The
seat was carved from precious wood and was strewn with cushions

stuffed with gaily coloured feathers plucked from parakeets taken from the heart of the jungle. The young Inca himself was wrapped in a huge, billowing cape of yellow cotton embroidered with gold. He turned his face away at Gabriel's approach, pretending not to see him.

Anamaya, sitting in the next palanquin and wearing a red belt around her white *lliclla*, smiled discreetly at Gabriel. But Gabriel saw her as some haughty princess now achingly distant from him. He found it hard to believe that she was the same woman whom he had once held in his arms. He found himself once more plagued by doubts.

He saluted the Inca stiffly, then said in a cold voice:

'Lord Inca, Governor Pizarro requests the pleasure of your company at the head of the column.'

Manco looked at Gabriel as though he was looking into the depths of his soul. He motioned to Anamaya to join him. They spoke a few words to one another, too quickly and too quietly for Gabriel to hear. She took her place at the Inca's feet with a submissiveness that fueled the jealous passion raging through Gabriel's veins.

He turned his horse around abruptly. He kept his back as stiff as he could as he accompanied the imperial palanquin to the head of the column.

As they approached, a great uproar rose from the crowd as they recognized their Emperor. The entire town and the sky itself echoed with the cry of:

'*Sapa Inca Manco! Sapa Inca Manco!*'

The clamor rose in waves from the crowd and made the hair on the Spaniards' arms and napes stand on end. For a moment the valley air grew thick with an unearthly exultancy.

Don Francisco Pizarro grinned. A broad smile, something rare for him, bisected the white beard on his emaciated face. He raised his feverish eyes to the sky and gave thanks to the Sacred Virgin, whom he considered his own blessed guardian angel and who he was sure was looking down on him from heaven at that very moment. He was so excited that he stood up in his stirrups and shook Gabriel by the shoulders.

'*Sapa Inca Manco! Sapa Inca Manco!*' shouted the crowd, over and over.

Don Francisco spun around in his saddle so that all the Spaniards could hear him and cried:

'Gentlemen, remember this noise. They hail their chief, but in fact it is *us* whom they unwittingly hail. Pay close attention to the sound of their cries, gentlemen, for you shall never forget it.'

Gabriel shuddered. Nearby, almost within his hands' reach, Anamaya stood beside Manco. Her beauty dazzled him and he became deaf to the shouting all around. When she turned her head to look at him he told himself that, yes, the Governor was right. He would never forget this moment.

Thousands upon thousands of Indians bowed down in front of the young Inca. Anamaya observed the extraordinary scene from where she rode in his palanquin. It was as though an enormous blanket of bodies had covered the sacred terraces, the streets, and the city square. The city of Cuzco, the 'navel of the world', was a great weave of men and women, a giant *unku* decorated with a pattern new to the world. And from this human tapestry rose the endless cry:

'*Sapa Inca Manco! Sapa Inca Manco!*'

'Do they call me to war or to peace?' asked Manco in a flat voice.

'They're asking you to become their Emperor.'

'Will you help me?'

Anamaya burst out laughing.

'You're no longer the young boy frightened of heights and of snakes, Emperor.'

'Yes, I am. Will you help me?'

Anamaya, surprised, turned her head away and looked at the crowd. But Manco was right. He still had the face of a boy, and the crowd was making such a strong impression on him that, instead of showing his joy, he clamped his lips tight to stop them trembling.

'You're coming home, Manco – home to this city, to Cuzco,

that for so long has given you only fear and pain. But today you are Emperor. Aren't you glad?'

'I don't know, Anamaya. My heart wants to shout out, and it also wants to cry tears. I cannot get it out of my mind that my brother Paullu is so far away.'

'You are emerging from a sea of chaos, my Lord. It is natural that there remains a little of it within you.'

Manco's expression relaxed a little.

'I shall show you Cuzco,' he said, 'I shall show you my Ancestors' palace . . .'

'I know it already: I lived there once.'

Manco was genuinely surprised.

'I thought you'd never been here.'

'Forgive me, my Lord, you are right. But the stones of your capital are so sacred that some of them were taken to Tumebamba, where I grew up in the *acllahuasi*, and the girls there told me stories about the city at the navel of the world. And then that night, that terrible night when your father Huayna Capac passed on to the Other World, he took me through all his palaces.'

'Was it my father who told you that I was the designated one?'

Manco touched Anamaya lightly on the shoulder. She trembled almost imperceptibly, but the young Inca still sensed it. He pulled his hand away without saying a word.

The road leading into the city ran alongside a river whose clear water flowed between the expertly constructed houses. Although it was a wide road, the Spaniards could only proceed two abreast, squeezed between the massive crowds stretching along the stone walls. A cacophonous din rose from the crowd, a noise like the rolling thunder of a thousand drums.

When the Indians saw the Inca's palanquin, they raised their upturned palms to the sky in a gesture of veneration and sub-servience.

Gabriel's fear slowly evaporated, as did his distress at being apart from Anamaya and his feeling of being a stranger to her.

Although he certainly didn't feel the heady joy that the normally impassive Pizarro was displaying, he felt himself nonetheless carried along by the general fervor greeting the Inca and those accompanying him. The Indians now surrounding them were a hundred deep, and although they surged forward at them, they made sure not to touch them. The newcomers were themselves extraordinarily quiet, speaking together only in murmurs.

'Are you dreaming, my friend?'

Bartholomew had appeared out of nowhere, and now walked alongside Gabriel's horse. He placed his hand with the deformed fingers on Gabriel's thigh, looked at him with his laughing eyes, and said:

'You have certainly come a long way since I first met you in the jails of Seville.'

'Don't delude yourself. That jail is as close to me here as it was there.'

Each time he spoke to Bartholomew, Gabriel felt conflicting emotions toward him. He felt a strong intimacy with the monk, so strong that he often felt the urge to reveal to Bartholomew all the demons tormenting his own soul. Yet Gabriel also felt instinctively suspicious of the man.

They came out onto a vast square, the surface of which consisted of fine sand rather than the usual flagstones, a sand on which the horses' hooves crunched. A magnificent round stone fountain stood in its centre. Water streamed from it toward the river bisecting the square.

To one side of the river – the side that they had just crossed over to – there were no buildings of any note, only a wall that had just begun being built. But on the other side stood the façades of palaces the likes of which the Spaniards had not seen anywhere else in the Empire. One of these was built of red-veined, green and white marble. A massive circular tower topped with a high, conical roof partially obscured its door, which was lined with plates of silver and other precious metals.

Here, an old, old Lord sat on an expertly chiseled throne under its magnificent lintel. The ancient nobleman sat perfectly still as he watched the Spaniards stream into the square. His evident nobility and impassivity intimidated the newcomers. A dozen women, dressed entirely in white, quietly busied themselves around him in a graceful ballet. Two of them fanned him with shimmering feathers, and two others looked after a fire burning at his feet.

He gave an impression of incredible power. The passing of the Spaniards, with their steel helmets and horses, seemed not to disturb him in the slightest. It was as though he was privy to the secret order of the universe.

The crowd poured silently into the square, careful to stay out of the old Lord's way.

'My God!' cried Bartholomew. Gabriel turned around.

'What is it?' he asked.

'Don't you see?' said Bartholomew, pointing at the old man's throne.

Sweat streamed down Gabriel's face, obscuring his vision. Everything seemed slightly blurred to him. He saw only the perfectly still Lord, surrounded by his faithful servants.

'He's dead,' said Bartholomew.

'Dead?'

'He's a mummy.'

CHAPTER 20

Cuzco, 15 November 1533

I T WAS A HUMBLE *CANCHA*, SET BACK A LITTLE FROM THE southern road leading to Collasuyu in the district known as Pumachupan – the puma's tail – and within sight of the Temple of the Sun. Whenever a ceremony took place on the Intipampa, those nearby could hear the priests' stentorian voices, the wail of trumpets, the rolling drums, and the chanting from within the *cancha*'s walls.

Anamaya passed timidly through the door in the simple, unadorned wall enclosing the *cancha*'s central courtyard. Its rooms, which gave onto the courtyard, were all dark and silent.

Yet she was sure that this was the place.

A roar made her jump, and she almost cried out.

She stood face to face with a puma that was tied to a post with an agave rope. Anamaya took several deep breaths to calm her beating heart, and then fixed her stare on the beast's eyes.

The great cat paced about imperially, never taking its gaze from hers.

'So, princess,' joked a voice from behind her, 'have you forgotten your old friends?'

A frieze made of gold, as wide as a man's palm and as thick as a finger, was fixed to the stone wall surrounding the Temple of the Sun. The fat Pedro Martin de Moguer pointed it out to the small gathering with proprietary pride.

A half-dozen of them, including the Governor and Don Diego de Almagro, craned their necks to see the gold more clearly.

'Here's some that you missed, de Moguer. Here's some you didn't ship back to Cajamarca.'

'Gold falls from the skies in these parts, Your Excellency. It grows from the earth. They replace it as quickly as we take it from their walls.'

De Moguer had 'discovered' Cuzco, along with Martin Bueno, a few months earlier, and he had organized the first shipments of treasure sent back from the capital to the ransom room in Atahualpa's Cajamarca palace. Now he moved his own massive bulk around the city with childish glee, proudly playing the guide to his compatriots. While the Spaniards were talking, an Inca priest wearing a long, fringed tunic appeared in a doorway. He was carrying a statue hidden under a wool covering. Gabriel was startled by his piercing gaze, and then he noticed the green coca juice dribbling from the priest's thin lips. Two warriors bearing spears, clubs and axes made of gold followed him. Two young boys in yellow livery preceded him and swept the flagstones with brooms, flagstones that seemed to Gabriel already immaculately clean.

The little group of Incas seemed astonished to find the Spaniards there.

'What are they doing?' asked Pizarro.

'We're interrupting their ceremony,' said Gabriel.

Juan and Gonzalo burst into laughter behind him.

'What things he tells us,' sniggered Gonzalo. 'As though we were interrupting Easter Mass at Saint James's.'

'De Moguer, how well do you know your way around this temple?' asked Pizarro, ignoring his brother.

'Well enough, my Lord.'

Pizarro grinned.

'In that case, gentlemen, let us go in and learn a little more about their ceremonies.'

'I'll come too,' said a gentle voice. Without waiting for Pizarro's permission, Bartholomew went ahead of them briskly.

They ran into the two Inca warriors beyond the trapezoidal door through which the priest had passed. The warriors crossed their spears, barring the Spaniards' passage. Their weapons could hardly be taken seriously, yet the Spaniards still hesitated for a moment.

Gabriel noticed a sort of cloister behind the soldiers. He watched as the priest placed the statue on a stone bench covered with gold leaf in the center of the cloister.

Having done this, the priest turned his gaze on the Spaniards. He looked at them for a while. Then, at a disconcertingly slow pace, he approached them.

'Every morning, I'm amazed to see the sun rise again,' said the dwarf. 'I'm amazed that I'm still alive.'

Anamaya smiled.

'I've missed you, dear friend.'

'And I have missed you, princess. Do you remember the day when that despicable priest abandoned me in the mountain?'

'Yes! How you cried, "Princess! Princess!" in a pathetic voice.'

'I might have died, yet you were utterly indifferent.'

'Oh, how silly you are,' said Anamaya, amused. 'I've thought of you a thousand times since.'

She looked around the room they were in. Although its exterior appeared humble, it was in fact sumptuously furnished inside. Its mats and luxurious blankets were made of feathers and wool. Finely worked stone statues of pumas, condors and snakes stood in its alcoves.

'You haven't done too badly for yourself, for a poor, abandoned soul.'

'The job of Guardian of the Puma is one that no sane, healthy Inca will touch. It is only right that it is duly rewarded.'

The dwarf was wearing one of his too-long red robes, its fringes sweeping along the ground. He couldn't stand still and kept bouncing nervously around Anamaya.

'How did you come to be entrusted with such a high position?'

'You mean you haven't heard?'

'I was told only that you were still alive.'

'Alive . . . in a manner of speaking, yes, I am alive. When we arrived here with the mummy of my master Huayna Capac, I went to the head of the cortege and, to banish my fear, danced around, shouting: "Here I am, I am Chimbu, the son of the great Huayna Capac! Make way, make way, here comes Chimbu!" But no one did. Instead, the local noblemen arrested me and threatened to carve me up into little pieces. "You little runt," they called me. They shouted, "Woe, why did the Sun God take our beloved Emperor, our father, who loved us and looked after us, and leave us this stunted fool in his place!" They insulted me thus, they spat on me, they hit me, they ignored my tears and my pleas. But, luckily for me, others came to my defence, and they arranged it so that I was put with the other prisoners.'

The dwarf's face darkened at the memory.

'Do you know the prison at Sanca Cancha?'

'No.'

'It is like your worst nightmare of the Under World. In fact, it *is* underground, a maze of underground caves. Deadly sharp flints are fixed to its walls, but the absolute worst—'

'The worst?'

'The worst is that there are no human guards in this prison: only wildcats, bears and vipers. They left us there for three days. For three days we howled in terror, for three days we cried until our eyes ran dry. For three days, we were so close to death that it was as though we were already dead. But we survived.'

'And then they freed you.'

The dwarf nodded.

'Of all the terrifying things that happened to me, that is the only thing that I can look back on with joy. I have died many times, but I'm far more attached to this particular life than to any of the others that I have lived.'

Anamaya was fascinated by the dwarf's tale. She murmured:

'And then?'

'I stuck as close as possible to the brothers, to Manco and Paullu, and I served them. That's it.'

'You served them?'

'Yes,' replied with dwarf, with an amusing affected air, 'I served them. I hid Manco in this very place, before he was able to slip away from the city. And I risked my miserable life time and again to carry messages to Paullu in the prison . . .'

'Paullu was *imprisoned*?'

'Yes, but not for anything serious, I promise you. He was rather forward with one of Huascar's favourite concubines, so . . . But when the northerners arrived, he pretended most convincingly that he had been persecuted because he supported them. So they freed him, although they remained suspicious. He didn't wait for them to change their minds, however, and he scampered off to Lake Titicaca.'

Anamaya looked pensive. She recalled the two young men she had helped all those moons ago, during the *huarachiku*. Now, one was the Sapa Inca and the other was in hiding.

'Manco spoke affectionately of you. He told me how to find your house.'

'He too frightens me. Who knows how he will change, now that he's Emperor?'

'Don't worry so much, my friend. Have you forgotten that we vowed to watch out for one another, you and I?'

'If I had forgotten it, princess, then a very important person took it upon himself to remind me of it.'

'Who?'

The dwarf came and stood directly in front of Anamaya and gazed up at her with his round eyes.

'Don't tell me that you don't know, princess.'

Gabriel watched as the green-lipped man walked up to the Governor, so close that he could have touched him.

'My name is Villa Oma, and I am the high priest of this Coricancha, this Temple of the Sun built by our powerful ancestor Manco Capac. Strangers are not permitted in here.'

Gabriel translated. Pizarro replied, with an appeasing gesture:

'Tell him that we have come to protect him and his people from the northerners.'

'And tell him as well that we have come to show them the one true God, and to put an end to their pagan practices,' added Gonzalo.

'As for that, my friend,' intervened Bartholomew, 'leave it to the men of God.'

Gabriel couldn't help but smile as he translated the Governor's words.

But the priest remained unmoved. He stood there, his arms outstretched from his tall, lanky frame like some crucified Indian Christ, barring their way.

'How dare you force your way in here like this when the law dictates that he who wishes to enter this sacred place must fast for an entire year, and then only come in barefoot and bearing a stone on his shoulders?'

Gonzalo burst out laughing.

'Tell this feather-head that we have fasted for much longer than one paltry year and that our shoulders are far more burdened than he can imagine. And as for our boots, well . . .'

Gonzalo pulled off one of his boots. The Spaniards guffawed when he shook it at the priest and said:

'You see, Brother Bartholomew? I have only the highest respect for the customs of these . . .'

A pebble fell from his boot as he put it back on with an exaggerated grimace on his face, provoking more laughter.

'. . . These barbarians. Let us leave the affairs of God to the men of God, then. As for the affairs of men – well, let us deal with them as men.'

He shoved the Inca priest aside and stomped into the temple.

The small group of Spaniards followed him into the center of the courtyard. They glimpsed their own indistinct reflections through the doorways into the rooms surrounding it. A strip of gold plate, set high up off the ground, ran all the way around the walls.

Four recesses, like church tabernacles, were carved into the walls. They were finished with extremely accomplished mouldings, their interiors gilded and set with precious stones – emeralds and turquoises. The Governor turned to Villa Oma:

'We are aware of the terrible threat that casts its shadow over your palaces and temples, and we have seen for ourselves the dreadful destruction brought upon some of your other towns by your enemies. But we are here in the spirit of peace.'

The priest Villa Oma narrowed his eyes. He looked at them for a while in silence. Then he said:

'I do not believe you.'

Villa Oma's voice echoed through the cloister. Pizarro didn't blink as Gabriel translated the priest's words. He smiled.

'Assure him that we shall win his trust. Meanwhile, we shall carry out a reconnaissance mission of this temple, in order to better guard both him and it. Don Diego?'

De Almagro's only eye shone avidly at the thought of all the wealth hidden in the temple.

'I am sure that you will take it upon yourself, as I do, to ensure that nothing from this temple is excluded from the King's fifth.'

De Almagro growled incomprehensibly in reply. The small group of Spaniards began moving toward the door of the building facing them, leaving the priest Villa Oma behind. He raised his arms to the sky and cried:

'Oh Noble Sun God, send us some tangible sign of your magnificent power!'

Mummies sat on their thrones to either side of the sun's path, mummies similar to the one that the Spaniards had seen earlier in the square. They were dressed in gold-sequined tunics made of the finest wool and spangled with precious stones. They all wore royal bands on their foreheads, from which colorful feathers stuck up. Gold discs hung from their ears. They were in remarkably good condition, though one of them was missing the end of his nose – a sight that made Pizarro's two younger brothers guffaw stupidly once again.

The Spaniards moved slowly around the courtyard, going from room to room. They found one room covered in silver and dedicated to the moon goddess. Here, de Moguer had to restrain himself from invoking Venus. They came across another lined with the usual gold plates, but with the added beauty of a jewelled rainbow, its colours running from one wall to another.

They had begun their visit in a state of excitement, like a

band of young lads setting out to drink and chase girls. But they became increasingly quiet, increasingly serious, with each room they entered.

Once they had visited the six rooms and had returned to the courtyard, they found that the high priest and his attendants had disappeared. De Moguer stood there in silence, and de Almagro had a dreamy look in his one eye. The Governor's younger brothers were unusually restrained.

Then the group walked through a passage on the courtyard's eastern side. They discovered that the inner sanctuary of the temple was far larger than they had at first imagined. They discovered more buildings in which they found servants who hid their faces as they appeared – and who were storing provisions in quantities large enough to wait out a siege of many weeks.

Gabriel's heart grew heavy as he saw the greedy looks in the eyes of his companions at the sight of all these treasures.

'There was a story going around,' said de Moguer, 'when we first arrived . . .'

'Well, what is it?' asked Pizarro impatiently.

But de Moguer didn't reply. No one asked him anything more about the story.

They had just unwittingly entered the garden of gold.

The dwarf continued telling his story to Anamaya in a muted, even voice.

'As soon as word arrived that the Strangers were approaching, Manco summoned me from Yucay, where I was living at the time. His men took me to him at Chinchero. When I found myself alone with him and that abominable high priest on one of the terraces below the *collcas*, I was sure that they had reconciled their differences behind my back and that they had some bloodthirsty plan in store for me.'

'Manco and Villa Oma together?' asked Anamaya, astonished.

'Yes. Strange, isn't it? At the time I didn't think about it much, because I was too busy working out how to save my own hide. But, luckily for me, they had something else in mind.'

Anamaya grinned, amused, as ever, by the irresistible mix of fear and humor that was always at the heart of the dwarf's tales.

'Perhaps, if you're lucky, you'll live long enough to tell me what it is,' she said.

'Mock me if you must, princess,' sighed the dwarf. 'But first let me tell you that they asked me to look after your noble husband, the Sacred Double.'

'You!'

Anamaya was unable to prevent the exclamation bursting from her mouth.

'That's exactly how *I* reacted. But they ignored me. They told me that the Strangers, who are despicably greedy, would try to get their hands on as much gold as they could. Manco and the priest were themselves indifferent to this because they know that there is gold in such vast quantities – limitless oceans of gold that the Strangers could never drain dry. But they were not to lay their impious hands on the Sacred Double, which was then at Coricancha.'

Anamaya was overwhelmed with emotion that sent hot and cold shivers down her spine.

'Is he here?'

The dwarf looked at her with the utmost seriousness.

'Do you think that I would be so foolish as to keep it here, even with a ferocious puma to guard it? No, we shall go to it under the cover of night. The Sacred Double is waiting for you.'

Everything in the garden that the Spaniards had stumbled upon was gold: The grass, the flowers, the trees, even the animals, whether big or small, domestic or wild, were made of gold. Gold lizards and snakes slithered along the ground, and gold butterflies and birds hung in the air, suspended by invisible threads.

There was a terrace with golden corn growing in it, and another with the grasslike plant that the Indians called *quinua*. There were gold llamas grazing, and a gold fountain from which silver water ran. There was a patch of golden vegetables, trees of golden fruit, and even piles of gold firewood.

The Governor stood there, flabbergasted.

'Touch nothing,' he said, his mouth dry.

'The story was,' began de Moguer at last, 'that there's a statue made of solid gold, one that is the exact image of one of those mummies we saw. It is said to be bigger and far more beautiful than any we have yet seen, and not hollow like so many of them are.'

'How big is it?' asked de Almagro.

'More or less life-size, I was told.'

'And how much does it weigh?'

'Several hundred pounds, surely.'

No one thought of disbelieving de Moguer. Each man silently calculated the value, in pesos, of that legendary statue, which doubtlessly increased in size in their own imaginations.

'Where is it?' asked de Almagro.

De Moguer shrugged.

'We have to find it,' said Gonzalo.

Juan agreed, his eyes ablaze.

'What's this statue of yours called?' asked Gabriel.

'Oh, *that* I know,' said de Moguer proudly. 'It has a strange name, which was translated to me as "the Sacred Double".'

Gonzalo glanced at Gabriel.

As they left the garden, his companions visibly overcome by the sight of this latest wonder in this land of gold, a land that had previously existed only in the most fabulous fairy tales or in their own overheated imaginations, Gabriel remembered Anamaya's words. He vowed to himself that he would never repeat them.

She had told him that she was the Sacred Double's wife.

His soul was confused: he didn't know what significance this had for the Incas.

But Gabriel knew what it would mean to his companions.

CHAPTER 21

Cuzco, evening of 15 November 1533

THE CITY OF CUZCO DIDN'T SLEEP.

The city of Cuzco never slept.

The hustle that kept the Empire running allowed for no rest. Young virgins continued weaving in their *acclahuasis*, goldsmiths and sculptors continued working at their art, and priests carried out their rituals. Clans continued maintaining their *panacas*, attending to their dead sovereigns, bringing them food and honoring them, transcribing their messages from the Under World and implementing them in this one.

In the square towers at Sacsayhuaman, guards relieved the previous watch. And in the round tower at Moyocmarka, the people were constantly ready for a visit by the Inca.

There was a lot of whispering that night, both in the palaces and in the more humble houses, and the waters of the Huatanay carried fearsome secrets.

The mummies slept, wide-eyed, in their palaces.

The mummies knew what the living didn't.

The dwarf ran ahead of Anamaya and guided her through the dark, narrow alleyways made slippery by the drifting fog, which penetrated her *añaco*.

Every time he heard a suspicious noise he froze, or else dragged her to safety under the lintel of a trapezoidal door. He led her across a bridge spanning the Huatanay.

Upon setting out, Anamaya had tried to figure out what part of the puma's body she was in. But all she knew now, as they rose higher and higher, and as the lights burning ahead of them in the towers of Sacsayhuaman came into view, was that they were heading toward the puma's head.

She came out at the top of a steep slope and, short of breath, discovered a vast esplanade covered in the same kind of sand as that at Aucaypata. She saw the evenly spaced recesses carved into a palace wall at its far end, at the base of a cliff. The lights of the city shone brilliantly behind her, and fires and torches burned on the mountain slopes.

'Where are we?' Anamaya asked the dwarf.

'Collcampata, princess.'

The very word made her heart beat faster. Collcampata was one of the largest districts of Cuzco, located just below Sacsayhuaman. It was here that the Chima Panaca, who were descended from Manco Capac, worshiped the founder of the Inca dynasty.

'What now?'

The dwarf didn't reply. Instead, he took Anamaya by the hand and led her toward the palace wall. All its niches were empty, their gold statues no doubt pilfered by the Strangers during their first visit. Where there had been a finely worked gold frieze, there were now only the ragged holes where it had once been fastened. And yet, even on that dark and damp night, the place still had a power about it. The sloping walls had a majestic quality about them that their perfectly fitted stones accentuated.

They followed the wall around a corner. The palace seemed to merge into the cliff here. Hidden now from the city's lights, they had entered the kingdom of shadows. They followed the wall, blending into its black rock, slipping through each new door they came to.

After they had gone through three, the dwarf leaned against the wall with all his weight. Slowly, silently, it pivoted open.

The veil in front of Anamaya's eyes was lifted.

*　　*　　*

On the great square, Don Francisco Pizarro gave his orders. He commandeered as his quarters the palace situated on its northern side, by the river. Its main room was so large that it could easily have accommodated sixty cavalrymen to play a game of *a cañas*. His brothers Gonzalo and Juan were given the neighbouring palace. De Soto was to stay in another across the square, the walls of which were decorated with snakes carved from stone.

'Let the tents be pitched,' said the Governor.

Gabriel stared at him, taken aback, and pointed at the palaces.

'I know, but I want us to remain on our toes, and I won't have any disorder. Let no one enter any house without my permission. I want to remain at peace with that young man.'

'Young man?'

'Manco. The Inca. I want his trust in return for our good behavior. De Almagro, de Soto, and my brothers shall have all they wish. But none of them properly understand that we are here to stay, and that now is the most critical moment for us. If we abandon our discipline, if we let ourselves go and start pillaging, then we are dead. I shall see the young man tomorrow. Together, we shall raise an army against the northerners.'

Pizarro's eyes were ablaze, and Gabriel sensed that strange mix of calm and excitement so characteristic of him during critical moments. He gave his orders to his lieutenants, and soon Gabriel saw a forest of tents begin to rise in the square.

'And afterward?' he asked.

Pizarro looked at him for a moment, smiling.

'Don't ask me questions whose answers you won't like.'

Gabriel began to move away. But Pizarro set his dry, bony hand on the young conquistador's shoulder and said:

'There's a matter I must discuss with you.'

The passage was broad enough for Anamaya and the dwarf to advance through the deepening dark with a degree of ease. But then they came to a flight of high steps and had to climb these cautiously, making sure that they found their footing with each tread.

It was said that Tupac Inca Yupanqui had had this tunnel dug all the way through the mountain to the Sacsayhuaman fortress, which was then being built.

Anamaya heard the dwarf's voice muffled through the fog. His face was wet from its dampness.

They followed a passageway round a corner, after which she made out a faint light flickering through a door-hanging up ahead. The dwarf passed through it ahead of Anamaya, then held it aside to allow her through.

They found themselves in a round room without any recesses in the wall. It was lit by only one fixed torch. There was no covering on the floor – no mats, no blankets.

There was only a simple wooden bench. On it sat the Sacred Double.

A shudder ran through Anamaya's body, and she had to close her eyes to keep her balance.

She stretched out her hand toward the Sacred Double but stopped short of actually touching it. She spread her arms in prayer and murmured to herself.

When she reopened her eyes, the dwarf had disappeared, and the room was dark.

But it wasn't a threatening darkness, for from its heart the Sacred Double's golden body burned like a night sun, calming and eternal.

Anamaya thought that she could make out on the walls traces of shapes familiar to her: forest animals, perhaps, or armies meeting one another on the field of battle – sling stones flying through the air like lightning bolts, axes raised, ready to strike.

Slowly the images of that shadowy battle dissolved, and as her heart settled she was overcome by a marvellous peace, a serenity that brought her to the ground, prostrate at the feet of the one whom she was to accompany and protect throughout his wanderings on the surface of the earth.

You are here.

Was it someone else's voice speaking? Or had she whispered those words herself? It didn't matter – she could hear him at last, he who she had thought had forsaken her.

You are stronger than peace, and stronger than war itself. You are older and wiser than the Inca, and you have crossed the deserts and the rivers to be at my side. All that is yours is given to you by the night.

All was silent. Anamaya could no longer feel cold or heat, dampness or dryness. She was now at the secret heart of the universe, at the junction of all the worlds, and she was filled with a wondrous tranquillity.

My words are eternal. You cannot forget them.

The voice traveled through stone and air to reach her. Sometimes it sounded very, very deep, sometimes as resonant as if it spoke through a sea conch. But when the voice uttered the words that she had been hoping for, hoping for without admitting it to herself, it was in an almost inaudible murmur:

Trust the puma.

Anamaya didn't have time to enjoy the sensation of well-being that now spread through her body, relaxing her every muscle.

The light returned, blinding her.

She cried out.

'Which one do you want?' Pizarro asked Gabriel, pointing at the palaces whose solid walls lined the street.

'None of them. I want my tent.'

Pizarro chortled quietly.

'You surprise me yet, my boy. God chased you out of Spain, and you aren't here for gold . . .'

'I thought that I was here for the same reason as you, Don Francisco.'

'Only God and the Sacred Virgin know why I'm here. There are times when I'm not so sure myself.'

Their boots clicked against the flagstones as they walked. A child could be heard crying in the night, its wail blending with the gentle sound of water running in the stream.

'You wanted to ask me something, Don Francisco.'

'Ask you something?' The Governor snapped out of his private thoughts.

'Yes, ask me something,' Gabriel said. 'Something important.'

Gabriel held his breath.

Pizarro looked intently at him and said: 'It's no secret that you've bedded that girl, my boy – that blue-eyed girl. Now, please understand, I'm not leveling any reproach at you, far from it: even an old dog like me grows warm in the company of some of those Indian girls.'

Gabriel felt his heart beating hard, and his mouth was dry. Pizarro pretended not to notice his discomfort.

'Still, for some reason unknown to me, our young man seems to attach some great importance to her. I have no idea what he plans to do with her. Make her one of his wives, perhaps, or maybe a royal concubine, or a priestess of his cult. I'm not happy about these idolatries of theirs, as you know, but there is a time and a place for everything, as it says in Ecclesiastes. In short . . .'

Pizarro paused and glanced at Gabriel, who was now shaking uncontrollably.

'In short, my boy, it seems to me that of all the women here that there are to choose from, you've chosen the wrong one.'

'I love her, Don Francisco.'

Gabriel regretted having said that the moment it left his mouth. What could the word 'love' mean to the Governor?

'Have you ever loved before, my boy, to use the term so blithely now?'

'No, Don Francisco, I haven't. That is why I now understand the meaning of the word.'

'It's a serious affair, then.'

There was no teasing in Pizarro's voice. Rather, Gabriel sensed an unexpected sadness in it.

'And yet you *must* end it, Gabriel. Or, at least, act with the greatest of care, so that the young man has no cause to give me any trouble whatsoever. Do you understand me?'

Gabriel couldn't reply. He felt Pizarro grab his arm and squeeze it, squeeze it until it hurt.

'Do you understand me, son?'

'I'm trying to.'

'Try harder. And I have something to help you forget this unhappiness of yours.'

Gabriel chortled nervously.

'You've found me another woman?'

'Better than that, my boy. I have a mission for you.'

'What is it?'

'Find me that statue. Find me the Sacred Double that they carry on about so much. I would like to see it for myself.'

Gabriel hoped that the Governor hadn't noticed it when the young conquistador's face had blanched.

The torchlight revealed Manco's face.

He came up close to Anamaya and stared at her without saying a word.

Anamaya had trouble regaining her breath, and she desperately tried to contain her rage at having been interrupted.

'Your father was speaking to me,' she said simply.

'I'm very sorry.'

Manco spoke these words with such simple sincerity that Anamaya's anger melted away.

'He was silent for so many moons. He hadn't spoken a word to me since the night of the Great Battle. I lived with a cold solitude within me.'

'Have you found him again?'

'He has never left me. I am his protector. Sometimes I think that he speaks to me only in order to remind me of what he had already taught me, back when I was but a young girl learning her lessons in the *acclahuasi*.'

'Does he speak to you about me?'

Manco's voice sounded touchingly naive. He was but a child, this Emperor, a child looking for reassurance.

'I told you, he marked you out a long time ago as the first knot of the future. Nothing that is happening now is new. Everything is as it should be, and the order of the universe is as your father told me it would be. You mustn't be frightened. You must be determined, and go onward. You must allow yourself to be guided by your own power and by that of the Sun God, just as you did on the day of the *huarachiku*.'

'You cannot stop me being frightened.'

'Your fear is an illusion. It isn't real. Your father never mentioned your fear to me, and I never spoke of it to the Elders when they elected you. Was your father frightened? Was Tupac Inca Yupanqui, frightened before him, or Pachacutec? Maybe—'

'And Manco Capac?'

The mention of the founder of the Inca dynasty left Anamaya wordless. She knew that Manco looked on him as his ultimate role model.

'Come,' he said.

She turned her palms reverently upward toward the Sacred Double before leaving him.

'I must return with *chicha* and corn, with coca and—'

'The dwarf fed him and quenched his thirst regularly. But you are right. He does need you.'

They passed quickly through the passage. Manco deftly pivoted the secret wall by placing both his hands on it. They found themselves back in the night outside, a night darker than the darkness that they had just come from.

On the esplanade at Colcampata, Manco took Anamaya's arm. He led her to the edge of the stone parapet overlooking the town and the valley. Although it was an inky-black night, moon-and starlight occasionally shone through gaps in the clouds, revealing the shadowy peaks of the Apus.

'My ancestor Manco Capac arrived here by crossing that mountain there, the Huanacauri. Mama Occlo was with him. They had made a long and difficult journey from the lake of origin, Lake Titicaca, from the depths of which the god Viracocha had created all that is. Manco saw this rich, fertile valley, and—'

Manco interrupted himself, and turned towards Anamaya.

'You are right. He may well have been frightened, but it is of no consequence. He had plenty of reasons to be frightened: travel fatigue; the certainty of his destiny, which he alone could see; doubt, that insidious enemy, which eats you from within and leaves you exhausted even before your battle has begun. The legends don't tell us which of these fears Manco Capac had to overcome before he took possession of his golden bar, his *taclla*, with which he tested the fertility of this valley soil for the first time. The legends are silent on that subject.'

Occasionally, the clouds would part wide enough to allow them a glimpse of the great river of stars in all its splendor. For a moment, the lights of the sky would match those on earth, the torches burning in the city, and for that moment the world would be in perfect harmony. Then a sudden gust would close the gap once again, and once again the black night returned, with its cold, its hostility, and its fearsomeness.

'The story goes that he was with Mama Occlo. The story goes that a woman helped him found the Empire.'

Anamaya suddenly realized what Manco was trying to say. She reproached herself for her slow understanding.

'I have stayed at your side as often as I could, Manco, and you know that I shall continue to do so.'

'That is not what I'm talking about.'

'Do you want yet another wife? It's impossible. I don't have royal blood running through my veins. Do you want another concubine for your bed? You have dozens already and, what's more, my skills in that particular art are negligible.'

'I know that, Anamaya, you've already told me so, and I don't want to lie to you with pretty words. And yet, I don't think that you would speak to me like this if it wasn't for . . .'

'If it wasn't for . . . ?'

Anamaya spoke defiantly. Manco lowered his tone.

'. . . If your heart wasn't already with another man.'

The silence of the night fell upon them. Anamaya controlled her breathing and made a concentrated effort to rid herself of the fear that had overcome her when she had sensed the violence underlying Manco's words. Manco, whom she had once protected in his youth, but who was now Emperor of the Empire of the Four Cardinal Directions.

'It's true,' she said at last. 'I love one of – of them.'

'A Stranger?'

'Yes.'

Manco had let go of Anamaya's arm some time ago. And yet she could feel him as though he were still touching her. She could feel his breath growing heavy. His profile, silhouetted in the night, looked something like that of a bird of prey, a hawk about to swoop, to attack.

'His arrival was foreseen by your father a long time ago.'

Manco shouted out in rage, and his fist came crashing down on the parapet.

'Manco!'

Anamaya's voice quivered with indignation.

'You know that I cannot tell a lie. Do you think that I would be so audacious, so *impious* as to invoke your father Huayna Capac's name in order to hide from you some sordid affair?'

'No, of course not. It's just that—'

He broke off. Manco's rage had passed as quickly as a squall. What remained was a moving, infinite sadness.

'Your father told me to wait for the puma's coming. This man is the puma.'

'This man is a Stranger. A Stranger cannot be the puma.'

'I find it as hard to believe as you do, Manco. And yet it is so. In my heart, I wished desperately for it to be otherwise. I've tried everything. But each time that I distanced myself from him, your father's voice reached me and told me to trust the puma.'

Manco remained silent.

'He is generous, Manco, and good. You have met him: you see that he already speaks our language, that he isn't like the rest of them, that he doesn't crave gold. What's more, I know for sure that he wants to help us. I've seen him try, with my own eyes.'

Manco let Anamaya list Gabriel's noble qualities to him. Or rather, he let the silent, black night absorb her words. Soon Anamaya, feeling a little ridiculous, stopped detailing the young Stranger's virtues.

'And now?' asked Manco.

'Now?'

'Now that union with the Inca is beneath you, now that you prefer some puma, come from who knows where . . .'

'Your rage is no better than your fear, Manco. It might even be worse . . .'

'I often speak to my rage, you know. I speak to it as though it were a person and as one does to become familiar with one's enemy. I ask it to let me be. Childishly, I believed that becoming the Sapa Inca would rid me of it. I know now that it's not the case.'

His joyless laugh rang through the night.

'He cannot have you, you know,' he said.

'I know.'

'You are the Sacred Double's wife, the *Coya Camaquen*, and you cannot be wife to any other, whether he is a puma or not.'

'I know, Manco. I didn't ask for this destiny of mine. But I accept it.'

As Anamaya spoke these words, her voice cracked despite herself. She had a vision of herself leaning over her mother's face – her mother who no could longer speak those tender words to her that reached into her very soul. Anamaya trembled as her old suffering returned. Then she said, with great dignity:

'I served at your father's side, and I never failed Atahualpa. I saved you from the snake, and it was my voice through which your father designated you to be Emperor. Do you need yet more proof of my loyalty?'

'I trust you, Anamaya,' said Manco in a conciliatory tone. 'I do not doubt you, and I know the difficulties that you have overcome. I am grateful to you, as I am to all those loyal to me. What's more, I need you for what is to come . . .'

'That which must be.'

'That which must be.'

Manco's words echoed Anamaya's, and the universe's natural order was restored. But still, he stopped short when he reached out his hand to touch her arm. True, he had given his pain a name: that which must be, must be. But that which mustn't be would not be – and that was just as cruel.

CHAPTER 22

Cuzco, end of November 1533

THE *ACLLAHUASI*'S ONLY DOOR OPENED ONTO AUCAYPATA Square. Its buildings were wedged between those of Hatun Cancha, where the Spaniards were setting up their quarters, and those of the palace of Amaru Cancha, which Governor Pizarro had allotted to Captain de Soto.

The twenty Inca guards supposed to preserve and protect the house of virgins had fled the moment the Strangers had arrived. Only one remained, either because he was unshakably loyal or else because his blindness stopped him fleeing. Anamaya called to him:

'You may let me pass, old man. I am not some bearded Stranger come to ravish a virgin or one of the Sun King's wives.'

'You shouldn't joke about such matters,' grumbled the old man. 'One day such a thing may very well happen.'

'Impossible. You'll be here to defend us.'

The ancient guard waved his hand wearily, and turned his white, unseeing eyes toward the sun.

Anamaya headed down the alleyway that ran alongside the *acllahuasi*'s buildings, passing first the workshops, then the warehouses filled with *piruas*, the large jars in which all that was needed to maintain the Inca empire was kept. She walked across the courtyard in which the idol of the Sun God was worshiped every morning, passed the buildings that housed the servant girls, the ordinary *acllas*, most of whom had already returned to their families, and finally reached the end of the alleyway, where the wives of the Sun King were lodged and where it was forbidden to enter under the penalty of death.

Anamaya was regarded as some kind of queen in the *acllahuasi*. Even Curi Ocllo, Manco's *coya*, did not dare challenge her authority. The women who had remained behind, priestesses who had devoted their lives to the cults of the various Inca divinities, felt threatened by the Strangers, who were steadily taking over the surrounding palaces and temples. Rumors of the rapes that they had committed in all the towns through which they had passed had reached Cuzco, and the women looked to Anamaya with a certain illogical expectation, perhaps because her blue eyes, the color of a peaceful lake, calmed them, or because she always had a kind word for the terrified young girls and their servants.

Anamaya's own room was located just before those of the Sun King's wives, and no one was allowed to enter it without her invitation. Her room was completely bare except for a simple mat, a woolen blanket, and a snake carved from stone in the room's only niche.

As Anamaya passed through the door-hanging, she heard sobbing.

'Inguill!'

The young girl was rolled up in a ball at the end of the mat and didn't rise to greet Anamaya, who had never before seen her gripped by such a terrible despair.

'Inguill! What happened?'

She turned her small careworn face toward Anamaya and said:

'What good did it do me to obey him? What good did it do me to cross great mountains and slip past soldiers who wanted to rape me and cut me up? What good did your protection do me?'

'Inguill, if you don't tell me what happened, I'm going to leave you to sob by yourself.'

'He's not going to take me.'

'Manco?'

'He promised me he would a long time ago, but he's not

going to do it. He despises me more than even the lowest of his concubines.'

'But have you lost your mind?'

'He hasn't spoken to me once since we arrived in Cuzco.'

'But he had to leave the very next day with Captain de Soto's horsemen and give chase to the northern armies, those who had mistreated you.'

'But I so hoped that he would have me, Anamaya, I so hoped for it.'

'Inguill, listen to me . . .'

Anamaya couldn't tell Inguill that she was responsible for Manco suffering the same pain that Inguill now suffered because of him. But she *could* tell her that this world was full of inexplicable emotions, and that one could never know whether to love and be loved was a blessing or a curse. And when she told the girl about the puma, about Gabriel, Inguill's teary eyes suddenly lit up with pleasure and surprise.

'A Stranger!'

But Inguill didn't seem disdainful or frightened, as the men had been. She asked Anamaya questions that only a woman would ask. She asked her if his hands were gentle and what his lips tasted like. Anamaya told Inguill the delicious details, told her of his tenderness, and of how she would have to hide her eyes from him whenever they filled with tears when he was in her arms, inside her.

'But I cannot see him anymore,' she finished, rather anti-climactically.

'Why not?'

'Manco has ordered me not to. He wants me to remain faithful to my husband, the Sacred Double, and to the service of the Empire.'

Inguill said nothing. Her feminine instinct fell short of knowing the mysteries of the Inca's destiny.

'I will speak to Manco about you,' said Anamaya after a pause. 'I won't leave you alone, my friend.'

Inguill curled up in her arms.

'The other women love you because you see and hear secrets

that they cannot understand. But *I* love you because you are good.'

Anamaya was hardly listening to the girl. Speaking about Gabriel, being able at last to share her secret openly with someone, had been a wonderful relief. But as soon as she had spoken her words she wanted to say them again, and her heartbreak was even greater than before. Obeying Manco was a burden that was hardly becoming lighter with each passing day. On the contrary, it was a pointless ordeal, and one that led nowhere.

Anamaya wished that there were no more words, that Gabriel would simply be there, with his eyes and his smile, with his way of silently desiring her, and that he would come to her, confident, noble – magnificent.

The first time Bartholomew stopped Katari, one morning on the gray, empty Cusipata esplanade, the young Kolla was startled. He stared at the Stranger whose black habit was girdled with a white sash, whose head was completely devoid of hair, and two of whose fingers were joined together. And then he stared directly into the monk's gray eyes with his own dark gaze and held his look until a smile lit the Stranger's face, a smile with no hint of malice, underlying violence, or fear. It was the smile of a man who had unexpectedly recognized himself in another.

Katari flicked his long black hair and pointed at the towers and thick walls of Sacsayhuaman rising over them. Then he swept his hand around at the entire city in its cradle of fields and terraces and at the slopes of the mountains surrounding them, before finally pointing at the first rays of the sun now rising in the east, from the direction of the distant and invisible ocean across which the Strangers had journeyed from their homeland.

The two men began walking along beside one another.

And they had been doing so ever since. Rarely a day passed when they didn't meet to ramble together through the more obscure corners of the city, or else into the mountains overlooking Cuzco, the mountains with their sacred stones, their streams, and their spirits.

Gradually, their silent partnership had given way to an exchange of a few words, and anyone observing them would have had the impression that the language of one somehow matched and intermingled with the language of the other, even if neither man ever understood more than a third of what the other was saying. Katari was frequently astonished to see the monk take from his robe a rectangular piece of fabric and some sort of paintbrush, similar to those used by potters, and trace a few patterns on the fabric. But he asked no questions. He breathed in the air and allowed the breeze to carry him. He showed the monk the steps that led, upside down, into the depths of the earth. He heard him pronounce the name of God.

Today a storm had forced them home earlier than they had planned. Bartholomew led Katari to the simple house in which the monk was quartered in Cantupata, a district where flowers bloomed with a magnificence that Bartholomew found richer and more beautiful than all the gold in the world.

Katari examined the few simple pieces of furniture with some curiosity. There were a table, four chairs, and some shelves on which sat a few books. He stared for some time at the crucifix attached to the wall. Bartholomew gave no explanation. Instead the monk pulled out a chair and invited his guest to sit down. Katari looked at him with some confusion, and the monk gently pushed him down by the shoulders until he was seated. Katari had the impression of floating above the earth. He was not lying down, nor squatting, nor standing. It was a position utterly alien to man.

The monk took out a piece of his white fabric and placed it in front of him, along with another brush. He dipped the brush in some black liquid contained in a tiny, narrow-necked jar, shook a drop or two from it, and then began tracing signs on his white fabric again.

'Look,' he said, 'and do as I do.'

He held his brush out to Katari, and the young man clumsily dipped it in the small bottle. He tried to trace a few signs on the fabric, but he managed only to make a mess, causing Bartholomew to burst out laughing. He looked at the monk

furiously, and Bartholomew simply started over again, patiently
guiding his hand.

'That's good,' he said eventually.

Katari looked at what he had traced. It was some kind of sign,
a poor facsimile of what Bartholomew had done on the other piece
of fabric, but he had no idea what it represented. He looked at the
monk inquisitively.

'*Amigo*,' said the monk, pointing at the signs.

Katari looked from Bartholomew to the piece of fabric and
back again.

Bartholomew pointed with his two joined fingers at each of the
signs on the fabric, saying patiently:

'A-M-I-G-O. *Amigo!*'

And, smiling, he placed his hand first on his own chest, then
on Katari's.

'You and me: *amigos!*'

Katari's face suddenly lit up with understanding.

'*Amigo!*' he said, nodding his head enthusiastically.

CHAPTER 23

T HE DWARF HAD WAITED FOR NIGHT TO VEIL THE CITY before daring to venture out into its streets. Whenever he heard the sound of hooves hammering the flagstones, he would duck into a doorway, or else flatten himself against a wall. He did not follow the Huatanay, which led directly to the Aucaypata, his destination, but rather took the long way through dark alleyways, stopping often to look over his shoulder.

When he reached the square, he stood for a long time in the shadow of a wall, watching the Spanish soldiers' tent city. Why had he said yes to Anamaya, he asked himself, and put his own life in danger once again? He sighed and stepped tentatively forward. She had told him that it was the tent closest to the Amaru Cancha. 'He speaks Quechua,' she had said, 'and I have told him about you. When he sees you, he'll know straightaway that you were sent by me.'

The soldiers the dwarf came across barely noticed him, or else elbowed one another in the ribs and burst out laughing. He felt his legs weaken as he approached the tent. Just as he was about to enter it, a voice burst out from within and startled him.

There was a strange atmosphere inside the tent. The sight of the Strangers, their bare torsos covered in black or red hair, quite alarmed the dwarf. He saw weapons bigger than himself lying about, along with those hollow metal carcasses that made the Strangers invulnerable. He was tongue-tied, unable to speak a word, but they wouldn't have understood him anyway. He rolled his eyes, looking from one to another, trying to stay as far away as possible from them while all the while hoping that some miracle would show him which of them was the one he was looking for.

But the Strangers, gesticulating and making odd sounds, approached him, and he scurried backward, waving his arms in front of him. He tried to scramble out of the tent, became entangled in the canvas, and fell over. As the Strangers' laughter pealed out, he thought, feeling somewhat ridiculous, that this time there was no Huayna Capac to protect him.

'What are you doing here?'

The Stranger had accidentally kicked him as he had entered the tent. He had blond hair and pale eyes, and he seemed less barbaric than the others. He perfunctorily helped the dwarf to his feet.

'Are you the one they call Gabriel?'

Gabriel looked at him, taken aback. Then comprehension flashed across his face and he muttered a few words to the others, who sniggered.

Gabriel wordlessly followed the dwarf through the sea of tents until they reached La Cassana, where they started down the alleyway leading to Colcampata. Here Gabriel grabbed the dwarf by the collar and growled, 'Are you going to tell me where you're leading me or not?'

'I cannot. You must trust me, and follow me.'

Gabriel shoved him away angrily but continued to follow him – never once noticing the shadows treading softly behind them.

As the dwarf placed his hands on the wall Gabriel suddenly felt very alone and very foolish. If this was a trap, he had walked into it carelessly, unthinkingly.

Why was he doing this? Some vague old story Anamaya had told him in Cajamarca about her friendship with a tiny man. And what of the dwarf's odd way of pronouncing his name: GA-briel?

The passage was completely dark. Gabriel called out, but in vain. He turned around and placed his hands on the wall to find his bearings, but he found nothing but empty air. He was overcome by a vertiginous terror, an old fear from his childhood that knotted his guts. He could feel the violent thumps of his heart beating in his chest and pulsing in his temples.

He went forward, feeling his way with his feet, checking that the ground was solid ahead of him. The ground had the same sandy quality as in the great square. Then he grazed his hands against the hard stone of the walls. This reassured him, and although he didn't advance any faster, he was less panicked now.

But a moment later Gabriel's hands met air again. He thought he could make out a gray light high above him, a light that illuminated nothing. He stopped in his tracks, and his whole body had a sensation of spinning and of falling into a pit.

'You're here,' his beloved said gently.

Gabriel grabbed her with a passion that he had not thought himself capable of, a passion greater than the terror to which he had just now almost surrendered. And as his hands took hold of her body, he growled like a wounded animal. He had conflicting urges to love her and hurt her at the same time, to cover her in kisses while beating her until she cried.

And even though he thought he was dominating her, it was Anamaya who pulled him down to the ground, to a pile of matting covered in blankets made of the softest wool, and it was her tenderness that inflamed both his desire and his rage. He desired her with an urgency he had never yet felt, an ardor without limits.

Gabriel slipped Anamaya's tunic off her shoulders, and he felt her abandon herself to him, give herself without any restraint, as though all the days that they had spent apart had removed all the barriers between them. Her hot skin quivered beneath his touch.

He felt as though every part of his body was charged with desire, that if she kissed his neck, if her breast brushed against his, or if her leg found its way between his thighs, he would have to cry out to release all the knotted tension contained within him. Perhaps he would also have to vent his anger at the fact that she had let so many days go by without contacting him, and had even seemed to avoid him deliberately.

Her belly writhed against his in a passionate frenzy of release, and her sinuous movements made him think of those snakes that she was friendly with. He allowed himself to be engulfed by her, overwhelmed by her, and he surrendered to her serpentine power. When he entered her, he sensed her holding her breath, and her long silence left him surprised and still. Then, slowly, she resumed her undulating movement, subtle and irresistible.

It was so dark that Gabriel couldn't make out Anamaya's face, and this accentuated his excitement. What man had not fantasized of a mysterious woman, a magical woman with perhaps malign powers, who would lead him into forbidden love during the blackness of night? He knew that it was Anamaya with whom he was making love but the sense that she had become a stranger to him provoked in him a fury of which he was terrified, and over which he had no control.

'Put your hands around my neck,' she said.

Gabriel was so startled by this that he almost withdrew, but Anamaya was so much part of him that she effortlessly controlled his rhythm. Then his hands, suddenly docile and obedient, left her smooth thighs and her arched back, its curve leading the dance of love. At first he simply stroked her neck, but then his fingers joined together around it, like the clasp of a necklace. He could feel her throat flesh palpitate like the wings of a fragile bird, while the rest of her body increased its pace frenetically. He squeezed her neck to the point where he felt her suffocating, as all the while her body continued to surge like a sea swell over his own, At the moment he released his grip on her, tears welled in his eyes as he let go of all his anger and released all his desire into her.

Anamaya wrapped a blanket around them and nestled her head in the hollow of Gabriel's neck. He couldn't stop crying, and she licked away his tears like a cat. Slowly he calmed down, and he realized that he still had more questions than answers.

'I didn't want to hurt you,' he said.

Then, after a pause, he corrected himself:

'No. I *did* want to hurt you.'

'I wanted you to do both. Not hurt me, and hurt me.'

'And?'

'You did both well.'

They laughed with relief.

'Ours is a strange world,' Anamaya said. 'A secret door opens in the middle of the wall of a *huaca*, and you fall through it to the center of the earth, and then, lost in the absolute darkness there, a light suddenly blinds you. When you go out again, you are reborn. You are changed, transformed into something else. I'll take you there one day.'

'Haven't you just done so?'

'You still know nothing.'

Gabriel whistled between his teeth, and Anamaya giggled once again.

'Where are we?'

'Are you like the other Strangers, then, who can't stand not knowing, and who want to know, to own, everything?'

'You seem to know everything about them. About the Strangers.'

'*You* taught me everything I know about them. We are in the only place in Cuzco where we may meet without your people or mine bothering us.'

'Manco, right?'

'Manco won't harm you. But he needs me near him, and I mustn't shirk my duty to my father.'

'Your father? But I thought—'

'My father Huayna Capac.'

'Anamaya, I don't understand any of this. I thought you were married to that king . . .'

'The Sacred Double, yes.'

'Where is he?'

He felt her stiffen, then slip out of his embrace.

'What's wrong?'

'Why did you ask me that?'

'To protect you against my people's greed. The younger Pizarro brothers – may their souls speed to Satan – have heard rumors of a statue made of solid gold, and they think of it now as the finest prize to be had in Cuzco, perhaps because they've never seen it. And to cap it all, the Governor has ordered me to find it.'

'And what would you do if you did?'

'Why, like the others, of course. I'd take possession of it and melt it down into ingots. I'd make myself rich. Wasn't it my avarice that seduced you?'

'Tell me what you would do, seriously.'

'I'd help you hide it from their greed. Because if I can find it, then so can they.'

Gabriel reached out to embrace Anamaya but she dodged him. His voice echoed into the void. He was naked and cold.

Just then a torch flickered into life, revealing the room by its feeble light. It was a circular room, like a baptistery, and before his eyes adjusted Gabriel saw only dancing shadows. Then he saw Anamaya, also naked, and despite their recent lovemaking he was still aroused by the sight of her supple body. In the center of the room was a gold statue on a plinth, glowing red in the torchlight. It was seated on a throne in the same posture as those of the other mummies Gabriel had seen. It was absolutely perfect except for its nose, the tip of which was missing.

Gabriel shivered, but not from the cold. They had barely had time to recover from their lovemaking, or to enjoy the delicious abandon that had been denied them for so long.

'Is it not a terrible thing with your people to disobey orders, as it is with mine?'

'Yes, it is. But when orders are merely a concealing cloak for immoral greed, then even what they call treason is a preferable course of action.'

'Perhaps you are disguising a simpler emotion with honorable words.'

'It's that very emotion which inspires honor in me.'

'You will be exposed to great dangers, Gabriel.'

'Hide this statue tonight.'

'We must not stay together any longer. You must trust me – no matter what you see, no matter what happens – you must trust me without being able to be with me, you must trust me despite all the evidence to the contrary.'

'What do you mean?'

But Anamaya's voice was already trailing off into the distance, even though Gabriel wanted to touch her once more, to hold her in his arms, to feel the fleeting caress of her lips.

'Trust me as I have trusted you. I will be there, Gabriel, when I need to be. Close your eyes.'

He obeyed her, using all his strength to resist the instinctive urge he was feeling to do otherwise. He wanted to take her with him. He wanted to defy Pizarro, Manco, and the Governor's brothers. But instead he listened to the soft echo of her words: *Trust me as I have trusted you.*

When Gabriel at last reopened his eyes, he found himself facing the dwarf's froglike stare. He didn't even turn back to look at the Sacred Double as the two of them set out down the passage. He felt empty and weak.

When they emerged into the night, he walked along the Colcampata esplanade. He looked up at the stars and made out shapes in the Milky Way, shapes that, one after the other, Anamaya had shown him after Atahualpa's death – the dog, the llama, the condor.

Suddenly, in the middle of that celestial disorder, Gabriel clearly saw a great cat looking at him, its paws raised, its mouth open.

The puma.

He walked fearlessly onward to the square.

CHAPTER 24

The Temple at Cuzco, 20 December 1533

A NAMAYA HAD TROUBLE DISTINGUISHING BETWEEN THE
silhouettes of the two men walking ahead of her through
the damp fog. Yet Villa Oma and Katari could not have
been more different in appearance. The fog seemed to stretch the
Sage's already unusually tall and lean body, whereas it flattened
the young Kolla's already compact one.

No one said a word.

They were only a short distance from Cuzco, but the weather
was so bad that they might as well have been lost in the mountains,
in the heart of the wilderness. The Sage was leading them along a
narrow path lined by two low walls to the temple in which Manco
had retreated for three days. Here he had to complete the ritual
fast decreed before he could receive the *mascapaicha*.

Turning around, they could see the city, indeed the entire valley,
engulfed in fog. The play of the light streaking across the sky sent
shapes of boulders, animals, and warriors to meet them, and the
gusting wind made these emit indistinct, doleful cries.

What was Viracocha's will?

The bulk of the Poquekancha temple now rose ahead of them,
with its vast esplanade and its blocks almost as perfectly hewn
as those at Coricancha. It was surrounded by corn terraces, the
widths of which exactly matched the height of the walls.

As Villa Oma greeted the guards standing at the only door cut
in the wall, Anamaya turned around and allowed herself to absorb

the harmony of the place. Majestic and shadowy, the view here of this world had never been more similar to that of the Other.

The temple's courtyard was thick with fog. It seemed to rise from the ground and was streaked with silver filaments, like a hummingbird feather. It muffled the regular lapping sound of the fountain, which was fed by a cleverly constructed system of pipes.

Manco sat alone at the entrance to his room.

Tomorrow, he would don the Inca's costume, which included an *unku* that a hundred virgins had woven in the *acllahuasi*, ensuring that each of its strands radiated gold and colour. He would wear a necklace made of many thousand *chaquiras*, a *llautu* and a *curiguingue*, heavy gold earlobe plugs, and the royal breastplate. But for the moment he wore only a simple white *unku* and straw sandals, and he was seated on his *tiana*, gazing at the pearly sky.

Anamaya, Katari and Villa Oma stood in front of him in silence, their heads bowed. He looked away from the sky to gaze at them. He gave them the most fleeting of smiles, a smile that in no way lightened his haggard expression.

'It looks like the Son of the Sun is lost in the fog,' said Katari.

Anamaya was taken aback, and Villa Oma almost choked. There was an awful, tension-filled pause – and then Manco burst out laughing, so hard that his whole body shook and he finished with a fit of coughing. Katari's face lit up and Anamaya relaxed, but the green-mouthed Sage remained unmoved, severe, disapproving.

'The Son of the Sun in the fog – you're the only one, Katari, whom I can forgive for such a transgression. Isn't it so, Sage Villa Oma?

The priest made no reply, but his moral disapproval was palpable. Anamaya found him more reserved and severe than ever, as though a deep, deep fury was constantly raging in his guts.

'Follow me,' said Manco.

He led them to one of the rooms giving onto the courtyard. Unlike many other temples, this one hadn't yet been ransacked by the Strangers. It still had not only its gold frieze running along the top portion of the wall, just below the expertly worked beam supporting the *ichu*'s roof, but also thick gold plaques on which, with a single, unbroken stroke of the awl, the outlines of animals had been etched. There were still idols in the niches, statues of gods with precious stones – turquoises and emeralds – as eyes, eyes that followed one around the room.

But, above all, there were still paintings.

Anamaya's breath was cut short at the sight. The paintings were on wood panels hung on all the walls around the room. She had never seen them before, but she recognized in the blink of an eye the most famous scenes of Inca history: the construction of Coricancha by Pachucatec and the battle against the Chanca. She was fascinated by them, and she could not dwell on one long before feeling the urge to go to the next. The scenes seemed so alive, so powerful, their colours so vibrant, the characters so close to reality that she wouldn't have been surprised to find the painter still there with them, hidden among them.

Even Villa Oma seemed impressed by the solemnity of the place. The entire mythology of the Inca world was painted here in strong, simple images, stronger than words and far more durable than any roar of battle. Anamaya suddenly felt her heart jump in her chest.

She had recognized, in one of the paintings, the great Huayna Capac's inscrutable face, as cracked as old wood, and so true to life that it left her dizzy with shock. He was pictured reclining on a mat, his body hidden by wool and down blankets that protected him from the cold. And at his side, her face half hidden in shadow, stood a little girl, her timid blue eyes revealing her dread as the old Emperor placed his hand on her.

Manco watched Anamaya as her eyes filled with tears. She could not escape from the role she had played in the Empire ever since Huayna Capac had died. But nothing could match this painting in making her realize how much she had now become part of its history.

'Tomorrow,' said Manco slowly, 'will be a great day for the Incas.'

Anamaya looked away from the painting to her friend's aquiline face. She saw a vital flame burning in his dark eyes.

'But tomorrow,' he continued solemnly, 'is also fraught with dangers. My fast has relieved me of many pointless concerns. But it has not dispersed all my confusion. I need your help to see clearly.'

He looked at Villa Oma, who didn't bat an eyelid, and then at Katari, who smiled faintly.

Finally, he rested his gaze on Anamaya. And held it there.

A few days before Christmas, Don Francisco Pizarro at last gave the order to strike the tents on the square, and commanded that the men should go to their quarters. Gabriel was staying with him in the La Cassana palace and not across the square with the rest of the men. He was alone in a modestly sized room and enjoying his only concession to luxury: a window, an exceptional little trapezoid of light that he had refused to cover in greased paper so that he might continue to enjoy the spectacle of the street, of the motley crowd of men and women flowing along beside the Huatanay.

'Gabriel?'

Gabriel made out Bartholomew's silhouette in the shadows, and did his best to suppress the nameless dread gripping him.

'What news?'

The monk approached him, smiled, and brushed past him. He stood by the window and watched the passers-by on the street.

'They're hopeful,' he said lightly.

'What do they hope for?'

'What all men hope for: peace, food, a woman's body. Our men hope for more: gold, silver, and the like.'

'True. The Governor has promised that the paying-out will begin immediately after the coronation.'

'You say that so joylessly.'

'You know very well that gold holds no glitter for me.'

Bartholomew looked at him curiously.

'You have only one motive for being here, then?'

'Which is?'

'The same as me: for the glory of God.'

A twinkle in Bartholomew's eye prompted both men into fits of laughter.

'By the faith, my friend, given the circumstances in which we met, I find it most generous of you to endow me with such religious zeal.'

'Am I so wrong?'

Gabriel, avoiding the monk's gaze, bit back his sarcastic reply.

'It's up to you to decide. But have you come here to ask me to help you prepare for Mass?'

'No, my friend. You know that for that purpose dear Father Valverde is unmatchable. He has already dedicated the palace that the Governor gave him to Our Lady of the Conception, after having exorcised it of demons, of course. I imagine the demons fled at the mere sight of him, howling at the tops of their lungs.'

'Will the church be built in time for Christmas?'

'Most likely not. But only because we no longer believe in miracles.'

'You don't think I can perform them, do you?'

'I wish you would stop mistrusting me, Gabriel. You have some problems that I can help you with. Come.'

The two men crossed the palace's vast courtyard, which was patrolled by soldiers night and day. It was here, in the Governor's own palace, that the treasures looted from the other palaces and temples were heaped in piles under the treasurer's watchful eye. It was also where these piles sat waiting to be melted down into ingots from which the royal fifth was levied, the remainder being divided among the conquistadors.

They came out onto the square which, now that the tent city had disappeared, had regained its normal appearance. Bartholomew led Gabriel to the fountain in its center. Dawn's thick fog had now dispersed and they stood in the light of a warm sun.

'They saw you,' said Bartholomew.

'Could you speak Castilian, so that I can understand you?'

Bartholomew raised his two joined fingers in an appeasing gesture.

'A few days ago, you were guided by night to one of their temples. You then "disappeared into a wall" – forgive me for the expression – before reappearing a few hours later.'

'So?' said Gabriel defiantly.

Bartholomew paused. Then:

'You can reply to me any way you wish. But I'm not so sure that the Governor will accept the same reply.'

Gabriel turned pale.

'I think I know who you visited that night. Believe me, I'm not judging you in any way, no matter what you might think.'

Gabriel scrutinized the bald-headed monk's expression to see if he could discern a trap. But he found only the wrinkles of genuine concern.

'Your first problem is that the two Pizarro brothers have a different theory. And your second problem is that they are trying at this very moment to bring the Governor around to their way of thinking.'

'And what do those two curs think?'

'They think that you've found this famous gold statue that the Governor commissioned you to find. But they also think that you've hidden it away safely and hope to keep it all to yourself.'

Gabriel felt the ground open up beneath his feet. Bartholomew stared piercingly at him with his gray eyes and said:

'In the name of God, is my Castilian clear enough for you now?'

It was a long and grim argument. More often than not, it was Manco and Villa Oma who disagreed as Katari looked on. While they carried on, Anamaya stared at the painting of Huayna Capac's death, experiencing the odd sensation of looking at her own memories.

'We must go to war, and we must do it now,' insisted Villa Oma. 'We must not repeat your brother Atahualpa's mistake. We must destroy them while we still can. We must raise an army from all the villages. We must summon your brother Paullu, and perhaps even make peace with Quizquiz and Guaypar . . .'

At that, Manco roared:

'No! I will hunt those two down unto the Other World if I have to. They elude me now, but—'

'—But only with the help of the Strangers! Do you really believe their false smiles, their sweet words? Do you really believe the things they tell you to lull you into complacency? Do you really want to serve under their king, and under their god? You will serve them like a slave—'

'Villa Oma!'

'You go too far, Sage,' intervened Anamaya.

'But I'm not accusing Manco of cowardice,' raged Villa Oma. 'I'm just saying that we know what the Strangers are now, we know that they only want to strip us of our treasures, to take our silver when our gold runs out, our turquoises when we have no more emeralds. We know that they want to destroy our temples. How much longer must we wait before we fight back?'

'We're not ready, Sage Villa Oma,' said Anamaya simply, motioning to Manco to say nothing. 'We're not ready yet. It's as simple as that.'

The Sage stared at the young woman to whom he had taught, many moons ago now, the most sacred rites of the Inca world. A sad smile crossed his gray, wrinkled face.

'You have changed, young Anamaya.'

'I have listened,' she said, 'and I have learned. I know these Strangers well.' She looked away from Manco as she said this. 'And I know their motives. But our father Huayna Capac's message is that Manco must reign, and that at first it must be the reign of the snake, who slides silently between the stones and disappears into the leaves. It is not yet to be the reign of the condor, master of the skies.'

Manco turned to Katari.

'What do you think?'

The young man flicked his long hair.

'Anamaya is right.'

'And you, Villa Oma?'

The Sage made no reply, but simply nodded, conceding defeat. For the time being.

'Is the Sacred Double secure?'

Manco had uttered the question like an accusation.

'He has left Colcampata and Cuzco for a secret destination,' Anamaya said simply.

'Will the blond Stranger be shown this place as he was the last?'

Anamaya, shocked to her core, grew pale with shame, but did not ask how he had found out.

'No.'

Katari and Villa Oma said nothing. The Sage wore a severe, disdainful look on his face. Anamaya felt an impulse to self-defence rise within her, but Katari stepped in front of her and said:

'It's not what you think, Manco.'

The young Inca wavered for a moment. He trusted Katari absolutely, but he was caught between conflicting emotions.

'The *Coya Camaquen* has always been the Empire's most loyal servant,' said Villa Oma, in his usual abrupt manner. But Anamaya sensed that his words carried weight. Manco touched her tentatively on the shoulder.

'I need you, Anamaya. The Empire of the Four Cardinal Directions needs you.'

His voice was so shy that Anamaya found it touching. She heard in it the echo of the adolescent frozen in fear of a snake, the adolescent for whom she had cleared the way.

'Everything is ready for the *capa cocha*,' said the Sage, green coca juice dribbling from his lips.

Anamaya froze, staring at him.

'But it's impossible!' she exclaimed, turning to Manco, who didn't react.

'Impossible?' chortled the Sage. 'The children of the highest families are arriving as we speak from every corner of the Empire. They are coming to receive the honor of being sacrificed for the glory of the Son of the Sun.'

Anamaya declared flatly:

'The Strangers will never allow it.'

'The Strangers!'

Villa Oma turned to Manco for support. But still the young Inca showed no reaction.

'Who are these Strangers,' spat Villa Oma, 'that they think they can interrupt our traditions that have existed since the foundation of the Inca empire? Who are they to impose their laws, their gods, upon us?'

Anamaya stared at the Sage. Her anger inexplicably gave way to an enveloping calm.

'You are wrong, Sage.'

Throughout this confrontation between the young girl and the old priest, Katari hadn't opened his mouth once, hadn't moved any more than Manco had. But at these last words, he came and stood close to Anamaya, his long hair brushing the *Coya Camaquen*'s shoulders.

Villa Oma spat on the ground to show his contempt.

'Well, Manco?'

Anamaya had tried to speak as gently as possible, but she hadn't been able to stop her voice from trembling. A bitter memory had flashed in front of her mind's eye: that of the very young girl who had been saved by the condor, many moons ago, on the summit of the mountain overlooking the secret city.

Manco looked away.

'The Strangers mustn't see a thing,' he said. 'But . . .'

'But?'

'. . . My reign cannot begin without the *capa cocha*.'

Anamaya said nothing. She tried to catch Manco's eye but he looked obstinately away. She held back from spitting out the words of disgust and great vexation that had formed in her mind.

The words *capa cocha* reverberated in her head like a terrible echo shrieking out into a narrow mountain gorge.

When they eventually left the temple and came out into the exquisite day, the sky a magnificent blue, the dreaded words were still echoing in her head.

The great hall of La Cassana was crawling with people. Local caciques, sporting colorful tunics and wearing gold discs in their ears, were gathered in groups not far from the soldiers. Some were looking for a step up or allies to plot with, while others were fishing for information on behalf of the Sage or Manco. Many were acting for both sides, keeping their options open, and

Gabriel, passing through this crowd, was uncannily reminded of the court in Toledo, that seething mass of ambition and mediocrity. Human nature, it seemed, was universal.

'Well, my boy?'

On the eve of his triumph – triumph, because Manco's coronation was Pizarro's victory – the Governor seemed to have relaxed at last. He wore neither his armor nor his chain mail, and he had slipped a crimson vest, of all things, over his usual black garb. Even his crisp white ruff suggested spring, as did the feathers in his hat, which jiggled as though still attached to the bird from which they had been plucked.

Don Francisco had broken away from the group fawning around him to join Gabriel, who noticed the Governor's brothers glaring at him malevolently, as well as de Soto and Pedro de Candia smiling at him more amicably.

'I haven't seen much of you, these last few days.'

'Don Francisco, I must speak with you.'

'I believe that is so, yes.'

It was the same friendly and paternal face, but Gabriel sensed an element of menace in his tone. He privately thanked Bartholomew for having forewarned him. Pizarro took Gabriel by the arm and led him back to the group, despite his reluctance.

'Gabriel wishes to speak to us,' he said smugly.

'I said I wished to speak to *you*,' Gabriel remarked pointedly.

'What is there to hear? Are my brothers' ears too delicate, perhaps? Captain de Soto's too large?'

Gabriel hadn't been mistaken: Pizarro's words, husked of their humor, threatened a severe reprimand. De Soto raised his hand in an appeasing gesture, and bowed before turning on his heels and disappearing without saying a word. De Candia was about to do the same, but the giant Greek stayed after Gabriel gave him a look imploring him to do so.

'Only traitors and thieves speak in such riddles as that fair-haired idiot, utters,' spat Gonzalo.

Gabriel reddened at the insult and placed his hand on the hilt of his sword.

'Hold your tongue, Gonzalo. Were you not the Governor's

brother, I'd have it out with you in an instant.'

'I know who you are, bastard son. My brother Hernando told me all about you, and I warn you . . .'

Gabriel glanced sidelong at Don Francisco. The word 'bastard' hadn't made him bat an eyelid. He even seemed to be deriving some strange pleasure from the dispute. All conversation had ceased, and a circle had formed around the group of men. Everybody awaited the logical outcome of the confrontation with baited breath. Gabriel noticed Sebastian giving him a friendly and slightly concerned look.

'I'll teach you a lesson, you cur. And I won't show you the mercy that I showed him.'

'I know all about you, you damned swine. I'll have your sword and your balls. And I'll have the gold statue you've hidden for yourself. And then I'll have your blue-eyed wench – I'll part her legs and show her what a real *caballero* is made of.'

Gabriel threw himself at Gonzalo, landing a roundhouse punch just above his eye. Blood burst from the split.

'Enough!' barked Pizarro, but to little avail. Gonzalo was as eager to fight as was Gabriel, and it took two or three men and his brother Juan to hold him back. There was no longer anything benevolent in Pizarro's dark eyes as he turned toward Gabriel.

Gabriel was breathing heavily, like a smith's bellows. He glared back at his master, the Governor.

'Gabriel,' Pizarro growled, 'when in God's name will you cease your childish capers? You have all the ingredients of happiness within your grasp: my friendship, my trust, and the respect of all those who have seen you in battle. Why do you insist on forfeiting it all? Why continue with these petty squabbles with a man whom I do not rate, even though he's my brother? Do you see me, the Governor, picking a quarrel with him over any of his idiocies?'

Gabriel brusquely freed himself, and eyed off Gonzalo, who was trying to stem the copious flow of blood from his split brow.

'You are, of course, in the right of it, Governor. Such idle prattle has no end. Follow me, then, those of you who crave so much to know where I've hidden my treasure.'

As he walked away, the rest of the group made to follow him. Gabriel stopped short, turned around, and pointed at the Governor's brothers.

'Not you. Don Francisco, de Candia, and Sebastian only. Not one more.'

And with that he turned on his heels. Pizarro pretended not to be surprised. He ignored his brothers' furious protestations and, winking at Candia, he fell into step at Gabriel's side.

Daylight was fading.

Gabriel and Pizarro hadn't said a word to each other since they had started out on the road to Colcampata. They entered the passage alone.

Sebastian and Pedro de Candia waited silently out on the esplanade.

'Well?' said the Greek.

Sebastian said nothing at first. Then:

'I hope so.'

The Greek spat out the end of the cord he had been chewing on.

When Pizarro and Gabriel returned at last from the passage, the two giants – one white, the other black – looked at them expectantly. De Candia was the first to give in to his anxious curiosity.

'Well, Gabriel?'

Gabriel pointed at Pizarro.

'There's nothing there,' said the Governor. 'Nothing but endless, infernal steps leading down a narrow passage, plus a few rats and snakes.'

'The statue?'

'There is no statue.'

The two friends withheld the sigh of relief that had simultaneously risen in their lungs.

'Leave us now,' said Pizarro.

Candia and Sebastian walked away. The silence between the Governor and his protégé had yet to be broken. Gabriel gazed away at the distant mountains, golden in the setting sun.

'I don't blame you for seeing her despite my express orders not to do so,' Pizarro said kindly.

Gabriel turned to face him, but didn't reply.

'And I don't hold it against you for having perhaps lied to me about that statue. I punish thieves when I catch them, but I know very well that if I rid my army of all its thieves and liars, then I would be on my own.'

He uttered his characteristic dry laugh.

'And perhaps I would have to get rid of myself.'

A smile flashed across Gabriel's face.

'In the end, I blame you for nothing. But I am a little grieved. You know that I love no one in this army. That is to say, I love them when I see them banded together, when I address them, when I see them in battle, when I hear their voices united in prayer. But as for them individually, well . . .'

He whistled disdainfully.

'They're thieves and liars, hypocrites, drunkards, criminals, almost to the man – my own brothers first and foremost. Do you imagine that I'm unaware of this?'

Gabriel shook his head.

'But you,' continued Pizarro, with a certain amount of emotion, 'you I recognized, I chose you myself. I adopted you.'

Gabriel was startled by that word 'adopted', although he still said nothing. But he felt the hostility that knotted his gut begin to unravel.

'And that you should lie to me, that you should hide something from me, it makes me . . .'

The Governor waved his pale, thin hands in the air, as though trying to outline the shape of the word he couldn't find.

'Look, Don Francisco!'

Pizarro looked in the direction where Gabriel was pointing.

'And over here! And there!'

Gabriel's arm moved around like a confused compass needle. The two men saw, through the dusk, entire columns of people coming from every direction at once, all slowly converging on Cuzco, and looking from a distance like an immense human compass card spread out across the entire area of the valley and its mountains.

'What's going on?' asked the Governor, stupefied. 'An army? I've never seen an army advance in such a manner.'

'It's no army, unless it's one that includes dogs, llamas, women, and children.'

'Then what is it?'

Gabriel stood shoulder to shoulder with Pizarro.

'It's something astonishing, Don Francisco.'

The two men fell silent once more, before Pizarro said in a low voice:

'You have found the right word for it, my boy. And that you should hide an important matter from me – that, too, is something astonishing.'

CHAPTER 25

Cuzco, 25 December 1533

THE DEEP BELLOW OF TRUMPETS FILLED THE ENTIRE valley. No one could tell if the effect was produced by horns answering one another from opposing slopes, or if it was the result of a natural echo. With each sustained note Anamaya, rolling gently in her palanquin with the movement of her bearers, felt the joyful yet grave anticipation of the forthcoming celebration grow within her.

At their departure from Coricancha, Villa Oma had been visibly delighted when Manco had ordered him to take the place of honor immediately behind him and right beside the palanquin bearing the mummified body of Huayna Capac.

That morning, Anamaya had suggested to Manco that the presence of both his father and of the great Sage Villa Oma, Atahualpa's most faithful servant, would show that the coronation of the thirteenth Inca was not a celebration of the triumph of one clan over another.

And now, in her palanquin, Anamaya was perplexed by the memory of the way Villa Oma's face had lit up when she had proposed this idea. For a fleeting instant, the Sage's expression had almost been one of rage: how dare she, once again, speak as though she were the authority running the Empire. But then he had realized what her words meant, and he had looked into her eyes with an irritated respect. 'The *Coya Camaquen* is right', he had admitted, conceding once again – and once had been one too many times – that although he was, in name, the second most powerful man in the Empire, this strange young woman held far greater sway over the Emperor's decision-making than he did.

Anamaya also ensured that the spot next to her in the procession would remain empty. The Sacred Double should have been there but, faced with the Strangers' greed, their lack of scruples, the tradition would have to be broken. They were capable, as soon as the procession was finished, of getting hold of the Sacred Brother and sending it to the smelting pot in the Governor's palace.

Anamaya's heart constricted at the mere thought of this and, more intensely than ever, she sought serenity in the acceptance of her destiny.

During the slow climb from Coricancha to the Aucaypata, the crowd thickened, and the pace of the procession slowed significantly. Anamaya heard singing but, above all, she heard the crowd's increasingly loud clamor as they laid eyes on the Inca. But which one: Manco or his father? Anamaya felt a certain pride – a guileless pride, devoid of vanity – that for the first time in many moons the energy of almost all the Indian tribes was united by a common purpose.

The war that Quizquiz and Guaypar persisted in fighting in the north of the Empire seemed to belong to another time, another world, one that gradually grew smaller and smaller. Oddly, she sometimes saw Guaypar's face in her dreams. In them he was always staring at her, his face severe and impassive, with an air of threat and defiance in his expression and with a fury that burned eternally in his eyes. But with the passing of time his features were growing less distinct, sometimes disappearing entirely, just as water erased any signs drawn in sand.

Anamaya felt the rhythmic caress of the drums pass through her body. She watched as the cadence rolled through the crowd like a wave passing along the entire length of the valley.

Then her spirits clouded over, and she had to close her eyes so that she could bear the distress that now flooded through her mind.

Gabriel.

She no longer found anything beautiful or serene in the rich,

colorful tapestries around her, or in the down pillows, or in the
seashell that was her palanquin, a shell floating on an ocean of
men. All hope drained out of her, and she was left with only a
feverish restlessness.

Gabriel.

Anamaya murmured his name, then said it again and again,
louder each time.

And just as the procession came out onto the Aucaypata,
amidst a cacophony of indistinguishable cries, chants, drums,
and trumpets, she shouted out the name of her beloved Stranger
at the top of her lungs.

Gabriel hadn't shifted his gaze from Bartholomew once throughout
the Mass. The monk was officiating alongside Bishop Valverde.
Whether he was holding open the Holy Book for Valverde, or
solemnly handing him the chalice, Bartholomew's unfeigned
humility and subtle discretion were such that no observer could
help but be impressed by the natural authority evident in the calm
precision of his actions.

There was an odd mood of combined reverence and excitement
in the great hall of La Cassana, temporarily converted into a
church nave. Gabriel had watched some soldiers bring in two gold
llama statues during the preparations for Mass. A plank had been
set atop them, and then a modest white sheet, and they now served
as the legs of an adequate altar. But the freethinking university
graduate couldn't help contemplating, grinning to himself as he
did so, the golden calf now being idolized here at the edge of
the world.

All the Spaniards were there, as were a large number of Indians,
including those who had already converted to Christianity either
through fear or opportunism. There were those, too, who had
come because of their curiosity to see from which gods the
Strangers drew their strength.

The first doors and the first locks ever to be made in Cuzco had
been made at the far end of this great hall. They had been made to
guard treasure, and behind them now lay piles of gold and silver.

Dozens of torches had been fixed to the walls, creating a slight resemblance to the lighting of a Spanish cathedral. A picture of the Virgin, painted on wood, sat on the right side of the altar. It was the one that Pizarro took with him everywhere, and it was the only religious image in the place.

The eyes of all the men were gleaming. They were happy to sing psalms, or at least to murmur them as best they could, for they didn't understand a word of them. And they fervently prayed that God would grant them a moderate – maybe even a great – part of the treasure that had been eluding them for so long, the distribution of which the Governor – God bless him – had repeatedly promised would take place 'Tomorrow, tomorrow'. But now tomorrow was today.

Alonso told himself that he deserved more than Diego, and Cristobal, the cavalryman, felt that he should receive at least double the share allotted to Pedro, the foot soldier. And yet, despite their avarice, which lit up their faces as much as the torchlight, Gabriel looked at them and understood what the Governor had meant when he had said that he admired them. Certainly they were brutal and coarse, but still they were courageous, untiring, and driven by childlike faith.

As Valverde gave the final blessing, Gabriel looked at Pizarro. The entire congregation was watching the bishop, but Don Francisco was staring at the Virgin. Gabriel knew that he was privately praying to her once again.

Gabriel then noticed Bartholomew's gray eyes looking directly at him. This made him feel distinctly uncomfortable, as though he had been caught committing some sin, and he was grateful to be carried along by the crowd of his companions as they streamed out of Mass.

With Pizarro at their head, they came out of the palace as a happy, disordered throng, Spaniards with Indians, *hidalgos* and *yanaconas*, rich and poor. They made their way to the center of the square through the crowd that had come for Manco's coronation, a crowd a hundred times greater than the one that had come to meet him on his arrival. Gabriel found himself a few paces behind Don Francisco and flanked by de Candia and Sebastian.

The sun shone brilliantly in the pure blue sky.

Manco, in his Inca tunic, was sitting on his *tiana* awaiting the Governor as a king awaits a vassal. All the mummies had been gathered and placed on their gold pedestals. The priest Villa Oma stood nearby, his tall and hostile silhouette visible to all. Smoke rose from the braziers amid the jars of *chicha*.

Gabriel saw all of this, but his attention was distracted by the flight of a white butterfly, a butterfly that had lost its way and now fluttered above the heads of the Elders before disappearing into a spiral of smoke.

Gabriel looked for Anamaya, but in vain.

'Do you remember, Your Grace?'

He didn't need to turn around to identify the speaker. And he didn't need to reply to prompt the memories to come flooding back. He could taste on his lips the bitter yet delicious flavour of a bowl of cheap wine. He could see the shop sign – The Bottomless Jug – in his mind's eye. And he could see the two giants sitting at a table, dreaming of the adventure that then awaited them, and that was now a reality – a reality, indeed, far beyond the limits of what they had imagined back then.

Gabriel felt a powerful hand take hold of his. He tried to catch Sebastian's gaze, but the African giant was staring directly ahead at the group of Inca noblemen. All that Gabriel managed to get from him was a sly smile, and the warm, brotherly handclasp of an old friend.

Bartholomew took in the entire scene of the gathering of Inca noblemen. He saw Manco, of course, on his gold *tiana*, resting on some cushions and with his feet planted apart on finely woven blankets. He saw the long-faced priest sitting on a silver bench. He saw all the caciques, sitting on progressively lower levels according to rank: on tin chairs, then on wood, then on bamboo, and finally, the lowest, on straw.

The monk could not help but be impressed by the beauty and order of this civilization. He drank in the harmony of the colors and of the precious metals, and the dignity and pride of the noblemen's faces.

Pizarro stood directly in front of him, dressed in his silk and velvet attire, his ceremonial sword on his hip. He seemed to Bartholomew like some petty provincial official, squeezed into clothes that were too small for him and with his white lace ruff doing little to hide the scrawniness of his neck.

But there wasn't a trace of self-doubt in the Governor's voice when he addressed Manco.

'Noble Lord, we came to you as friends, guided by the One True God . . .'

As Felipillo translated, Bartholomew searched the Indian faces for a glimpse of his new friend. He couldn't see him, however, and his absence gave the monk an uneasy feeling in his stomach.

'. . . And you shall now hear the *requerimiento*, as our law dictates. We ask that you state that you have understood it and that you accept it, both on your own account and on behalf of your Council of Elders. After that, we shall be friends forever, and we shall undertake to protect you against all your enemies.'

Manco gave a very slight nod to indicate that he had understood, and Pizarro signaled to Pedro Sancho de la Hoz.

Pedro's grating, lackluster voice was infamous among the Spaniards. But he was the Governor's secretary, and the only one in a position to read such a significant proclamation. His voice was even duller than usual on this momentous occasion, perhaps to ensure that his words weren't heard or that the Indians fled before the end of the reading.

The words themselves were heavy, majestic boulders of language but the voice reading them rendered them more like pathetic pebbles.

'*On behalf of the Emperor and King Don Carlos, and of Doña Juana, his mother, Sovereign of Castile, of Leon, of Aragon, of the two Sicilies, of Jerusalem, of Navarre, of Granada, of Toledo, of Valencia, of Galicia, of Majorca . . .*'

Pedro tried, in vain, to amplify his voice with each enunciation, to accord every province and every country an equal solemnity.

'*. . . Count of Roussillon and of Cerdagne, Marquis of Oristan and Gothie, Archduke of Austria, Duke of Bourgogne and of Brabant, and Count of Flanders and of the Tyrol. To the Rightful Sovereign*'

*of the Barbarian Peoples of Peru, and to your Subjects, we profess to
you and testify to our utmost ability that the One True and Eternal
God created Heaven and Earth'*

Pedro's voice conveyed even less solemnity than Felipillo's
unpleasant squawk.

Bartholomew had great trouble suppressing a terrible urge
to laugh.

*'Because of the great multitudes of generations that have prolif-
erated in the five thousand years since the world was created, it has
been made necessary that some men go one way and others the other
and that they divide themselves into a great many separate Kingdoms
and Dominions. Our Lord God chose one man amidst all of these
to be Sovereign over all of the men of the world, a man called Saint
Peter . . .'*

When Bartholomew at last spotted Katari, he realized that the
Indian had been watching him closely for some time now, a smile
on his lips. It was not a mocking smile, but rather a questioning
one, as though he was saying, 'You'll explain the meaning of these
strange words to me, won't you?'

*'As a consequence of this, we beseech you and call upon you to
understand clearly what we have just told you . . .'*

Thus continued the interminable *requerimiento*. Phrases like
'Catholic Faith', 'malicious prevarications' and 'Their Majesties',
and the repeated promise of God's blessing echoed back from
the walls of the palaces and mingled with the sound of the water
flowing from the fountain.

Bartholomew looked away from Katari a number of times, as
though he felt embarrassed. But whenever he looked back again,
the Indian was still staring at him, his expression friendly but his
eyes full of questions.

*'But if you refuse to do so, we testify to you that we will use all
our power to make war with you, with God's help. We will place
you under the yoke, and extract your obedience to the Church and
to Their Majesties. We will make slaves of you, your wives and
your sons. We will sell them as slaves. We will take your goods and
chattels and we will bring upon you as much harm as is right to bring
upon disobedient vassals who deny and resist their Lord. We strongly*

declare to you that the death and damage that would result would be your fault and not that of Their Majesties, nor ours, nor that of the knights accompanying us here.'

Bartholomew watched Katari's face cloud over and his entire expression change as the translation continued, and the Indian now bore a look of alarmed incredulity. When the monk tried to give him some signal indicating his friendship, some sign to mitigate the extreme violence of the words being spoken, he could no longer catch his friend's eye.

Pizarro approached Manco and bent toward him as though to kiss him. But the Inca did not move from his bench.

Trumpets sounded as the standard bearer unfurled the royal banner.

Only then did Manco rise.

'She's not here.'

Gabriel had felt at a loss throughout the ceremony on the great square, a stranger to his own people, and a stranger among the Indians' inscrutable faces. All he could hear was the horrid droning sound of the *requerimiento*.

Anamaya wasn't there, and that was the only thing he could think about, the only thing he could feel.

Their last embrace lingered on his flesh like a burn that wouldn't fade, a wound that wouldn't heal, inflaming a desire that made him regret not having been even more violent with her – more violent than she had asked him to be, more violent than his fear had allowed. Violent? Gabriel wondered at himself, and reined in his raging anguish. Not more violent, but more gentle, infinitely gentle, caressing her entire body while whispering those little words that had no meaning in themselves yet were the very currency of love.

Occasionally a breeze sprang up that lifted the hems of the Indians' tunics and their splendid feathered costumes, ruffling their enormous fans.

Occasionally a trumpet call echoed across the valley.

Occasionally a beam of light would illuminate the idol of the

Sun God that had been uncovered near the Sage Villa Oma in the center of the square, just beside the fountain.

Occasionally Gabriel imagined that he had detected one of the mummies moving slightly, the mummies that had arrived one by one on the square, each one majestically seated on a gold throne, surrounded by the crowd and by wealth, representing the past reigning over the present.

But Gabriel knew only one thing for sure: that his beloved Anamaya was not there, and that as a result his loneliness was excruciating and his blood boiled with rage at his lack of power. He stared at Manco with a cold hatred, privately cursing him, secretly challenging him to bloodthirsty duels. But Manco didn't look at him once, no more than he had looked at Pedro Sancho de la Hoz during his proclamation, or at Felipillo as he had translated it. His gaze stayed fixed on Pizarro.

When Manco stood and Anamaya at last appeared behind him, Gabriel opened his mouth to cry out to her, and he had to bite his lip to stop himself.

Pizarro embraced each of the Inca noblemen. A clamor of shouts and songs rose from the crowd as it overflowed from the square into the surrounding alleys and palaces, a rumbling noise rising from the entire valley, the mountains – and, perhaps, even from beyond.

Perhaps it was some absurd joy, some hope for something undefined, but whatever it was rose up in Gabriel as well. His body began to tremble with the same joy and hope, despite the jealousy still poisoning his blood.

The entire world seemed to be celebrating, to be preparing itself for a celebration that was to last for days and days, a celebration that would blot out all fear and the memory of war.

Who was being crowned? Whose victory was this?

What did it matter?

Everyone began to dance.

Only Gabriel and Anamaya remained motionless, facing one another from a distance – together, yet each one alone. They could see nothing but their love.

CHAPTER 26

Cuzco, January 1534

EACH NIGHT WAS INDISTINGUISHABLE FROM THE ONE before. The hours of darkness were filled with shouting and singing, drinking and feasting. On the Aucaypata, as on the all the city's other squares and in the palaces and the most distant *canchas*, the jars of *chicha* were constantly emptied and refilled, and the braziers burned endlessly, illuminating both the living and the dead. And after watching the mummies come out of the temples and palaces and take their places on their golden thrones, surrounded and served by the celebrating people, men and women ended up actually hearing the murmur of their voices, the echo of their ancient power.

Even Gabriel had heard them.

The mummies spoke of the Empire's legends, of fierce battles, of Gods revealing themselves, of vanquished enemies. They spoke of the Sun God and of the Lightning God, and of the solitude to be found in the mountains, where the air was thin and the condor ruled.

Gabriel hadn't seen Anamaya again since the day of the coronation, and he trailed around the endless festivities feeling intensely frustrated and sick at heart.

At La Cassana, the councils between the Governor, his brothers, de Soto and de Almagro soured the air night and day. But it mattered little, because Gabriel was no longer welcome to join them. Don Francisco himself had gone out of his way to avoid him ever since the affair of the missing statue. And so Gabriel's 'treason' had made of him a grateful pariah. He had no desire whatsoever to participate in these ridiculous festivities. Still, he had to find something to do with his days, otherwise the depression caused by Anamaya's absence would engulf him. So he wandered around the strange city, smiling only at children and old women, and was a stranger even to his friends.

'Gabriel!'

The shout startled him, and he reached instinctively for his sword.

'*Holà!*'

'Whoa, my friend! I know that you're well versed in the art of fencing because I taught you all you know, and I don't want to be at the wrong end of your blade.'

The two threatening silhouettes resolved into the friendly forms of his tall companions, Pedro and Sebastian.

'Forgive me, my friends, I was looking—'

'—To avoid us, by the Virgin! As you have been doing these past several days.'

The Greek grinned amicably as he said this, but his smile and goodwill did little to relieve Gabriel's unhappiness.

'We've been looking for a remedy for your languor,' said Sebastian, 'and we think we might have found something.'

Gabriel couldn't help but be curious, despite his dejection.

'And what might this powerful antidote be, I wonder? Condor sperm? Llama shit?'

'Better! Come, stop your grumbling and follow us.'

Gabriel hesitated for a moment, then went after them.

The long shadows of afternoon loomed over the *cancha*, and Gabriel could hear women's voices rising from it like birdsong.

He shrank back from the building, but both his friends urged him on, and he allowed himself to be led.

They entered a cheerful room. Like all Inca interiors, it had no furniture to speak of, but it was rich with tapestries, bed-mats, wool blankets, and resplendent feathers. Three young girls

stopped their talk as the Strangers entered, but their beam-
ing smiles showed that they were already well acquainted with
Gabriel's two companions, and that they were evidently looking
forward to becoming so with him.

Colorful tunics covered the alluring shapes of their bodies.
Their legs were bare below the knee and Gabriel could see the
honeyed colour of their flesh that so pleased the Spaniards.

'We have been campaigning,' began Sebastian with feigned
solemnity, 'against the barbarity that drives the ignoble among
us to force themselves on young ladies. Once we had learned
that the *requerimiento* had been accepted by the Inca and his
council, we took it upon ourselves to teach the true chivalry of
the *caballero* to the local population.'

Gabriel couldn't help but smile. The girls' zeal to please made
it clear that his companions' lessons had borne early fruit. He felt
soft hands touch his shoulder, urging him to sit with his friends
on a pile of mats covered in fine blankets.

'I don't . . .' he began, rather weakly.

'You don't say a word, and you follow our lead,' said Pedro.

And, in fact, Gabriel found it enjoyable to do so. Why should
he exhaust himself by struggling in vain against ill fortune? The
young girls busied themselves around him in what almost seemed
to be some graceful ballet, bringing him drink in gold goblets and
murmuring to him, in their language, that they found the Strangers
handsome and strong. They giggled as they looked at one another,
like all young girls anywhere in the world do, and they spoke with
an astonishing candor.

'I don't mean to be impious,' said de Candia, crossing himself,
'and may the Reverend Valverde forgive me, but I find that
paganism has a lot to offer.'

'My friend, I've known that since birth,' replied Sebastian.

'Yes, but you've spent years among us, in Don Diego de
Almagro's service, and you've been baptized and been awarded
your sword – well, all that's enough to change a man. But look
at these girls. The merest misreading of the Holy Book would
corrupt them, and they would resist us.'

'Yes. And I would add that they seem to have read some other types of books, in which it is written that it was their destiny to become better acquainted with us.'

Gabriel grinned as he listened to his friends' banter. Fatigue, disappointment, and a slight intoxication was having an affect on him, gradually leading him into a state where letting himself go in the arms of an agreeable young woman was the only thing that mattered.

The women's deft hands had already undone his friends' jerkins and shirts and the two tall conquistadors now sat bare-chested. He caught a glimpse of Sebastian's powerful torso, and also of Pedro de Candia's slighter but still impressive build. Then he saw a pair of dark eyes staring at him, two young, innocent, and questioning eyes that promised him pleasure.

'You're very pretty,' he said in Quechua.

The young woman showed no surprise when Gabriel spoke in her own language to her. Her gaze grew even more intense and her slightly parted lips revealed two rows of delicately chiseled white teeth, teeth that could nibble as easily as they could bite.

She squatted down beside him on the mat, close enough to kiss him, but she didn't yet go so far as to touch him. He breathed in her scent of trees and flowers, and he closed his eyes to better savor this perfume, allowing it to waft over him.

Gabriel heard a piece of wood crackle in the fire, followed by a muffled laugh. Then there was only the silence of pleasure, a silence redolent of harmony and sensual abandon. The young girl put her hand on his forehead, ran her fingers down his nose, rested them for a moment on the bump on its bridge, a relic from a fistfight long ago, then lingered on his lips. He remained still, his eyes closed, and despite the desire rising up inside him he didn't kiss her fingertips. His breath grew shallower and he felt his entire body tingle when she undid his shirt and placed her hands on his burning flesh. *By God, how I want her*, he said to himself.

But a troubling thought slipped in amid all these sensations, amid his instinctive urge to abandon himself to those fingers. Gabriel tried to shoo away the thought as though it were a fly, but it had taken root firmly in his mind. *Anamaya, Anamaya, you run away from me yet you seek me out. You elude me now, but you won't forever.* The girl slipped his shirt off his shoulders, and Gabriel felt his manhood harden with desire. He opened his eyes.

He looked around the room, and saw his two friends lost under a soft shower of caresses. and now he saw the young girl looking at him, her eyes half shut. She let him take her wrists in his hands, halting her caresses. Still she showed no surprise, only willingness to give him anything he wanted. Her ease and candid sense of her power made him smile.

He lifted her up from the mat and stood her in front of him. He ran his hands through her hair as she purred like a cat and closed her eyes. He stood up, put his shirt back on, and allowed her to lean against him.

Gabriel was teetering in the balance.

He was dancing to a silent tune that led him gently from the urgency of desire to the slow rhythm of tenderness, and he didn't rush her any more than she had rushed him. 'I want you,' he murmured, as much to himself as to her. 'But I want to wait for her more than I want you. How much suffering there is in waiting. But thanks to you I now know that there is nothing more tender than that wait.'

The girl's body relaxed slowly, and she smiled at him when he moved away from her.

'You're very pretty,' Gabriel repeated. 'But . . .'

He blew her a kiss and left the room, crossed the *cancha*'s courtyard, and came out onto the street. He inhaled in great gulps the clear air of the Andes.

A moment later, the first punch struck him.

For a moment, Gabriel's body clung to the warmth of the room he had just left, to its caresses, to the intense desire he had felt there, and to the wonderful lightness that had entered his spirit. But the rain of blows eventually shattered this illusion and he felt a rage rise up inside him as he stood there, helplessly, being beaten.

There were four of them – the two who had grabbed him from behind and who were now holding him despite his furious efforts to break free, and the two who were punching and kicking him methodically.

None of them said a word, and Gabriel could hear only their exhalations and grunts – and another odd sound that he couldn't identify for a moment. Then he realized that it was his own furious cry, a cry that carried in it all his rage at his own weakness, and at the futility of his own efforts to escape or dodge the beating he was receiving.

Night veiled his assailants' faces, and in any case they had gone to the trouble of wearing bandannas across them. Gabriel could only see their dark eyes flashing in the gloom.

Then a red fog passed in front of his eyes, and he began to feel increasingly weary. Warm blood was flowing from a head wound, blurring his vision, mixing with his tears, his sweat, and his snot. Some vital instinct in his gut urged him not to faint, to fight on. To fight on? He could manage a few ungainly movements, about as useful as those of a frog. But his resistance only urged his attackers on to further violence.

Fragments of thoughts passed through his mind: 'If they wanted to kill me . . .' If they had wanted to kill him, he would already have been dead.

And so, resisting uselessly to the last, Gabriel eventually fainted. He had a vision of Gonzalo's curly brown locks, of his smiling, charming face, floating above him like some fallen angel.

Had he seen this before passing out? Or was it just the first image of a nightmare?

Gabriel writhed on the ground in the middle of the alley like some drunkard.

Blood flowed from his mouth into the gutter.

CHAPTER 27

Cuzco, January 1534

'M Y POOR FRIEND.'
Pizarro looked at Gabriel with a mixture of irony and
regret, of disdain and pity. Gabriel felt as though not a
single part of his body had been spared. He still hadn't had the
courage, since he had dragged himself to the La Cassana palace,
to look at himself in the mirror.

'Have you seen Juan de Balboa yet?'

'Don't concern yourself for me, Don Francisco. I need no
surgeon.'

'I don't know what it is that you need, my boy. Words of advice,
perhaps? You would do well to heed a few.'

The Governor had always ensured that his quarters were laid
out in exactly the same way no matter where he was, whether in
a tent or a palace. He had a narrow bed, a table with two chairs,
and the painting of his beloved Sacred Virgin. He motioned to
Gabriel to sit, but the young man preferred to remain standing,
broken as he was.

'Well, as you won't listen to anyone, then I shall listen to you.'

'You haven't even asked how this happened to me, Don
Francisco.'

'Do I need to?'

An enigmatic smile flashed across the Governor's thin face.

'There is only one reason why you have no need to ask me:
because you already know very well what happened.'

'Are you accusing me?'

'Accusing you, Don Francisco? By the faith, I don't even know what to call what I may suspect you of.'

'Tell me what happened to you anyway. That way you may not have to give your suspicions a name.'

'Your brothers, Don Francisco, your brothers,' said Gabriel, growing pale at the mere mention of them. 'Your fucking brothers, may their souls speed to Hell.'

'What about my brothers?' asked Pizarro quietly, pretending not to notice Gabriel's rage.

'Not content with being thieves and having less dignity than swine, Don Francisco, not satisfied with heaping dishonor on your name by their cowardice, their greed, their hypocrisy . . .'

Gabriel began to choke on this litany of evils, and Pizarro raised his black-gloved hand to interrupt him.

'Enough, young man. Not another word.'

The two men defied each other with their glares. Gabriel was trembling.

'I am happy to forgive you,' said Pizarro slowly. 'They were very severe on you, and it is your sense of your own humiliation that speaks now . . .'

'It's my humiliation that drives me to tell you a truth that is on everybody's lips, and that everybody hides from you.'

Pizarro burst out laughing.

'Do you imagine that I am unaware of what my brothers are? Do you think that I do not know why they are with me here, and what they are after? Do you think that I arrived in Cuzco blinded by blood ties?'

'I haven't known what to think for a long time, Don Francisco,' said Gabriel with uncharacteristic bitterness.

'That's right, young man: you no longer know where you are. You have forgotten yourself ever since you laid eyes on that blue-eyed priestess, ever since you carried out I know not what subterfuge with that golden statue. Your sense has given way to your sentiments – and now you dare to insult my brothers.'

Gabriel said nothing for a moment, absorbing the shock of Pizarro's statement The Governor had raised a problem that

Gabriel knew was less than straightforward. But he also knew from experience that it was at such moments that calm and lucidity returned to him, as they often did during the chaotic height of battle.

'You're right, Don Francisco. But despite that, and even in my confusion, I believe that you are still the one at fault.'

'Oh? Explain to me how.'

'You think that your brothers are a necessary evil, one that has limits, and that you can control them just as you do Don Diego de Almagro and all the men who follow you. You are superior to these men. You have more stamina, more courage, and you see further than others. You are not blinded by gold as they are. You think things through, and your hand is steady. You are a captain whereas they are dogs. But what you don't see is that these men – your brothers and Don Diego – are ready to turn against you the minute you show the slightest sign of weakness.'

'My own brothers?'

'Yes. Oh, they won't confront you directly. But they will do you so much harm that the blows I received from them will be like a woman's caress by comparison.'

For once, Pizarro looked slightly astonished. His face wore a perplexed expression that was most unusual for him. The two men stared at one another in the ensuing silence. The memory of their long and strange acquaintance remained as a bond between them, as well as their affection for each other, a feeling that persisted despite the clash of their wills.

Don Francisco spread his arms.

'You still love me, then.'

'Without a doubt, Governor.'

'Without a doubt . . . those are truly the words of a schoolboy. Bah, it's not important. I shall help you, my boy.'

'Help me?'

'Yes. I might even save your skin.'

Gabriel listened to what the Governor said next without interrupting. And as Pizarro talked, Gabriel felt defeated, more beaten than he had been in the alley.

When he finally staggered out of the La Cassana palace, the

light of early morning blinded him, and he groped his way along towards the fountain.

It began to rain. He was alone.

The day passed.

Gabriel didn't move.

He felt the wet, the cold, and then the heat, as well as all his shifting pains. But nothing affected him as much as the Governor's words still echoing in his head.

Dusk fell.

His fellow conquistadors passed by and looked upon him with pity or with mockery. He ignored their taunts. He kept his gaze fixed obstinately on the mountains. He watched the shadow of the fortress as it grew longer with the setting sun.

Gabriel slipped into the cool of the night.

A torch flickered from the shadows and illuminated his face. He raised his hand to shield his eyes from its glare.

'Who wishes me well now?' he muttered sarcastically.

'Me.'

'You too want to save me, then, like him?'

Bartholomew said nothing. He took Gabriel gently by the arm and pulled him up. Gabriel didn't resist. He had done nothing but resist since the previous day. He had resisted the girl's dark eyes, he had resisted the blows, he had resisted the Governor's words. He'd had enough of fighting against the whole world.

They walked slowly through the La Cassana palace, and Bartholomew led him to his room.

The pale yellow reflection of a candle flickered across their faces. Gabriel lay down with infinite care, barely managing to stop himself groaning with pain. Bartholomew sat down beside him on the bed and placed his two joined fingers on Gabriel's chest. Gabriel didn't resist. Bartholomew didn't speak until Gabriel's breathing had grown more regular. Then he asked:

'Well?'

Gabriel was suddenly overwhelmed by sorrow. He wanted to speak, but no words came from his mouth, and all his powerlessness, all his loneliness and rage rose up and constricted his heart. He broke down, sobbing.

Bartholomew said nothing, letting the young conquistador's tears flow. His curious gray eyes shone with sympathy for Gabriel.

'I'm not much of a warrior,' Gabriel sighed eventually.

'Who told you that warriors don't shed tears?'

'You speak well, my brother.'

Bartholomew only smiled.

'Don Francisco told me that I had to go with him,' Gabriel said. 'He told me that he would soon leave Cuzco to found the capital of the kingdom and that he needed me with him. He said that if I stayed in Cuzco I would be killed and that then I would be no use to anyone. He said that if I stayed in Cuzco *she* would die because his brothers would stop at nothing to satisfy their hatred. He ordered me to go with him. He said that we would return one day.'

'What are you going to do?'

'I'm going to obey him, of course. Because he's right, because what he said was terrible but true. He knows that I'm not frightened by his damned brothers. But he also knows that I fear more for her life than for my own.'

'What can I do for you?'

Gabriel looked at Bartholomew, astonished.

'For me? Nothing. What would you want to do for me?'

'Anything you ask.'

'Is that all? Brother, the Lord reveals to you his greatest mysteries . . .'

'It goes without saying.'

Bartholomew grinned. Gabriel tried to express his deepest desires:

'What I want . . . what I pray for . . .'

'I'll do my best,' said Bartholomew.

Gabriel stared at him in surprise.

'How . . .'

'Isn't that what you want? I'll do my best, believe me.'

The monk rose and left the room, taking the candle with him, before Gabriel had a chance to say another word.

CHAPTER 28

Kenko, January 1534

G ABRIEL HAD NO IDEA HOW LONG HE HAD BEEN FOL-
lowing the dwarf.

Sometimes he felt as though he was sleepwalking. At
such moments he couldn't tell whether he was moving forward or
whether the path was sliding backward under him, like some giant
ribbon pulled by an invisible hand, and he was actually staying in
the same place, held there by some unseen force.

For a while he considered a few possibilities about where he
might be heading. The fortress at Colcampata? But soon there
were no more houses to be seen, they encountered fewer walls,
and the towers of Sacsayhuaman were behind them. He had
noticed that they had set out to the northeast, but now that
knowledge helped him little. He went forward with his hands
stretched out in front of him, and he had the odd notion that
he was swimming among the stars. It was a grand, infinite night,
one that swallowed up the earth.

His injuries bothered him less now, although he still felt
somewhat numb. *What a strange thing is man*, he thought philo-
sophically as he limped along. A man might be overcome by
despair in the morning, and then be light-hearted, almost carefree
as soon as night, with all its promises, had fallen.

Even the fact that he would be leaving Cuzco tomorrow,
perhaps later, no longer seemed so cruel. Truth was hidden
somewhere in this night sky, not in the Governor's words.

He didn't know where he was but he had the impression of having left Cuzco below for a higher world. The air was thinner here, there were no trees, and the stony scree was all around him in the liquid night. He was a traveler through time and space, and it seemed as though he could feel the presence of the gods.

The dwarf had remained silent throughout their journey. Perhaps he was the first citizen of this higher world in which Gabriel was now arriving.

When the dwarf suddenly veered away from the path, Gabriel didn't hesitate to follow him toward a rocky declivity, the size of which he didn't see until the very last moment. It was, in fact, a large natural amphitheater with niches carved into its walls, niches similar to those he had seen in the city's temples and palaces. When he had turned around again, the dwarf had disappeared.

He walked to the center of the amphitheater and stopped in front of a boulder there. He didn't know what it was meant to represent, but he could feel its power.

'The hand of man worked on this stone. But a god was born of it.'

'I thought I would never see you again,' said Gabriel. A giggle was his answer.

'And you still don't see me. Follow me.'

And in fact, no matter where he looked, Gabriel saw only a fleeting shadow. He followed it down a gentle slope to a cave carved out of the cliff face.

'Anamaya . . .'

He hesitated at the top of the broad stone steps leading into the cave.

He walked down a few steps, then stopped, surrounded by a blackness darker than the night outside. His hands searched for a wall, for something solid, but they met with only the cool, moist air rising from the ground. He smelled the odor of herbs burning, a sickly sweet scent that both lured and repelled him.

Gabriel took a few more steps, tripped, and fell heavily to the ground. His cry echoed through the cave.

'Anamaya!'

But there was no reply other than his own voice echoing back at him.

'ANAMAYA!'

'Come . . .'

Her whisper came from close by, and as she guided him to her, his fear evaporated. He made his way to her step by step, until he could see her eyes gleaming in the night. She took hold of his wrists and placed his hands on a stone table, a sort of altar.

'I told you that I would be here.'

'It was so long ago.'

'I told you to trust me.'

Anamaya's hands stroked his and then moved up his arms, over his shoulders, around his neck – he was bruised and injured everywhere, yet she didn't hurt him at all. Still, he flinched slightly.

'Don't be frightened.'

Gabriel closed his eyes and let her explore his body with her hands, soothing him like a flowing brook or a gentle breeze. He felt a splendid warmth spread through him, and he let himself slip into it. His breathing slowed, his body relaxed.

'Your gray-eyed friend found Katari and told him that you needed me.'

'Bartholomew?'

'I don't know his name. Katari and he often meet and exchange knowledge with one another.'

Gabriel sighed in frustration and said:

'I've been ordered to leave, Anamaya.'

'I know.'

Gabriel was astonished by how calm Anamaya's voice was. He looked into her eyes as she said:

'You are in too much danger here. You must leave . . .'

'Manco?'

'I told you that Manco would do you no harm. I'm talking about your own people.'

'Are there other dangers I don't know about?'

'There are always dangers of which one is unaware,' said Anamaya, smiling. 'He who believes otherwise is a fool.'

'Or else very wise.'

He could see her smile.

'Or else very wise, yes. But be that as it may, you must leave Cuzco.'

Gabriel listened to the silence surrounding them, and inhaled the strange odor in the air.

'Where are we?'

'In a *huaca*, one of our sacred places. There are hundreds around Cuzco, arranged in a circle with the capital at its hub. Some hold treasures that your people will steal soon enough. Others are so secret that you will never find them.'

'Do sacrifices take place here?'

He noticed that Anamaya hesitated before replying:

'Sometimes, yes.'

And suddenly Gabriel realized what the smell was. It was the smell of burned flesh, of boiled blood. An icy shiver ran down his spine.

Anamaya noticed his discomfort and led him away.

'Come, let's leave.'

The fresh air outside relieved him somewhat and, after the darkness of the cave, so did the starlight. They climbed a flight of stone steps to the summit of the *huaca*.

'Difficult times are upon us,' she announced.

'And must I disappear during these difficult times?'

'The peace we are living is a lie. It is riddled with lies and deceits.'

'Are you talking about Manco? About your people?'

'I'm talking about all of us, Gabriel.'

'Is that why I have to disappear? Answer me.'

He spoke with reluctant harshness. Anamaya was clearly a little taken aback when she answered:

'Of course not. You must go because you must live.'

Gabriel immediately calmed down. Still, even the undeniable love apparent in her words didn't relieve the black torment in the pit of his soul.

An odd channel carved into the rock zigzagged across the top of the hill. Figures too were carved into the rock, and two blocks, like mooring posts, rose up in the middle of nowhere.

Gabriel gave Anamaya a questioning look. She said nothing, only smiling and hugging him closer.

They lay down on a rock.

Gabriel could no longer feel his injuries.

'Tell me why—' he began.

'Look at the sky,' she interrupted. 'Look at the stars, and stop asking why.'

He dreamed with her.

He forgot all about what he didn't know, all his questions and doubts. He bounded like a puma, flew like a condor, he crossed the sky like a bolt of lightning, all the while holding her hand. Not a word was spoken between them.

She curled up against him.

Anamaya let Gabriel see her own weakness, her own sadness, and he was moved by her trust in him. Together, and still without a word, they shared the simple, human sadness of their impending separation.

When she eventually moved away from him, she looked at him for a long, long time, and he saw everything he wanted in her eyes: he saw their entire story, he saw all he knew about it, all he sensed unconsciously, and all that she kept hidden at the bottom of her heart.

'Look,' Anamaya said.

The moonlight outlined a shape between the two monolithic rocks, and the rocks themselves had become two pale eyes shining in the night. The shape was that of a great cat, peaceful yet menacing.

The puma.

Gabriel asked no more questions.

By the time day dawned, Anamaya was long gone.

The puma's eyes were once again two round rocks atop a boulder.

Gabriel didn't return to the cave.

He headed back down the road to Cuzco, knowing in his heart that the road ahead of him would be much longer than the one he had travelled so far.

PART 4

CHAPTER 29

Cuzco, July 1535

T HE GOVERNOR'S BROTHERS REACHED EMPEROR MANCO'S
palace so early on that day in July that the sacred cornfields
facing the Colcampata were still covered in early-morning
fog.

Gonzalo had stuck some splendid blue and yellow feathers into
his hatband. As for Juan, he had wound an odd-looking swathe of
white silk around his own headgear. They were laughing loudly
together, and their laughter reverberated between the high walls
of the alley, rising above the stamping of their boots and those of
the dozen or so henchmen armed with pikes and crossbows who
followed them.

A group of Indian warriors, commanded by a lieutenant whose
helmet had been stripped of its gold ensign, made a show of
defending the entrance to the royal *cancha*. Gonzalo Pizarro
shoved the lieutenant aside. Juan feigned indignation, grabbed
his brother by the collar, and said:

'Please, Gonzalo. We come here as friends.'

Gonzalo burst out laughing, and his companions followed
suit. After this outburst, they readjusted their somewhat worn
doublets as the Inca soldiers stared at them, their eyes burning
with indignant powerlessness. The Spaniards formed a double
column, orderly enough to pass review in an Andalusian palace, and they marched thus through the *cancha*'s outer courtyard into the inner one. All the servants and lords they came

across stopped dead in their tracks, astounded at their intrusion.

Don Gonzalo, a radiant smile lighting his handsome face, led his men straight to the door of the *cancha*'s biggest building. The young Indians guarding it crossed their spears at the Spaniards' approach. One Spaniard bounded ahead of the Governor's brothers. He didn't even need to raise his hand for the Indians, after only the slightest hesitation, to drop their pretense of defense.

Gonzalo led them in. Inside, they stopped short, surprised as much as they were amused.

Emperor Manco was standing bare-chested, surrounded by his wife and concubines. With his head slightly titled, his torso bowed forward, and his eyelids lowered languidly, he was examining the range of tunics, each one as delicately woven as a bird's feather, being offered to him by his women. One of his concubines noticed the Strangers. She uttered a short, involuntary cry without raising her head. Manco stiffened. An expression of rage passed over his face, but he immediately suppressed it.

'Greetings, Sapa Inca,' began Gonzalo, bowing.

Manco ignored his greeting, turning his attention back to the *unkus*. He deliberately took his time selecting one.

'Let's let him get dressed,' suggested Juan, turning away.

'But of course, brother. We're not savages, after all,' sniggered Gonzalo, walking further into the room.

He moved so close to one of Manco's wives that the young woman stepped back, looking away. Gonzalo grabbed the tunic she was holding from her hands. He waved it at his henchmen, who burst out laughing when he held it up against himself, tilted his face upwards, and batted his eyelids like a coquettish girl.

'The king's costume becomes me, no?' he said with cold irony, eliciting a few guffaws from his men.

Manco maintained his appearance of indifference, not even glancing at the Spaniards. He pointed at a midnight blue *unku* decorated with crimson geometric patterns. Two trembling women helped him into it despite the Strangers' gibes, while another held out the royal headband on a folded *manta*.

A crowd drawn by the scene had gathered in the courtyard.

Men and women, servants and lords all murmured disapprovingly among themselves. In the morning sun their eyes glowed with terror at the irreverence their Emperor was being subjected to.

'Gonzalo—'

Juan stopped short to look at whatever it was that had caused an outcry of laughter around him. Gonzalo had ripped one of the tunics rejected by the Inca from a servant-girl's hands.

He approached a concubine and offered her the *unku*, urging her to try it on. More terrified by the profanity than by the Stranger's brutality, she defended herself as best she could.

'She wants to, really,' said Gonzalo. 'She just needs some encouragement.'

'Gonzalo . . .' said Juan, increasingly embarrassed.

The other women had gathered in the corner furthest away from Gonzalo. Manco, his face as impassive as ever, hadn't moved an inch. He seemed to be paying no attention at all to the scene, not even when the young Indian woman fell to her knees to escape Gonzalo's unwelcome advances.

Then a voice known to them all cut through the air:

'Gentlemen, the Emperor never receives guests in his chamber. Please go out into the courtyard, where he will grant you an audience.'

The Spaniards, startled, moved aside. Anamaya stood at the threshold of the room, her blue eyes blazing with rage. Gonzalo shivered, then laughed when he caught his brother Juan looking reverently at her.

'To tell the truth, fair lady,' he said, 'you timed your arrival well: It is you whom we seek.'

Anamaya stared at the two brothers. Apart from the fire in her eyes, she gave no sign of the hate, anger, and fear raging inside her. She stood tall and proud, and even Gonzalo had to turn his eyes away, unable to bear her gaze.

'You lied to us,' growled Gonzalo. 'You promised us gold. Where is it?'

He waved his arms angrily as he paced about in the sun. Manco remained seated calmly on his *tiana*, not saying a word. Anamaya was standing a little behind him, looking tense and staring at the Spaniards. The Elders, who had rushed to the royal *cancha*, were gathered on the other side of the courtyard, keeping a safe distance between themselves and the threatening line of Strangers.

'Three months have passed, Sapa Inca,' continued Gonzalo, pointing at Manco. 'Three months since the day you promised us more gold. You pledged yourself a friend to our King, who is also yours, and you did so to prove to us that the rumors of an uprising against us were groundless. Time has fled since then, yet all we have received are a few plates and some baubles you stole from your servants.'

He stopped speaking and silence filled the courtyard.

A flight of birds passed overhead. Their shadows crossed from the Spaniards to the Indian lords as quickly as arrows. Juan Pizarro kept trying to catch Anamaya's gaze. But she gave him no more attention than she did any of the others. Finally, Manco smiled wanly and pointed at the palace courtyard, the buildings' walls, and the threshold of his room.

'Do you see any gold here, my friend?' he asked in a disturbingly calm tone. 'Winter has visited us twice since you arrived in the Puma's City. Cast your mind back to that day: wasn't there gold here then? Gold on the walls, gold in every room of my *cancha*, gold in my gardens, gold in the palaces of the noblemen of my court? Didn't my wives and concubines wear gold in their hair then? You amused yourself with one of them a few moments ago. Let me ask you: Was she wearing any gold? Turn around, brother of my friend the Governor. Look at the noblemen in my court. Look at their ears. Do you see any gold earlobe plugs in them? No. Only wood. Look at their chests and arms. Are they not as bare as those of peasants? They have already given you all the gold they have. Where could I possibly get more gold, when you have it all already? Where would I hide it, now that you are masters of this country?'

Gonzalo grinned at Manco malevolently.

'You're lying to me,' he said, emphasizing each word and

pointing at him. 'I know that there's more gold in this country. A lot more gold.'

'Have you seen any, foreign friend? Tell me where, so that I may send for it.'

Gonzalo hissed maliciously, then padded up to Manco as softly as a cat. He looked as though he was about to spit in his face, but instead he turned his gaze upon Anamaya.

'You know very well what gold we're talking about. Where's the big gold statue that my brother the Governor demanded? He has run out of patience, as have I. You've been telling us tales for months. I want that statue in my house no later than three days from now.'

Silence followed. Juan stepped forward.

'That is impossible,' said Anamaya in a clear voice.

'Ah? And why is that, milady?' asked Gonzalo, his tone chillingly courteous.

'Because that statue is no longer in this world. It lives now with the Noble Ancestors in the land of the setting sun.'

Gonzalo stared at her for a moment in silence. One eyebrow was raised in astonishment, and he looked as though the meaning of her words was slowly dawning on him. He raised his hand as though to strike her, and a shocked murmur rose from the Indians. But instead he set his hand on Manco's shoulder with a measured gentleness.

'Isn't my friend the Inca the Son of the Sun?' he said, 'Isn't he sovereign over the dead as he is over the living?'

'You are forbidden to touch the Emperor,' said Anamaya flatly.

'Come now, my friend the Inca will surely not spurn this gesture of intimacy, so natural between friends. With us, you see, friendship is expressed naturally, with smiles and hugs. And with gifts.'

Still smiling, Gonzalo let go of Manco as abruptly as he had grabbed him. The Inca tried to recover his dignity as Gonzalo turned to one of his soldiers. He motioned to him to approach. The man was carrying a large leather saddlebag over his shoulder. He opened it and drew a large-linked chain from it, together with manacles and a steel padlock. Gonzalo dropped the irons at Manco's feet.

'See, I'm not like you,' he said. 'I've brought you a splendid gift.'

Manco and Anamaya looked at the irons.

'Do you know, my friend Sapa Inca, that this is the very chain with which *your* brother Atahualpa, the late Inca, was protected from the affections of his own people by *my* brother, Governor Don Francisco Pizarro? The thought occurred to me that this device might find a place of eminence among your treasures. Am I right?'

Not a sound rose from the courtyard.

'I hope that, in return, you will present me with the gift that I am seeking.'

Neither Manco nor Anamaya reacted to the threat. The Elders, meanwhile, along with the palace guards, had closed in on the Spaniards. They slowly formed a defensive line around their sovereign. Juan took his brother by the wrist and smiled at the Indians nervously.

'Wait a moment, brother. Don't you remember that we have another proposition for the Sapa Inca?'

He removed his hat and bowed to Manco, a belated attempt at respect.

'Sapa Inca,' began Juan in a conciliatory tone, 'it is true that we are disappointed not to see this famous statue, which we are told is without rival in its beauty and value. But people do us an injustice when they say that we prefer gold to beauty. What disappoints us, you see, is not the fact that we don't have possession of the statue, but the way your attitude reveals your mistrust of us. Some even believe that it's a sign that you're preparing to go to war with us. We don't agree with them, of course, and that is why I bring this proposition to you, a proposition that, if you accept it, will make it clear to the whole world that we are friends and shall always be so.'

Juan paused to let his words sink in. His calm, conciliatory tone defused the tension. Even Manco relaxed a little. He nodded and stared with a slightly confused air at the hat Juan was waving about.

'Today, Sapa Inca, I have put a white silk ribbon in my hat. In my country, this means that I wish to take a wife.'

Juan turned toward Anamaya. He stared at her intensely for a few moments, and then, sticking his chest out a little, declared:

'I have chosen you, fair lady. I was told that you are without a husband – or, rather, that your gold statue was, according to your customs, your husband, and that this forbade you any other marriage. Now you tell us that this statue is no longer in this world. This is sad news, but also good news. You are thus free to come to the church and share the benediction with me, a benediction that will bless you forever.'

The blood drained from Anamaya's stunned face. Juan took a step toward her and tried to take her hand, but she instinctively held it tightly against her stomach. Meanwhile, Manco had stood up. His face had turned scarlet, and the veins in his neck had swollen with rage.

'The *Coya Camaquen* belongs to my father,' he cried, 'and no other shall lay a hand upon her!'

'Ha! That's a likely story!' Gonzalo guffawed loutishly. He looked at Manco defiantly, then said in a low voice:

'She's as much a virgin as a Panama whore. Everybody knows for whom she parts her thighs . . .'

Manco was now standing in front of Anamaya. He pushed Juan aside so roughly that the Spaniard stumbled and fell to his knees.

The courtyard was in turmoil for a few moments. Gonzalo leaped forward and grabbed Manco's arm, prompting the Indian guards to rush forward to protect their Emperor.

The brothers' Spanish henchmen confronted them, and the ensuing scuffle distracted everyone's attention from Anamaya. Women were fleeing from the edges of the courtyard to the outer enclosure, uttering high-pitched cries as Juan too tried to get a grip on Manco.

A dark shadow suddenly emerged from nowhere, causing Juan to release Manco immediately. But Gonzalo froze, his hand gripping the Inca's arm tightly.

'Have you all gone mad?'

Anamaya recognized Bartholomew the monk, Gabriel's friend.

He was as pale as a sheet. He pointed his joined fingers at Gonzalo and thundered:

'Have you lost your mind, Don Gonzalo? By what right do you brutalize the Indian lord?'

'By my own. This is outside your domain.'

'Release him!'

Bartholomew's gray eyes burned with a wolflike ferocity. But it was the quiet intensity of his composure that carried the most weight.

A ghost of a smile passed across Gonzalo's lips. He relaxed his vicelike grip on Manco's arm a little. Juan took hold of Gonzalo and tried to land him away from the Inca, but his brother shook him off.

'This savage is playing a game with us,' spat Gonzalo. 'We came to take this woman,' he said, jutting his chin contemptuously at Anamaya, 'as a wife for my brother, then he claims that she's untouchable. Untouchable!'

Bartholomew glanced briefly at Anamaya as though he had just noticed her. He stood between her and Manco and said in a voice loud enough for all to hear:

'Sapa Inca Manco is sovereign over the Indians of this nation. Emperor Charles the Fifth has placed him under your brother the Governor's protection. Have you forgotten this?'

'Spare us the sermon, Brother Bartholomew, it's not Sunday today,' sneered Gonzalo. 'I'm well aware that my brother is the Governor. I'm also well aware that he is far away from here, busy founding capitals and building empires. Meanwhile, he has placed us in charge of this city.'

'And you shall answer for it to him! Just as you will for the way you have treated this man.'

'It is for us to decide who is a man and who isn't,' said Gonzalo furiously. 'I don't think that my brother Francisco is in any position to teach us a lesson about that.'

'The eyes of Spain are upon you!'

'Spain? Where's that?' scoffed Gonzalo. 'But enough. Who are you to play the saint? By what authority do you preach at me thus?'

'Gonzalo, please!' pleaded Juan.

'I have no authority over you, Don Gonzalo,' replied Bartholomew calmly.

'Just so,' hissed Gonzalo. 'So be gone – go and save some souls. But spare us your pieties.'

Gonzalo looked viciously at the monk before bending over to pick up his hat, knocked off during the fight. Juan looked utterly dejected. Bartholomew smiled modestly and said:

'It is true that I have no authority over any of you, gentlemen. The ultimate judgement belongs to God. He is the God of divine mercy, the God of the humble, and the God of vengeance against the proud.'

'Brother—' began Juan miserably.

'Shut up!' cried Gonzalo.

Gonzalo gave Bartholomew one last look of hatred as he left the courtyard.

Anamaya hadn't stopped trembling throughout the entire scene.

Bartholomew leaned unobtrusively against the *cancha*'s wall and watched Anamaya entering and leaving the enclosure. He waited until a degree of calm had returned before going to meet her.

He said to her in his somewhat stilted Quechua (of which he was nonetheless very proud):

'I know that it is very difficult to forgive one man for the actions of another, *Coya Camaquen*. Nevertheless, I must ask your forgiveness for the insults that you and Sapa Inca Manco have just endured. If it were in my power to banish such insolence, then it would never have happened. I loathe boorishness and I'm ashamed of it.'

Anamaya looked at him for a moment, then gave a slight wave with her hand and said:

'I know you do. And allow me to thank you for what you did.'

'No, please don't thank me. I wish only that you explain to Emperor Manco that he mustn't think that we're all like the Governor's brothers.'

Anamaya said nothing for a moment. She returned Bartholomew's gaze, then shook her head gently and said:

'I don't think that there are enough of your kind among the Strangers for Sapa Inca Manco to be at ease.'

Bartholomew nodded, a thin, sad smile on his lips. He pulled a small packet from his cowl with his oddly deformed hand. He clicked his tongue as he unfolded the brownish sheets densely covered with writing done in a neat hand.

'There are at least two of us, I believe,' he murmured. 'Don Gabriel asked a favour of me, one that I am glad to carry out. His letter reached me yesterday. In truth, I came to bring it to you, not to save you from the claws of the Pizarro brothers. But it seems that God, and your Ancestors, had willed things differently.'

He laughed quietly.

Indeed, Bartholomew found it easy to be at ease in Anamaya's presence, as though the simple fact of her beauty was enough to calm and comfort him. He pointed to a patch of shade by a building in which servants, returned from their daily chores, were now preparing the soups and game that constituted Manco's dinner.

'Let us move into the shade, if you will, so that we may be at ease while I read this letter to you.'

A few moments later Anamaya, her eyes aglow with a happiness that spread through her like the intoxication caused by *chicha*, found herself listening to Gabriel's words through Bartholomew's voice. She listened with the utmost attention, with her eyes closed, and his words became as tangible as caresses.

City of the Kings, 18 June 1535

Brother Bartholomew, dear friend Bartholomew,

I hope that very soon your eyes will be reading these words that I scribble on this poor-quality paper, paper that is far too moist but is the only kind to be had here.

Possibly you will be surprised by this letter. I have frequently told myself that it would do me good to write to you, that it would help me ward off my black moods and melancholia. And then some vile impulse intrudes to spoil this good intention. Days have gone by not in a flash but with an appalling slowness, so deep is the hole I feel within myself. In short, it will soon be eighteen months since we saw each other last. I carry a memory of our somewhat abrupt farewell, when I failed to thank you properly for your friendship and your help during the difficult times that I went through, and that led to the exile to which I am still constrained. The mistrust that I once felt toward you seems completely foreign to me today, even childish, and it now feels quite natural that I should confide in you.

I have often had occasion, during my travels at the Governor's side, to think of you and to miss both the calming warmth of our conversations and your expert understanding of human character. I must say that I have missed the first cruelly, constrained as I am to this isolation that Don Francisco has imposed upon me in order to appease his brothers; and I have found myself sadly wanting in the latter on far too many occasions.

No doubt I can tell you little that you haven't already heard through one rumor or another: you know as I do that the problem with rumors is not their untruthfulness but rather that they are in fact too often true. My friend de Soto has sailed for Panama after having become convinced that the Governor's brothers will never permit him to become as wealthy and as honored as his worth and his actions lead him to believe he deserves. His absence is a great loss for me, for we worked well together despite the fact that everything was done to separate us, and I hope to keep many good memories of him.

Your bishop, Fray Vicente Valverde, has also sailed: he left for Spain with Don Francisco's fulsome blessings. The Governor is increasingly becoming the avuncular sage, with a manner befitting his white beard and twinkling eye. It is a role that suits him well, I believe. There is a virtuous core beneath the shell of madness that originally lured him to this land. The more I watch him grow old, never overly susceptible to the infirmities of age but seeking peace and quiet far more often than he used to, impregnating his wife – who is one of the late Inca Atahualpa's sisters (the Governor's way of honoring his promise to watch over his family for him) – and behaving with true kindness, the more I tell myself that there are two Pizarros. I loathe the first, the one capable, in his single-minded pursuit of his goals, of anything: violence, lying, an abominable toadying that taints his otherwise impressive valor. That man is not far separated from a mere beast. He has strength and will the likes of which the world has rarely seen. Then there is the other man, the attentive, intelligent one, the one with great political acumen. A man who has but one extraordinary objective: to found a nation, no less. The truth is that gold interests him no more than it does me, except that he needs it to establish his power. I believe that he is capable of sharing this power with the Inca lords in Cuzco. At least, I hope he is.

I'm never quite sure which of these two men is the one who calls me 'son'. Please don't laugh, Brother Bartholomew. I haven't been deceived by the studied charm of this. But I have, nonetheless, felt the sincerity of it. Don Francisco chose me over his brother Hernando, over the vile Gonzalo, and over the wretched Juan. He chose me even though others foisted themselves upon him and would have liked to be rid of me – you witnessed it for yourself – by whatever means possible. I sense that he has a genuine affection for me that is evident even in his occasionally bad treatment of me, an affection that might be described as fatherly. You know my story, Brother Bartholomew. It was what landed me in the jails of Seville, where we first met. You know, then, what significance it has for me, and why I live in the Governor's shadow a little.

In order not to dwell on the time I am spending away from her, I keep myself busy each day with tasks great and small.

One of the more important of these, as you may well be aware, has been to find a site on which to found the capital of Peru. I must admit that during this search I experienced one of the most beautiful moments I have known during these long, long months that I have been away from Cuzco.

Not a day passed since last autumn when Don Francisco didn't search for a site worthy of his grand project. He was of the opinion, as were we all, that the ideal spot would have to be on the coast of the South Sea so that a port might be built, which would facilitate communication with Panama and Spain. So we surveyed hundreds of leagues of desert before finally reaching, one day in early January, around midday, a true Garden of Eden. Imagine a valley so rich and bountiful that one might ride through it for three hours under branches bowed with fruit without once having to squint against the sun. Imagine an orchard dotted with fields of corn and sweet potato, and with houses made of dried mud bricks or cane with beautifully kept little gardens in which guavas, avocados and tomatoes grow like flowers, the whole place kept irrigated with a brilliant system of canals that never run dry. From a distance, the pattern of its layout reminds one of the subtlest Toledo marquetry.

We reached a shallow river in the center of this enchanted valley. Near its bank we came across a mound common to Indian temples, set in a glade surrounded by flowering bushes and shrubs with purple or yellow leaves.

We entered the glade at a trot, as though fearful that such a magical place might evaporate before our very eyes. The Governor gave me one of those looks, like the one that he usually gives only to his blessed portrait of the Sacred Virgin during moments of great victorious excitement. 'It shall be here,' he said, and removed his hat.

As it was the day of the Epiphany, he added: 'The capital shall be called *La Ciudad de los Reyes*.'

It only took a few days for the wish to become reality. On the 18th day of January of this year 1535, the foundations of the capital were laid in this place, which the locals call *Lima*. Pegs were placed to mark out the royal square, the future cathedral, the future marketplace and, of course, the future palaces of the Governor and the municipality. A cleric fresh off the boat from Panama blessed these imaginary places. The poor fellow was not yet used to the way things are done here, and he trembled horribly. He was convinced that the Indians watching him were surely going to roast and eat him at the first opportunity.

I must admit that the moment moved me more than I had expected it to. To say to oneself, 'We have arrived in a country and today we are founding a city' was more stirring than I had imagined it would be. To imagine that tomorrow there would be carriages moving noisily down streets between buildings and shops, that there would be monks and – forgive me – thieves, life in all its seething chaos, in a word, on the very spot where today there were but a few freshly painted white lines on the green grass moved me to my very soul. Yes, I can promise you that I felt something then that tied knots in my guts tighter than any battle has ever done. I can at last believe – or at any rate hope – that we have come to this strange and marvelous country for reasons other than looting it of its gold. I can finally believe that we are here to build something that is, if not exactly God's work, then at least that of men of dignity.

At least, that was how I wanted to see things during that arousing moment.

Brother Bartholomew, my friend, I imagine your thin smile as you read these lines, wondering why I have sent you this detailed description.

The truth is that I wanted to find some good news for you. As you are no doubt aware, things are going badly between the Governor and Don Diego de Almagro. After a hundred disagreements, reconciliations, and even outright threats of war, a solution had to be found to separate them, so volatile was their antagonism.

The news reached me the day before yesterday. As you doubtlessly already know, it has been decided that Don Diego de Almagro will set off to conquer the south of Peru. The region is said to be richer in gold than anywhere we have seen until now, and this somewhat appeased de Almagro's noxious voraciousness for the stuff. However, it seems to me that that rumor should be taken with a grain of salt.

Don Francisco asked me to join Don Diego's expedition and, to be frank, to be the Governor's spy.

It is a task that I cannot love, and I loathe especially what it entails: another year of traveling, perhaps longer. And what a journey it will be, when every day I shall be burdened by the thought of what I have left behind.

Dear friend, permit me to write her name: Anamaya.

Not one morning, not one evening, not one quiet moment passes when I do not think of her. Not a day passes when I do not see her face whenever I close my eyes, so clearly it is as though she has been branded into my mind with a white-hot iron. Dear friend, my love for her boils within me, and I tremble with anxiety for not knowing what to do about it. I grow anxious whenever I imagine the thousand caresses of love we are missing, caresses that never end. I tremble for the fear of ever forgetting her voice, her lips, or the scent of her skin.

I shudder, and then I tell myself that it is over. We have been apart too long now. And I fear that this latest departure of mine will tear us apart forever.

I shiver with fear whenever I think how vulnerable she is, and I grow furious for not being able to protect her. I know what the Governor's brothers are capable of.

I know that I have good reason to be anxious.

Dear Brother Bartholomew, forgive me for confiding in you, a man of God, these feelings that I myself cannot separate from the heat of desire, its frustration, and that rapture that makes us human. Yes, truly human, because one loves with all one's being. Knowing that another human being exists who is so different from me, so foreign to me, and yet from whom I cannot separate myself without finding in her place a bottomless void, gives me a taste of the infinite happiness that fulfills me as a man.

But in these circumstances, you are the only person who can help me. Could you let Anamaya know that I am leaving?

Could you let her know that I go against my will? Above all, could you offer her some protection? Could you consider her a friend and warn her of Gonzalo and Juan's ill-intentioned excesses? They are bound to return to their old villainies once de Almagro has left Cuzco. They will be masters of the city, but not of their own folly.

Will you help her leave Cuzco, if necessary? I will let you be the judge of any such necessity.

As you can see, I am in great need of paper. I must end here. I put myself in your hands as a drowning man surrenders himself to the will of God.

Sebastian will bring you this letter privately. You can trust him and ask him for help and even for gold. He has just pulled off a great stroke at Jauja. Having become an expert at dice, he relieved Mancio Sierra de Leguizamon of his wealth in only one day and one night. Sierra looted the great temple in Cuzco of all its gold two years ago. So now Sebastian is Don Sebastian. His skin is still black, but he is rich and free. Your God sometimes shows Himself capable of the greatest irony.

I say *your* God. Today, I wish I could sincerely pray that He is also mine. Adieu, dear friend Bartholomew. Take the greatest care of Anamaya, I beg you. I love her more than I do my own life, and I will not forget her, even in the hell to which I am heading.

Yours, and hers,
Gabriel.

Bartholomew looked up from the letter to see, for the first time, that the *Coya Camaquen* was crying. She had tilted her face upwards and was gazing at the magnificent mountains far beyond the *cancha*'s walls. She didn't bother to wipe away the tears glistening on her cheeks.

Slightly embarrassed, Bartholomew raised his hands in a small fatalist gesture. He said gently:

'I am considered, in my country, a man close to God, just as here you are admired for being close to invisible presences. That should make us incomprehensible to one another, for God knows no invisible presence other than Himself. Yet, each time I see you, I feel that this draws us closer together.'

Anamaya frowned in concentration, as though she was trying to suppress the thoughts that were tormenting her.

'I know that you find it difficult to understand us. Even he does,' she said, pointing at the letter as though it was Gabriel himself. 'Even he finds it difficult. But I thank you for trying, anyway.'

'I'll be there for you whenever you need me,' said Bartholomew. 'Gabriel is right. You are indeed in grave danger here. You must be very cautious.'

'I know what that word means, but it plays no part in my life. I do what I must do, with or without caution.'

A flash of a smile lit up her still-wet blue eyes as she stared at Bartholomew, who couldn't help but be disturbed by the depth and intensity of her gaze.

'Perhaps,' Anamaya said gently, '*you* are the one who needs to be cautious?'

CHAPTER 30

Tiahuanaku, August 1535

GABRIEL HAD BEEN ON THE ROAD FOR TWO WEEKS now, trying to catch up with de Almagro's column. He had followed the coast along the South Sea for some time before an Indian had guided him inland into the valleys and hills.

For two days he had been on his own again, and as far as he knew he was completely lost in the barren wilderness. For two days he had seen nothing except the wasteland and had fed more on the dust and wind than on the victuals that still filled his saddlebags.

He occasionally felt he was on the roof of the world. The insects here didn't flee at the sound of his bay's tread, softened as it was by the dry, yielding earth. The vast plateau extended smoothly to the horizon, with patches of *ichu* – short, thick grass – scattered here and there. It was in turn whipped by squalls and burned bone dry by the sun. The sun was setting now, and the whole land turned a rusty color beneath the somber blue of dusk.

Gabriel had covered his face with his kerchief, to protect himself from the dust. He felt as though he had gone blind, so long had he been staring at the same unchanging landscape. Suddenly he heard a cry, or at least something like one, shiver through the air. He stared for some time before making out, due west in the gathering shadows, some tall shapes rising from the flat horizon. Perhaps he was finally getting somewhere!

He wetted his kerchief with water from his gourd and wiped his face with it. Then he gently urged his horse into a trot. It would take him another half-hour at least before he reached the strange objects.

They turned out to be enormous angular statues that rose from the barren ground, two or three times bigger than a living human. He could make out, carved in the dark stone, faces, hands, and limbs. They looked like giant, crude dolls. The ground beyond them was strewn with massive polished boulders, half buried in the dusty soil as though a monster from the core of the earth had tried to swallow them.

Some of the sculptures looked like giant doors, with their strap hinges and lintels carved from a single boulder. How was such a thing possible? How could these prodigious objects, over thirty feet long and fifteen wide, have been worked, sculpted, polished, and transported here, where there was nothing but sky, wind, and dust? With what instruments, what tools, what craftsmanship had they been chiseled from boulders that could only have been even larger in their original state?

A man was moving in a strange manner in front of the immense monoliths, twirling around as though dancing with them. He was slightly shorter than Gabriel, but of far greater bulk. A mosaic of wrinkles covered his broad face from his forehead to his neck, and he looked out from slanting eyes set above a flattened nose. His only remaining teeth were two skewed black stumps through which he flicked his nimble tongue. His clothes were mere rags, and his legs were bare despite the freezing wind blowing across the upland. He wore a square, brightly coloured embroidered cap, a very strange headpiece indeed, with each corner angled upward like a billy goat's horn.

As Gabriel approached, the man stared intently at the conquistador's horse. But he didn't show the slightest trace of fear, as Indians usually did upon seeing the animal for the first time. He said nothing in reply to Gabriel's greeting or to his question about whether he had seen a long column heading south.

'A column of strangers dressed like me and with beasts such

as this one,' continued Gabriel, patting his horse's flank and dismounting. His voice was a little husky from lack of use.

The man screwed up his eyes, but said nothing. Gabriel thought that he hadn't made himself understood. He had discovered, ever since he had left the coast for the interior, how many different tribes of Indians there were, and how many different languages were spoken in this country.

The old man suddenly started windmilling his arms. He exclaimed in passable Quechua:

'*Taypikala, Taypikala*! This place is the *Taypikala*! You are in the center of the universe, Stranger. What you see here are the humans of the past, who were human before we were. They're made of stone, but they can see you. And they can see me. That's why I come here every day to salute them. Every day that the sun is over my head. Yes, yes, yes! You should salute them too, Stranger. Do as I do.'

The old man rolled his eyes back into his head, bent his knees, and raised his arms to the sky. He muttered incomprehensibly in his high-pitched voice in a language unknown to Gabriel.

Gabriel stood there looking vaguely amused, the reins of his horse flung lazily over his shoulder. He watched the man raise his arms to the sky and shake his torso back and forth while making a clucking sound like a chicken. When he noticed that Gabriel had remained standing motionless beside his horse, the man stopped short and stared at him furiously.

'Why do you not salute the Men of Stone?' he reprimanded Gabriel in his broken Quechua. 'They can see you, you know, and they will certainly become very angry with you. Salute them as I do, or else you'll regret it.'

The man spoke with such earnest conviction that Gabriel almost believed him. The otherworldly aspect of the place, one of the most extraordinary he had ever seen, also increased his inclination to believe.

As though he had read Gabriel's thoughts, the man approached him. He didn't show the slightest fear of the horse, ignoring it completely as he grabbed Gabriel's shirt with his long nails, as black as claws. His breath carried the stench of the starving. He muttered:

'A long time ago, Stranger, Viracocha, the maker of the beginning and the end, wished to put humans on the earth. But the beings that he originally created didn't walk upright. Or else they behaved like animals. They killed, grunted, and ate one another like animals. They copulated like animals, and their offspring did the same. There was no difference then between humans and animals, Stranger. So Viracocha destroyed them. He turned them into stone. You see them in front of you now. Viracocha said to himself, "I'm going to create perfect men, human beings who are strong, wise and beautiful. I shall give them a perfect city to live in. They shall educate the ones that aren't perfect, that aren't yet complete human beings." And then he created the Inca clans and Cuzco, the City of the Puma. There everything is perfect, Stranger.'

The old man fell silent. He winked at Gabriel, clicked his tongue, and released his grip on the Spaniard's shirt. He turned toward the immense sculptures, now bathed in the golden glow of dusk, raised his arms to the sky again, and said:

'Such was Viracocha's work, Stranger. He went on to create all the nations loyal to Cuzco. He sculpted what you see here — he modeled from giant stones men old and young, women, and children, one for each nation. He accorded each one a headpiece particular to them, a particular color for weaving, and *quipus* without a single knot in them. He built them a *cancha* here with enormous doors so that they might learn to live both indoors and outside. Then he gave them the country around Cuzco's sacred mountains.'

The old man clicked his tongue harder with each succeeding sentence. His eyes bulging, he shouted as though he was worried that the icy wind would whisk away his words as soon as they had left his mouth.

'Viracocha said to them, "Humans, here are your nations: here is the nation of the Canchis, there that of the Kollas, here the Yungas. And you shall all serve the Noble Lords, the Sons of the Sun, the Cuzco clans. They will teach you how to cultivate land and build roads. They will teach you how to be wise, as humans should be." Then Viracocha had guides brought for each nation.

He ordered them, "Submerge yourselves into the earth with the Men of Stone and come out only onto the land of the nations that I have designated," and this they did. They travelled through the earth, coming out only at springheads, caves, and great broken rocks. There, Viracocha's guide blew on their massive stone bodies and said, "Rouse yourselves, humans of *Taypikala*! Come to life! Become human, and go forth and populate this desert land. Propagate yourselves, respect the will of Viracocha and of the Sons of the Sun!"

The old madman screamed these last words. Gabriel felt a shiver run down his spine. He grabbed his doublet, which he had slung over his saddle, and put it on. The old man turned around. Still completely ignoring the horse, he grinned and clapped his hands. Gabriel smiled back at him, feeling rather ill at ease. The man nodded and pointed across the plateau.

'The ones you seek are over there, Stranger,' he said, his voice now back to normal. 'They are many. There are some Cuzco Lords with them, and other men, Strangers like you.'

'Thank you!' said Gabriel.

The man laughed through his two black teeth. He said:

'They are over there, Stranger. Viracocha is going to have to start all over again.'

He waved his arms as though he wanted to grab the monoliths and fling them off the plateau.

'The *Taypikala* is over,' he exclaimed, 'look around you: you will see that everything is disintegrating. Those whom you are joining are like animals. They kill, grunt, and fight among themselves like animals. They steal women, without distinguishing between old or young, in order to copulate with them like animals. There is no longer any difference between humans and animals, Stranger. Things have returned to what they were before Viracocha put humans on the earth. It's a new *pachacuti*. The *Taypikala* is over.'

Gabriel shivered again, not from the cold wind but at the old madman's sinister laughter. He bid him farewell, remounted and set off at a trot. He heard the man's laughter growing fainter behind him, his cries still echoing through the cold air:

'The *Taypikala* is over! Viracocha must begin again!'

*   *   *

Night had fallen by the time Gabriel had crossed the plateau and reached de Almagro's column. He could see and hear it from afar, an immense body of men camped in a fold of the plateau lit by a thousand torches. At first it reminded him of the army raised two years before at Cajamarca. It was as numerous as that one, with perhaps ten thousand Indians now following de Almagro and his conquistadors.

Gabriel spurred on his bay, and galloped across the plateau to the head of this giant human herd, where the Spaniards were usually to be found. But there were so many Indians that he came upon them before reaching the end of the column. What he saw left him dumbfounded.

He saw Indian men chained together in groups of ten. He saw two dozen others standing almost naked despite the wind and the dark, their ankles tied together with leather straps. By moonlight he saw women, both young and old, in the same position, their faces twisted with pain. He couldn't see fires for them to keep warm by or tents to take cover in anywhere. They were all terrified, they all avoided his gaze, and they would not answer any of his questions.

The old madman's cry came back into his head: *'There is no longer any difference between humans and animals, Stranger.'*

With his heart in his mouth, Gabriel rode for an hour amid the horror. When he at last reached Don Diego's camp, lit by a row of torches mounted on halberds, the screams and laughter rising from it warned him of what he would find there.

He lifted the tent flap and was hit by the noise, the brightness of the lamps and the heat from within. There was more space than he had imagined there would be. The pallid one-eyed man sat dozing in an armchair at the end of a long table on which sat the remains of roasts. Two dozen drunken Spaniards sat around with goblets of beer in their hands, shouting, guffawing, and tormenting a number of half-naked young Indian women. Indeed, some of the women were already completely naked, their eyes wide with terror, or else they too were drunk, laughing and crying at the same time.

Don Diego de Almagro emerged from his daze and was the first to notice Gabriel enter the tent. His only eye came alive, mocking and agleam. He cried out, bringing silence to the room, and everyone turned toward Gabriel. Looking at each person, Gabriel realized that he knew almost none of them.

'Why, Don Gabriel,' exclaimed de Almagro. 'What a surprise!' He jumped up out of his chair. He brought both his palms slamming down onto the table, startling the women and making the men laugh.

'Gentlemen, allow me to present to you Don Gabriel Montelucar y Flores, a very dear, very close friend of my friend Don Francisco.'

The evident venom in Don Diego's voice was enough to focus the drunkards' attention more keenly on Gabriel. They clearly shared Don Diego's hatred of the Governor. Gabriel refused to let himself be provoked, however.

'Don Francisco sent me to assure you of his support. He bid me tell you that his support extends beyond the merely financial, and that should you require something of him, you need only send him word and he would be honored to send you whatever you need.'

Almagro began laughing again.

'I am most grateful for his generous attentions. Don Francisco's pockets overflow with gold. At this very moment he sleeps in a bed of down, whereas we continue to march along roads, finding nothing but dust and more dust. But he has a pair of eyes whereas I have but one. And in front of you, gentlemen, you see his second pair—'

'Don Diego,' interrupted Gabriel, 'save your fatuities for the rest of the trip. I have just spent an hour riding through the hell that is your column. You treat these people like animals. Do you hope that the entire country will rise up against us?'

A silence as cold as the wind outside followed. De Almagro replied icily:

'Do you dare to lecture me, Don Gabriel?'

Gabriel did not have time to reply. A man rose from the table. He grabbed one of the young women nearby, drew his dagger and cut her entire tunic off her.

She touched her bare breasts and then looked at the blood on her fingers with an expression of terrified bewilderment.

'Here,' bellowed the man as the woman tried desperately to escape his grasp, 'we do as we please. Here our Governor is Don Diego.'

Gabriel had already drawn his sword. But his action was met with the sound of twenty others being pulled from their scabbards. A line of steel blades bristled at him.

Almagro's thin, pockmarked cheeks started quivering uncontrollably.

'You see how generous my men are, Don Gabriel. You see how naturally they call me by the title that was refused me. And that's not all: you see how far they're willing to go for me. Come now, I know you're a brave man. But there are five hundred of us, whereas there's only one of you. I fear that the odds are too great, even for you. As Don Cristobal de Narvaez has just explained to you, I am the ultimate authority here. And I march as I see fit. If my ways displease you, then run back to Don Francisco and clean his boots for him.'

Gabriel slowly sheathed his sword. His limbs were heavy with fatigue after his long trip, and he had a bitter taste in his mouth.

He heard de Almagro's men sniggering as he turned on his heel and left. The old madman's words echoed sadly in his head:

'The *Taypikala* is over. Viracocha must begin again.'

CHAPTER 31

Cuzco, August 1535

'H ELP, MILORD!'
       'I'm going to stab right through you!'
       'Ouch, *caballero*!'
   'Titu! Lloque! Be careful with those sticks or you'll hurt yourselves.'
   The two boys, five or six years old at the most, paused for a
moment and looked at the sticks in their hands that had become
swords in their imagination. Then they looked at their mother.
She was busy, along with the other servants, cleaning the great
common hall, shaking out the beds' *mantas*. She turned away as
soon as she had finished reprimanding her offspring, and the two
children burst out laughing as she did so. They bounded about
like puma cubs, continuing their game, their splendid new game:
sword fighting, just like the Strangers did, and with the same
weapons as them.
   Anamaya sat perfectly still in the shade, watching them. She
was smiling, but it was a grave, melancholic smile, one that put
no light in her blue eyes.
   'What are you dreaming about, *Coya Camaquen*?' murmured a
soft voice nearby.
   'Inguill!'
   Anamaya, surprised, turned around to see her young friend's
sweet face.
   'I didn't hear you arrive. You always move about as quietly as a
current of air,' she said warmly.

'Not so. I've been standing here behind you for some time now, but I didn't dare interrupt your thoughts. You seemed so fascinated by those little ones. I told myself . . .'

Inguill hesitated and nibbled on her lips before whispering:

'You were thinking of *him* as you watched them, weren't you?'

Anamaya simply nodded, and looked again at the children. They were running now, chasing one another from one end of the courtyard to the other, running themselves out of breath, laughing and yelling out the few Spanish words that they had picked up from the Strangers.

'You're missing him,' said Inguill, 'yet so many moons have passed since you saw him last, you could almost forget his face. Not like me; I don't have your strength, and I would have died long ago from crying.'

Anamaya suppressed her urge to stop the young girl saying anything more. Inguill's affection was sincere, and she wasn't aware of the hidden cruelty of her words. What was more, she was right: Anamaya had had to keep her love for Gabriel stifled for a very long time now, and she confided her pain and her loneliness only to the darkness of the night and the silent, looming mountains.

'Sometimes things happen that way,' she said in a low voice. 'Sometimes I manage to forget about him for a whole day. Sometimes I sleep through an entire night without waking up with him on my mind. Sometimes I'm frightened that I'm forgetting his face, as you say – forgetting what he looks like, the shape of his mouth, the gentleness of his touch. But then I remember without knowing why. Nothing is ever forgotten. Walking across the courtyard earlier, I saw these boys playing. And suddenly there he was, in front of my mind's eye.'

'But why do you go on thinking about him even though you're not sure he'll come back to you? Worse yet, you know that he can never be your husband, not in the proper way. You suffer in vain, *Coya Camaquen*.'

Anamaya could tell from the smarting in her eyes that she was about to cry, and she blinked to block the tears. She let out a little laugh, her eyes shining. Inguill held out her hand, and Anamaya took it in her own.

'No doubt you are right. But that is how it is. What can I do about it? I think about him because he's in my heart. I think about him because he's in my soul, and maybe also in the soul that waits for me in the Other World. I think about him because my body yearns for his caresses, his and nobody else's.'

'It must be terrible for you.'

'No, not always.'

They fell silent again as the boys' mother called out to them for a second time. This time she confiscated their sticks, triggering an outburst of tears.

'Gabriel isn't here, and yet I feel him so close to me, so close that I keep a space for him between my breath and my skin,' murmured Anamaya as she watched the scene between the mother and sons. 'On certain days I feel him so strongly, so violently, that it's as if he has only just left Cuzco. On those days, I imagine that if I were to turn around he would be there, and I could touch his face, and he would take me in his arms. But you are right: the rest of the time, I know the truth. He is far away, so far that I have no way of knowing if he still lives in this world.'

A single tear rolled down Anamaya's cheek. She wiped it away furtively. Laughing almost self-mockingly, she grabbed hold of Inguill's arm, led her to the *cancha*'s door and said in a firm voice:

'But come now, let's stop our prattling. Come with me to the great square at Aucaypata. The mummies of the Ancestors of Manco's clan were brought this morning. I want to pay my respects to them.'

Inguill, looking pensive and blushing with emotion, nodded and followed Anamaya.

A trumpet blew a brief call as they approached the *cancha*'s surrounding wall. Six guards, armed with spears decorated with feathers in Emperor Manco's colours, arrived to escort the *Coya Camaquen* without any verbal order having been given.

As they set off down the steep road toward the Aucaypata, Inguill suddenly asked in a low voice:

'Anamaya, is it possible to love a Stranger in the same way as a man from our own race?'

Anamaya, surprised, slowed down. She glanced at the guards

escorting them before answering to make sure that they couldn't hear.

'Gabriel isn't a Stranger like the others. It's difficult to explain. He has a strength of spirit that makes him stand out from other men, whether they're from here or from his own country.'

Inguill shook her head and smiled an impish and embarrassed smile. She asked again, in a whisper so low as to be practically inaudible:

'What I mean is, do they make love like men from here do? I've heard women say that they attach a greater importance to it than our own men, that they like doing it more than our own men, and that for us, for women I mean, well . . .'

Inguill dared not finish her sentence. Anamaya came to a halt. They could see the great ceremonial square from where they were, with the mummies lined up to the left, each with a brazier burning before it maintained by a priest.

'Why are you asking, Inguill?'

'I want to help Manco. I might be able to if you help me, Anamaya. I know that the Strangers came yesterday to torment him, demanding that he give them your husband, the Sacred Double made of gold. They shouted at him, even threatened him. I couldn't sleep at all last night, so much did the thought of what they asked of him torment me.'

Anamaya knew too well what Inguill was talking about. The memory of Governor Pizarro's two brothers' threats still lingered unhappily in her mind. What was more, those two devils Juan and Gonzalo were the main reason why Gabriel was so far away from her now.

Manco had once again bravely refused to give them the gold statue. Once again they had insulted him, insulted the Inca, the Son of the Sun, as though he was nothing but a mongrel dog. Then they had made a vile proposition to him: that the *Coya*, his own wife, should leave his bed for Juan's.

'I'll never allow it, never!' growled Anamaya furiously.

The men of the escort looked at them curiously. Anamaya set off toward the square again, with Inguill at her side. Anamaya said, in a low but still furious tone:

'Manco must no longer allow them to treat him with such disrespect. He cannot give them the *Coya* any more than he can give them me. Curi Ocllo is Queen. The Sun and the Moon have blessed her womb so that the Emperor may seed his lineage in it. She is even more sacred than I am. What an infamy it would be were a Stranger to take her. The Elders would lose all their trust in Manco. His authority would evaporate.'

'Anamaya, he has no choice,' protested Inguill, a resigned look on her face. 'Manco cannot refuse them again. The Strangers will certainly put him in chains. Oh, may Viracocha help us.'

Anamaya sternly waved the escort away from them as they reached the last paved steps before reaching the square. Not many people were on it, just a few Inca noblemen, some priests, and a gaggle of boys around the mummies. A small group of Spaniards stood a little way back, looking on with a bored, idle curiosity. They had stopped being fascinated by the ceremony long ago.

'No, Inguill,' continued Anamaya sharply, turning to face the young girl, 'don't let fear overwhelm you, for fear is always the worst of counselors. We must leave Cuzco. It's for the best. It's no longer possible to share this city with the Strangers.'

'Anamaya! That would be madness! It would mean war!'

'It's a necessary risk,' replied Anamaya calmly. 'Did you see the children earlier? They were pretending to be Strangers and they spoke words that they had learned from them. Their sticks weren't the clubs or spears or bows used by Inca warriors but the weapons of the Strangers. What will become of them as they grow up here if we leave things as they are? They'll stop loving Inti and Mama Quilla. They'll no longer be the children of the human beings to whom Viracocha gave the Empire of the Four Cardinal Directions. They'll be nothing but slaves to the Strangers, despising all our Ancestors and calling our nation "Peru". You know very well, Inguill, that I did all I could to prevent war breaking out when Chalkuchimac wanted only that. I had to do it so that Manco could be crowned Emperor. But today, Emperor Manco must be prepared to make war.'

'But he can't!' cried Inguill. 'Forgive me for interfering in matters that are beyond what an ignorant girl like me can understand, *Coya*

Camaquen. But everyone says, in the *acllahuasi* as elsewhere, that we aren't strong enough, that we don't even have enough warriors to fight the Strangers.'

'Circumstances will be different a few moons from now.'

'A few moons from now, Manco will have chains around his feet and neck, just like Emperor Atahualpa!' cried Inguill. 'The Strangers are coming for the *Coya* in just three days!'

Anamaya turned away with an exasperated sigh. She concentrated on the priests for a moment in order to calm herself and avoid speaking harshly to Inguill. They wore long, fringed tunics and were offering oblations to the mummies, throwing corn kernels and strips of meat into the braziers with precise, composed movements. Then they raised the jars of *chicha* to the preserved bodies, as though inviting them to drink.

Without looking at her and without being able to withhold her sarcasm, Anamaya asked Inguill:

'Very well. You seem to have worked everything out. Can you offer a better solution?'

'Yes! Please don't be angry with me, Anamaya. I only want to help you and Manco.'

'How do you hope to do that?'

The young girl stiffened before blurting out:

'The Strangers can have me.'

'*You*? Inguill, don't talk nonsense. You're not the *Coya*.'

'I know that, but they don't. And everyone says how much I look like Curi Ocllo.'

Anamaya, flabbergasted, stared at Inguill's tender, innocent face for a few moments, at her broad and high cheekbones, at her small but well-defined lips, and at her slightly hooked nose. It was true that she looked like Manco's wife. Anamaya, moved, shook her head nonetheless.

'No, Inguill. It would be madness. You don't know what you're saying.'

'Anamaya, listen to me. You know that I love Manco more than anyone in the world. I love him as much as you love your Stranger. I owe him my life, remember. So now, even though he doesn't want me in his bed, I want to show him how much I love him.'

'By becoming a Stranger's wife?'

'By helping him avoid a war for which he isn't yet prepared.'

Anamaya was shaken, and stared at her friend.

'But do you understand what would happen to you?'

'I've thought about it for a long time,' said Inguill, smiling wanly. 'That's why I asked you earlier how the Strangers made love. I would be wife to the oldest, the one called Juan. I've been watching him, and I don't think he's as cruel as his brother.'

Anamaya shook her head again, incredulous. Tears rose to Inguill's eyes as she laughed and said:

'At least I'll get to be Queen for a short while! Help me, *Coya Camaquen*. Take me to Manco so that I can tell him my plan.'

Hidden behind the *manta* hanging over the doorway, Anamaya watched the festivities going on in the courtyard. Manco had prepared matters well. The Strangers looked gratified for once.

There were only a dozen or so Inca guards and Spanish soldiers in the courtyard. A number of pretty young women came and went, all wearing brightly colored ceremonial tunics and garlands of red *cantutas* on their heads. They set dish after dish before the Emperor and his guests, platters laden with sweet-smelling delicacies such as roast vicuña stuffed with prunes, roast turtledoves and partridges served with tiny potatoes, and a purée of *quinua* and peanuts.

Juan Pizarro was wearing a new coat with voluminous sleeves and a lace ruff as broad as a hand that hid his beauty spot. He held his gloves in one hand and a white cattleya orchid in the other, and he brought this to his nose every now and then, making a great show of inhaling its scent. Gonzalo, standing beside him, received the fruits and honey-laden corn cakes offered to him with such grace that no one who saw him then would have believed him to be a blackguard. Both brothers sat on a bench made more comfortable with fine woolen blankets. Manco sat in front of them on the three-legged seat reserved for Emperors.

'Everything's going well,' said Anamaya in a low voice. 'The

Strangers are pleased. Manco is playing the happy host. But they're bound to ask for the *Coya* soon.'

Inguill murmured from behind her. The girl was squatting in the shadows, and only the glint of her gold headpiece could be seen.

And indeed, as the servant girls, their necks bowed and eyes looking down, brought forth the jars of *chicha*, Juan Pizarro declared:

'Sapa Inca, your table is delicious, and your hospitality generous, but I don't want you to forget why we are here.'

Manco, saying nothing, held up his right hand. The servant girls immediately stopped what they were doing and formed two lines up to the door to the outer courtyard.

The first of Manco's concubines appeared. She came forward slowly, gracefully, preceded by two young girls dressed in white tunics. The two Spaniards examined her broad face, her small waist, and her well-defined lips as she slowly made her way through the two ranks of servant girls. She was perhaps more robust than she was beautiful, but she was clearly a sensual woman. She went straight to the Emperor and prostrated herself in front of him, not even glancing at the Strangers.

But before Manco had even ordered her to her feet, Gonzalo had a derisive look on his face.

'Why, Sapa Inca,' he carped, 'would you have us believe that this woman is your wife?'

'Certainly she is,' replied Manco, grinning.

'Of course she isn't. You're trying to deceive us. She doesn't look anything like the *Coya*,' complained Juan, piqued. 'Look, Gonzalo, she's older than I am.'

'Sapa Inca,' sighed Gonzalo, rising to his feet, 'surely we're not going to quarrel yet again. My brother needs the most beautiful of your women. Your favorite wife, in fact.'

Anamaya saw the restrained anger in the Spaniard's smile. Manco must have noticed it too, because he laughed quietly and said:

'Well done! You're absolutely right, dear Governor's brother. You spotted it right away. But this woman is indeed one of mine. She is the one who, a long time ago now, taught me how a man is to behave between his wife's thighs.'

The two brothers burst into laughter as Manco continued:

'It would displease me to give my most beautiful woman to a man who doesn't recognize beauty. I am happy to learn that your taste is as exacting as mine.'

He clapped his hands. Twenty young women emerged from the great communal hall opposite his private chamber. The Spaniards, turning around to look at them, stared wide-eyed and open-mouthed.

'My dear friends,' began Manco in a friendly tone, 'here are my most beautiful women. I cannot do better than to let you choose.'

From her inconspicuous position in the shadows, Anamaya watched the amazed expressions on the Strangers' faces as the young women, looking fearful but resigned, approached them. They were all wearing the same light blue *añaco* and white cape brightened with only a few colorful patterns on their hems.

'It has begun,' murmured Anamaya. 'The concubines are here.'

Inguill, nervous and tense, had drawn so close to Anamaya's shoulder that Anamaya could smell the heavy scent of oil musk that the young girl had covered herself in.

'Look.'

Anamaya pushed the *manta* very slightly aside so that Inguill could watch the scene.

Under the sun beating down on the courtyard, the Governor's brothers inspected the concubines. They would lift the chin of one, take another's hand, stroke another's shoulder, have one and then another turn around so that they could ogle the young women's figures. Gonzalo's gestures and giggles became increasingly coarse. Now he would feel a breast, next a belly, and would stroke the girls so immodestly that Anamaya shivered with disgust.

'Inguill, are you sure about—'

'Yes! Absolutely,' interrupted Inguill. 'My only fear is that they might choose a concubine before even seeing me.'

But that didn't happen, and everything went as planned.

Gonzalo frowned and drew his brother aside, even though Juan seemed completely enchanted by the women and was endlessly saluting them with flourishes of his hat. The two brothers spoke privately together for a few moments. Then Gonzalo turned to Manco. Now his eyes were glowing with rage, and he walked right up to the Emperor.

'Sapa Inca, by the blood of Christ. When will you understand that you must not lie to us?'

His loud words echoed across the courtyard, causing the servant girls and concubines to stand stock-still.

'You must never lie to us again!'

Inguill instinctively gripped Anamaya's arm as though she was frightened that the Spaniard's anger alone would destroy her.

Manco, meanwhile, reacted with disarming calm. Ignoring Gonzalo's cries, he asked Juan, his voice quite unfazed:

'Do none of these women please you, then, dear Governor's brother?'

'Why, it's not that they aren't pretty, Sapa Inca,' said Juan, embarrassed. 'They're pleasant enough to gaze upon, it must be said, and they're young and shapely.'

'But none of them is the *Coya*!' interrupted Gonzalo angrily. 'And you know very well that—'

'Dear friends,' sighed Manco, 'you are indeed very exacting.'

'No more games, Sapa Inca. I am growing impatient. We want to see the Queen this very instant.'

Manco's face suddenly clouded over. He stared dead ahead of him, as though his heart was shattering into pieces. Anamaya shivered and drew Inguill closer to her.

'He's about to send for you,' she whispered. 'Look after yourself, my friend.'

Anamaya noticed that Inguill's cheeks were wet with tears. As she kissed Anamaya's hand, the young girl muttered, against all evidence to the contrary:

'I'm not frightened! I'm not frightened!'

Anamaya pressed her face against Inguill's. They heard Manco calling out:

'Curi Ocllo! Fetch me the *Coya* Curi Ocllo.'

'Don't forget that I love you always!' whispered Anamaya urgently. 'And promise me that you'll run away if he hurts you.'

Now the servant girls had lifted the *manta* aside and were prostrating themselves on the threshold of the room. Anamaya retreated further into the shadows as Inguill stepped forth into the light.

The Spaniards' expressions immediately became more relaxed and self-satisfied. Inguill had never looked so beautiful. She was dressed in an ocean-green *añaco*, one so finely woven that it was impossible to make out its stitches and which accentuated her slender figure. A violet *lliclla* floated as gracefully as smoke from her shoulders to the ground and was embroidered with ingenious geometric designs that matched those on her belt. A number of gold-gilt seashells were strewn through her hair. Her face was immaculately made up, with her eyelashes curled by an expert hand. The fact that her eyelids and lips were trembling and that she was on the verge of tears only accentuated her beauty.

'Aaah,' cried Gonzalo. 'Here she is at last, my brother. Here is the *Coya*. I recognize her.'

Juan seemed to be greatly troubled by the vision of beauty in front of him. Anamaya saw that his discomfiture was more genuine than she had thought him capable of. He stared at Inguill as he approached her hesitantly. He bowed to her courteously and when he stood straight again, his expression still full of awe, it was clear that there was true respect mingled with his excitement.

'Yes, yes, this one!' Juan stammered to Manco. 'That's her, Sapa Inca, I recognize her, she's the *Coya*. I must have her right now.'

As he reached out to take Inguill's hand she began screaming, as had been arranged. She turned away from him, cried out, covered her face with her hands, trembled, and cried out that she didn't want to leave her master and husband the Emperor, and that these people frightened her. The faces of all the concubines and servant girls still present reflected Inguill's fear and pain. Some of whom began murmuring in distress and even crying. A mood of apprehension gripped the room.

'*Holà!*' laughed Gonzalo. 'Calm down, Lady *Coya*. What kind of welcome is this for your new husband?'

As Juan looked on in consternation, Inguill threw herself at Manco's feet, ruffling her beautiful clothes. She was like a magnificent flower suddenly unfurling its petals all at once. She cried:

'My Lord Emperor, don't forsake me. My Lord, I love only you. Emperor, my heart beats only for you and for the Ancestors in the Other World. My Lord, split open my chest and tear out my heart, but don't give me to the Strangers.'

Despite the fact that she had rehearsed these words with Inguill previously, Anamaya couldn't help but shudder at the sincerity with which the girl delivered them. Anamaya saw that everyone, including the Strangers, was sincerely upset.

'Rise, woman,' said Manco gravely. 'Go with my friend, the Stranger Lord. Don't concern yourself that he's a Stranger. You may serve me by becoming his faithful wife. Such is my will.'

'Oh Lord Emperor, have pity on me! Please kill me, for I have no reason to live if you leave me in the hands of another man.'

Anamaya winced once again. Inguill's words were like arrows in her heart. At that moment Manco, who was meant to cruelly ignore her tears, instead leaned forward toward the young girl. He took her by her arm and lifted her to her feet. He pulled her swiftly to him and kissed her on the mouth. It wasn't a long embrace, but the silence that accompanied it filled the courtyard for what felt like an eternity.

Anamaya caught a fleeting glimpse of Inguill's face as Manco pushed her away. Her face and eyes were lit by a marvelous smile that lingered even when Juan roughly snatched her up, and even as Spanish soldiers dragged her away toward the courtyard's gate.

In no time at all, it seemed, the Governor's brothers had disappeared with their catch. Anamaya came out onto the threshold of the room, her heart aching with shame, anger and a terrible feeling of loss. The faces of those gathered in the courtyard seemed more like masks than faces, all wearing the same fixed, wretched expression.

Manco stood up and went to Anamaya. He brushed aside the concubines and servant girls who ran up to him. His gait was that of a heavy-hearted man. He wore a tense smile on his face, or at least an attempt at a smile that was in fact no more than a strained, joyless grimace.

Beneath the deep blue sky, Anamaya raised her eyes and looked at the walls of the Sacsayhuaman fortress with its three seemingly indestructible towers.

'We did it,' said Manco earnestly.

Anamaya looked at him and nodded. She sensed the sadness and bitterness now taking root in the depths of his soul.

'That's what remains of your power,' she said, pointing at the walls of the fortress on the mountainside. 'The façade of power beneath the sun. The memory of power . . .'

'*Coya Camaquen*, please don't.'

'A power that reduces us to sacrificing a pure-hearted young girl to satiate those monsters' hunger . . .'

Manco's face turned white, and he clenched his fists as he said:

'Don't think that I don't know it. Don't think that Inguill's suffering doesn't tear at me like the claws of a puma.'

Anamaya said nothing. The word 'puma' had startled her. Her own puma was strong, but so far away.

'Come back,' she murmured to herself. 'Please, come back and help me.'

CHAPTER 32

Cuzco, September 1535

A GENTLE RAIN WAS FALLING. ANAMAYA LISTENED TO IT pattering on the roof above her. The rainwater was soft. It streamed down gently from her hair, across her forehead, and wetted her *añaco*.

Anamaya listened to it splashing into the mud puddles outside in the courtyard. She felt an urge to leave her bed, to go outside and watch the rain falling gently through the night. She saw herself wake and get up. At that moment she realized things were not as they should be.

How could her hair and forehead be wet with rain if there was a roof above, sheltering her? What was more, the *cancha*'s courtyard was paved with flagstones. How could mud puddles form there?

She got up and went to the door. Yes, she had been mistaken. She wasn't in the *cancha* but in a hut in the jungle village of her childhood, the one where she had been born. Now the rain grew heavier, as it had on that night so long ago, that last night before the beginning of everything.

Before she had become the *Coya Camaquen*.

Anamaya told herself quickly that she was still asleep, that she was dreaming. Perhaps she should wake up and end the dream. Still, she couldn't help but be fascinated by the village, with its four great communal huts surrounding the central courtyard. It was exactly as it had been then, except that the huts now were totally empty. She had a presentiment of danger, and was frightened that Emperor Manco's warriors were about to attack.

She was frightened, and she knew that she should try to wake up.

But the silvery flash and gentle patter of the rain falling through the night were so mesmerizing that she couldn't tear herself away. It was extraordinary to be back in the village where she had been a little girl. And if she mustered up all her courage, she might perhaps see her mother's face.

Anamaya was grateful to her husband the Sacred Double for having granted her this dream. She would go and thank him after she woke up. She felt both light-hearted and frightened.

A sudden sound made her jump – a scurrying sound, like that of an animal. Another noise followed it. She thought she could make out the grow – and the silhouette – of a light-coated beast bounding toward the outer fence.

But no, she was mistaken. What she heard was the sound of steps on the wet ground. It was a particular step, one that she recognized instantly: the sound of a Stranger's boots.

Anamaya's heart leaped the moment he walked into the hut. Gabriel took off his hat, and his face shone luminously in the night. He was dry despite the rain. His golden hair was dry. He smiled. He spread his arms out to Anamaya, whose belly and breast quivered with happiness. She had waited for him for so long. At last he was back, as alive and as handsome as he had been the first day they had laid eyes on one another.

A marvelous happiness surged through Anamaya when Gabriel embraced her. She could feel the heat of his body through his shirt, and she listened to his breathing quicken as he kissed her and began undoing her *añaco*. She laughed at his eagerness. He lifted her as though she were a feather and carried her to her bed. She wanted to see his face, his eyes. She had missed his face for so long now, his soft lips, his aquiline nose, and his bronzed cheeks. But he was impatient, so impatient that he became violent. As she tried to shove him away, she realized that a beard covered his mouth and chin. His face had changed.

She screamed.

Now she was awake, wide-eyed. The man sprawled on top of

her wasn't Gabriel. His fingers were frantically grasping for her breasts, and he was trying violently to strip her clothes off. She realized that he was trying to rape her, and she screamed again.

This time her attacker retreated, his eyes full of hate. He swore in Spanish, slapped one hand over her mouth and reached for her throat with the other.

'Don't resist me, bitch!'

She didn't understand the words coming from that mouth foaming with desire and hatred, but she recognized the voice. Gonzalo, the Governor's brother.

Anamaya's fear gave way to rage. She tried to roll away but the man held her in place. She struggled and shook her head violently from side to side, trying to get free. The Spaniard's fingers slipped into her mouth, and she bit down on them as hard as she could. She tasted blood on her tongue and heard the man scream out in agony.

'Spread your legs, damned Indian whore!'

She took advantage of his shock to fold her knees back over her chest. Gonzalo moaned with pain. He had trouble holding her with his injured hand. He fell on top of her, trying to pin her down. But Anamaya managed to slip the soles of her feet against his gut, and she used all her strength to kick him off. He stumbled back and slammed into the wall, but not without first ripping her *añaco* from her and scratching one of her breasts with his nails.

Anamaya jumped to her feet and cried out for the servants to come to her aid. She realized that it really was raining and that Gonzalo's breeches were soaked. Even his shirt, under his unbuttoned doublet, was wet. His hair was plastered against his demented face. He was grimacing and sniggering as though it were all a game. He groped around for his sword, which he had taken off and placed near the bed. He found it and stood up.

'Shut up, slut!'

But before he got a chance to unsheathe the weapon, Anamaya kicked him with a strength that until then she hadn't thought herself capable of. Gonzalo tried to dodge her foot, but in vain. Anamaya's whole being was concentrated on killing him. She felt

her heel slam into the Stranger's face, slide up his cheekbone and
dig deep into his eye cavity. She fell back down onto her bed.
Gonzalo's head bounced off the stone wall that Anamaya's kick
had driven it against like a rag ball.

'*Coya Camaquen! Coya Camaquen!*'

The servant girls rushed in, screaming, and surrounded her.
Then the guards arrived with torches, spears and clubs. Everyone
stared at the scratches on Anamaya's face and at the bloodstains on
her torn tunic. They all began speaking at once, but she silenced
them with a wave of the hand. She gathered her breath as best
she could.

'I'm all right,' she said, speaking to herself as much as to them.
'I'm all right. He didn't do anything to me . . .'

The Governor's brother still lay unmoving at her feet. Blood
flowed from his temple and zigzagged in a thin stream down his
neck to his shirt.

Anamaya wrapped a cape, given to her by a servant girl, around
her shoulders and asked:

'Is he alive?'

A guard leaned over the Spaniard and put first his hand on
Gonzalo's chest, then his cheek next to his mouth. He smiled
and nodded.

'He's only knocked out, *Coya Camaquen*. But I can kill him if
you want.'

Anamaya closed her eyes and took a few deep breaths to
suppress the desire to give the order.

'No,' she whispered. 'No, let him live. Just call the Emperor.'

When Gonzalo came to, he was still slumped against the wall
in the room, and his left eye was swollen crimson. He felt
it with his fingertips, moaned, and shoved away the servant
girls trying to put a plaster on his temple. He was stupefied
to discover that there were two dozen spearheads pointed at
him.

The Emperor's guards stood to each side of Manco and
Anamaya. A few noblemen from the court were also present.

The dancing light from the torches flickered over their severe faces and accentuated their stern expressions.

The Governor's brother tried to laugh, but the effort made him grimace with pain. His face no longer had anything angelic about it, making one think instead of a cruel and wounded beast. He looked at Anamaya through his uninjured eye with such ferocity that she felt a chill run down her spine.

'What I promised you earlier is mild compared to what I'm going to do to you now,' Gonzalo murmured savagely.

He leered at her obscenely, and Anamaya felt a terrible fear spread through her body.

Gonzalo swayed as he tried to rise to his feet. But his pride drove him on and, his face twisted with pain, he managed eventually to stand up and lean against the stone wall. Then Manco said in an even voice:

'Governor's brother, I should kill you for what you did. I'll repeat what I told you already: No one is to lay their hands on the *Coya Camaquen.*'

Gonzalo stared at him with a surprised look on his face before uttering a dreadful little laugh that twisted his face even more.

'It is our law,' continued Manco, 'that we hang a man guilty of raping a woman by his hair in the jungle and leave him there until the beasts have eaten all of him but his bones.'

'Well, then, try it. Kill me!'

Gonzalo took a couple of unsteady steps. The circle of bristling spearheads closed in around his chest, forcing him to stop. He glared at Manco and Anamaya with his good eye. Then, recovering his arrogance, he growled:

'You think that you scare me! You're nothing but a coward, Sapa Inca. You're not a man. You don't have what it takes to kill me right here, right now, even with two dozen warriors to do it for you. And I'll tell you why . . .'

He spat and cleared his throat. His wicked smile broadened.

'Because you know that my death means your own, and you love your own life above all else. More than your gold, more than your women, and more than your honor . . .'

He stared at Manco with utter hatred, and spat insults at him as though he was striking him with a sword:

'See what we've made of you, Oh Son of the Sun, Oh divine Sapa Inca! A mere puppet, a bawling, gesticulating doll. The sounds that come out of your mouth have no more meaning than the wails of an infant . . .'

Gonzalo went on and on as the warriors pushed their spears toward him. The bronze spearheads were touching his dirty shirt now. He brushed a few of them violently aside, but the effort made him dizzy. He stumbled backward like a drunkard and leaned against the wall before continuing:

'Oh great King of Kings! You think that you can dupe me? Me?' He laughed coarsely and spat blood onto the flagstones.

'Your *Coya* is nothing but a servant girl. That poor fool Juan thinks he's fucking your Queen, but in fact he only has some courtesan in his bed. And you thought that I didn't notice!'

Manco signaled to the warriors to step away from the Spaniard. He held Gonzalo's sword in his hand and, pointing it at the would-be rapist's gut, he came up so close to the conquistador that only the bare blade was between them. The Spaniard's good eye clouded with fear.

Anamaya also stepped forward. She made as though to hold Manco back. But the Emperor, moving so quickly that the startled guards jumped back, raised both the sword and his leg. He slammed the blade down, snapping it in two across his knee.

'We're the ones,' sneered Gonzalo, 'who decide who lives or dies! We're the ones with the power over life and death!'

Manco, his eyes bulging with rage, grabbed a club from a guard and swung it above his head.

'NO!' cried Anamaya. 'Emperor, no! Don't do it, not yet!'

Everything stopped for a moment. All eyes were on Manco's raised fist and the club it gripped. The whites of his eyes were now as red as Atahualpa's had been.

The only sound was the Spaniard's raucous, wheezing breath.

'Let him go, my Lord,' continued Anamaya gently. 'There is truth in his lies. He will do you more harm dead than alive.'

Manco let his arm fall, then flung the club down at Gonzalo's feet.

'Get out of here, Stranger,' he growled. 'Leave this *cancha* immediately.'

Gonzalo grinned. He shook himself free of the warriors holding him and ran his hand over his cheek, which was bleeding again.

'Yes, listen to your untouchable whore, who I'll be touching again soon enough. It's best for you that I stay alive.'

The servant girls and the guards moved aside to let Gonzalo pass. He turned around in the doorway, spat on the ground again, pointed a bloody finger at Manco, and said:

'Give up your high and mighty airs, Sapa Inca. You're nothing here, nothing more than mule shit. From now on, *I* am Cuzco's true ruler.'

As Anamaya watched the guards reluctantly move their spears and clubs to let Gonzalo leave, she thought about his parting words.

What he had said was horrible, grotesque, contemptible.

And true.

'We must leave tonight, Emperor,' said Anamaya as soon as the guards and servant girls had withdrawn. 'You must go as far away as possible from Cuzco.'

'You shouldn't have stopped me killing him earlier,' growled Manco, not listening.

'Gonzalo's brother would have come to kill you tomorrow. You must harness your rage and not allow it to rule you.'

Manco cried out in anger and raised his fists to the night, as though he was trying to expel all the violence stifled inside him. The rain had at last stopped.

'You should have let me kill him! He sullied you with his hands, yet you spared him! Where is your pride, *Coya Camaquen*?'

Anamaya met his gaze directly with her own cold, stony stare.

'Killing him would have started a war. Fighting would have broken out tomorrow! You aren't ready to go to war with the Strangers, Emperor. First you must leave Cuzco and gather your troops. You know as well as I do that we don't have enough warriors at the moment. The Strangers are still stronger than us.'

Manco stared at her.

'Do you believe that the time for war is upon us?'

'The time to *prepare* for it is upon us. We must leave Cuzco this very night. You can no longer remain in this palace.'

Manco continued staring at her, as though the meaning of her words was slowly dawning on him.

'Prepare for war . . . but how? Villa Oma and my brother Paullu are with de Almagro, on their way to the southern provinces. We have split our forces in order to force the Strangers to split theirs, since they are divided among themselves. Villa Oma and Paullu must be at least two moons away from Cuzco now. I have only five thousand men left in the mountains around the sacred valley. If I flee Cuzco without a real army under my command, the Empire of the Four Cardinal Directions is doomed. Who will believe that I am strong enough for them to want to join me?'

'If you are placed in chains, if you become the Strangers' prisoner, then your people will certainly shed their tears. But they won't rise up, Emperor. We will be like a body without a head. But if you go into the mountains, then your Ancestors will surely help you. Most of the *chaskis* are still loyal to you. You only have to say the word and they will mobilize all the provinces. We'll form the army that you need. Villa Oma and Paullu are ready to come to you with thousands of troops the moment you send for them. Everyone will help you, because everyone will be proud of you.'

'Did my father tell you all this?'

There was a trace of sarcasm in Manco's voice that disturbed Anamaya. But she held his gaze and said in a low voice:

'Manco, you know very well that your father Huayna Capac hasn't visited me for a long time now. But I'm just like you: not a day passes when I don't yearn to hear his voice. Tonight I had a dream and I thought . . . I thought that he would come to me.'

She fell silent for a moment and tears welled up in her eyes. The memory of Gonzalo's attempted rape passed in front of her mind's eye and mingled with her memory of Gabriel, unnerving her.

Anamaya felt the weight of Manco's gaze and continued in a stronger tone:

'Trust me, Manco. I know what the Strangers are made of. What happened just now clearly shows that nothing will stop them. As the Governor's brother said to you, he'll do everything to humiliate you. We must flee now, tonight, without losing another moment. We must leave before it's too late for you to call the people of the Son of the Sun to arms. I beg you, Manco, please listen to me. Dawn brings with it many dangers.'

But Manco still hesitated. He ran his fingers along the edge of Anamaya's torn *añaco* beneath her cape, and he brushed his hand along her cheek that had been scratched by the Spaniard. Then he gave a resigned nod and said:

'Yes, I trust you, *Coya Camaquen*. Have the necessary arrangements made. We shall leave Cuzco by the secret staircase in the Tower of the Sun.'

The light of dawn was already visible over the mountains to the east by the time they emerged at last from the vast secret labyrinth that linked the terraces of Colcampata to the high Tower of the Sun of Sacsayhuaman. The fortress's enormous walls overlooking Cuzco looked like the head of a giant sleeping monster in the early morning light.

There were about thirty of them. Manco wanted only a few of his favorite wives and servants and five or six noblemen from his court. The rest were ordered to remain in the royal *cancha* and go about their business as usual, so that the Strangers shouldn't discover Manco's escape for as long as possible.

Breathing heavily, their chests burning from the effort of the climb, the escaping Incas spread out on the terrace at the base of the tower. A film of sweat covered Anamaya's forehead, and her thighs were stiff from the quick ascent of the stairs. She watched the dwarf jump around with surprising agility on the low walls that led to a terrace overlooking the city. Then his small form stood still and became obscured in the lingering darkness.

She heard the bearers setting down the palanquins and then saw the dwarf returning.

'All's well,' he announced, grinning. 'Not a sound to be heard. The Strangers are all dreaming of gold. We aren't going to wake them.'

His smile faded when he saw Anamaya.

'Are you all right?' he asked, taking her by the hand.

'I'm fine,' she said hoarsely. 'Just tired from the climb.'

But, in truth, the memory of her dream of Gabriel and the horrible vision of Gonzalo tearing at her clothes kept coming back into her mind, utterly draining her spirit. She had already vomited twice, and her nausea had only increased as they had climbed to Sacsayhuaman.

'Come,' said the dwarf, leading her to the palanquins, 'you must at least rest for a little while. Try to eat something. I brought these for you.'

As Anamaya lay down in her palanquin, he pulled out a roasted corncob and a mango from a little woven bag he wore slung across his shoulder.

Anamaya, touched by his kindness, smiled. She stroked the dwarf's hand as she took the fruit and the corn from him, but she placed them at her side rather than eating them.

'I can't possibly eat anything now. But I'll keep them for later.'

Manco, standing nearby, surprised them both when he said loudly:

'Eat. The dwarf is right. You must eat and recover. We have a long day ahead, and I'm going to need you.'

She tried to smile, but she felt almost too weary to do so. She was there – she was always there – to aid Manco when he needed her. But who was there for her when she needed help?

Loneliness – her old, familiar, terrible loneliness – invaded her soul like a shadow.

They skirted around to the east of the town in almost complete silence. They walked quickly but did not run. The cortege made its way along the outer walls of the noblemen's *canchas* before heading down an alleyway into the goldsmiths' section of town. In the square bordered by adobe houses, they saw the red glow of furnaces still burning. Then they crossed the part of town adjoining the plain where those who had not been born in Cuzco lived. The houses were spaced further apart here, and were set in well-kept gardens, but were without any protective outer walls. A man or woman occasionally appeared, their arms laden with firewood. They would stop in their tracks and, astonished, would watch the column slowly disappear into the haze of dawn.

The fleeing men and women passed the city's great storehouses before heading south on the well-paved royal road. They walked in total silence for over an hour, hearing only the sound of their own sandals shuffling along the flagstones and the noise of birds greeting daybreak as the sky above them slowly turned a vanilla colour.

Anamaya had made space beside her for the dwarf, so that he wouldn't exhaust himself running on his short legs. She hadn't left the *cancha* for months, and she was surprised to find how beautiful the fields and the mountains beyond them were. The previous night's rain had sharpened the reds and ochers of the shimmering terrace plots stepped one above the other, and the mountain looked as though it had been covered in some giant, finely woven ceremonial *unku*. Banks of pearly fog slid down from the peaks into the folds of the valleys. The sight of Mother Earth's beauty all around her somewhat eased Anamaya's anxiety. She dared to hope that this serene loveliness was in fact a sign from the Ancestors, happy to see them leave a city now sullied by the Strangers – as Anamaya herself had almost been.

But her hope faded quickly.

As the first rays of the sun reached the peaks, a soldier ran along beside the cortege until he reached the litters, his eyes bulging with panic:

'Emperor! Emperor!'

Manco pushed aside the curtain and ordered the young man to speak.

'My lord, a *chaski* has just caught up with us. The Strangers have discovered your escape. They know that you've left your *cancha*. They have destroyed it, and—'

'Oh no, they're already at our heels!' cried the dwarf, looking at Anamaya.

'They'll catch up with us in no time with their horses,' cried an old Lord, fidgeting with his gold-gilt wooden earlobe plugs. 'May Viracocha help us!'

'Now isn't the time to panic,' interrupted Manco harshly.

He ordered, in as few words as possible, the noblemen, women and servants to continue south along the royal road.

'There's no point hurrying. If they catch up with you, tell them that I ordered you to join my brother Paullu and their friend de Almagro. I'm going to disappear into the valleys to the east. The *Coya Camaquen* is coming with me.'

'Me too, Emperor, please!' cried the dwarf, prostrating himself.

'Let him come,' said Anamaya, seeing Manco frown. 'You know that he'll give his life for you if necessary.'

'Even better,' muttered the dwarf, 'I shall strive to stay alive so that you may remain free.'

Manco shrugged his shoulders, then ordered the bearers to set off – which they did at a run, despite the weight of their load. They were no longer on the royal road, and the unpaved paths they were now negotiating were littered with slippery stones and mud puddles. But they ran as though they had claws on their feet. They reached the edge of the valley in very little time. Day was now well established. One of the porters suddenly cried out and pointed. The dwarf, who had been watching the horizon, cried out at exactly the same moment:

'There they are!'

Manco and Anamaya saw the troop of Strangers appear beyond the gray-green *quinua* fields. They looked like giant black-shelled insects skimming with supernatural speed along the tops of the plants. And their horses did more than just allow them to travel quickly: from their elevated positions, the riders were able to see further across the plain.

'They're on the royal road,' said Manco hopefully. 'They're chasing the women. They won't see us.'

Anamaya shook her head.

'I'm afraid they will. The palanquins are clearly visible above the fields.'

'She's right, Emperor,' agreed the dwarf, abandoning all the proper etiquette due a monarch. 'If we can see them, then they can see us.'

The remained frozen in indecision for a moment and watched the troop of Spaniards galloping on. The wind carried cries like those of animals hunting to them across the plain. Then the dwarf suddenly clapped his hands and jumped down to the ground.

'Emperor, there is a marsh over there,' he shouted, pointing at a clump of bushes at the edge of the plain. 'The Strangers avoid them because they're no good for their horses. Let the porters continue with the palanquins up the mountain path while we hide there.'

Manco agreed.

The dwarf was right. The clump of bushes a few leagues beyond the terraces marked the beginning of a bulrush-covered marsh.

The dwarf snapped off a number of reeds and mixed them with others, either dry or rotten, with astonishing speed. He gathered a pile of dead wood and of mud, and with them made a great heap of debris that looked as though it had been lying there for ages. But when he invited Manco to hide inside it, the Emperor hissed disdainfully between his teeth.

'Do you take me for a guinea pig?'

'Emperor—'

'No!' shouted Manco angrily. 'The Son of the Sun shall not hide under a pile of rotten twigs! What would my father say?'

'Manco, it's only for a little while, to get away from the Strangers,' said Anamaya gently.

Manco gave her a furious look.

'*Coya Camaquen*! Do you think that I'm going to begin my war against the Strangers by hiding like a coward? Do you want Illapa and Inti to see me huddled up like a child beneath this stinking pile of bushes? Do you want to lend truth to the Governor's brother's words that I'm nothing but a coward?'

'I just don't want you to get caught,' replied Anamaya, but in vain. Manco had turned around and now haughtily declared:

'It is for my father and for Viracocha to decide, and I shall remain standing for as long as it takes them to do so.'

And with that, he marched off to hide amid the bulrushes, ankle-deep in water.

Anamaya couldn't think of a way to explain to him that he wasn't talking to Gonzalo now, and that he would do better to use crafty military tactics rather than proud, useless speeches to regain his dignity.

They stayed like that for a long time, with Anamaya and the dwarf squeezed together beneath the pile of branches and Manco waiting, only partly hidden, among the bulrushes. But the wet and the cold very soon chilled them to the bone, and Anamaya had to clench her fists to stop herself from trembling.

For a while, however, Anamaya told herself that they had succeeded. The Strangers' shouting stayed distant, and occasionally even seemed to fade further away. Then, suddenly, she felt the dwarf's fingers tighten around her shoulder.

The first thing she noticed was the thudding of hooves on the earth. Then she heard shouting close enough for her to make out what they were saying.

'Over there, Beltran. Go have a closer look at those bushes . . .'

'They're coming,' whispered Anamaya.

The dwarf replied by tightening his grip still further.

They watched, through the crisscross of branches, two riders approaching side by side. They were moving slowly, looking around carefully. They were coming toward the hideout. One of them leaned over in his saddle and peered more closely into the bushes. Anamaya closed her eyes. She listened to the hooves thudding past them. Past their hiding place. The Strangers hadn't seen them. They were continuing through the swamp.

At that moment, they heard cries echoing from the direction of the mountain.

'By the damned spit of the llama,' cursed the dwarf. 'They've caught the bearers. Now they'll see that the litters are empty.'

They heard more shouting. They stared at the rushes in which
Manco was hiding. They heard the sound of a horse walking
through water, and then a cry in Spanish:

'Ho, Don Pedro! Have you found him?'

There was no reply, and the two cavalrymen came back along
their tracks, passing the hideout once again. At that moment, a
very large Stranger rode over from the other side of the marsh. His
horse, foaming at the mouth, splashed water in every direction as
it turned around in circles.

'We've found their palanquins,' he cried. 'He can't be far away.'

As the man's sweating horse reared up, Anamaya recognized
him as one of Gabriel's few friends.

'*Holà*! I've found him! Here he is, friends!'

'No!' murmured Anamaya, 'No!'

'Shhh – keep quiet,' whispered the dwarf hoarsely.

The horses splashed through the mud as their riders pushed
aside the reeds. Manco was revealed, standing proud and tall.
His calves were covered in black mud. He looked as though he
was wearing Spanish boots.

'Don't move,' said the dwarf, gripping Anamaya's arm again
tightly. They listened as the big Stranger gave his orders.

'Beltran! Go and inform Don Gonzalo that we've found him.
And have the Sapa Inca's palanquin sent here.'

For a fleeting moment, Anamaya thought that Manco was
looking into her eyes through the pile of deadwood. She had
stopped breathing and if it had not been for the dwarf she would
have immediately come out of hiding.

Now Manco turned away, his face utterly expressionless, as
though this was no greater a nuisance than having to get out
of his bath. His bearers arrived running. The Greek smiled and
respectfully invited Manco to get into his litter. Manco pushed
aside the curtain and climbed in.

'I must go with him,' whispered Anamaya.

'Are you mad?'

'We can't let him go by himself.'

'And what exactly will you do to help him, once the Strangers
have their hands on you?'

'I must go—'

The dwarf slapped his tiny hand over her mouth.

'Please, say nothing more! Have you already forgotten what happened last night? What do you think the Spaniard would do with you now?'

At that moment, as though emerging from the nightmare that the dwarf had evoked, Gonzalo himself appeared, galloping at full pelt on the edge of the swamp, accompanied by three other horsemen. He rode right up to the palanquin, so close that one of its bearers was struck by a hoof and fell to the ground, crying out in pain.

The Governor's brother yanked back on his reins and turned his horse, splashing stagnant water on everyone around him. He wore a scarlet kerchief around his head, hiding his wounded eye.

'Well, I must say that I'm very happy to see my beloved King, my soaking wet Sapa Inca, once again.'

His voice was calm and loaded with venomous irony. He rode up as close as he could to the litter, leaned forward swiftly in his saddle, grabbed Manco by the hair, and dragged him off his seat.

'Manco . . .' breathed Anamaya.

'Shut up! Don't watch!' hissed the dwarf.

'Don Gonzalo,' de Candia rebuked him, 'you cannot treat the Emperor like that.'

Gonzalo ignored him. He pulled Manco out of his palanquin.

'Don Gonzalo!'

'Enough from you, Candia the Greek! Why don't you go check if your mother doesn't need her ass wiped!' shouted Gonzalo, dropping Manco to the ground. 'Have the chains fetched here, and shackle this monkey king.'

Anamaya couldn't watch anymore. She felt as though her heart would stop beating. She heard the clanking of the chains, the shouts and insults, and she felt the light in her soul go out. The dwarf was clasping her to him as though he wanted to squeeze the breath out of her.

'Oh Lords of the Other World! Oh Viracocha! Why have you abandoned us so?'

'Shut up,' whispered the dwarf. 'Please, shut up.'

The Spaniards made away with their prisoner, and silence returned to the marsh.

When there was no other noise but the whisper of the breeze and the lapping swamp water, the dwarf held her tight with an unbelievable strength.

'Now there's only you, Princess, there's only you. Don't let them catch you, you hear me? Never let them catch you.'

CHAPTER 33

Tupiza-Grand Salar, November/December 1535

THERE WERE HUNDREDS OF THEM, YOUNG AND OLD, shackled in groups of ten or twenty.

Each one had the same type of grimy iron collar clapped around his neck. Their shoulders were all grazed and bruised from the swinging of the chain linking them together. They all had the same hollow look brought on by hunger and fatigue. And they all had the same vacant stare in their eyes, eyes that could no longer tell the difference between the blinding brightness of day and the chill dark of night.

They had been marching together for days now. They had crossed mountains and traversed bare plains, and they strained their emaciated muscles to carry baskets that weighed as much as their bearers did, baskets laden with clothes, food, pewter plates and goblets – in short, all the supplies needed by the Spaniards.

Around midday, under a sun beating straight down, one of them stumbled. He righted himself for a moment. Then his knees gave way and he passed out. A whip cracked in the air above him, but he didn't wake up. The chain linking him to other men tautened. It cut into the other men's necks, half strangling them. But no one complained about this by now familiar occurrence.

Oddly, the basketful of goblets and platters on the man's shoulders remained in place. But he was definitely dead. His muscles had contracted in spasms, and his arms now seemed to be fused to his burden while the rest of his body had given up.

At last the basket tipped over, and all its contents tumbled to the ground with a loud chinking sound. The men chained together came to a halt. A low murmur rose from those men immediately around the dead man. His head was held gruesomely upright by the chain, his body hanging limply beneath it.

Gabriel, riding fifty paces away, turned around in his saddle when he heard the metallic sound. What he saw chilled him to the core and made him feel as though his own body was nothing more than a pile of bones.

A horseman wearing a broad-brimmed hat was standing in front of the dead man suspended from the chain between two other Indians. The Spaniard passed his whip nonchalantly from his right hand to his left and drew his sword from its scabbard. Gabriel only realized what he was planning to do when the blade was glinting high in the sunlight.

He circled his horse around and spurred it violently on, shouting at the top of his lungs:

'NO! NO!'

But the blade was already sweeping through the air. The Spaniard leaned forward in his saddle and, stretching his arm out as though swinging a scythe through wheat, he sliced off the dead man's head. It rolled away between the clumps of *ichu* grass as the headless body collapsed in a heap, under the terrified gazes of the corpse's companions.

Gabriel only caught a glimpse of the body crumpling to the ground as he galloped along. He drew his sword as he rode, provoking a cry from the mass of bearers watching him approach. The Spaniard turned around in his saddle, looking bewildered beneath the broad brim of his hat. He didn't have time to cry out or even to defend himself. With his fist clenched within the basket hilt of his sword, Gabriel struck him in the chest with incredible force.

A sound like dry wood cracking cut through the air as the man flew from his saddle. He tumbled over the rear of his horse and fell with a thud on the ground. He tried to stand, wide-eyed with incomprehension, blood streaming from his mouth. His eyes were level with Gabriel's boots, and when he looked up he saw a man with a demented look in his eye, as though he was ready to destroy the entire world. Now Gabriel pressed his blade against the man's throat, blocking his breathing and cutting off the air to his brain so that he barely heard Gabriel cry:

'I'm going to cut your swine-head from your body, you whoreson cur!'

The man felt the steel dig into his flesh. He grabbed Gabriel's sword with both his hands and was about to try and push the blade away when a voice thundered through the air:

'I wouldn't if I were you, Don Gabriel. Make one false move and your brains will be lying splattered on the ground.'

Gabriel turned his head slightly and saw a crossbow pointed at him from not five paces away.

For half a second he felt the urge to go ahead and kill the man on the ground. He felt as though hearing the sound of the crossbow releasing its quarrel at him would at last put an end to the shame that had been eating at him for days.

'Move back slowly, or else I'll order him to shoot!' cried de Almagro again, sensing Gabriel's hesitation.

Don Diego sat on his horse behind the crossbowman who was pointing his weapon at Gabriel. The familiar ugliness of his face was heightened by his present crimson rage. His lips had turned violet and his cheeks, already severely pock-marked by his many earlier battles with syphilis, seemed about to explode like balloons. His body, inordinately thin, looked ridiculous beneath his cratered, puffed-up face.

The man whom Gabriel had felled crawled away, moaning. Gabriel let him go. The column had come to a complete halt, and hundred of Indians were watching the confrontation with fearful and uncomprehending expressions on their faces. Not one of them had done anything about the headless body from which a steady stream of dark blood continued to flow.

De Almagro cracked his horse's reins and rode up to Gabriel.

'By the blood of Christ!' he growled. 'What's come over you?'

'You're a dangerous lunatic, de Almagro. Look around you. Not one man here walks free. Every single one is in chains. They're dying like flies from hunger and thirst, yet you never relieve them of their burdens. You even have them carry your foals on palanquins. And by night, you hobble them together like animals, without shelter, even when it rains, even if it hails. The children are the lucky ones; at least they die within a week. As for the women, they're raped by dozens of your men until blood flows freely down their thighs. If villagers try to flee your cruelty, you burn their villages, or else you remove the roofs from their huts so that you can cook your meals in them. And now your vile henchmen have taken to decapitating corpses so as to save themselves the bother of having to actually unlock the irons. You are the scum of the earth, de Almagro, it's written on your face. You leave your foul stench lingering behind you with every step you take.'

Gabriel fell silent, trembling with anger. De Almagro's laughter had grown louder with each declaration Gabriel had made, and now it erupted into a frank guffaw, the captain's entire emaciated body shaking with mirth. He had two dozen Spaniards now gathered around him, both cavalrymen and foot soldiers, and they laughed along with him.

'Poor soul! Poor delicate little bird!' chuckled de Almagro, eliciting more chortling from his men. 'D'you hear, gentlemen? This fop presumes to teach us our duty! Well, I suppose there's an explanation for it. Having licked Don Francisco's ass one too many times, His Eminence Don Gabriel has become accustomed to the scent of roses!'

Gabriel stepped forward and stiffly pointed the tip of his sword at de Almagro's scrawny form. The laughter instantly stopped. The Indians, who had been watching warily, now stared in disbelief. A group of cavalrymen surrounded Gabriel and drew their stiletto daggers. De Almagro, smiling contemptuously, raised his hand to stop them.

'In all his time here, the Governor has never allowed the people of Peru to be treated with such brutality,' shouted Gabriel for the benefit of all. 'De Almagro! When you arrived at Cajamarca, you brought with you shame and disgrace. You have spread nothing but terror around you. Atahualpa died because you lied and hoodwinked good people. You are nothing but a stain on the

honor of the conquest. I pray that there is such a place as Hell.
It cannot be different from what you have created here. And if
God exists, then I'm sure He'll welcome you there.'

Gabriel, beside himself, almost thrust his blade home, but his
bitter diatribe had opened the floodgates of bile within himself.
He suddenly felt sick. He broke out in a cold sweat, and was
obliged to set one knee on the ground. He leaned against the hilt
of his sword as though the weapon were a walking cane. He felt
all his strength drain from him, his eyes welled with tears, and
he bent double as he vomited out his guts.

Laughter broke out again from all around him.

Don Diego spurred his horse closer and set his heel on Gabriel's
bowed neck.

'*Gabrielito*,' he warbled, 'I feel that this journey is bad for your
health. Your poor little heart is so fragile, as is your soul. The way
you're going, I fear that this journey might be your last. Take my
advice: leave us to continue along our road to Hell and return to
your own lovely Garden of Eden.'

Gabriel said nothing in reply. He heard the jeers and laughter
all around him. He felt a new emotion rise up inside him, a
bitter brew that he was forced, despite himself, to drink to the
last drop.

He was forced to listen to every jeer, to every snigger, and to
look at those faces twisted by the free rein given to Man's most
ignoble instincts.

He forced himself to get up and swallow the bile that had
collected at the back of his throat, swallow it as though it
was nectar.

In his humiliation Gabriel found the fountainhead of his
strength.

Gabriel, a bitter taste still lingering in his mouth, galloped along
the length of the entire column until he reached the palanquins of
the Inca grandees. Their leaders, in theory at least, were the Sage
Villa Oma and Paullu, Sapa Inca Manco's favorite brother. They
were, also in theory, meant to be leading the column itself.

There were no chains or starved faces here. A few guards, dressed in tunics as clean as they had been on the great square in Cuzco, tried to halt Gabriel with their spears. An order thundered out from behind them. The guards uncrossed their spears and now escorted Gabriel to Villa Oma's litter. The hanging enclosing it opened, as did the one of the neighbouring palanquin. Gabriel recognized Paullu's noble and wily face.

The two Inca lords looked at him with a degree of incredulity. Gabriel made a deliberate effort to slow his racing mind and get a hold of himself, and he made sure to salute them appropriately before saying:

'Sage Villa Oma, in the name of the Governor, Don Francisco Pizarro, I have come to ask you to put an end to the appalling suffering being endured by your people in this column. It is not possible to continue south in such a manner. Your people will all be dead before we arrive. I can promise you that Don Francisco would never allow such unspeakable horror. It is a clear violation of his orders.'

Young Paullu shot Gabriel a furtive look of fury before turning away. The Sage, however, remained impassive. He went on passing his ball of chewed coca leaves from one cheek to the other, offering Gabriel no hint of a reply.

'You must know what I'm talking about,' insisted Gabriel. 'You must intercede; you must go to Don Diego. You must insist that the bearers be freed of their chains. You must demand that the women and children be allowed to leave the column. In the name of Emperor Manco—'

Now the Sage's dark eyes stared at Gabriel so intensely that he fell silent. All around him, there was nothing but silence.

His bay, ill at ease and stamping at the ground, snorted loudly. Gabriel had to gentle it and calm it down before continuing:

'Sage Villa Oma! I know who you are, and you know me. I was at Cuzco when Emperor Manco placed the royal *mascapaicha* on his head. I know that he designated you as second in command of the Empire of the Four Cardinal Directions. And I am a . . . a friend of the *Coya Camaquen*. I beg you, listen to me: It is not Governor Pizarro's wish that your people should be abused so. Lord Paullu, Sage Villa Oma – how can you stand by and watch?'

Despite his fury and his frustration, Gabriel could tell that the silence greeting his words was like a bottomless well. All the noblemen and all their bearers and guards were looking at him now, their expressions utterly indecipherable. And together they presented him with a wall of silence.

Then the sage spat a thick green line of coca juice onto the ground between Gabriel's horse's hooves. He clicked his tongue, ordered the bearers on, and let the curtain fall back across his litter.

Gabriel had a long, cold, sleepless night.

He sat with his back against a boulder that partly sheltered him from the wind, on the edge of a talus less than a quarter of a league from the long column. For hours he watched the torches glowing red in de Almagro's camp. At the other end of the column he could see the torches burning in front of the Inca lords' tents. Between these two beacons was darkness, a darkness that cloaked suffering and shame.

And at the blackest moment of the night, when the moon had gone and the sky above was empty, apart from a few stars low to the south, Gabriel let his anger and powerlessness overwhelm him. He clenched his scabbard between his teeth so that his howls wouldn't carry too far, and he cursed God, mankind, the earth, and life itself.

And then he saw Anamaya's face in his mind's eye, and the mere thought of her was like a breath of purified air. He was trembling again, but this time not from rage at being human in this god-forsaken place at this godforsaken time. For a moment, his entire body became light. For a moment, he imagined reaching out his arm and touching the warm and reassuring flesh of his beloved.

Dawn approached. It rolled, like some pale celestial wave, over the mountains rising majestically to the east. Gabriel was still wide awake. He shivered every now and then, his blanket heavy with dew. The fire he had built the night before was now nothing but embers. He knew that he had to make a decision soon. He had to decide which was the lesser of two evils. He could either continue on the road to Hell with de Almagro and his henchmen and thereby suffer their jeers and taunts, or he could return to Don Francisco in Lima, his 'Garden of Eden' as the vile de Almagro had called it. Either way, he would need all his strength to carry his shame.

His bay stood a few paces away from him, half asleep. It opened its eyes every now and then and gave him an anxious look, pricked up its ears, snorted, and shook its mane from side to side, before coming over and nuzzling him.

Suddenly the horse stiffened, bristled its mane, and paced nervously in a tight circle. Gabriel heard stones crunching beneath an approaching footfall – a light step, like someone treading softly to avoid being heard. He quickly drew his dagger, concealing it beneath his blanket. He looked to the right, expecting the intruder to come from there, so he was surprised when he heard someone whispering to him from the left.

'Don't be frightened, my Lord. Don't be frightened.'

But Gabriel was already on his feet, dagger in hand.

He saw an old dried-up hand with deformed fingers emerge from beneath a dark red cape. The hood of the cape fell back and revealed a face so wrinkled and so old that at first Gabriel couldn't tell whether it belonged to a man or a woman. The face gave him a toothless smile and its pale gray eyes, the color of melting snow, shone brilliantly.

'Don't be frightened, my Lord,' the figure repeated.

The visitor offered Gabriel a cloth package, its four corners tied together.

'Here is some food that I put aside for you.'

Astonished, Gabriel took the package and began untying it. Inside was a handful of corn and a few shriveled and blackened potatoes, potatoes that had been frozen in the ground for a long time before being cooked.

'Thanks,' he murmured, then: 'Why have you done this?'

The visitor uttered an elfin laugh, revealing herself to be a woman.

'Because of your courage and decency yesterday, Stranger. We saw your fire burning by itself out in the night, and we wanted to thank you.'

'We?'

The old woman pointed at the column with her buckled hand and said:

'All of us. Everyone knows what you did. People talked about your rage throughout the night, and of how you went to the Sage and told him to rise up against your own people.'

'Oh yes? Then perhaps you can explain to me why Sage Villa Oma didn't even answer me.'

The old woman hesitated for a moment. She stared intensely at Gabriel, making him ill at ease.

'Because he had already made up his mind. He left last night to free Emperor Manco and prepare for war with the Strangers in Cuzco.'

Gabriel's body hairs stood on end beneath his doublet.

'What are you saying?'

'Emperor Manco is held captive in Cuzco. The *chaski* brought us the news two days ago. The Strangers there are of the same mold as those here. They placed a chain around the Emperor's neck.'

'Oh sweet Jesus!'

At first, Gabriel didn't dare ask the question burning on his lips. But he stared at the ancient face before him and finally asked:

'And the *Coya Camaquen*? Do you know if she's being held captive too?'

The old woman shook her head slightly and curled her lips.

'Who is the *Coya Camaquen*?'

Gabriel said nothing. He had a nightmare vision of Gonzalo and Juan mauling Anamaya. He saw Anamaya with a chain around her neck. Anamaya . . .

He had to stop his imagination running riot. The road to Cuzco was too long – he would go mad before getting there.

He stood up, folded his blanket, and picked up his saddle. His horse snorted and came up to him as though it had been waiting for this.

'Which way did the Sage go?' asked Gabriel as he saddled the horse.

The old face smiled at him.

'He took the hidden paths through the mountains, but you'll catch up with him quickly if you follow the guide who brought us here. You should take water and more food with you. I'll help you find some.'

Gabriel slipped the saddle strap through its buckle, then turned around, frowning, and asked:

'Why do you want to help me so much?'

'Because I like you.'

'Well, I like you too, Grandma. You're cute.'

'Cute – ha, ha, ha!'

The old woman laughed as daintily as a girl.

Gabriel listened to her laughing still as she headed back to the column and he finished saddling his horse.

For the first time in a long while, Gabriel's soul was at peace. A glimmer of life had appeared in front of him, a crack in the wall of wickedness.

Now he had only one task ahead of him.

And that reassured him, even if it was the height of reck-lessness.

CHAPTER 34

Huchuy Qosqo, December 1535

IT WAS A COOL EVENING. ANAMAYA STRETCHED OUT HER
hands toward the fire that the dwarf had lit. A soup boiled
slowly in a terracotta pot, releasing the sour odor of wild
onions and tomatoes into the damp air.

Anamaya glanced surreptitiously at her loyal friend. She hadn't
recognized him when he had arrived in the village a little earlier,
shivering after having walked through the rain for two days, and
his face still showed signs of his ordeal.

The high red walls of the *canchas* of Huchuy Qosqo loomed
over them in the gathering dusk. The walls glowed carmine in
contrast to the sharp greens of the potato and maize fields that
covered the plateau right up to the edge of the cliff overlooking the
valley. In more peaceful times, Anamaya had enjoyed the pleasing
symmetry of this city suspended between sky and earth. But now
it seemed as though Pacha Mama, the beloved Mother Earth, was
suffering the same agony as the dwarf.

That morning a terrible storm had lashed the Valley of the
Royal Cities.

While the sky directly above them had been concealed only by
a thin mist, a thick bank of clouds as black as smoke had gathered
at the edge of the plateau.

A short while later, the entire valley had turned into a cauldron
spewing steam from the Under World. The terraces of corn and
quinua, spread like giant butterfly wings on the banks of the river

Willkamayo, had disappeared, as had the slopes and the steep road leading to Huchuy Qosqo.

And then a wave of liquid silver had billowed across that sea of clouds and everyone had heard Illapa growl, although the thunder rolled from the valley rather than from the sky.

The peasants had begun murmuring among themselves. The women had brought their children indoors. The Elders and priests of Huchuy Qosqo had gathered at the wall at the edge of the plateau. They had all had the same thought: The world was being turned upside down.

The fields and alleyways of Huchuy Qosqo had been bathed in Inti's light filtered through the mist. Over in the distance, beyond the Valley of the Royal Cities, the eastern mountains were glowing beneath Inti's glare. But the sea of clouds had continued to seethe between the two, forks of silver light occasionally ripping through it.

And then it had ended. The clouds had spiraled upward into whorls that had been torn apart quickly by the wind. A humid fog had rolled in over the fields, had combined with the light rain, and had left a lacquer of moisture on the *canchas'* mud walls. The sky had darkened. It had rained non-stop until late in the afternoon.

That was when the dwarf had arrived, filthy and exhausted after having trekked along the arduous mountain paths.

The sky was cloudless now. The only turmoil was on the dwarf's face. Anamaya filled a big terracotta bowl with steaming soup.

'Eat,' she ordered him gently, 'Eat – you're trembling from hunger as much as from cold. You can tell me your news later.'

The dwarf held out his hands like a child and took the bowl. He stared at the rich, reddish stew for a moment, then shook his head and looked up at Anamaya from under his thick eyelids.

'No,' he said, 'I can't eat. First I must tell you . . .'

But he fell silent. His eyes burned feverishly and stared at Anamaya. She reached out and caressed his temple lightly with her fingertips. He set the bowl down on a stone next to the fire, took hold of her hand, and pressed his forehead into it as though he might draw from it all the strength that he lacked.

'First of all,' he murmured, 'they dragged him across the lower city. They led our Emperor, Emperor Manco, before the Coricancha with chains around his neck. Then they kept him on Colcampata Square for three days, their chains around his neck and ankles.'

The dwarf paused, as though expelling the poison with which these words were contaminating him. He pushed away Anamaya's hand and curled up on himself.

'They left our Emperor there, outside and in chains. His *unku* was torn and filthy. He wore the same one for three days. Three days, Anamaya! The Son of the Sun appeared thus before the mummies of his Ancestors, before the eyes of the people of Cuzco. And the Strangers came to taunt him from dawn till dusk.'

The dwarf fell silent again. Anamaya couldn't even bear to look at him. She kept her gaze fixed on the distant peaks. She looked at the snow-capped mountains rising in the night, and she felt as though their snow was chilling her to the bone.

'When they took him at last from Colcampata, the entire City of the Puma wept for him,' continued the dwarf. 'They took him to the house in which the foreign devil tried to rape you. The Emperor's servant girls wailed with grief when they saw how he was being treated. Some ran away, others used the Strangers' weapons to slit their own throats or cut open their own bellies. All the concubines went to the Strangers and begged them to treat the Emperor with more respect. The Strangers laughed at them. They locked the concubines in the courtyard, brought Manco to them, bound in chains, and tore his women's clothes off them in front of his very eyes. Then they raped them throughout the night, forcing him to watch. Many were dead by the next morning. Their lives drained out of them from between their legs.'

The dwarf was having trouble breathing. He was trembling so much that he had to press his hands hard against the mat to stop himself toppling over. He dared not look at Anamaya. She was sitting extremely still, and her stillness belied a tension that seemed on the point of exploding.

Suddenly the dwarf let out a sob and swiped his fist through the air, knocking over and breaking the pot of soup. The fire went out in a hiss of steam.

'They threw him in a pit and pissed on him by the dozen,' he said.

'That's enough,' said Anamaya, rising to her feet.

Her face looked as though it had been carved from a block of chalk.

For Anamaya, war had always been something remote – the sound of fighting in the distance, the always baffling sight of thousands of warriors facing one another across a battlefield.

Now, she felt the spirit of war burning within her own soul.

The Sacred Double glimmered in the torchlight.

The statue so coveted by the Strangers was set on a cotton-filled woven cushion on a large polished stone in a small temple. Coca leaves were burning in a brazier at his feet, their heady odor filling the room.

Anamaya entered to find two young women sprinkling *cantuta* petals on the ground. They had just presented the Sacred Double with his meal. Anamaya waved them away.

Her face was empty and expressionless. Two silver strings held a long woolen cape around her shoulders, but still she shivered with such violence that her teeth chattered.

She filled a ceremonial goblet of painted wood with *chicha* from a jug. She raised it above her head. She stared into the Sacred Double's golden face. He was as impassive as she strove to be.

But instead of saluting her husband from the Other World, Anamaya let her arms fall back down to her side. She didn't pour the *chicha* on the ground as an offering. She held the goblet tight against her chest and closed her eyes. She barely opened her mouth as she whispered:

'Why do I offer food and drink to you day after day, Oh Sacred Husband? Why do I pray to you and tell you of my suffering if you cannot hear, Emperor Huayna Capac? What have we done, that you should remain silent for so long? What have we done to deserve the shame that we are suffering here, in this world?'

She fell silent. She was swaying from side to side, perhaps unwittingly.

She frowned, compressing her lips into a thin, tight line. Then she cried out, exhaling so violently that the torches flickered and were almost extinguished:

'Why have you abandoned us?'

Anamaya stepped forward without opening her eyes and stretched out her arms. She let the goblet of *chicha* fall to the ground, and she sobbed as she hugged the golden statue.

'Are you there, Noble Lords of the Other World? Can you not feel our love for you, or hear our cries? Do you not see our suffering? Oh Noble Lords of the Other World, no day passes when we do not obey your will in everything. You are on our minds from the moment we wake until we lie down to sleep at night. We watch the flight of birds and the patterns of clouds to better understand your will. We grow the finest ears of corn for you, we offer you the blood of our best llamas to please you and so that you will be proud of us. We weave tapestries of the finest colors to honor you in this world as in the Other. We obey all your laws. But still you give us only this silence. Are you frightened of the Strangers' gods? Have you become as weak as us?'

All Anamaya's muscles seized up with pain and anger, and she felt as though she was being torn apart. She shook the Sacred Double on its cushion, unable to stop herself, and shouted:

'Are you there? Didn't you hear what the dwarf said? Didn't you see your son Manco being pissed on by our enemies?'

Her words tore through the still and empty night.

'Oh Emperor Huayna Capac! You, who held my hand before you joined Inti and when I was still just a girl – do not forsake me! Do not turn your back on me. Do not let me think that we are all alone, like children lost in the mountains. Would you let us be destroyed in war as you let us be conquered in peace? Do not abandon our people's fate to the Strangers. If I, the *Coya Camaquen*, have offended you, then I am ready to be burned to ashes.'

But her passionate pleas were met only with silence.

The villagers of Huchuy Qosqo had gathered outside the little temple to listen to the *Coya Camaquen*'s despair. Now they trembled with her, and they bit their lips as she did. They hoped, as she did, that the silence would give way to something greater.

But the only sound was the regular drip-drip of rainwater streaming off the *ichu* roofs onto the flagstones.

It was almost dawn when Anamaya finally decided to leave the temple.

The torches had gone out, and no one had dared relight them.

Although the night was still dark, when Anamaya came out of the temple she had to blink to adjust to the light.

It happened in a flash.

The plateau, the Sacred Valley, and the eastern mountains were illuminated in a light as bright and as harsh as the sun's. The plain looked as though it had been covered in an even, bone-white blanket of salt. The whole world seemed to have suddenly turned into a desert. The earth's surface was nothing but an old, cracked layer of dead skin. There were no more shadows, no more trees or bushes, not a single sign of life. Not even an insect.

Anamaya felt her knees collapse beneath her. She didn't notice the dwarf's small but strong hand reaching out to her. She didn't hear the murmurs as she fainted. All she saw was what the world of Man would look like when it was finally and irreversibly dead.

And then she saw him. Gabriel.

She saw his blackened skin and his clothes torn to rags. First he appeared far away on the endless plain. Then, suddenly, he was right up close, so close that she could hear his labored breathing and see his swollen lips and his cheeks cracked like old leather. She saw his pupils burned by the white death. Sweat dripped from his eyelashes, which the sun had turned into minuscule salt crystals. She saw his hands and fingers covered in clotted blood. He was swaying like a man on the edge of death. Like a man who had nothing left but his own shadow. His gaze was empty, absent.

Each time he took another step forward through the white desert, his heel kicked up a little cloud of dust that immediately settled and covered his tracks. He wasn't even leaving a trail behind him. Suddenly he stumbled and fell.

Anamaya cried out.

She had understood two things at once: that Gabriel was dying somewhere at that very moment – and that the Lords of the Other World had heard her cries after all.

CHAPTER 35

The Grand Salar Desert, December 1535

A S FAR AS GABRIEL'S EYES COULD SEE, EVERYTHING looked white.

They had just reached the top of the last hill. The path ahead of them twisted back and forth down a steep slope, then came out onto a broad desert valley, a sea of salt stretching beyond the horizon and flanked by steep mountains. It looked white, hard and ominous, like a road leading into the void.

'*Lloc!*' said a raspy voice. 'Now is the wrong time to cross.'

The owner of the voice looked completely at home in the landscape that Gabriel had been traveling through these last few days. He was short, very dirty, and very tanned. His long, filthy hair fell in matted knots from under a large hat of faded colors. His only clothing was a threadbare, stained tunic and a long llama-leather cord around his waist. The muscles of his thighs and calves were so well defined that they gave the appearance of being raw and without a cushioning layer of skin. But his feet were the most remarkable part of him. They seemed to have molded themselves to the shapes of all the stones and paths that he had ever walked across. They looked more like animal paws than human feet. The separate toes were no longer really distinguishable, and the toenails had been overgrown by a skin so thick that it didn't bleed when it cracked open.

Gabriel had met him the previous night. After having vainly

tried to catch up with the Sage Villa Oma, he had had to admit to himself that he was well and truly lost.

Ever since he had left Tupiza, the Sage's slender lead had incomprehensibly grown. Yet Gabriel had cracked on, only resting his horse when it was absolutely necessary. In the villages where he stopped for a little food, he learned that the Sage had been recruiting men wherever he passed. All of them had been ordered to the north. Villa Oma thus had an inexhaustible supply of bearers, and he was traveling day and night, eating and sleeping in his palanquin.

Gabriel's first thought had been that the Sage's haste was an indication of the gravity of the situation in Cuzco. And if the Sage was mobilizing every man he came across, then war was certainly imminent.

His second thought had brought him to the brink of despair. He knew that there was no longer any way he could catch up with Villa Oma and cross the Empire safely with him, getting to Anamaya more quickly as a result. Instead, he would have to make his own way, and that meant getting lost, taking the wrong turns, doubling back, and generally advancing at a snail's pace. And all the while the Pizarro brothers would certainly be submitting Anamaya to the worst atrocities. What he had just witnessed among de Almagro's thugs left him without a trace of hope. Now, not a day passed without the most appalling visions assailing his imagination.

Gabriel reproached himself both for his rashness and for his misguided devotion to Don Francisco. The Governor had once again drawn him too far away from his reason for living. From her.

He fantasized about how he would rid the earth of Gonzalo. He dreamed of changing into a bird and soaring away from the excruciating slowness of travel on the ground that left him unable to do a thing to help Anamaya. He dreamed of meeting her, of finding himself once more in her arms, of rediscovering the joy of her breasts, of finding her as beautiful and as unharmed as the day they had parted.

Gabriel had pushed his bay harder than was sensible, forcing it to carry on into the night. And in doing so, he had become lost.

He had wandered about in frustration until this ageless man, like some demon who had emerged from his cave, appeared before him as he was traversing a scree slope.

The man was now looking at him through eyes as black as night. He warned Gabriel once again in his poor Quechua, repeatedly clicking his tongue:

'*Lloc*! If you cross now, then you'll either arrive quickly or die quickly.'

One only had to look at the great emptiness of the salt pan ahead of them to believe him. The sun was rising behind the mountains and their incredibly long shadows stretched across the pale desert. The northern horizon, blurred by morning fog, was as visibly curved as it would have been on a calm ocean.

'Three days, you say?' asked Gabriel for the tenth time.

'Three days – if you make it. Three days, if the sun doesn't consume you first.'

'Perhaps we could travel by night instead of by day.'

'You'll get lost at night! The clouds will hide the peaks of the Apus from you, and they are your guides. You'll die. And if the clouds are absent for too long during the day, you'll also die. Inti will devour you.'

Gabriel gave his horse a reassuring pat. The animal had grown skittish, as though it had understood the Indian's words.

'Three days,' repeated Gabriel. 'Whereas if I go through the mountains, you say that it'll take me six or seven.'

'*Lloc*! Yes. Seven or more, because it's the rainy season, when all the paths turn into rivers. Seven or more. But at least you won't be dead.'

'What good will it do me not to be dead if *she* is? Come, no more talk, we're wasting time. Will you guide me?'

Gabriel asked the question without much hope. So he was surprised when the man nodded.

'You're even crazier than I am,' he said.

They entered the desert.

*   *   *

As Gabriel entered the Grand Salar, what he saw astounded him. He had expected to find nothing but salt: instead he found nothing but shallow water. The sun was veiled behind a light haze that obscured the horizon. The overcast sky and the water blended together into the same washed-out color. Gabriel felt as though he was traveling into an untouched canvas. Both men shielded their eyes, as though to avoid glimpsing any evil spirits that might inhabit this strange world.

The Indian showed him how to save his sight. First he soaked his hat with water from one of the four jugs firmly attached to the horse, and then he pulled it low over his forehead, covering his eyes.

'You do the same for yourself – and for your horse,' he ordered in his gasping voice. 'Otherwise the glare of the salt will burn through your eye sockets and set your head on fire.'

Gabriel pulled his last shirt from one of his saddlebags and ripped it to shreds, then wet the cloth with water from the jug. His bay didn't complain when he tied a dripping shred around its eyes. The horse looked so comical in its makeshift eyeshade that Gabriel grinned at it. Like a Moor, he wrapped his own head in a piece of cloth, leaving only a small slit through which to see ahead of him.

He set off in silence with his horse's reins over his shoulder. He followed the Indian into the pale waste ahead of them. The Indian's silhouette seemed to float on the void.

The shallow water disappeared within an hour. It gave way to a world so still that it seemed as though nothing in it would ever move again. It was a harsh world, one that crunched beneath their feet. Its ground was cracked into thousands of salt plates as hard as rock and which stretched ahead as far as the eye could see.

The haze had also evaporated, revealing a sky so deeply blue that it unnerved Gabriel. He fell into step with the familiar rhythm of his horse's hooves.

The mountains' long shadows had long since retreated. The air was still. The Indian looked straight ahead as he trekked on, not once turning his head. They walked for a while with a patch of rocky scree to their left. It was scattered with cacti so tall that to Gabriel they looked like warriors from another world. The spaces between the mountains at the edge of the sea of salt gradually grew larger, and the peaks themselves appeared and disappeared mysteriously on the horizon, wavering in the shimmer of the rising heat.

The sun became a giant, burning orb long before it had reached its zenith. Gabriel felt his skin burning on his unshaven chin and cheeks, burning as though a naked flame was being held to the parts of his flesh not protected by the piece of cloth. It was very tempting to drink some water from one of the jugs. But he managed to resist the urge to do so.

Suddenly the Indian stopped in his tracks without saying a word, so abruptly that Gabriel almost walked right into him.

The man turned around slowly, checking the sight lines to the mountains on the horizon. Then he looked at Gabriel. He tilted up his hat and shook his head.

'What is it?' asked Gabriel, his mouth dry. 'Are we going the wrong way?'

The man pointed at the sky and said:

'*Lloc*! Too much sun.'

'What do you mean, too much sun?' asked Gabriel, widening the eyehole in his head covering.

'Not enough clouds. The sun is going to eat us.'

Gabriel didn't seem to understand, so the man waved his swarthy hand at the expanse of desert and again at the crystal blue of the sky.

'There's too much sun today, as there will be tomorrow and the day after. We cannot cross the desert. The sun will eat us. We can make it back to the hills by nightfall.'

'No!' protested Gabriel. 'That's out of the question. I won't turn back.'

The man retreated a couple of steps and shrugged his shoulders.

'Your animal will also die,' he said quietly. 'No one can cross the sea of salt without clouds above them.'

'You're just frightened, that's all. I will cross.'

The man looked at him for a moment, then murmured:

'Sometimes it's right to be frightened.'

He pulled his hat back down over his eyes and said:

'Tomorrow, if Inti wills it, he will show you a mountain shaped like two hands holding one another by the fingers. He's called Apu Thunupa. Before becoming a mountain, he was a human being, a nobleman like those of Cuzco. He marks the end of the sea of salt. But you must still have eyes to see him.'

And with that, the man headed back toward the hills to the east without so much as a good-bye to Gabriel.

Gabriel hesitated. He knew that the Indian was right. He knew that being alone would make crossing the sea of salt even more difficult. But he urged himself on by telling himself the only truth that mattered: What good would being alive be to him if she wasn't?

He watched the man heading back toward the hills, and noticed that his shadow was very short. He wondered how the Indian managed to walk barefoot over the vast cracked salt pan when his own feet felt as though they were boiling in their boots.

When the Indian had walked about a hundred paces without looking back, Gabriel turned away and stroked his horse's mane.

'Come, old friend, come. We'll do fine on our own.'

And he started walking before he had time to doubt his own words.

They set off into the desert again before dawn, the sea of white gleaming beneath the night sky. Gabriel found comfort in the myriad of stars twinkling overhead. He used the Southern Cross as his guide. Even after sunrise it stayed cool enough, for a few hours at least, for him to ride his horse instead of leading it by its reins. Then a fog rose up. Gabriel told himself that the Indian had been wrong, that the sun wouldn't eat them after all. It appeared intermittently through the clouds, a white orb hanging over a white sea.

All seemed well. The heat wasn't such an ordeal, and the

sun's rays weren't so deadly. Gabriel dismounted and began to walk, leading his horse. He maintained a brisk pace for almost half a day.

He only began to feel the fatigue that had been creeping imperceptibly up his legs when the sun was already low in the west. At first it was only a dull, faint pain. But soon it felt as though a thousand needles were stabbing into his muscles. He took a break for the first time that day and lay down for a while before setting off again, his bay looking at him with concern.

Then, less than a league further on, he had to stop once more. The pain had become unbearable. He felt as though all the muscles in his thighs had been twisted hopelessly into knots.

He stopped and started so many times that the horse began to put his big head in the small of Gabriel's back and push him forward.

Suddenly Gabriel heard a horrid cracking sound as the bay neighed. The horse's head smacked violently into Gabriel's back, sending him tumbling over. The horse itself collapsed to the ground, neighing terribly again.

Gabriel, dazed, was too tired to get up off his knees. His worst nightmare had become reality.

His blinded horse's right hind leg had got stuck in a hole the size of a hand in the thick crust of salt. And it had snapped clean when the animal had stumbled.

'The bay,' murmured Gabriel, pulling off his head covering. 'The bay.'

The horse pulled back its lips and showed its yellow teeth. It stuck out its neck and whinnied plaintively, its nostrils quivering. It made a desperate effort to get up. But its legs just waved helplessly in the air, and Gabriel could tell that its terrified round eyes were glimpsing its own death. It fell back down onto its side with a thud and neighed again.

Gabriel at last emerged from his daze and crawled to his horse. He grabbed its head and felt a terrible shiver run through his faithful companion. The bay was now breathing fast and hard. Its barrel shook as it gasped laboriously. Blood flowed from its belly and stained the salt beneath it.

Only then did Gabriel realize that the horse had collapsed onto the jugs of brackish water and that a shard had pierced it like a dagger, perforating one of its lungs. Blood was already trickling from its mouth.

'The bay,' whispered Gabriel, holding its head against him. 'The bay. I never gave you a name, and now it's too late.'

The horse's eyelids trembled over its glassy eyes.

Gabriel made one last futile effort, ignoring the pain in his legs. He removed the horse's curb chain, bit and harness. But the horse looked at him as though asking him only to stroke it. It shuddered again from pain or terror, its whole body shaking.

Gabriel laid the horse's head down across his aching thighs. He stroked it for a long time, scratching its ears, caressing its nose.

He knew what he had to do. But he couldn't steel himself to the task.

He pulled his dagger from his belt and set it on the ground at his side.

He told himself that he still had some time, although he could feel the bay's breathing growing increasingly labored as its lung became painfully flooded.

He cried salty tears. His chest shook with the sobs of fear and of a terrible sadness.

And then he did it without thinking about it any further. His fist closed around the dagger's hilt and he plunged the blade into the softest part of the animal's throat.

At the moment of dying, the bay shoved its head so strongly against Gabriel's chest that he fell backwards, covered in his horse's blood.

Another night passed. Gabriel no longer knew how long he had been walking for.

He was still covered in horse blood. It had coagulated into a crust that protected him from the sun. The sun had returned, and wanted to devour him. Gabriel knew that his time had come.

His lips were so cracked and distended that he had trouble breathing. He thought that if Anamaya were to see him in this horrible condition, she would turn away from him in disgust.

But he forced himself on. He could no longer feel the pain in his legs. He walked as though walking was the only thing his body could do. His hands dangled at his side, the fingers as swollen as balloons and burning as though they had been baked in an oven.

Gabriel raised an eyelid every now and then and pushed back his head covering with his knuckle. He thought he saw Thunupa's jagged peak – the mountain that had once been a human being. But he knew that he would never reach it. The soles of his leather boots had split, and his feet were becoming like those of the Indian who had been wise enough not to accompany him on the road to death.

'You're even crazier than I am,' he repeated over and over, not sure of whom he was talking about.

He pictured Anamaya in front of him, and he walked toward her. He smiled at her, and she at him. He told her:

'I can't join you now, but I'll wait for you. Never forget that I love you.'

She nodded and told him that she was all right, that he mustn't worry about her. She said to him:

'Never forget that you are the Puma.'

He laughed. He had a vision of her standing in the rich green mountain grass on Thunupa's slope. She was far away now, and he couldn't make out her eyes. She was standing in front of a little cottage made of sun-baked red clay, her arms stretched out toward him. She cried to him again:

'Don't forget that you are the Puma, and that you can always find freedom!'

Gabriel told himself that he had lost his mind, and that he should pray to God to save him and her as well. He told himself that he still had time to say a prayer, and that he shouldn't offend God.

Once again he heard Anamaya call to him, much closer this time, no more than fifty paces away. He knew that he shouldn't believe it. But he did.

His heartbeat slowed right down, and he felt a sense of peace come over him.

At last his long, futile journey was coming to an end. He stopped walking. He raised his bandanna awkwardly with his monstrously swollen hands.

He didn't see the green slopes of Thunupa, only the same infinite white desert of the sea of salt. But he was astonished to see a long train of silhouettes shimmering through the heat in the distance. They seemed to be heading toward him. The silhouettes were dancing, singing, spinning around on themselves.

He smiled as he realized who they were. Angels.

Gabriel felt Anamaya's breath on his cheek, he felt her kiss, and he knew, as he collapsed to the ground, that she would be waiting for him in Paradise.

CHAPTER 36

Huchuy Qosqo, February 1536

A T DAWN, HUNDREDS OF THEM CAME POURING OVER the peaks overlooking Huchuy Qosqo. With their shields on their shoulders and their studded clubs in their hands, they streamed through the potato terraces and reached the red walls of the *canchas*. Hundreds of llama-leather sandals tramped along the flagstones like some warlike murmur rising from the bowels of the earth. Everyone, noblemen and commoners, young and old, came out to admire the warriors. Their distinctive tunics showed where they came from: some of them were from the north, others from the south, and still others from the distant provinces on the coast.

The warriors gathered in an orderly fashion on the great ceremonial terrace overlooking the valley. Most had serious looks on their faces, but some were smiling happily. Some wore the insignia and carried the spears that marked them out as generals while others were only junior officers. Most had fought under Atahualpa or Huascar's commanders. But today, this long-awaited day, all old quarrels were forgotten.

Inti Himself was happy to see them. The rain had stopped, the weather was clement, and only the lightest clouds were scattered like feathers through the sky. The smoke from coca leaves burning on the braziers rose straight up in the still air. The sun, the Emperor's beloved father, rose above the peaks.

Young virgins served jugs of fresh water and fermented llama

milk to the warriors as they arrived, and offered them fruit and
corn bread. Priests stood at the four corners of the terrace and
around the Sacred Stone to which Inti hitched Himself every day.
They ceremoniously poured sacred beer onto the dark earth. A
drum roll announced the arrival of the Sage Villa Oma and the
Coya Camaquen.

The Sage carried a heavy gold spear, the symbol of the army's
supreme commander. He wore a green and crimson *unku* decorated with geometric patterns that only he was permitted to wear.
His leather helmet, covered in gold and with a crescent of blue
and yellow feathers rising from it, shone like anther sun throwing
its light into the Empire's four directions.

A few of the younger warriors murmured with proud approval
as they watched Villa Oma approach the *Intihuatana*, the Sun's
hitching post, in the centre of the *ushnu*. The gold disks set in the
Sage's earlobes were bigger and finer than any they had ever seen.

The *Coya Camaquen*, walking at Villa Oma's side, was also
wearing magnificent jewels that everyone else thought had disappeared into the Strangers' coffers long ago. She wore a white tunic
and had a heavy gold disk, the disk of Inti, hanging from her finely
woven sash. Gold ornaments shaped like the snake Amaru were
coiled through her hair. Amaru, like the *Coya Camaquen*, was
known for traveling between the visible and the invisible worlds.

A conch shell sounded loudly as Anamaya and Villa Oma came
to a halt facing the mass of armed men. Its deep tone reverberated
through the mountains, echoing back from further and further
away, fading swiftly as it streaked across the Valley of the Royal
Cities like a falcon. The warriors gathered on the square bowed
to the two most powerful people – apart from the Emperor himself
– in the Empire of the Four Cardinal Directions.

Anamaya advanced towards the bowing warriors and took hold
of the gold disk hanging on her chest. She raised it up above her
head and in a strong voice she chanted:

> *Oh Viracocha, Oh Inti,*
> *Great Fathers of the Universe,*
> *Beloved Fathers of all that will be,*

Hear our supplication!
Oh Viracocha,
You reign in the sky above!
Oh Inti,
You reign in the sky below!
Oh Viracocha, Oh Inti,
Beloved Fathers of the origin of the World,
Cast your eyes upon us!
Exalt us with your strength!
Oh Viracocha, Oh Inti,
We want nothing more than to experience your Being
In the Day that follows Night.

A brief silence followed as the warriors straightened up. They fixed their fiery gazes on Anamaya's blue eyes as she said in a loud voice:

'Noble Captains of the armies of Tahuantinsuyu: I am overjoyed that you have answered my call. I wanted to tell you the news directly: Emperor Manco will soon be free. The chains that the Strangers had shackled around his neck and ankles are already broken, and soon he will suffer their indignities no more. Two moons from now, his father Inti will cast His shadow over the Sacred Valley, where the Emperor will join us.'

The murmur that had been rumbling through the crowd now exploded into a roar, a raucous, violent outcry that whipped through the crisp morning air like a thousand slings being swung.

Villa Oma smiled a brief, bitter smile, revealing his green-stained teeth. He approached Anamaya as the roar quietened, and motioned to four soldiers standing at the edge of the terrace. The men brought him a large basket. They opened it and tipped its contents onto the ground so that all the warriors could see.

A torn doublet, black with coagulated blood, a pair of boots, and a sword snapped in two tumbled out onto the grass. Then something else fell out of the basket, an odd, round package that somehow seemed both hard and soft. Villa Oma stuck his spear into it.

His face impassive, he slowly raised the bundle of flesh – for

that was what it was – into the air. It was the white skin of a
Stranger who had obviously been flayed alive.

The older, more experienced officers didn't bat an eyelid. But
a shocked murmur rose from the younger ones. Anamaya looked
away. She did her best to suppress the nausea rising up inside
her. Villa Oma thundered:

'The man who used to wear this skin had his dogs devour
our children. He was the first of the Strangers to have sullied
the Coricancha. His name was de Moguer. His agonized cries
were music to my ears, because they blocked out the sound of
those laughing as they humiliated our Emperor Manco. This is
our answer to the Strangers.'

Villa Oma's face was as hard as a bronze ax as he carried the
trophy past the warriors on the point of his spear, making sure
that everyone saw it. He continued in the same stentorian tone:

'While I was away the *Coya Camaquen* obtained the support
of the Elders of the Other World. The Sacred Double of our
beloved Huayna Capac proposed to come and free his son,
Emperor Manco, himself! We must all be grateful to her. Even
though she's only a woman, she carries herself like a warrior. But
tomorrow, when the Emperor joins us here in this valley, free at
last and with the light of Inti upon him, we must provide him
with the force necessary to punish those who laid their hands
on him.'

Villa Oma flicked his spear dismissively and de Moguer's hide
flew through the air, flopping down in front of the younger
officers.

'I, Villa Oma, second in command of the Empire of Tahuantinsuyu,
declare that, before the month of Aucaycusqui, we will retake the
City of the Puma from the Strangers, and we will celebrate the
great Festival of the Sun within its walls. We shall purify Cuzco
with a great battle so that our Emperor may return to his rightful
throne in his *cancha* and our Ancestors' mummies may once again
enjoy peace in the great temple of the Coricancha. From today
onward, each of you must begin recruiting men and gathering
weapons. I want enough men to cover the peaks of all the hills
surrounding Cuzco. On the day of battle, I want Emperor Manco's

warriors to form a noose around the city as strong as a belt made of llama leather. And then we will tighten it around the Strangers' throats so that not one of them remains alive.'

Villa Oma mimed strangling the enemy with his hands. But the shiver that ran up the warriors' spines wasn't caused by this gesture.

A rain shower had been moving from one mountain to another as the Sage had been speaking. When he fell silent, the seven-coloured Arc of Cuychu suddenly appeared. Its curve rose up high into the sky and its ends disappeared into the steep slopes falling away at the end of the Huchuy Qosqo plateau. It shone clear and splendidly for all the warriors to see.

Anamaya, Villa Oma, the residents of Huchuy Qosqo, the warriors, everyone raised their palms up toward the rainbow, the messenger from the Gods of War, and chanted:

'We see you, Cuychu, *we see you clearly. Welcome here among us, you who bring us the strength and joy of battle.'*

In the small temple's gentle half-light, the beams of sunshine that filtered through from outside drew a smile on the Sacred Double's face. Villa Oma looked at the statue for a long time before glancing at Anamaya, who had the offerings ready.

'*Coya Camaquen*, I'm happy that we find ourselves together once again for this momentous occasion,' he said. 'And I'm very proud of you. What you've done for Manco is invaluable.'

Anamaya shook her head unceremoniously and said:

'It's only the beginning of something that I'm longing to see the end of. The older of the Governor's brothers has returned from his country. He now commands the Strangers in Cuzco. He is vain and proud, and he takes advice from no one. He smiles at the Emperor and pretends to be his friend only because he wants more gold. We managed to get some vases and plates to Manco. He gave them to the Governor's older brother, and his chains were removed. Then the priests agreed to sacrifice a statue of Viracocha, and we sent that too. It's as big as my husband the Sacred Double, but it's hollow. Manco presented it to the Strangers and they were so gratified that he is now allowed to come and go as he pleases. Soon he will suggest to the Governor's brother that he should go and fetch the Sacred Double. All the Strangers talk about it, about how heavy it is, and how it's made of solid gold. Then Manco will leave Cuzco, and will only return with our armies.'

There was real joy in her smile.

'I am only putting into practice what you taught me, Villa Oma,' she added.

The Sage's laughter sounded like sand crunching beneath someone's feet. He stroked Anamaya's wrist nervously.

'Oh, I might have taught a few of the more elementary things to a strange child called Anamaya. But the *Coya Camaquen* is no longer that child, and hasn't been for a long time.'

Anamaya blinked and lowered her eyes. Villa Oma's compliment confused her.

'May I ask you something, Sage?'

Villa Oma's screwed up his eyes, and she felt herself blush under his sharp stare.

'Ask whatever you want, *Coya Camaquen*. There is nothing I know that you cannot know too.'

She almost backed away from the opportunity, but her desire to know was too strong. She had spent too many sleepless nights worrying recently, and the uncertainty had become unbearable.

'Have you seen . . . him?' she whispered.

Villa Oma stiffened like a bowstring pulled taut. His mouth became tight and his eyes burned with anger.

'Who are you talking about, *Coya Camaquen*?'

'You know. You were with him on the road to the south, and—'

'How *dare* you?'

'Villa Oma!'

'How dare you! You, of all people! And today of all days, when we have just decided to go to war with the Strangers.'

'Villa Oma, Gabriel isn't like the rest of them. He's the Puma.'

'Shut up! Do not pronounce his name in this place. Do not dishonor the temple. All the Strangers are the same, *Coya*

Camaquen, d'you hear? All of them without exception. I watched them for days and days destroying everything in their path. Men, women, children, houses and animals, temples – everything! They spread destruction day and night. They are demons, *Coya Camaquen*, and he is one of them.'

'No, he isn't! He's the one that Emperor Huayna Capac sent to me.'

'You're mistaken.'

'In that case, Sage Villa Oma, I must have been mistaken about everything else. I must have been mistaken about the comet that designated Atahualpa as Emperor. I must have been mistaken when the Sacred Double designated Manco as our Inca to me. If I'm wrong about Gabriel, Villa Oma, if he isn't the Puma who is meant to guide me, then I've been wrong ever since that first night when Emperor Huayna Capac held my hand.'

The Sage spat a long stream of green coca juice onto the temple's threshold.

'Believe what you want, *Coya Camaquen*. But I am the supreme commander of the Inca's armies, and I warn you: You will not save this Stranger from the fate that awaits him. I will personally make sure that he is one of the first to die. And think about this as well, if you can: If you betray your husband the Sacred Double with this man, then you are putting all of us in danger. If you behave like an adulterous young girl yearning for a lover's caresses, then you are going to destroy Manco and the entire Empire of the Four Cardinal Directions, Anamaya. And if you do that, I will kill you myself.'

Anamaya watched him storm away. He seemed absolutely certain of himself.

Trust the Puma.

For the first time, she wondered if she hadn't made a mistake.

CHAPTER 37

Lake Titicaca, February 1536

G ABRIEL HEARD THE SOUND OF GLASS BREAKING, OF crystal tinkling, of shouts and laughter. Then an icy chill came over his body. Everything went red. The pain was excruciating, as though he had been caught in a workman's vice. He wanted to cry out, but his voice produced no sound.

Night returned, bringing relief with it.

Again, everything was red, as though he was swimming in a sea of his own blood. Perhaps he was in the process of being born: He felt as though he was being carried in a liquid, enveloped in its protective bubble. The red grew deeper, more intense. He heard the laughter and the sound of crystal again. He felt a bitter cold bite into his head, and he opened his eyes.

His teeth were chattering and he felt as though he couldn't breathe. But he managed to inhale deeply and after that he calmed down a little. His vision cleared – and what he saw was wonderful, almost too good to be true.

He was surrounded by blue. What he had taken for crystal was in fact clear water. He was submerged in a vast, icy sea, one surrounded by mountains so high that he couldn't see their peaks.

Gabriel took another breath, shivered, and discovered twenty faces staring at him intently, including those of several women and children. They looked deeply amused and heartily satisfied. Some were in the water with him, others were standing on the shore nearby. They came up to him and stretched out their hands toward him. He worried that he had landed in some supernatural world, and he wanted to get up and run.

His feet struck sand and stones at the bottom of the icy water, and he managed to stand. The children's laughter grew more intense, as though this action of his had gratified them amazingly. Gabriel turned around. He saw the peaceful half-moon of a sandy beach by a creek. A few houses stood next to it. He saw trees that looked like pines, and others that could have been olives. For a moment he thought that he must have been dreaming of his native land in Spain. His heart beat joyously. He wanted to run to the shore, but his muscles wouldn't carry him. He collapsed with a splash after only three steps, causing another outburst of laughter.

He gathered his strength, got on his hands and knees, and crawled forward through the shallow water, his beard trailing in it. But soon he felt hands reaching for him and supporting him. They belonged to perfumed young women with long, oiled hair. He found them to be real, very real, and very beautiful, and he found too that he was as naked as the day he had been born. He shook himself free and tried to cover up his nakedness, causing another hearty outburst of laughter. Eventually they managed to carry him up onto the beach.

A small, stocky man sat there observing him. He looked friendly and serene. His long hair hung loosely over his shoulders. His hands were disproportionately big and strong. He greeted Gabriel with a nod as the young women laid him down on the sand. Only then did Gabriel recognize him.

'Katari!' he cried, then immediately stopped. He didn't recognize his own voice.

'Greetings to you, friend of the *Coya Camaquen*,' replied Katari quietly.

'Please, tell me which world we're in.'

In reply, Katari silently opened his right hand and revealed a small black stone in his palm. He flicked his wrist and launched the stone into the air. It hung in the air for a few seconds, defying gravity for an unnaturally long moment before falling back into his palm.

Gabriel watched this, then gazed about at the surrounding landscape.

It was a place both of this world and of another, set in the present moment and in its parallel in time. Katari grinned at him and said gently:

'Welcome to the world.'

Gabriel was lying on a pile of finely woven *mantas*. A woman was patiently smearing a balm over his body. The unguent warmed him and loosened up his muscles, which felt as though they had melted like snow in the sun.

They were outdoors, just above the beach where he had regained consciousness. The bay in front of him could easily have been taken for a Mediterranean one had it not been for the dozens of agricultural terraces lining it, and the similarity moved him deeply.

A number of boats whose design was completely unfamiliar to him lay sheltered from the wind in the bay. Some were small, others were large enough to carry twenty passengers, and all of them were designed as rafts rather than as hulls. Fishermen came and went from them as though they were walking on water, which was a vision Gabriel had had while unconscious. What most surprised him, though, were the materials of which they were built. Their bodies were not made of wood or their sails of canvas, but of a clever assembly of yellow reeds.

What Gabriel had taken to be a sea was in fact a lake. But it was a lake of such vast proportions that its furthest shore could not be seen. The horizon to the north disappeared into a thick bank of fog. To the east, the sparkling slopes of the highest mountains Gabriel had ever seen stood beyond a steep and arid shore, and he could see their snowy peaks reflected in the calm water below them. To the west and south, the slopes were covered in agricultural terraces as far as the eye could see. These rose up high toward the peaks, without a break between one and the next, and they formed a giant tapestry of rich, velvety greens, the folds of which, supple and silky, fell gently down the mountainsides into the blue abyss of the lake. It was as though the mountains had been created not by some divine will but by vast numbers of men who had raised them terrace by terrace and wall by wall until they soared into the sky.

The sheer grandeur and beauty of the landscape completely absorbed Gabriel, and as he contemplated it, uncertain whether he was truly awake or not, he became oblivious to the caresses that were bringing his body back to life.

'This lake is called *Titicaca*,' explained Katari, squatting a few paces away. 'It is here that the world envisioned by Viracocha was born. Those mountains that you see, the strongest and the tallest, those are called Apu Ancohuma and Apu Illampu, and they were the first beings to be born here. The Lord Mountains saw you come back to life today, and they are rejoicing.'

Gabriel looked at Katari to make sure that he wasn't making fun of him. But the Inca Master of Stones was contemplating the snow-capped peaks with an earnest expression on his face. He was fiddling with the black stone that stayed with him always.

'You are on an island,' he went on. 'The very island where Inti, on the day He was born, emerged from the sacred rock before rising into the sky. There's another island over there, behind that hill. It's a smaller island than this one, and that is where our Mother the Moon rested the day She was born. Just as you are doing here today.'

Now Gabriel sensed a slight element of irony in Katari's tone and in his expression. The young woman nursing him, clearly unencumbered by any Spanish sense of modesty, was now massaging the cheeks of his buttocks so firmly that Gabriel felt like a pampered baby.

'Must she really manipulate me like that?' he asked.

'It's for the best,' said Katari, amused. 'You spent a long time completely immobile. If you want to be able to stand without feeling great pain, then you need to be massaged a lot. But don't worry about your modesty. This girl is familiar with your nakedness.'

Gabriel ignored the girl's smile, and pushed away her hand when she tried to confirm Katari's words physically.

'Katari, I must return to Cuzco as soon as possible!'

The Master of Stones uttered a little laugh.

'You won't be able to for at least another moon. You no longer have a horse to carry you. You'll have to walk. You'll need all your strength.'

'That's no good. I must leave sooner.'

'If you're worried about the *Coya Camaquen*'s safety, then you needn't be,' said Katari gently. 'She's fine. She's living in a city in the mountains that the Strangers in Cuzco don't know about.'

Gabriel propped himself up to look at Katari. The girl halted her massage.

'You said "Strangers in Cuzco", Katari. Is that because you don't want to hurt my feelings or offend my pride? No one knows better than I do how evil those people are. A terrible madness now plagues those whom Governor Pizarro brought here. Blood and gold are their only goals, the only things they think about, and their very reasons for being. They can no longer tell good from evil. They can no longer tell what is human from what is base. Their madness terrifies me and, I can promise you, it isn't mine.'

'I have observed them,' said Katari gravely. 'They are worse than animals because animals are never cruel for no reason, and animals have no knowledge of slavery, and animals only kill to feed themselves. But it's true that you aren't like them. If you were, then I doubt the *Coya Camaquen* would hold you in such high regard.'

'Thank you.'

'I can tell good from evil in this world, in my world.'

'There's going to be a war, isn't there?'

'No doubt.'

'Anamaya must get away from Cuzco,' murmured Gabriel.

Katari shook his head and said:

'No, the *Coya Camaquen* cannot go far from Emperor Manco's side. She is going to free him, then help him run the war. Anamaya is the Son of the Sun's only source of direction. She's the only one left who can hear the Ancestors speaking to us. Villa Oma, whom you were pursuing, is no longer a real sage. He has become a mere warrior bent on vengeance.'

Gabriel said nothing for a moment, absorbing everything that the Master of Stones had said. Two things, at least, relieved his anxiety: Anamaya was alive, and far away from the Governor's brothers.

'How did you come to save me?' he asked suddenly. 'How did you find me in that hell, that sea of salt?'

Katari's laugh was almost tender.

'As for that, you must thank Anamaya, not me. She had a vision, and in it she saw you dying in the salt desert. A *chaski* told me of it, and I set out to find you. You were almost in the Other World when I did. We had to look after you here for a long time to make sure that your soul didn't leave your body.'

'I've been asleep for a long time?' murmured Gabriel, greatly surprised. 'But I feel like I've been asleep since only yesterday! I remember when I fell. I remember my horse dying, and I remember watching my own shadow refuse to go on. I remember my thirst as well, and the burns on my skin. But . . .'

He looked at his hands and arms. He felt his shoulders, glistening with oil and still being massaged by the servant girl.

'My skin has recovered!' he said, a little nervously. 'I am intact. It's as though I dreamed the whole thing, as though I never crossed that hellish sea of salt.'

Katari's dark pupils glowed. He launched his black stone into the air once again. And once again Gabriel thought he saw it hang a moment too long at the top of its curve before falling back into the Master of Stone's palm.

'You slept for weeks,' he confirmed. 'It was necessary for you to do so because the salt had started desiccating you from the inside and you were turning into a mummy. Had you woken up, the pain would have been so unbearable that you would have died straight away. So I made you drink herbs that kept you asleep. Slowly, very slowly, we put the water back into your body. Right up to the day when you woke up and crawled out of the water!'

Katari laughed with pride at having saved a life. He motioned to the servant girl, who finally finished her massage and handed Gabriel a yellow *unku*. He slipped it on. He had trouble getting his beard through the neck hole, and the young woman helped him with special gentleness.

'I need a shave,' grumbled Gabriel, embarrassed. 'I hate wearing a beard.'

'You'll upset all the women on the island if you do,' joked Katari. 'They're very partial to the gold hairs on your face. They think that you're a gift from the Mountains, and that soon all men will look like you. If you lose your hair, I'll have to cure them of a malady far more serious than yours!'

At last, Gabriel smiled. He extended his hand toward the Master of Stones and said:

'I owe you a lot, Katari my friend. I don't know how I'm going to be able to repay you.'

Katari took his hand firmly in his own.

'There's nothing to repay, in this world or the next. We have what we have to give it away, my friend, and to give it away again.'

Katari was right about everything.

When Gabriel shaved off his beard, all the women on the island cried for a week and hid their faces in their hands whenever they crossed his path. As for being able to walk, at first all he could manage was ten paces, and he had to labor every day until he got to twenty, then fifty. He was as worn out and exhausted as if he had just climbed the highest Apu in the mountains.

But after only about ten days, he was able to walk slowly along the lakeshore for an hour without too much trouble. Soon his walks led him further and further afield, and he discovered all the island's wonderful sights, including the vast plateau overlooking the beach of his 'rebirth'. Trees softened the sharpness of its edge, and herds of llamas grazed on it in utter peace.

Gabriel gradually came to experience for himself the almost supernatural power of the high mountains to the east. Their deep valleys and tall peaks rose up from the stillness of the sleepy lake. But they also seemed to contain a latent threat, as though in some great, prodigious movement, they might drag the entire earth into the abyss of nothingness.

After two weeks, Gabriel managed to climb the highest hill on the island, and from there he was afforded a staggering view of its western aspect. There wasn't a llama or a single corn or potato terrace to be seen. What little vegetation that survived there was dismal, almost doleful in appearance. The wind tore away at the bushes, whipped the grass, and scoured the stones until they shone.

From time to time, Gabriel observed the great Sacred Rock and Inti's temple on the other side of the island, although he was careful never to get too close, for fear of arousing suspicion. The inhabitants of the lakeshore all congregated there on sacred days.

His walks grew longer with each passing day, and Anamaya occupied his mind completely. His need to be with her became increasingly urgent. With his eyes fixed on the lake's horizon, he tried to conjure up each part of her body and to remember the details of every moment that they had spent together. He half hoped that the wind out of the west would carry her scent to him, that he would hear her words transported on its breezes. He looked at no other woman on the island, living instead only with the image of his beloved.

At night, she came to him in his dreams, and when he woke with a start, his arms grasping at the emptiness beside him, her absence became even more cruel and unbearable.

The island itself seemed to have a quality that protected his love for her, a love that at times laid him low far more effectively than the fatigue he was recovering from. He saw himself living out the rest of his days with Anamaya here, living in one of the houses by the beach, at last fulfilling the destiny that binds a man and a woman together in love.

Gabriel made something of a ritual of it. Every evening, at sunset, he sat on the same rock facing Lake Titicaca's vast expanse and daydreamed about what their life would be like in this wonderful and tranquil place.

One night he caught a glimpse of a bright green flash on the horizon. A fearful shiver ran down his spine. But he couldn't deny what he had seen. The sun had just disappeared behind the western peaks, and a crimson bank of clouds was suspended above them. He saw long green trails drawn through the darkening sky. He sat up, expecting to see some further sign that the world was about to change irrevocably. He jumped with surprise when he heard a voice behind him hum:

> The Sun,
> The Moon,
> Day and the night,
> Spring and winter,
> Stones and mountains,
> Corn and cantutas.
> Nothing exists without a reason, Oh Viracocha.
> The shores of Titicaca are the source of everything.
> It was here, Oh Viracocha, that you held the rod of
>   origin,
> And it is here in the Titicaca that I am with my soul mate,
> The soul from above and from below.
> Oh Viracocha, it is your will
> That he who leaves Titicaca
> Is already on the road home.

It was the girl who had looked after him so well during the past few weeks. She smiled at him, but her eyes were sad. She pointed at the point in the sky where the green streaks, now gone, had been.

'When the sky becomes green,' she said, 'it means that Viracocha is bestowing peace upon the human race. Viracocha is telling you that he loves you.'

She took Gabriel's hand and squeezed it tenderly.

'It is time for you to go, Stranger. The lake has begun showing you that which your eyes do not see. One day you will wish to return here because although your skin is white and your hair gold, Viracocha has recognized you. You come from his rod of origin, and a soul from below waits for you here.'

After she had spoken these strange words to an astonished Gabriel she squeezed his hand again and hummed:

> The Sun,
> The Moon,
> Day and the night,
> Spring and winter,
> Stones and mountains,
> Corn and cantutas.
> Oh Viracocha, it is your will
> That he who leaves Titicaca
> Is already on the road home.

CHAPTER 38

Calca, April 1536

I N CALCA'S TEMPLES, THE PRIESTS AND SOOTHSAYERS HAD
been pressing the oracles for answers for two days now.
Quantities of coca leaves had been burned, and the hearts
of both black and white llamas had been closely examined. In
the stone tower outside the *huaca*, those who counted time
endlessly went over their calculations, and in the warehouses
the *quipu* knotters carefully manipulated their bundles of knots.
The generals appointed by Villa Oma took stock of the number
of weapons and supplies amassed in the secret *tambos* and tallied
the number of warriors recruited.

The royal *cancha* had been a hive of activity for the past two
days. The servants prepared a hundred different dishes, the virgins
wove piles of fabulous tunics ready for the Inca to wear, and his
wives and concubines spent hours grooming themselves.

For two days the men, women and children of Calca had been
fasting and drinking only water, no matter what physical condition
they were in.

All this because, two days previously, Emperor Manco had
been freed. And that morning, as the sun rose, trumpets had
sounded throughout the valley. From the slopes surrounding
Calca, everyone could see the cortege forming around the Emper-
or's palanquin. They could see a hundred virgins sweeping away
the dust ahead of him and they could hear a hundred others
singing and drums beating. They could see a thousand warriors

wearing immaculate tunics and carrying bows or clubs following him.

In the royal *cancha*, Anamaya ordered the Sacred Double to be placed in the center of the courtyard. Offerings of coca, food, and *chicha* were spread out all around him.

Then the heads of the Cuzco clans and some provincial ones as well came to pay their respects to the golden Sacred Double before taking their places at the sides of the courtyard, each one standing behind a heavy rectangular stone. The wives and concubines followed and stood in a row a few paces back from the royal stool, which was set on a long *cumbi* woven from bat hair.

Everyone knew his place, and their faces revealed their pride. Not since Manco had been crowned with the *mascapaicha* had so much pomp and ceremony been witnessed. It seemed to everyone present that the glory of the Empire of the Four Cardinal Directions was at last restored, and that it was as intact as if the Strangers had never set foot on the land created by Viracocha.

Anamaya's face was radiant, and her every movement was suffused with a dignity that inspired the warriors watching her.

But she had to hide the lake of melancholy and yearning in which her heart was drowning.

Before the sun had reached its zenith, the sound of trumpets and drums echoed from between Calca's walls. The wives and concubines prostrated themselves on the ground in the royal courtyard. Then the Lords and generals picked up the heavy stones at their feet. Each man placed one on his shoulders and, bowed under their weight, waited for Emperor Manco to arrive.

The hundred virgins stopped singing. The trumpets and drums played a final flourish.

Now complete silence fell over the city as each person held his or her breath.

Indeed, the silence was so complete that everyone heard the rustling of Manco's very fine *cumbi* as he stepped out of his litter, and even the swish of the feathers with which the virgins swept the flagstones ahead of him.

And everyone heard him clearly when he touched Anamaya's shoulder and said:

'You may stand up, *Coya Camaquen*. Stand and look at me.'

Anamaya stood. She had to hold back her tears when she saw Manco, saw with her own eyes that he was truly alive and free. He seemed as radiant as the sun itself, and the gold on his helmet and tunic was as resplendent as the Sacred Double.

'I am overjoyed to see you, Emperor,' Anamaya said joyfully. 'I've missed you terribly. We've all missed you.'

Manco smiled faintly before turning away from her to look at the Lords bent under their stones. Only then did she see him properly. Anamaya was shocked by his appearance.

Now he seemed as dark and as hollow as night. He was terribly thin. His cheeks were hollow and his lips were narrower than before. He now had crow's feet around his eyes. And his eyes themselves looked like they belonged to a man whose spirit had retreated so deeply within himself that life barely showed in his pupils.

Everything that was young, spirited and alive had been wiped off Manco's face. It was hard to believe that this was the same man who, as a boy, had won the great race at the *huarachiku*.

The Strangers had left the terrible scar of their torments on his face, and it had been frozen into place by the icy breath of hatred.

He turned back to Anamaya, raised his hand and caressed her cheek with his fingertips. She shuddered as he touched her, and she had to suppress an urge to shrink away.

'I too am happy to see you again, sister Anamaya. I know that I owe you much.'

His words were warm, but they were spoken in a cold and distant tone. Anamaya could feel Villa Oma's burning gaze directed at her from behind Manco.

Manco drew his hand away and whispered:

'You find me changed, don't you?'

Anamaya hesitated before replying:

'No, my Lord. You just need rest, good food – and a little peace.'

Manco smiled a cruel smile.

'No, *Coya Camaquen*, you're wrong. I just need to go to war.'

'The war is waiting only for you, Emperor.'

She smiled at him. She felt more alone than ever before.

'Anamaya!'

Anamaya didn't hear the dwarf's call the first time.

The moon was high in the night sky. The festive noise of celebration rose up from the royal *cancha*. The Lords were drinking heavily both to steel themselves for the battle and to mock their enemies. They shouted more than they spoke, especially when they told the stories of past battles and of the Ancestors' glorious victories.

Anamaya, standing alone outside the courtyard, watched them from afar. Their faces looked both childish and terrifying in the torchlight.

'Anamaya!'

This time she turned around and saw the dwarf's diminutive profile against the corner of the building. He motioned to her to come closer.

'Why are you hiding?' she asked him.

'So no one sees me,' the dwarf whispered hoarsely, grabbing hold of her cape. 'Bend down so you can hear me.'

'Why all this subterfuge?'

'Bend down!'

She complied, sighing wearily. When her face was level with the dwarf's, he whispered:

'He's here.'

Anamaya twitched. She reprimanded herself for the thought that crossed her mind. She forced herself to frown as she asked the dwarf.

'Who are you talking about?'

'About *him*. He's here.'

The dwarf laughed mischievously, but when it became clear that Anamaya was refusing to understand, he grumbled:

'Don't play the fool. HE's here. The Puma.'

She gripped the dwarf's hand as though her legs were about to give way. She closed her eyes and tried to pull herself together before asking:

'Where?'

'I put him in a wool warehouse. It's the safest place. I'll take you there.'

The dwarf indicated a basket beside him.

'I've brought you a black cape. You'll be less visible leaving the *cancha*.'

Anamaya held his arm.

'Chimbu . . .'

'Why, Princess, it must be serious for you to call me by my real name!'

'I'm frightened.'

For a moment Anamaya doubted that it was really him.

He was wearing a yellow tunic and peasant's trousers. A four-cornered hat like those commonly worn around Titicaca covered his shorn blond hair.

He stood a few paces away from her, took off his hat, and laughed nervously.

'I know I must look strange in these clothes,' Gabriel murmured, 'but they allowed me to get here unnoticed. The hardest part was getting the dwarf's attention . . .'

But Anamaya wasn't listening: his laugh was still echoing inside her, fanning a flame of happiness. She took a few more steps, and now all the stiff self-restraint appropriate to a *Coya Camaquen* disappeared in a flash.

He was still laughing when he wrapped his arms around her. She extinguished his laugh with her lips and melted into his warmth.

Then she abruptly broke the embrace and stared at him by the poor light of an oil lamp. Now she was the one to laugh uncontrollably, and she caressed him and danced around him as she said over and over:

'You're alive! You're alive!'

He caught her and started kissing her neck almost violently before moving down to her breasts and kissing those as though he wanted to feast on her skin and her scent. Between kisses he whispered:

'Yes, I'm alive, but only because of you! I was already dead!'

They ran their hands over one another's faces as though their long, long separation had made them blind. Their desire, frustrated for too long, and for too long being satisfied only in their imaginations, now fired their loins so much that their caresses became almost brutal. Anamaya pulled Gabriel's tunic off and ran her fingers over the birthmark on his shoulder.

'Puma,' she moaned. 'My puma.'

He took her up in his arms and carried her to a pile of raw wool. There he ran his hands over and over her body as though discovering it for the first time. They lost themselves in one another, fusing together, flesh to flesh, belly to belly, breath to breath.

Far away, beside a mountain lake, Katari threw his black stone into the air for them. It stayed suspended in the night, stopping time so that their love could find a moment of refuge amid the chaos.

Afterward, the shyness common to young lovers arose between them. They helped one another find words between caresses, telling one another the experiences that each of them had suffered during their months apart. The gravity of their situation slowly dawned upon them, and each was eager to sustain the fleeting lightness of their present happiness.

Eventually Gabriel declared:

'The dwarf told me about everything that happened in Cuzco to Manco and you . . .'

Anamaya didn't reply but closed her eyes, entwining her fingers in his. She surrendered herself to his caresses once more, offering him her breasts, her belly, and her thighs.

Gabriel continued stroking her for a while. But then he closed his hand around hers and whispered:

'I know about Gonzalo. I know what he tried to do. I promise you that I'll kill him for it.'

'It's already disappeared from my soul,' she replied. 'I've forgotten it as though it never happened.'

But the tears pearling up beneath her eyelids gave the lie to her words. Gabriel drank the salty droplets with little kisses.

'I think I know who the puma is,' he said, deeply moved, 'I saw him . . .'

Anamaya said nothing.

'I saw him in the shadows and by the light of the sun, in the night and in the stones. I saw him in your lake of origin where I was reborn. On my way to you, I realized that the puma was within me, that I am the puma. And my fear left me.'

Anamaya stayed silent. Nothing she could say could bring anything more to the universe. And yet none of what Gabriel had said had truly relieved her of the loneliness that was within her, and that had always been there.

'We're leaving,' he said, his eyes shining. 'I came here to get you, to take you with me, away from this chaos. We're going to live on the island in Lake Titicaca, where we'll find peace and where no one will be able to destroy our happiness – no one, not the Pizarros, and not Manco . . .'

She stiffened and glanced away from him. She heard an odd sound rise out of her throat, almost a sob. Wordlessly, she took Gabriel's face in her hands and kissed him for as long as it took for desire to return to her. She gave herself to him more slowly this time, as though she was trying to banish the reality of the visible world, and to become herself a lake of promises.

It was a long night. But day always follows night eventually, and soon the light of dawn would rise over the distant hills.

It was a night that Anamaya and Gabriel wished would never end. But its end was nonetheless near.

They were lying side by side and cheek to cheek, naked and perfect.

'I must stay with Manco,' said Anamaya finally.

'No!'

The cry had burst involuntarily from Gabriel's mouth, and she placed her hand over it tenderly.

'Gabriel, we're going to war. We *must* go to war, otherwise there will be no more Sons of the Sun.'

Gabriel looked away from her.

'You can't stay here,' she continued. 'You can't stay with me. Villa Oma wants you dead.'

Gabriel nodded, a look of cruel, ironic awareness on his face as his eyes welled up with tears.

'I came to you with love, and you turn me away! I travel all this way, and you turn me away! I tell you the things that I feel in the depth of my heart, but they mean nothing to you. You talk to me about your war . . . your people respond to the madness of mine with their own!'

She hesitated. She pulled her black cape up over her shoulders.

'You are the puma, and you are the only man who can reach me in this world or the Other.'

'But you'd rather I left for the Other!'

'Please, stop it!'

Gabriel began trembling uncontrollably, like an inconsolable child. She tried to hold him to her, but he pushed her away angrily. When she turned away, he took her by the throat, he dug his fingers into her flesh, he held her tight, he caressed her – and then he pushed her away again even more brutally, as though he needed to be violent to release the words burning in his mind.

'You cannot win this war. You're weak, and your world is collapsing. Our conquest is unjust, I know. It has been accomplished with crimes of which I'm deeply ashamed. But you will lose just as you did at Cajamarca and everywhere else. Don't you see?'

'We must have this war. The mountains and our Ancestors need us to fight, otherwise they will disappear into the void. And I must be at Manco's side. That is my proper place.'

Gabriel stood up and uttered a cry of rage. He pushed aside the hanging over the warehouse's door. The cold outside made him shiver.

'In that case, we're going to fight against each other.'

'You don't have to,' she murmured.

'If your proper place is at Manco's side and not at mine,' said Gabriel with icy calm, 'then it's because you think I'm a "Stranger" like the others. Well then, my proper place is with the Strangers.'

They stared at one another for a long time, both searching for some sign of hope in the other's eyes.

'I must fight this war,' murmured Anamaya at last. 'I must, don't you see? Otherwise Emperor Huayna Capac might as well never have held my hand!'

A terrible calm filled Gabriel, as though all his rage had disappeared like an ebbing tide.

'Very well. I understand. I don't know what it means, but I understand it to the very depths of my soul. And I accept it.'

His calm rattled Anamaya more than his cries, more than his words of outrage. Now he really was the *puma*, the one she had been waiting for. And at this moment of their separation, they were as close as two beings could be – two beings who had once, in the lake of origins, been one, like twin souls reunited after crossing an ocean of stars.

'I hope . . .' he began. 'I hope against hope, I hope against this war. It's so difficult, so very difficult . . .'

His voice faltered, and he cleared his throat before continuing:

'. . . It's so difficult to leave you after everything I have gone through to reach you . . .'

'I love you.'

Gabriel nodded. Tears blurred his vision. He came close to her and this time it was he who took her head in his hands and kissed her on the mouth.

Later, during the time of darkness, in the weapon-loud din of battle, when he would lose all sense of the meaning of life, he would use, as a defence against loneliness and despair, the memory of how soft her lips had been when he had kissed her after she had spoken those last words to him. And they would give him the utterly illogical certainty that in every death there is always another birth.

GLOSSARY

Acllahuasi	– House of the Chosen Women (*acllas*).
Añaco	– A long, straight tunic reaching to the ankles worn by women.
Apu	– Quechua word meaning 'Lord' or 'Governor'; also used as a title preceding the names of mountain divinities.
Ayllos	– A throwing weapon similar to a bola: it consists of three leather strips ballasted with rocks, designed to entangle the legs of a running quarry.
Balsa	– A wooden raft made of balsa wood.
Borla (Spanish) or *mascapaicha* (Quechua)	– Along with the *llautu* and the feathered *curiguingue*, this woolen fringe makes up the royal headpiece of the Sapa Inca.
Cancha	– An open inner courtyard; also, a collection of three or four buildings around such a courtyard, forming a single living area.
Chaco	– Large hunt in which hundreds of beaters flush out game.
Chaquiras	– Small pearls from pink shells (*mullus*), which are made into necklaces or woven into ceremonial costumes.
Chaski	– Runners who carry messages by relay.
Chicha	– Ceremonial beverage; a fermented beer, generally made from maize.

Chuño	– Naturally dehydrated potatoes that keep for months.
Chuspa	– Small woven pouch decorated with religious motifs and used to carry coca leaves.
Collcas	– Circular or rectangular buildings made up of a single room and used as warehouses to store foodstuffs, weavings, weapons and luxuries.
Coya	– Title accorded to the Inca's principal wife.
Cumbi	– The finest quality of woven cloth, usually made from vicuña wool.
Curaca	– Local chief or official.
Curiguingue	– Small falcon, the black and white feathers of which were used to decorate the Sapa Inca's headpiece.
Gacha	– Soup or stew made from a base of cereal or starch; one of the mainstays of the medieval diet.
Hatunruna	– Quechua word meaning 'peasant'.
Huaca	– Quechua word meaning 'sacred'. By extension, any location or sanctuary in which a divinity is kept.
Huara	– Shorts. Boys were given a pair of these during the initiation rite called the *huarachiku*.
Ichu	– A type of wild grass that grows at high altitudes and is used mainly to thatch roofs.
Inti Raymi	– One of the major festivals of the Inca calendar; occurs during the winter solstice.
Kallanka	– Long building with doors that generally give onto the square of an administrative centre.
Kapak	– Chief
Llautu	– Long woolen plaits wrapped several

times around the wearer's head to form a headpiece.

Manta — Spanish word meaning 'blanket', but also used to denote the cape worn by Inca men (*llacolla*) and women (*lliclla*).

mascapaicha — See *borla*.

Mullus — Shells from the Pacific coast, usually of a red or pink color. They were widely used during Inca religious rites, either in their natural state or after having been worked.

Pachacuti — A great upheaval signaling the beginning of a new era.

Panaca — lineage from an Inca sovereign.

Plateros — Spanish word denoting those metalworkers who specialized in precious metals.

Quinua — An Andean cereal rich in protein.

Quipu — A device of colored strings in which knots were tied. The knots served as a mnemonic system for keeping records.

Sapa Inca — Literally, 'Unique Lord'. The title of the Inca sovereign.

Tambo — Inns set at regular intervals along the Empire's roads. In such places the traveler could find food and shelter, as well as fresh clothes, all provided by the State.

Tiana — A small bench or stool reserved exclusively for the Inca and for *Curacas*, and which was a symbol of power.

Tocacho — A tree, five to eight meters high, that resists the cold well.

Tocapu — A geometric motif with symbolic meanings used to decorate Inca weavings.

Tumi — A ceremonial knife, the bronze blade of which is set at a ninety-degree angle to the handle.

Tupu — A long needle made of gold, silver, bronze

or copper, used to clasp a cape, or *manta*, together.

Unku — A sleeveless knee-length tunic worn by men.

Ushnu — A small pyramid set on the square of an Inca settlement and reserved for the use of those in power.

Viscacha — A rodent of the genus *Marmota*, with a tail similar to a squirrel's and which lives in scree.